This Is The Fall

Book One

LynnErin Faye

First Edition

ISBN: 979-8-9995896-0-6

TYPESET & PUBLISHED BY: SNOW FOREST PRESS
COVER ART BY: SAIRA IQBAL

For You, the epitome of bravery, curiosity, grit, try, and the stubborn will to survive at all costs. I'll love you forever.

Author's Note

Buried deep within the forgotten stacks of The Snow Forest Library, I discovered a relic of *The Time Before* lying benignly at the bottom of a dusty crate. A stack of small journals, bound together by a strap so ancient, the leather crumbled at my touch. Upon opening the first journal, it's leather cover cracked, its pages yellowed and fragile as autumn leaves, I knew what I had found was as rare as it was precious—a firsthand account of *The Fall*.

I am LynnErin Faye, one of many humble scribes who wander the halls of this library searching for stories to inspire, challenge, entertain and bring joy to the hearts of our city's patrons. Perhaps one day, the stories I transcribe will travel beyond the confines of our borders, maybe this is one such story? I hope that it is, for the words of these journals spoke to me with an urgency I could not deny, and I immediately began the painstaking task of preservation and translation.

Scant firsthand accounts of *The Fall*, and the time before that deadly moment in our world's history, have ever come to light, leading us to speculate that the people living in *The Time Before* must have possessed some means of information preservation that eludes our understanding today. Be that as it may, upon further research, I found that these journals were delivered to us nearly four centuries ago by a woman known only as *The Messenger*. She conveyed that the woman who passed the journals to her, a certain enigmatic soul named Amber, had no family left to carry her legacy, and in light of that fact, chose to send them off into the world with a stranger—The Messenger—so that the tale of her greatest adventure would endure and not be left to wither and rot away in the wilds where she once made her home.

The story you are about to read is based on Amber's own words, so before you embark on this journey, know that her tale does not shy away from the darkness and shadows of her world. It is a story that touches on **violence, PTSD, panic attacks, physical assault, threats of sexual assault, themes of coercion, suicide, suicidal ideation, blood, gore, death, dead bodies, kidnapping, manipulation, and strong language.** For those sensitive to such topics, I urge caution. Your mental health matters. But, for those who dare to venture forth, this is also a story of adventure, survival, camaraderie, triumph, and love.

And so, dear reader, it is my fervent hope that you enjoy *This Is The Fall.*

Eight Months Ago...

THE LENS OF THE CHANNEL 2 NEWS camera bore into me, and I suddenly forgot how to speak, my mind and heart racing as the newscaster, Becca Boyce, smiled encouragingly and tipped the puffy microphone in my direction.

"Umm, can you please repeat the question?" I asked, feeling absolutely foolish as heat slowly crept up into my cheeks. I brushed a stray hair away from my eyes and fidgeted.

God, this was a horrible idea. Being behind the camera was much more comfortable than being in front of it. Capturing single moments in time, preserving that minuscule portion of life for generations...that I loved, but the thought of my own awkward image preserved in the same fashion made me squirm. *Hooray for social anxiety.*

"Of course," the pretty reporter said, voice calm and gentle, like she had dealt with hundreds of nervous interviewees. "We aren't live so we can try as many times as we need to. It'll probably help if you focus on me and pretend the camera isn't even there."

I nodded nervously and took in a shaky breath. My armpits itched as I broke out in a nervous sweat and I tried to focus on her rather than the camera, but there it was, staring into my soul.

"We're here at the Panther Creek Campground trail head, a popular stop for through hikers on the Washington section of the Pacific Crest Trail. I'm speaking with Amber, a local avid hiker and solo car camper. Now, Amber, in light of the attacks and disappearances happening in national parks and forests all across the country, do you still plan on getting out into the wilderness this summer?" Again, she tipped the microphone in my direction.

My mind went blank. I'd heard the question, processed the question, but I just couldn't seem to force a response through my lips. As if on cue, a group of three 'through hikers' passed beside us cheering and hamming it up for the news camera. Their wild gestures and fist pumping managed to cut the self-imposed tension building in my chest and I let out a breath I hadn't realized I had been holding. Becca and I both fought down a laugh.

When the group was several paces away, I squared my shoulders and with a determined breath, I spoke, "Well, yeah, I suppose so. There haven't been any attacks reported here locally, and until then, I'm gonna keep playing in the forest. But I have started bringing a few extra things with me just to be safe."

"What kind of extra things?"

"I have an extra can of bear spray, and I carry a Personal Locator Beacon. PLB for short." I was starting to relax a little bit; thank goodness I was nearly as passionate about outdoor safety as I was about photography and wrenching on cars. I held the large can of bear spray and PLB up for her to see.

"That's a very interesting gadget. How does it work?" she asked.

"It's basically a lifeline," I explained the particulars of my unit's operation and a few of its features, words finally began to flow, and I smiled back at the reporter. "If I'm late coming back from a trip, or if I'm lost, injured or otherwise can't make it out of the forest on my own, I can call emergency services, and this will bring them straight to me using satellite location."

"That is an impressive piece of technology and could very well save a life. Thank you for sharing that with us," the reporter said as she turned her attention back to the cameraman and delivered a perfectly rehearsed safety spiel before closing the segment. "This is Becca Boyce, back to you in the studio." She smiled for a solid five seconds then lowered the mic. "How was that, Colin?" Her entire attitude shifting from being on stage, to chatting with a friend.

"We got it," the cameraman said flatly, nodding his head. "Let's get some B-roll and we should be good to go."

Becca turned back to me, "Would it be alright if we borrowed you for a bit longer? Maybe we could get a shot of you getting out of your car and walking down the trail? And how about a close-up of the bear spray and that beacon?"

"For sure."

All was done in a few short moments, and Becca handed me her card. "There are several of us working on this story, as of now its set to be the headliner on the seven o'clock news. Keep your eyes peeled and feel free to email if you think of anything else we might be able to add."

"Sounds good, thanks, Becca. Colin. It was great to meet you both," I said, shaking each of their hands in turn.

"Stay safe out there," Becca said, then she and Colin turned to go.

I hopped back into my old Jeep excited to tell my mom and brother that I was about to be on the news, but the drive home gave me more than enough time to over analyze the entire event and convince myself that I was about to look like a complete idiot on broadcast television.

"Well, it's too late to change anything now," I mumbled to myself with a groan. I ran a hand over my face as I slammed the car door closed, gazing up the short walk to my house. Our *home*. The only place I'd ever felt safe and fully accepted. It wasn't much to look at, just a cookie-cutter two story home that was a few years older than I was; the shutters needed repainting, the yard was full of dandelions, and the same shabby welcome mat had sat in front of the door since I had been in grade school, but everything I had ever loved rested inside those walls. At least I knew my mom and brother would never judge me as harshly as I judged myself most of the time.

As I opened the door, the scent of lemon floor cleaner mingled with my brother's favorite microwave pizza and I smiled to myself. Slipping off my shoes and setting them in the bin beside the door, I called out into the still house, "I'm home! You guys are never going to guess what I just did!"

Hours later, my attention was violently pulled away from my idle photo editing by my mom's excited shriek, "It's on, it's on! Get in here!"

My younger brother, Joey, and I sprinted down the stairs, through the hallway and into the living room, shoving each other and laughing the whole way.

"Turn it up," Joey said, his eyes twinkling with excitement. "I gotta see this."

Mom grabbed the remote and cranked the volume up as the intense news introduction played.

The nerves from earlier in the day came back as butterflies to dance in my stomach. "Here's to hoping I didn't make a complete fool of myself." I crossed my fingers and plopped down on our worn sofa.

Amid the flashy, digital bulletins and scrolling ticker, two efficiently somber newscasters gazed into the camera. "Thank you for joining us on this Saturday edition of the seven o'clock news, I'm Ben Holmes." Ben glanced to his right at a striking woman with dark hair.

"And I'm Andrea Anderson," she stated. "We begin, of course, with continuing coverage of the bizarre attacks and disappearances that have been plaguing national parks and forests across the country."

The picture on screen cut to an idyllic scene at Yellowstone National Park. The lodge, roads and surrounding attractions were chocked full of visitors wandering the park while marveling at its rugged beauty.

The disembodied voice of Andrea Anderson floated from the television, mingling with the sounds of a busy national park during peak season. "Yellowstone, the worlds very first national park, has been a popular summer tourist destination since the spring of 1872. Since 2008, the park has welcomed over three *million* visitors each year. But this season, Yellowstone stands empty." The lines were delivered with the perfect William Shatner pauses for dramatic effect.

Yellowstone? Completely empty at the height of tourist season? It was about as likely as a desert without sand. The cameras cut to a recent clip of the normally bustling park. It was a ghost town.

Ben picked up where Andrea had left off. "For the first time since the devastating wildfires of 1988, the park has closed off all five of its entrances and is completely evacuating its guests."

"Wait, what?" I squeaked, quickly glancing back and forth between my mom and brother.

"Holy shit," Joey mumbled.

Mom waved a hand at us both. "Shut it, I can't hear what they're saying."

The newscasters continued to speak while my mind reeled. "Since March of this year, current estimates point to more than two-hundred people either found dead or missing in Yellowstone and Teton National Parks alone. And that number is growing every day," Ben finished before the cameras cut to a short clip of the administrators of the two parks.

Standing behind a small podium bristling with microphones, a gentleman in a starched ranger uniform spoke slowly and carefully to the gathered press before him, "It was an easy decision to close the parks, but not one that we took lightly. These killings and disappearances are highly disturbing and very real. At this time, we don't know what has caused this tragedy, animals or humans, but this

5

is a matter of public safety. We will be closing the parks indefinitely to allow for proper investigation of the scenes and surrounding areas, and we are urging citizens in the greater Jackson area to use extreme caution when out at night."

"What a nightmare," I whispered more to myself than anyone else.

The cameras flashed back to the newscasters and Andrea reported, "Disappearances and animal attacks are not uncommon in our country's national parks. In fact, people go missing in those remote areas every year. From Yosemite, to Olympic, Denali to the Great Smokey Mountains, every park has had a missing persons case, but until recently, the numbers reported were quite low. One website states that there were only twenty-nine open cold cases for missing individuals at our national parks from 1958 to 2021. This year, nearly every national park has reported at least ten missing persons with more than a dozen mutilated and half eaten bodies found in these remote areas across the country."

Mom's hand drifted to her chest. "My God, this is getting out of hand," she breathed, her voice just above a whisper.

Interviews come and go as the news story rolled out increasingly staggering facts and numbers. A knot began to form in the pit of my stomach. Perhaps I *was* being reckless, even with my extra bear spray and PLB?

I turned my full attention back to the television when a woman's face graced the screen. She was a scientist, a volcanologist to be specific, and had rocketed into the limelight two months ago after going public with a controversial theory; the killings and disappearances were somehow connected to a record number of small earthquakes that shook the Yellowstone caldera area in early spring. Her colleagues dismissed her theory as nothing but bonkers pseudoscience, stating that there was no actual evidence behind her theory, and it was only a gut feeling that she had. But I believed her...along with a good portion of the public at large.

"Ya know, a gut feeling should never be discounted," Mom said, poking her chin out while looking more than a little self-righteous. "Your head and your heart can pull you in every different direction, but your gut will never lead you astray." She crossed her arms over her chest and scowled at the television, no doubt wishing all those stuffy science men would just leave that woman alone.

Mom had always been a bit of a man-hater. Since my dad had just up and left us all more than fifteen years ago, she hadn't gone on a single date, and I could tell she still kicked herself for not listening to her gut when it came to him. A bit of her angst rubbed off on me over the years, but unlike her, I still held out some hope that eventually, I'd stumble upon a good guy. Not that it's happened yet.

"Pseudo-science, my ass," Mom snorted. "I think she's right."

The story continued while Mom, Joey and I talked over the reporters.

"My gut has never let me down, and the few times I didn't listen to a gut feeling, I instantly regretted it," I said. Like that time I almost put the Jeep in a ditch trying to avoid hitting a deer after my gut told me I should take a different route home. I shivered visibly and Mom laid a hand on my shoulder.

"What about that time—" Joey started, but Mom cut him off with a happy little squeal.

"Look, look! There she is!" Mom sat forward and bounced in her seat on the edge of the couch.

"You look like a rabbit in the headlights, Sis," Joey snickered, playfully punching me in the shoulder.

"Shut it, dweeb." I glared at him then burst out laughing. I *did* look scared to death.

Becca Boyce's pretty face smiled out from the screen while I twitched and shifted nervously to one side of her. I groaned and buried my face in my hands with utter embarrassment. I could hear my own, slightly squeaky voice telling her and the entire metro area (if not the world) that I was still going to go play in the woods because no one had been killed or gone missing here in the Gifford Pinchot National Forest.

"Oh, I'm an *idiot*," I moaned and flopped to my side on the couch, curling into the fetal position.

"You look so cute, sweetie," Mom said while playfully jostling my balled-up form. "Look."

I peered at the television from between my fingers just in time to see myself clip the can of bear spray and PLB onto my belt and start walking down the trail, my own disembodied voice talking about the locator device.

"Why didn't anyone ever tell me that I'm so freaking pigeon toed?" I groaned. I was never going to be able to take a single step again without picturing myself waddling down that trail.

Becca's voice-over was sweet and cheery, "You see, it's important to be prepared and aware of your surroundings at all times when out in the back country. Know your limits, stay on the trail and always let someone know where you're going and when you expect to return. This is Becca Boyce, back to you in the studio."

The image on the screen flashed back to Andrea Anderson's pretty face, "It is always best to be prepared, right Ben?" she said with a slight smile.

"Exactly. My own mother always used to say, 'It's better to have it and not need it, than need it and not have it.'" Ben said, chuckling.

Mom sat up tall and wagged her finger at the screen, "Your mom's a wise woman, Ben. A wise woman."

"Definitely words to live by, especially during times like these," Andrea said solemnly.

The news casters continued to speak with other correspondents out in the field covering different areas of the country. Things sure did seem to be growing worse by the day. Several doomsday preppers graced the screen talking about food stores and water supplies, others were convinced that the deaths and disappearances were nothing more than a government cover up; the Yellowstone super volcano was going to erupt.

I rolled my eyes at most of the interviews and then the image of a man with a truly crazed look in his eye filled the screen. He gazed straight into the camera lens, straight at *us*, completely unblinking. "The people that get chewed up and taken to the hospital, they tell us that all those people died because of some novel bacteria. No modern medicine can stop it, right? But did you know that none of the family members were able to retrieve the bodies of their loved ones? My wife—" the man's voice cracked, and he cleared his throat, eyes shimmering. "Yeah, every single body needed to be kept for study." His voice began to take on a decidedly sinister tone. "You know what that means? It means that those people never died. They had to have been taken to some top-secret facility for more study. I think they changed. It's the only logical answer. We've got a zombie apocalypse on our hands!"

"You've got to be kidding me," Mom groaned. "I can't believe they're letting this quack speak. He's going to start a panic."

"This is why I never watch the news, Mom. All they do is sensationalize everything just to get the people riled up. He's obviously nuts," I said. "Just look at him."

The man prattled on and on about his conspiracy theory, his wild gray hair standing out at odd angles while his eyes darted from one thing to another somewhere behind the camera. "This isn't like zombies on tv though. No one is ever injured during daylight hours..." he trailed off, his expression dropping into uncertainty. "Maybe they're—" his voice cut off and his eyes widened, as if he had just connected two *very* important dots. Without another word, the man turned and sprinted away from the camera, leaving the reporter scrambling to close his segment.

"Ugh, lay off the meth, bro," Joey said with a disgusted snort then turned to mom and I with a mischievous twinkle in his eye. "Top-secret facility...that reminds me! Did you guys see the video of the angel escaping from that facility?"

"The-*what*?" Mom and I said in unison, both whipping our attention from the television to Joey.

9

"Yeah, it's trending on Reddit. It's all-over social media but the mainstream media hasn't touched the story." A wry smile quirked his lips as he pulled his phone out of his pocket.

We both shrugged and motioned for him to continue. Mom muted the television while Joey searched for the video. She and I had social media accounts, but we never really used them. I posted my photography to Instagram and used Facebook for my off-road-gals group, but other than that, they were just a time suck, and I enjoyed the outdoors too much to just sit and stare at my phone for hours on end...but Joey was a social media addict.

"Here, look. They're saying it happened in South America." Joey turned his phone our way looking smug.

Through the fingerprinted screen of his phone, the image of a female form crashed through the large, glass doors of what looked like some sort of high security 'facility', just as Joey had said. She hit the ground completely naked, cut, bruised, and bloodied, but that wasn't what really took my breath. She had wings. Enormous, actual feathered wings. She pulled herself up and scrambled on hands and feet for a brief moment, before breaking into a desperate sprint. Then, the unmistakable pop of gunfire rang out. She stumbled slightly before unfurling her pearlescent, cream-colored wings, taking to the air with a single beat, and disappeared out of the video frame.

"What the Hell?" I glanced over at Mom who had a hand to her chest.

"Play it again," she whispered.

Joey laughed, "I knew you'd freak out."

Mom hadn't even taken a breath. We watched the video again and I was left completely speechless. It looked so real but there was no way it could be. My mind scrambled for some way to logically explain what I was seeing. It had to be some sort of AI deepfake. I studied the video again but try as I might, I could find no flaw in it. It wasn't just the power in her movements, or the determination etched into the planes of her beautiful, battered face; it was the subtle nudging of my gut telling me what I had just witnessed was *real*. The

10

entire video was stunningly, *terrifyingly* clear leaving me gaping and shaking my head.

"She's pregnant." Mom's whispered gasp brought my attention back to the video.

"No way," Joey scoffed, "I've watched this thing a dozen times and never noticed that."

Mom didn't answer, didn't even make eye contact with either of us, she only brought trembling fingers to her lips as she stared at the phone screen, her expression a mixture of deep concern and heartache, like the realization had struck something deep within her. When Joey played the video a third time, it was clear. The woman, or angel, was definitely pregnant.

I had never been to church a day in my life, but what I had just seen forced me to question more than a few things. Mom didn't think church was a necessity to raising good humans. We celebrated Christmas and Easter, like most of the people in the country, but our celebrations were more about family coming together for dinner than celebrating the birth and resurrection of a deity. We all took the Lord's name in vain daily and had never even said a formal prayer. But that single video made me wonder if I *should* be subscribing to all the 'Father in Heaven, Jesus our Lord and Savior, and The Hosts of Heaven' stuff. But it all seemed wrong to me somehow. Like, if we had a Heavenly Father and Jesus is supposed to be his son...our brother, where was our Heavenly *Mother?* Or Heavenly Grandmother, for that matter? And, from what I knew of pop culture movies, tv shows and books, Angels were either all male or genderless...and the 'angel' I had just seen in high definition was most definitely female. It didn't make sense.

"Seriously, what is going on?" I murmured. "Earthquakes, wars, gas shortages, supply train interruptions, storms, climate change, fires, people getting murdered in national parks and forests, and now a pregnant *Angel?* Maybe those doomsday preppers aren't so crazy after all?" I brought my fingertips to my forehead, "This can't be happening."

"You really need to do some research," Joey said through his crooked smile. "So, yeah, they say some hackers pulled it off the surveillance cameras of a top-secret facility. The government is *obviously* hiding something from the public."

"Alright, you've convinced me. I'll crawl out from under my rock and get with the times," I said sarcastically to Joey, and he beamed triumphantly.

"You're about to fall down a rabbit hole, Sis," Joey said with a conspiratorial chuckle and a cryptic smile. "Enjoy the ride." He wagged his brows at me.

The news story must have ended because when Mom turned the volume on the TV back up, they were talking about the ten-day forecast.

"Well, I guess that's it, then," I said slapping my knees and pushing up off the couch. "My thirty seconds of fame has ended. Thank God."

"I'll text you the link to that post on Reddit. There's a huge group of people trying to figure out exactly where the video came from. I can't wait until they figure it out," Joey said, rubbing his hands together.

"Well, I'm gonna go hide in my room and hope that nobody I know saw me on the news looking like an idiot," I laughed. "Do you need help with anything, Mom?"

She seemed lost in thought, eyes distantly staring at nothing in particular.

"Mom?" I said again, a little bit louder.

She shook her head and looked up at me. "Umm, no sweetie, I'm okay."

I nodded and started back up the stairs to my room.

"I'm proud of you, Amber. I know how much being on camera unnerves you and you did a great job. You should be proud of yourself," she said earnestly.

"Thanks, Ma," I sighed and tried to hide my smile. "Love you."

"Love you more."

I continued up the stairs to my room and sat down at my computer. I had been editing a portrait but just could not seem to get back into it. So, I opened my web browser and started searching.

Is this the end of days? I typed into the search bar. Article upon article from bible thumping websites and blogs popped up. Not what I was looking for.

Real life angel in South America. That yielded some interesting articles. From what I could gather, the video in question really *had* been taken from surveillance cameras by a hacker and released to the public and it was 100% authentic. I kept searching and found a blog dedicated to all things Yellowstone Disappearances and was immediately sucked into a whirlwind of conspiracy theories.

"These people are as bad as the folks that think Elvis and JFK Junior are still alive," I mumbled to myself, clicking away from that website and searching for more information on disappearances farther away from Yellowstone and Grand Teton. I watched video after video on YouTube and before I knew it, it was after midnight. Yawning and rubbing my tired eyes, I stretched and changed into my pajamas.

For the next two months, almost every spare moment I had was spent researching the disappearances, and then, as suddenly as they had begun, they stopped. Across the nation, there were more than three-hundred people confirmed dead and close to fifteen hundred missing or otherwise unaccounted for. The Pacific Northwest, oddly enough, counted the fewest number of casualties. The authorities stated that even though the bloodshed seemed to have stopped, there was no reason to lapse into complacency. They urged the public to stay vigilant and to always travel in groups of two or more. The buddy system from childhood making a comeback into our adult lives.

By Christmas, most folks had stopped talking about the killings altogether and chose to focus on some other weird, extraterrestrial happenings—like the deaths of nearly two-thousand people didn't matter at all. They were old news. Even I welcomed the return of some normalcy, but those dead and missing people were never far from my thoughts. What had happened to them? And why in the hell did it all just suddenly stop?

The emergency preparedness community never stopped discussing it though, and the public at large, no matter how hard they tried to get back to their ordinary lives, seemed changed somehow. Everyone knew something was terribly wrong, but like the herd animals we are, we tried to hide that fact by looking toward other things to fuss about.

It was all a terrible mistake.

1

A Chance Meeting

THE CHILL OF A LONG AND WET WINTER still clung to the shadows around the trees, but the unseasonably warm, early March sun tickled the side of my face. I turned so that I could welcome the morning glow head on with a grateful smile, glad that the weather seemed to be cooperating during my outing, for the moment at least. Bright white and cottony, the cumulus clouds floated in the otherwise brilliant blue sky. I had four days off work and planned to make the most of them.

I slung my day pack over my shoulders and readjusted the heavy, antique camera that hung around my neck before continuing down the walking trail that ran through Miller Park. To my left, a small river ran high and fast, nearly overflowing its banks and I wondered absently at how much more rain it would take to flood this entire area.

The past winter had been a rough one; rainfall records were broken every month from October to February, and in the higher elevations, the snowpack was the deepest anyone had seen since the mid-1900's. The past week though, a peculiar warm front pushed in from the pacific bringing mild temperatures and a much-needed respite from the constant rain.

The grass and leafless trees glittered with silvery water droplets while mist rose from the ground in wispy clouds and I sighed, relishing the moment. Spring was on its way. I could almost smell the fresh cut grass and blossoming trees.

"On your right!" a voice called out from behind me, pulling me out of my reverie.

I quickly stepped to my left as a morning jogger flew past and I wrinkled my nose. Why on earth would anyone want to run for fun? *Eww.* The jogger did cut a striking figure though, silhouetted against the sun, surrounded by glistening trees. Just him and the trail.

I quickly gathered the old camera in my hands and brought the view finder to my eye. Shooting with 35mm film, I only had one chance, maybe two if I was fast enough, to get the shot. I pressed the shutter and quickly advanced the film. Adjusting the focus, I snapped one more shot before the man was lost to sight around a bend in the path.

With a deep sigh I lowered the camera. I wasn't out to photograph people; I was supposed to be practicing nature photography. Portraiture was my niche and passion though, and I couldn't allow myself to miss out on a golden opportunity for a beautiful photo simply because it wasn't supposed to be my focus for the day. I continued down the path, pausing to capture an old arched bridge over the river and a few birds that were busy looking for things to eat, but I was left feeling uninspired.

I needed a different environment to shoot. I turned on my heel and began the short walk back to my Jeep. Once there, I popped the hatch and sat down in the cargo space. Feet swinging, I scrolled through a hiking app looking for something close by with a good view. Nothing was standing out to me, so I tucked my phone into the pocket of my hoodie and sighed again.

Maybe I could take an overnight trip to one of my favorite camping spots? I hadn't been out all winter and even though there hadn't been a single reported national park disappearance or killing since last October, I was still a little bit gun shy. As I mulled the idea over, I glanced back to the walking path. The parks in town really weren't that bad, I could just go to one further out. It was then that I saw the jogger coming back.

Nope, don't feel like saying word one to anybody right now.

I hopped down from the back of the Jeep and stretched up to pull the hatch closed just as he arrived. Our cars, parked side by side, were the only two vehicles in the small parking lot.

He flashed me a friendly smile as he pulled his keys from a small waist pouch. "Beautiful morning, isn't it?" he said, slightly out of breath.

I was momentarily struck dumb. He was tall...and very fit, his athletic frame obvious under a snug, long sleeved shirt. He had a great smile and a dimple on his left cheek.

Shit, was I staring? I shook myself, heat creeping up my neck, and I finally spoke, "Uh, yeah—it's gorgeous. Nice break from the rain." I slammed the hatch down and returned his smile hoping it looked natural. *Frikkin' awkward...*

"Enjoy the sunshine." He winked at me before turning to pull his car door open.

The heat rose from my neck to my cheeks, and I was suddenly grateful that he had his back turned to me. "Yeah, you too," I said, rather lamely as I shook my head and made my way to the driver side door. After settling myself behind the steering wheel and plugging my phone in, I shifted into reverse and turned to back out of my parking stall, but the jogger was waving at me through my passenger window.

I gasped and raised a startled hand to my chest before rolling down the passenger side window a crack, chuckling to myself for being so jumpy.

"Everything okay?" I asked as our eyes met.

My God, he's like...super good looking. Dark hair curled out from under his ball cap and his hazel eyes crinkled lightly at the

17

corners with his broad smile. Beard stubble shadowed his jaw and the dimple I had noticed before reappeared on his tanned cheek.

"Sorry, I didn't mean to scare you. Uh, do you have any jumper cables?" he asked with a sheepish grin.

I paused before answering in a stammer, "Um-yeah. I've got some in the back, hold on." I shifted back into park and popped the hood.

"Thank you so much," he said with a grateful sigh as he stepped away from my window. "I hope it's not the starter or something."

I unplugged my phone and stuffed it back into the pouch of my brown hoodie and hopped out of the SUV, quickly making my way to the back hatch again and pulling out my roadside safety kit.

"Hopefully not," I said as I handed the jumper cables over awkwardly.

Together we connected the batteries, and he tried cranking the ignition to his car. It turned over slowly but wouldn't fire up. My brows knit together as I took a close look at the grimy battery under his hood. I smeared away a layer of oily dust covering the label with my thumb and wiped it on my pant leg. It was five years old.

"Looks like your battery is toast," I said pointing to the date.

He stepped closer and leaned over the engine, then made a noise that was equal parts relieved and disappointed. I tried to hide a smile. Guys hated it when a girl figured things out before they did, especially when it came to cars. But I was more than comfortable under the hood. Mom had insisted that I learn at least the basics of car care before I was even allowed to get my driver's license. The result...she'd unwittingly created a gear head—when it came to cars that were about as old as I was, anyway.

Taking a deep breath and a half step away from the jogger, I fidgeted with the tattered cuff of my hoodie. I'd hoped that the whole interaction would have been over and done with in less than a minute, but knowing his battery was shot and we'd be sharing space for a few minutes, I could feel my anxiety starting to build.

I hope he's not the chatty type, I thought to myself.

I didn't have many friends and am the type of person that goes grocery shopping with ear buds in to avoid having any type of conversation...with anyone I didn't know. I had a hard enough time speaking normally, let alone trying to form a coherent sentence while a guy with a million-dollar smile was making hard-core eye contact with me.

"So, uh, I like your rig," he said, dimple flashing. My heart kicked up a notch as his eyes roamed my face.

Good lord, this man is fine. Deep, cleansing breaths, Amber.

He was obviously just trying to break the odd silence with small talk.

"Don't see too many girls driving around in cars that look this capable." The nonchalant tilt of his head toward my car had the corner of my mouth inching into a crooked smile.

You wanna talk cars, eh? Okay. I can do this. Just don't come off like a weirdo.

"It's my first car," I said with a shrug, trying to downplay how much I loved it, not to mention the butterflies dancing around in my stomach. At least he'd unwittingly chosen a topic that I could talk to almost anyone about though. The Jeep was my pride and joy. "I like hiking and camping, so I started building it while I was still in high school." I described a bit of the build process and tried not to look at his face so I could keep my thoughts straight.

"You did the work yourself?" he said, sounding impressed.

I nodded, "Most of it. I had help with the suspension and exhaust though."

My entire friend circle, which was really just an online community of outdoorsy, gear-head girls in the area, centered around wrenching on trucks, wheeling out in the forest and camping. We had large meetups on holiday weekends all summer and some smaller gatherings whenever we could find the time. We would circle the rigs around the campfire, eat, drink, and laugh under the stars. Sleep, wake, hike, take pictures, rinse, and repeat. It was my favorite thing ever.

I told the jogger as much and he nodded appreciatively. "I can see why so many people are getting into that overlanding style. I bet it's pretty cool knowing you can just head to the mountains and get lost for a while without having to set up a tent." He lightly kicked the toe of his running shoe into the sun faded, green fender of his older, hatchback sedan. "Can't do anything like that with this bucket of bolts."

I laughed lightly and returned his smile, "Are you joking? That's a Subaru. I bet you could get down more than half the trails I go down." He looked doubtful. "You'd be surprised." I smiled up at him, beginning to feel a bit more comfortable...as long as I didn't look directly into those hazel eyes of his. "So-uh, what's jogging like?" I asked, as I leaned back against the fender of the Jeep and studied my tattered sneakers.

He chuckled, "Not nearly as much fun as those crazy fitness people will tell you it is." He glanced down at his own shuffling feet before continuing, "I had to run every day in the military, so it just turned into a habit. Keeps me in shape. Helps me think."

I couldn't help but notice the hint of something melancholy in his voice. "Sounds like how hiking is for me."

"Yeah, the repetitive movement and steady breathing works wonders," he said, and we lapsed into another uncomfortable silence.

Even more awkward...

After a beat, I mustered up some courage and asked, "Do you ever go trail running? Like on a hiking trail?"

"I have a time or two. I really liked the Hidden Falls Trail, but I stuck to the gym after all that creepy stuff happened last summer."

"Man, that was wild, wasn't it?" A shiver crawled up my spine at the memory.

He nodded in response.

"Speaking of Hidden Falls, have you ever stopped at the camp store on the way up there? The one with the deli? The guy there makes the best huckleberry milkshakes in the world."

"Ya know, I never have. I'll have to do that one of these days," he said, the corner of his mouth twitching.

"Some of my favorite camp spots are up there on that mountain. Every time I get a chance, I stop at the store in the summer. I told the folks that work there that if the world ever ended, I would head straight for the store just so I could have one last milkshake before I died." I breathed a small laugh and then realized the jogger was looking at me strangely.

So much for not coming off like a weirdo.

I had started rambling like I always did when talking about my favorite things. At least I hadn't started prattling on about how otherworldly *gorgeous* the owners of the store were too. I cringed inwardly and tried not to wither in embarrassment.

Suddenly, he rapped his knuckles on the fender of his car and said, "Let's see if this turd will start now."

He cranked the ignition and to my relief, his car roared back to life. As I helped him disconnect the jumper cables and began tucking them back into their case, I had an attack of conscience.

Should I tell him that I took his picture on the trail? I knew it would be the honest thing to do. He was just another human before, but after our short conversation, he felt more like a *person* who obviously had feelings, and it seemed to me that he might be struggling with some things as well. Having an artsy, black and white photo of himself might make him feel better. And as much as I hated to admit it to myself, I kind of wanted to see him again.

"Thanks for the jump," he said, raising a hand before turning away from me.

I zipped the case closed and took a deep breath. *Just say 'you're welcome' and get on with your day, Amber.* I didn't want to come off as even more awkward and weird than I already had, plus he was already walking away...but before I could stop myself, I'd said it, "Before you go, I have a confession."

"Oh?" he said, turning back toward me, raising his brows.

"So, I'm a hobby photographer," I said gesturing to my pack and camera bag in the back of the Jeep, "and I'm playing with an old 35mm camera. I took a couple of shots of you when you passed me on the trail earlier."

He took a step back and crossed his arms, "Really?" It sounded more like a statement than a question and he eyed me with a suspicious arch to his dark brow, head canted to one side.

I withered a bit; definitely shouldn't have said anything. But it was too late to backpedal.

"I hope you're not mad," I said in a rush. The look on my face was probably some sort of a cross between a grimace and a sheepish grin. "I know I should have asked but you were way past me already and it was a great shot. I didn't wanna miss it."

He remained silent, so I pressed on. "It's just a silhouette shot. After I develop the pictures, I can give you a copy if you want one. I mean, if they even turn out."

He paused, seeming to process what I had just said, then his eyes lit up, "Wait, you mean like, *real* film? Not digital?" He uncrossed his arms and leaned forward a bit.

At least he wasn't upset with me. If anything, he sounded slightly impressed. I breathed a small sigh, trying to shake off the nerves. "Mm-hm. I'm going to shoot the whole roll today so I should have a print in a couple of days, I think."

"That's really cool. I'd actually love a copy. Hang on," he said, dipping into his car and pulling out his phone. "What's your number?"

I recited the ten digits, and he dialed the number. After it rang through to my phone, he hung up. "There ya go. Shoot me a text if it turns out."

My heart pounded in my chest. *Did I just give my number to a random guy? Yup. That happened.*

"O-Okay," I stammered lightly. I was way out of my wheelhouse with this whole situation, and I started to sweat even with the chill in the air. It had been close to two years since I had last exchanged numbers with a guy and that hadn't led anywhere. "So, should I save you as 'random jogger' or 'stranded motorist'?" I asked with a small smile, phone in hand, waiting to add him to my contacts.

"You can call me DJ, and you are?" His eyes met mine with that intense gaze he seemed to like so much. *Did he already know that it made me squirm?*

"I'm Amber," I said, all traces of the humorous confidence I'd just been feeling vanished to be instantly replaced with a riot of butterflies in my stomach. I wet my lips and swallowed.

"Amber-what?" The corner of his mouth curled as he looked down at me.

Oh, that smile is dangerous. He has got to stop looking at me like that or I'm gonna forget how to speak.

"Just Amber." I shrugged a little and tucked a stray hair behind my ear, then immediately chided myself. *You are not flirting, Amber! He could be a total womanizer. Just look at that face...and that body....?* My eyes took a quick tour of the man standing before me and damn it all if he didn't notice; his crooked smile morphing into a full-blown, sexy smirk. My face heated, no doubt going pink all the way to my ears.

Yeah, definitely a womanizer. Best to tread carefully.

"Alright then, 'Just Amber'." He spelled my name aloud and hit save.

Despite all my self-chiding, I saved his number too, curious about what the initials stood for but too nervous to actually ask him about it. Clearly, I was lacking in the self-control department; a fact that raised my hackles a bit. I couldn't recall a single moment in my life that I had been so easily charmed by someone I had just met. I would definitely need to evaluate my behavior and make some changes if we ever saw each other again. But, for all I knew he could just be humoring the awkward girl that helped him jumpstart his car and he'd totally ghost me.

"So, where are you off to for the rest of the day?" DJ asked, snapping me out of my thoughts.

"Well, talking about the camp store made me really want a milkshake," I said. "I think I'm gonna head up that way. I can use the trip to finish shooting this roll of film." I turned to close the hatch of the Jeep. "Maybe I'll make it an impromptu camping trip even? What about you?"

"I've got work," he shrugged.

"Bummer,"

"Eh, I'm just a bartender," he said with more than a touch of self-depreciation, "It's an easy job, and I get to talk to a lot of middle-aged couples during happy hour, so that's fun." We both laughed and he continued, "Some of those ladies about my mom's age scare me though. I flip one bottle, and they turn completely feral."

I guffawed then howled with laughter, but I could understand. I might have a feral moment if I watched him flip a bottle and wink at me over the bar. My hormones did a little dance and I immediately questioned my sanity. Why was it so easy for him to get me laughing? I'd never been so disarmed by someone in my life. Why him? Why now? Best not to think too deeply on it.

"Well, on that note," I extended my hand, "It was very nice to meet you, DJ, the jogging bartender.

"Nice to meet you too, Just Amber."

As he took my hand in his I couldn't help but notice how broad and calloused they were. I'd imagined the hands of a bartender being a bit softer and wondered what else he did in his spare time that would cause calloused like that—and why I suddenly cared so much about it. Fighting a suspicious look, I smiled squeezing his hand a bit harder than I normally would.

He raised an eyebrow at me. "Good grip."

"Thank you?"

We both laughed again before parting ways.

During the drive home, I couldn't stop thinking about him. His smile, his friendly, easygoing manner, his mysterious hazel eyes, or the way my hand had felt so small in his. For a short moment, I let myself wonder what it would be like to get to know him, maybe actually go on a date for once, like a normal person in their mid-twenties would, but then pushed it out of my mind. I couldn't let myself get distracted with a guy...especially one like DJ. If I even mentioned him to Mom, she'd call him a walking red flag.

A super good looking, super fit, charming, friendly, funny, bartender? *Queue the alarm bells.* There was a ninety-nine percent chance that I would never hear from or see him again, even after I got his photo finished and texted to let him know it was done, so I needed to quit daydreaming.

I rolled my eyes and cranked the volume on the stereo. Who was I kidding? Guys like DJ never went for girls like me, and if they did? Well, I didn't even want to think about what that could mean. I had a trip to the mountains to pack for—and no time for daydreams, no matter how handsome and annoyingly charming they might be.

2

Stranded

WHEN I ARRIVED HOME TO PACK for my impromptu trip, I caught a little flak from my mom.

"I just don't like the idea of you going all the way out there by yourself, Sweetie." She was only halfheartedly pleading with me. After I graduated high school, I had desperately wanted to move out on my own, but there was just no way I could make ends meet alone, so Mom and I had come to an agreement. If I worked a steady job, paid rent and bills on time, contributed to the house upkeep and shared the grocery expenses, Mom wouldn't hover, and I was allowed to come and go as I pleased; just like I was living on my own.

The arrangement worked out so well, that when Joey graduated a few years back, he had made the same agreement. But even though we all got along...even in a house as roomy as ours is, sometimes we just want a weekend away...alone.

"You know I've been doing this since I bought the Jeep, Mom. I'm going to be fine." I tried not to let out an exasperated sigh while I loaded my bedding and cooler in through the back hatch and failed.

"But the stories about the hikers going missing..." she trailed off, brows knit, lips pursed.

I knew the news stories last year really spooked her and I softened my tone a bit, taking her hands in mine. "That happened way out near Yellowstone and the Teton's. No one has even been attacked by a bear or cougar around here in decades. Besides, all that mess stopped last fall."

I looked into her very pretty, very concerned green eyes, and I almost caved. But I had to finish that roll of film for DJ, and I really wanted that huckleberry milkshake, (ok, maybe I wanted to gawk at the store owner a bit too) and some time alone in the forest.

I continued in an even softer tone, "I'm gonna be fine, Mom. I promise. I have my PLB and I'm gonna stay where I have reception anyway," I said while pointing to the cell signal booster attached to the roof rack.

"That could be in the middle of nowhere with that booster and you know it," she countered with a mock scowl that quickly morphed into a crooked smile. "You have to keep in touch, send me the GPS coordinates when you get set up for the night—"

"—And call as soon as you wake up," we said at the same time, me in a slightly mocking tone. Her instructions were always the same. Mom was a worrywart, but I supposed that all good parents were. Plus, she was the best mom and dad that I could have ever hoped for.

I gave her a tight hug and kissed her round cheek. "Love you, Ma."

"I love you too, Sweetie." She patted my shoulder and smiled just as Joey pulled up in his cherry-bombed Honda. We both rolled our eyes when he revved the engine and it backfired. He thought he was so cool.

He cut the motor bringing blessed quiet back to the neighborhood and sprang up out of the car, quickly noting that the Jeep was packed for a trip. "Where you off to this time, Sis?" he called out across the lawn.

Still wearing his grocery store uniform, he somehow looked scrawnier than he did in his regular get up of oversized jeans and tee-shirts. He still didn't look like he was old enough to even be driving, let alone old enough to buy liquor, but there he was in all his twenty-two-year-old glory, lopsided grin and all.

"Into the national forest," I said.

"Well, duh. You always go to the forest. Which part?" He acted like he was going to pull my hair, then stepped on my toe instead and laughed heartily.

"Ow, you turd!" I socked him on the shoulder. "Little brothers are so overrated," I said, looking at Mom while I rolled my eyes and smiled. Then to my brother, I said, "You need to get yourself a real car and come with me one of these days."

"You can keep your 'Heep'. Club Honda for life!" he said, waving his arms and trying to look tough.

Glaring at him, I said, "It's not a 'Heep', it's a Jeep and its way more fun than your backfiring, bucket-of-bolts will ever be."

"Hashtag Overlander is so three years ago,"

I cranked back my fist to sock him again and he bounded out of my reach, laughing. "I bet you'd finally find yourself a girlfriend if you did. There're lots of pretty, outdoorsy types out there that like a guy with a capable truck. But they won't even look at a dude in a Honda."

"Those girls *actually* scare me." He had the nerve to shudder dramatically.

I poked a finger at his chest, half laughing, half serious, "That's because we're tougher than you, and you know it!"

"Alright you two. Chill," Mom cut in wagging her finger at us both, "or I'm gonna tear your arm off and hit him over the head with it."

We both chuckled at the threat she had used on us our entire childhood...and obviously still used when we were acting like children. I slammed the Jeep's hatch closed and turned back to face Mom and Joey.

"I'll probably head up past the reservoirs and toward the mountain, but I may head down The Gorge and then go north from there. I'm not sure yet but I'll keep you guys posted. I promise. I'll turn on location sharing too."

They seemed satisfied with that last bit, and I hugged each of them in turn. "Love you guys. See you day after tomorrow."

I drove away from the house waving out the window and watching Mom and Joey shrink away in the rearview mirror. After the first few miles through town, the traffic thinned, the roads narrowed, and the drive through the foothills was incredibly scenic. Scattered farms and a few rural towns passed by in a blur. I loved the area, with its scattered meadows littering the flatlands, while small mountains rose steeply at their edges, covered in thick undergrowth and evergreens. I rolled down the window and let the cool air whip my hair around while I sang along with the radio, joy and the thrill of adventure harmonizing in my veins. Yes, I was definitely overdue for a camping trip.

As I crossed over an ancient, single lane suspension bridge that spanned the narrow portion of a lake, I held my breath for good luck, my childhood superstitions refusing to die. The driving surface of the bridge was nothing more than thick, wooden timbers that bumped and creaked under the Jeep's weight. Once back on solid ground, I let my breath out in a whoosh and laughed to myself.

Not much further down the road sat the old log cabin camp store I had told DJ about earlier that morning. It had been there, in the middle of nowhere, since some time in the 1940's. Run by the same family for its entire existence, it was a staple and a must stop destination for anyone traveling this road through the forest. Unfortunately, as I pulled up to the front doors, the tattered 'Closed' sign hung in the window.

"Dang it," I mumbled to myself. I squinted to make out the hours of operation.

October 16th – May 15th: *Friday – Sunday 8:00am-5:00pm*
May 16th – October 15th: *Thursday – Monday 7:00am-7:00pm.*

Inclement weather may delay peak season hours.
We're sorry for any inconvenience.

I wouldn't be getting the milkshake I had been dreaming about that day, but when I made my way back down the mountain on Saturday, I could stop in again.

My phone chimed and I pulled it out of my bag expecting a text from my mom or brother. I almost dropped it when I saw that it was from DJ.

"No way," I said aloud. I tapped the notification and read.

Hey, wyd?

"What you doing?" I squealed in spite of myself and bounced a bit in my seat remembering the wink he shot at me and the way his dark hair curled out from under his ball cap. Oh, to hell with the 'walking red flag' mess. I wanted this to be something fun. The beginning of a great friendship...maybe even more.

My fingers raced to type out a response. *Sitting in front of that camp store being sad that they aren't open today. Wyd?*

He immediately began typing a reply. *Trying to convince my coworker that a pretty photographer in a built Jeep saved my ass this morning and I actually had the good sense to get her number.*

I stared at my phone dumbfounded. Wait, he was talking about me? Me? Pretty? Really? I could feel my face heating while I grinned from ear to ear.

I do drive a Jeep and like to take pictures. Is your coworker convinced? I typed and hit send.

He was quick to respond again, *He says pics or it didn't happen. lol*

Great, I thought. My hair was a wind-blown mess, and I didn't have a stitch of makeup on. But he'd seen me that morning looking much the same as I looked now. I hopped out of the car for a picture anyway. I held my phone out in front of me making sure to get the SUV and the old store in the frame and tapped the shutter. The chilly mountain breeze bit my cheeks and tossed my hair in wild directions, but my eyes were still visible. It was the best I was going to be able to get. I hit send and climbed back into the Jeep. It wasn't long before another text came through.

PrettyJeepGirl confirmed. When r u heading back to town? You should come have a drink. It's on me.

I had the sudden urge to tear out of that parking lot and head straight back to town, but I had come all the way up here for nature photos. Plus, I needed to shoot the whole roll before I could get him his picture, so I responded,

I might head back tomorrow evening but probably first thing Saturday morning. Will you be working then?

He wrote back, *I'm on shift 3-midnight Friday, Saturday and Sunday. The Martini Bar on the Waterfront. Come see me.*

I was still internally squeeing as I typed, *Martinis? So boujee. I'll text you when I leave the house...and I'll bring your picture.*

DJ responded with a winking kiss emoji.

Throwing caution to the wind actually felt great. Bouncing around on cloud nine and still grinning like a fool, I tossed my phone in my bag, put the car in gear and guided it back out onto the road and continued deeper into the forest.

The asphalt dipped and curved, winding its way through the tunnel of vegetation and I kept my eyes peeled for the sneaky turn onto the tiny dirt road that led to one of my favorite dispersed camping areas. But then the Jeep just...shut down. No stuttering, no flashing idiot lights on the dash, nothing. It just went dead. One moment I was cruising down the forestry road dreaming of drinks with a handsome stranger, and the next, everything went silent. *What, the...?*

In all the years that I'd had it, the Jeep had never given me problems before, so I switched gears into neutral while it was still rolling and turned the key. Nothing happened so I coasted to a stop, put it back in park and tried to crank the motor over again.

Nothing.

The road was narrow and had no actual shoulder so I pushed the hazard light button and not even those would come on. Had something happened to the battery after jump starting DJ's car? Everything had seemed fine, there hadn't been any idiot lights shining, no sparks, and it had started up just fine a few minutes ago at the camp store.

Absolutely befuddled, I pulled my cell phone out of my bag praying that I still had a signal...the booster could only do so much and if there was a hill or in this case, the side of a mountain in the way of a cell tower, I was gonna be completely out of luck. The screen of my phone was black. I tapped the screen and lock button.

Nothing.

Okay, now *that* was weird. *How the heck could the battery have died already? There's no way. I'd had it plugged in for most of the drive. What the heck is going on?*

"Well, shit," I mumbled to myself as I elbowed the door open and hopped out listening hard for the sound of an approaching car. I tucked my short, dark hair behind my ears and looked around. I was still on a paved road, but I was also pretty far away from the more well-traveled areas, especially this time of year. All I could hear was the chilly spring breeze through the conifers and the river running just beside the road. I reached back inside the Jeep and popped the hood. After checking everything that could have possibly caused a complete electrical malfunction, all the fuses were good, and the wires, hoses and cables were tight. Nothing that I could see would have caused a complete shutdown...unless something fried the computer, but the chances of that were slim and nil.

"Shit!" I yelled out to the forest, my echoing voice bouncing around the trees. "Okay, don't panic, Amber. Think."

With fingers laced behind my head, I looked in the direction I had come from, then back to where I had been heading. A curving tunnel of trees bordered the pavement of the road, the broken, yellow line down the middle disappearing over a small hill. I was very alone.

A deep sense of unease started to take root in the pit of my stomach, and I took in several deep breaths to try and calm myself.

Should I start walking? Should I stay put and wave the next car down or maybe try to hitch a ride back down to the old camp store I'd left a few minutes ago? What the heck did people do when they broke down before cell phones?

I was completely stranded on a deserted road, well over an hour away from home with no idea what to do.

After a long talk with myself, I decided to stay put. The bright, puffy clouds had closed ranks, changing the sky from blue and white to a muted gray, and before long, it began to drizzle. Even after the morning had been so beautiful, the Pacific Northwest weather decided that half a day of sunshine was all that we needed. I should have known better, the weather always changed so fast in the mountains, especially in early spring. The rain wouldn't have even been an issue had the Jeep been operational, but...

I sighed and tried to look at the bright side; at least it wasn't snowing. Staying with my vehicle was definitely my best option. The last thing I needed to do was head out into the weather and catch my death. It was still very chilly up in the mountains. The road itself was clear, but there were several large patches of icy snow still clinging to the narrow shoulder and the ditch. Being cold was bad enough, but being wet *and* cold? I shuddered. Hard no.

My habit of being a hopeless over-planner helped to put me at ease a bit. I had a tendency to pack enough food to feed three people for every trip I took rather than just myself. My ice chest and food tote were stocked full of drinks, snacks, and freeze-dried backpacker meals. I had my pillow, sleeping bag, an extra blanket, jet-boil, and a cooking pot. When car camping without proper refrigeration, I only kept shelf stable foods, water and shelf stable juice bottles filled the cooler along with a few pieces of whole fruit and a couple bags of candy. The Jeep was the safest place to be and would be more than comfortable. I would just be doing my car camping while broke down on the side of the road.

Waiting would be easy. Someone was bound to pass by before too long, or before nightfall at the very latest. Forest service personnel or construction maybe?

After I popped the hatch of the Jeep, putting my roadside safety kit to work for the second time that day, I set out two cones and a flare about fifty yards down the road. Then I opened the awning to give myself a little more space while I waited and snapped a couple of shots of my roadside setup.

Joey was going to give me hell about the Jeep breaking down when I finally made it home. I could already hear his voice in my head, teasing me about my crappy choice of a Jeep when I should have picked out a Honda or Toyota. I chuckled to myself as I eased down into my camp chair.

With my Jet-Boil rumbling away, heating water for some coffee, I almost felt comfortable, but the asphalt beneath my feet reminded me that I was not out in some cozy little camp site in the woods. My car was dead. The nerves quickly inched their way back up.

I crossed my arms protectively across my chest and settled in to wait. Hours passed. Somebody—*anybody* should have passed by during the time that I waited, but no one did. When dusk approached, I told myself that I should try and get some sleep then head out walking back to the camp store at first light.

Settled onto my foam-topped bed platform and snuggled into my sleeping bag, I hardly slept a wink. Every rustle of wind, every creaking tree, every tiny sound in the night had me poking my head out of my blankets to peer out the windows of the Jeep. I couldn't risk missing a potential car passing, but the sounds were never anything more than the wind.

Somewhere close to midnight, the thick bank of clouds broke, and the night sky cast a colorful glow through the windows of the Jeep. I sat up and gazed out the window in wonder. Through the breaks in the trees and clouds, the northern lights danced across the sky in yellows, greens, pinks, and purples, while shooting stars, several every minute, flashed bright in the unpolluted darkness, some even appeared to trail fire as they streaked through the sky. Even through my anxiety I couldn't help but marvel at the sight, wondering what on earth would cause the northern lights to be visible this far to the south?

I was sure that Google would have known but my phone was still not working, so all I could do was wonder. After staring at the sky for what felt like hours, I finally drifted off fairly close to dawn, but my sleep was violently interrupted by a deep rumble followed by a sudden, vicious shaking.

"What the heck?" I popped my head out of my blankets and looked out the window. Through the shadowed, blue light of dawn I could see the road rolling while the Jeep bounced and heaved on its shocks.

"An earthquake? You've got to be kidding me!"

I watched in terror as the enormous trees trembled with the motion of the quake and my heart raced. The rolling asphalt buckled in several places then began to crack. Trees swayed then toppled across the road while dry fir needles and branches fell all over my car. A broken tree limb bounced off the windshield, sending a spiderweb of cracks across it and I couldn't watch anymore. I closed my eyes and hid in my sleeping bag like a terrified child. The quake seemed to last forever. My heart thundered in my ears nearly drowning out the loud clatter of the debris hitting the roof of the Jeep.

"Shit, shit, shit!" I squeaked, fighting panic and threatening tears while my thoughts raced. "Please don't let a tree fall on me." In the midst of the chaos, all I could think about was that I had left so many things unfinished. "I don't want to die. Please, please, please," I whispered into the dark interior of my sleeping bag.

The shaking ended as suddenly as it had begun, and the forest once again grew silent.

I lay there for a moment just breathing, trying not to cry, waiting for an aftershock. When none came, I threw the car door open and frantically began packing my bag. My heart never slowed, pounding in my ears as I quickly rolled up my sleeping bag with my pillow still inside. I strapped it to the bottom of my pack then stuffed the bag with as much food and drinks as it would hold. With all that I could carry slung across my shoulders, I closed the hatch of the old Jeep and took a deep breath. It was at least five miles back to the camp store, but that was the best hope I had of finding someone to help. With all the trees down across the road, there was no way any vehicles were going to be able to make it up here let alone a tow truck. I would have to leave the Jeep behind.

I hadn't taken more than half a dozen steps from the car when I heard the faint echo of a human voice off the trees.

My heart soared. *Oh, my God, I'm saved!*

I listened intently for a moment suddenly realizing that the voice was male, and he sounded angry. My heart dropped and an ice-cold sliver of fear settled into the place that had just been warmed by hope. It *would* be just my luck to run into a complete maniac while alone on a deserted road in the middle of nowhere...without a weapon of any sort. But I had to do something. I couldn't just stand there in the middle of the road waiting for my very likely demise at the hands of a possible psychopath.

Whispering expletives under my breath, I scurried back to the Jeep and threw my pack inside. If he found me and I had to try and escape from him, the pack would just slow me down. It was too darn heavy. I locked the door, darted off the road and crouched down into the leafless bushes and ferns.

As the sounds of the voice got louder—closer—I began running through every worst-case scenario possible. The guy is crazy; he tries to break into my car. The guy is crazy; he finds me hiding in the bushes and murders me. Or he finds me in the bushes, tortures and violates me, then murders me.

My eyes darted around my immediate area searching for an equalizer of some sort. A stick or a rock maybe? The man's head bobbed into view over a small hill in the road. He had to be tall, and he was walking so fast he was practically jogging. At that distance I couldn't make out any of his features, but he was waving his arms around in wild gestures while cursing every living thing on the planet.

Yup. Definitely crazy.

With my mind made up about this man's sanity, I sank further back into the bushes and crouched, praying that he wouldn't stop at my car. He did though, growing quiet as he approached. I let out a quiet groan.

He looked at the Jeep and then spun in circles, eyes canvassing the surrounding area. I could tell that he didn't see me in the bushes and breathed a tentative sigh of relief. But then he cupped his hands around his eyes and peered through the windows of the Jeep, checking each one before finally stopping at the driver side rear window. He had to have seen my pack.

Well, that was stupid, Amber. I should have just hidden it in the ditch somewhere close by. *Damn it.* I had panicked, and in my rush to hide, had made a huge mistake.

"Hello?" he called out, looking around again. "Is anyone still out here?"

I held my breath and sat motionless. When no answer came, he began trying the door handles. Finding them locked, he scanned the ground and picked up a softball sized river rock, testing its weight.

What? A smash-and-grab? Oh, no you don't, bro.

Forgetting my fear and thinking only of my poor Jeep, I popped out of the bushes with a bent twig in my hand brandished like a sword. "Don't break my window!" I yelled.

The man screeched and nearly jumped out of his skin at my sudden appearance and dropped the rock.

"Please?" I added, letting the crooked twig fall from my hand. My arms shot up, palms facing forward.

He mirrored my position for a moment before dropping a hand to his chest.

"You scared the absolute hell out of me, girl." He laughed nervously before continuing, head canted to one side. "Why are you in the bushes?"

I thought about moving toward him but hesitated. I had to be careful. I didn't know what was going on or why he was walking down a deserted road in the mountains, but I was generally a terrible liar. Honesty would probably be the best choice given the situation.

"I—uh, I panicked. My car just died, and I've been stuck here since yesterday."

He raised his brows, "Yours is dead too, 'eh? Its really happened then." His voice trailed off and his hands went to his hips, while a genuinely concerned look spread across his face.

"What do you mean? What's happened?" I asked as I awkwardly lowered my hands. Maybe he wasn't as crazy as I had first imagined, only frustrated, confused, and scared, just as I was?

"S.H.T.F." he said, like I should know what that meant.

The look of confusion on my face must have cued him in to my lack of understanding and he elaborated with an exasperated sigh. "Shit Hit the Fan, girl. It's the end of the world as we know it. The *fall* of our civilization."

"Wait, what?" I asked, my voice sounding shrill and more panicked than I intended. "How do you know that?"

"Climb up out of the ditch and I'll tell you," he said, motioning me towards him.

I shot him a skeptical look and considered. He was a big man, tall, well over six feet, and he had an athletic build, but he was easily twice my age with thinning, salt and pepper hair, graying beard stubble, and a bit of a potbelly. He wore sensible pants, sturdy shoes, and a plain, puffy vest over a tucked in shirt. This man's entire look smacked of 'Outdoorsy Dad'.

"Look, I'm not going to hurt you. I have a wife and kid to get home to. I've been walking since before dawn and I'm thirsty, not to mention being out in the open for that earthquake...my nerves are pretty well shot. You got some water in that cooler you'd be willing to share?" He pointed to the window of my Jeep.

So, he was after the ice chest and not my pack? I paused a beat and listened to my gut. He wasn't throwing off dangerous vibes anymore and he certainly *seemed* normal now that he was talking to me rather than himself. Plus, he had confirmed my 'Dad' suspicions without my asking.

"Okay, but no sudden movements," I said as I scrambled out of the bushes and pulled the car keys out of my pocket. I had to take a chance, but I could still be cautious.

He raised his hands and took several steps away from the car to reassure me.

At least he's polite. "I'm Amber, by the way. And I do have some water," I sighed, a little of the tension leaving my body then mumbled to myself, "I wish I woulda packed some frikkin' whisky though."

As I unlocked the passenger door, he chuckled and introduced himself, "Ya got that right. I'm Dan."

Still eyeing him cautiously, making sure he stayed on the opposite side of the car, I reached in and jerked open the cooler. Several bottles of water, juice, and a bag of candy I couldn't fit in my pack stared back at me. Pulling a water and juice out, I tossed them over the hood of the Jeep. He caught each one and nodded in thanks. I waited while he took a drink before asking again about how he knew it was the end of days.

"Have you not been paying attention to the news the last couple of years?" he asked, all exasperated disbelief.

I shook my head. With the exception of last summer's research obsession, I hadn't watched the news in over two years and had completely dropped off social media over the winter. Staying disconnected from current events kept my stress levels low and the worst of my anxiety at bay. Not that I explained that to *him*, though.

Dan rolled his eyes but continued, "Our way of life has been deteriorating for a long time, the economy is in the toilet and the country—no, the *world* is in shambles. It was just a matter of time before something, natural or man-made, happened to bring about a reset."

I shrugged and shook my head, "So, what does that have to do with both of our cars breaking down on the same road?"

Dan looked smug, "That, girl, is caused by an electromagnetic pulse. It could be some crazy country detonated a nuke in the atmosphere, but I'd bet my eye teeth that it was a solar flare or coronal mass ejection. We're in the middle of a solar maximum right now and judging by the northern lights and all the shooting stars last night, there is a ton of solar radiation in the atmosphere. A blast like that from the sun can take out every electronic component on the side of the planet that was facing it. Shoot, it might even wrap around most of the planet if it was large enough."

He sounded so sure of himself, but how could I know? How could *anyone* really know?

I raised my brow in blatant skepticism. "So, you're telling me that the sun did all this and that we have basically been pushed back into the pioneer days?" Leave it to a man to think he's got it all figured out—especially when there is no way to prove him right...or wrong, for that matter.

"Pre-pioneer days. No trains, no telegraphs, no internet, no power, no running water, no infrastructure. Nothing. Think pilgrims, girl. We might as well be back in the dark ages."

I stared at him gaping. He couldn't be serious, could he? But what if he really was right? "Damn," I said under my breath then paused. What were Mom and Joey dealing with back at home? No infrastructure meant no emergency services, no law. I didn't want to think about it. I didn't want to believe it. There had to be some other explanation. "What about the earthquake though? Do you think it was connected to the solar—corona...whatever you called it?"

"Solar flare. Coronal mass ejection," he corrected. "And I dunno for sure...except maybe Mother Earth is pissed that we've been neglecting her these last couple hundred years?" He shrugged, "Coincidence, maybe? Whatever the reason, there have been some unexplainable sightings in the news lately, from all over the world. Things no one fully understands."

A muted chill tickled up my spine and I shuddered inwardly as I thought back to the national park killings and the missing people that were never found. Then there was the 'Angel' video. Did he really think all of that was connected to the power going out?

I thought back to the volcanologist that had killed her career with the controversial theory that the killings and disappearances were linked to the cluster of earthquakes that happened around Yellowstone last year. My mind quickly connected the dots. We had just been through an earthquake, the entire Cascade Mountain Range was volcanic, and we were standing in the foothills of the most active volcano in the range. My mind reeled at the thought.

Dan sighed and took another long drink of water before he continued, "I see your bag is packed. Are you planning on hiking out?"

Perceptive, wasn't he? My eyes narrowed. "Well, I was going to head to the camp store down the road to try and make a phone call."

Dan grunted in response.

"You headed there too?" I asked.

"That was the plan," he nodded. "It's either that or trying to walk out the back way, which would involve higher elevations and snow. I'm not prepared for that." He cranked the cap back onto his water bottle and continued, "Ya know, land lines probably aren't working either."

My heart sank. How was I going to get a hold of my family and let them know I was okay? Were *they* okay? A dull ache began to form in my chest. "No regular phones either?"

"Nope. I mean, it's possible that they could work, but those old school copper phone lines are being decommissioned. Pretty much every communication system is digital now, so it only makes sense land lines would be down too."

I nodded numbly, grappling with all the implications of his words.

"I spent a lot of time watching videos on what an EMP would do to our electronics after all that crap with North Korea a few years ago. Opinions were split. Some people swore that everything electronic would be toast and others said cars and phones would most likely keep working." He shrugged. "Judging by the fact that both our rigs are dead in the water, so to speak, I think we know now." He took a deep breath, fidgeting with the bottle in his hands and looked at the sky. "Your cell is dead too, right?"

"Yep," I sighed and looked up at the sky as well. Fast-moving clouds piled thick around the mountain tops, like a gray harbinger of things to come. Maybe we really were in bigger trouble than I could have ever imagined.

"Ya know, I think the camp store has mountain bike rentals during the summer." Dan spoke mostly to the sky then turned back to me, "I'm not sure where they store them in the off season, but they've gotta be somewhere close, and a bike is going to be the best way to get around from here on out. I'm going to stock up on what I can at the camp store and get back to my family. The wife is probably worried sick."

I nodded, a vision of my worried mom appearing in my mind's eye. I needed to get home. "I live with my mom. She has got to be beside herself. My little brother too."

He pegged me with a 'kids these days' look and shook his head.

"Rude." I scowled. Who was he to judge? "Not that I should have to justify my living situation to a complete stranger, but I'm the oldest sibling and I'm helping my single mother make ends meet. Things are tough these days."

I dipped back inside the car and opened my pack then sent a bag of jerky and an apple flying toward Dan's head. He caught both with ease. "You're welcome," I snapped before he had a chance to thank me.

He droned out a long suffering 'Thank you' before turning back towards the road. "Do you want to walk together? There's safety in numbers and some company could be a good thing."

I wasn't too keen on staying put alone, but walking with this stranger wasn't a great option either. He seemed harmless enough since we had been speaking, but something in my gut was urging me to stay put.

I felt a bit like Forrest Gump as I thought about what my mom always said, *'Your mind and your heart can absolutely lead you astray, but your gut will never do you wrong. Trust it.'* I had rationalized away gut feelings in the past and always wished that I had just listened when something bad inevitably followed.

Also, what if Dan was lying? Was I really going to bite into his story and swallow it hook, line and sinker? I might not have as much world experience as Dan had, but I was far from clueless. What I needed was a second opinion, but I had no way of getting one, so I had to go with what my gut instinct told me.

"I'm going to wait a bit. It looks like we're gonna get wet, and I don't have any rain gear." I tugged at the shoulder of my hoodie and sighed. The ever-present cloud cover did seem to be hanging rather low at the moment, so my decision came across more like solid reasoning instead of a hastily thought up excuse.

"Fair enough," Dan nodded, but I could see concern etched into the lines of his face.

The wind kicked up just then bringing a light mist with it and I shivered. "Yeah, definitely going to stay put until the weather blows over."

"Alright then," Dan sighed. "But I'm not thrilled with the idea of leaving you alone out here. Just doesn't sit right. How about I send up a flare when I make it to the store assuming it still has supplies? Shouldn't take me more than a few hours if I huff it." He tucked the water and juice bottles into the pockets of his vest. "And if the shop owners are there, I'll let them know you're up here. On the off chance that communications are still up, they should have a way to get in touch with rangers or the forest service."

"I'm sure I'll be fine, and I'll keep watch," I said wondering if I would even be able to see a flare through the trees and misty rain.

Dan raised a hand as he walked away. "Thanks again for the snack and drinks," he said around a mouthful of jerky, shaking the bag. "I hope you and your family have some food stored up. It's gonna get really ugly in the coming months if you don't. There are only nine meals between peace and anarchy."

"Well, that's freaking chilling, bro," I called out to him.

"Just dropping truth bombs." He mimicked a mic-drop and resumed his overly fast walking pace down the road and around some fallen trees.

Another gust of wind blew through the area causing the bushes at the road's edge to sway and a shadow seemed to dip and move through them at the same moment. The sharp scent of sulfur and earthy decay briefly brushed my nose and I cringed, the forest around me suddenly looking much more sinister than it had just a few short moments ago. A knot formed in my stomach while an icy chill tickled down my spine. It wasn't the smell that nearly froze my feet to the pavement, it was the light scratching sound of something moving through the undergrowth. *Is something out there?*

"Dan!" I yelled. "I have a bad feeling. Maybe you should wait here with me?"

"It's just the winds of change, girl!" he called in response turning to face me while walking backwards.

"But," How did he not feel the same sense of wrongness that I did? I knew what Mom would say, *Men never pick up on the little things that could keep them alive. And they always seem to ignore women's intuition...too much testosterone.* "I really feel like you should stay—"

"Keep an eye out for the flare!" He pointed to the sky with a confident smile, completely brushing off my concern. Guess you really couldn't talk any sort of sense into a pig-headed man's brain.

With a small scowl, I reluctantly raised my hand, and he turned back in the direction he was going. I watched him until he disappeared around a curve in the road then hastily got back inside the Jeep. Something was definitely off. I couldn't put my finger on it, but a deep sense of dread had settled in my chest.

The rain began falling in earnest streaking the windows of the car and distorting the dark trees around me. Hours passed in an indistinguishable blur and as the rain darkened sky began to blacken with the coming of night, I unpacked my bag and settled in for another night alone in the woods. There was no way I would be walking out of the forest before dark. The rain showed no signs of letting up either, not to mention the queasy, nervous feeling I had in my gut. I couldn't see anything in the forest surrounding me, but it felt like something was out there. Lurking in the shadows. Waiting. I hadn't seen any sign of the flare Dan said he would send up and I found myself hoping with all my might that he was alright. A deep and primal sense of unease gnawed at the pit of my stomach, and I shivered as I lay down to try and get some rest

3

To Fight and Survive

Dan

THE CHILLY FOREST DRIZZLE SEEPED through Dan's vest as he trudged along the narrow road toward the camp store. The earthquake had stirred up chaos, dumping branches and whole trees across his path like some sort of twisted obstacle course. Each natural barricade he scrambled over or around was a not-so-subtle reminder of the list he'd dreamed up after his time in the service.

Three Rules to Survive the Apocalypse:

#1. *Stay sharp as a goddamned tack.* Complacency will get you killed.

#2. *Lend a hand whenever you can.* Next time it might be your ass on the line. Being in need could get you killed.

#3. *Don't ever be a hero.* That's a one-way ticket to getting yourself killed.

He dug into his vest pocket, retrieving a pack of jerky. Tearing the ziplock open, he snatched up a hefty chunk and stuffed it into his mouth whole. A small smirk crept across his face and was immediately replaced by a scowl. Barely half a day into the apocalypse and he'd already violated rule number one. That girl, Amber, had scared the living daylights out of him when she'd popped up out of the ditch. His wits were nowhere to be found in that moment. Truth be told, he'd nearly pissed himself. Not the finest example of staying sharp, but at least he had recovered quickly.

He grunted to himself, "Amber. Probably should have insisted she come along."

She was just a kid after all, but damned if that would have broken rule number three. He wasn't supposed to play the hero, plus she was better prepared than he was at the moment. She'd even given him food and drink, a perfect example of rule number two. Hiding in the bushes at the sound of his approach—rule number one. She had shelter in that old Jeep as well. Yeah, she seemed smart enough. She'd be alright for a while. Once he got to the camp store, he could send help back up to get her, or go back up there himself with a better grasp of the situation he'd found himself in.

"She'll be safe up there," he muttered, as if trying to convince himself that he had made the right call in continuing on without her. A seed of doubt sprouted in his mind, and he paused in the road, turning to look back at the way he had come. Debris littered the broken asphalt while the tall fir trees swayed in the wind.

Try as he might, he couldn't shake the memory of her worried voice as he had walked away.

Dan! I have a bad feeling. Maybe you should wait here with me? She'd called out to him, her voice quavering while she wrung her hands and furrowed her brows.

Had he let his toxic masculinity rear its ugly head when he'd dismissed her fear and left, telling her that it was 'just the winds of change'? He let out a heavy sigh. There was nothing he could do about it now; she was over an hour and a half behind him. She'd just have to hang on until he got to the camp store and then he'd figure out how to get her off the mountain.

He turned back in the direction he had been heading as the smell of earthy decay laced with sulphur floated in on the breeze and hit him square in the face. He cringed, wrinkling his nose.

That stink had to be from the earthquake. With all the down trees and cracks in the ground, it was no surprise that some strange odors had taken to the air. Most likely it was just a dead animal, its body disturbed by the quake making the odor more pungent.

Glancing around, he quickly took note of his surroundings. To his left, a steep drop led to an icy river, while to his right, a steep incline ran up around fifty feet before the loose soil and rocks gave way to forest.

A flicker of shadowy movement on the mountainside, just inside the tree line, caught his eye, and he squinted trying to see through the misty rain. After several tense moments, he dismissed the stirring of the bushes for a gust of wind and continued his march down the road, tucking the bag of jerky back into one pocket and retrieving a bottle of juice from another.

Rule number one: *Stay Sharp.* There is no sense in flinching at shadows; they're everywhere in a forest. But that didn't mean he should brush them off either.

Dan may not be as young and spry as he once was, but he still had his health and strength, not to mention the combat knife he always carried on his belt. Genuine military surplus. He unsheathed the knife grinning at the familiar muted gleam of razor-sharp steel. It gave him a sense of security. His rifle would have made him feel even better, but he hadn't taken it with him on his drive. He'd only planned to be gone from home for a couple of hours. Boy had he ever picked a shit day to go enjoy the mountains. At least his wife had the rifle for protection until he made it home.

Juice bottle in his left hand and blade in his right, he walked on. There was no need to jump at shadows, but there was also no excuse for being ill-prepared either. *When in doubt, whip it out.* He tossed the blade lightly in his hand as he walked.

Another hour passed and he was making great time. At well over six feet tall, his lanky stride ate up the distance and for the first time since leaving Amber, he felt a sense of accomplishment. The camp store was close—maybe half an hour, tops. As his focus on the road ahead drifted, his ears picked up the faintest scraping sound coming from the underbrush just beside the road.

There was no way that was just the wind.

He froze mid-stride, heart knocking, grip tightening on the knife in his hand as he strained to hear anything above the patter of rain in the conifers. He scanned the bushes, gut clenching, raw survival instincts firing. Then he heard it; another swish followed by the sharp, staccato clicking of claws on pavement directly behind him.

Dan wheeled, knife raised, adrenaline searing through his veins. The odor of sulfur hit him first then mingled with the sickly-sweet stench of rotting meat a heartbeat before a shadow with teeth and claws launched itself directly at him. It was *fast.* Unnaturally fast; nothing but a blur of glowing red eyes and long, sinewy limbs. The creature crashed into him.

He didn't even have time to brace. The impact drove him into the pavement, knocking the breath from his lungs and sending the juice bottle flying. It was instinct alone that kept the survival knife tight in his grip. His mind flipped to combat mode, years of training finally kicking in.

Move fast. Strike hard.

But the creature flowed like smoke and black flames, whip-fast, and wild; nothing but a blur of movement. It defied all logic. In an instant, sharp claws ripped through his shoulder and raked down his ribs. White-hot pain screamed through his body, but he pushed the sensation from his mind as the creature's jaws snapped for his throat.

Dan twisted, slamming his forearm into the creature's neck, pushing it back just far enough to keep his jugular intact. His knife hand was pinned, the blade grinding uselessly into the damp asphalt, as the thing lunged and thrashed above him, its claws shredding through the thin fabric of his shirt.

Keep moving. Create space.

Dan bucked his hips and pushed against the creature with his knees. It was just enough to put it slightly off balance. With a roar, he wrenched his arm free and drove the blade upward with all his strength, targeting the vulnerable spot between the beast's neck and shoulder.

Black blood spilled out, splattering his face and chest as the creature reared back howling in pain.

It lashed out, claws tearing down the left side of Dan's face. A guttural cry tore from his throat, the sound mingling with the beast's own unearthly screams.

The creature slammed into him again, the stench of sulfur and rotting meat clawing down his throat, turning his stomach. *Jesus*, it was like death itself had lungs.

He twisted his head to one side narrowly avoiding snapping jaws. It was too strong. He was going to lose this fight.

As the creature's claws dug into Dan's chest and it leaned closer— straining to sink its yellowed teeth into his throat—he spotted an opening. The beast's red eyes shone with malevolence and Dan stared back with a twisted grin.

"Got you, fucker," he growled, and plunged the combat knife into one of the creature's eyes with a sickening squelch. It howled and leapt back before Dan could drive the knife through its eye socket, dragging one front leg as it went. Silently, it disappeared back into the shadowy depths of the forest.

Dazed and bleeding profusely, Dan hauled himself to his feet and continued lurching down the road to the camp store.

Keep moving, he thought, *just get to the store.*

As he stumbled along, blade still in hand, he kept his gaze fixed on the forest never letting his guard down. Searing pain throbbed through his body with every frantic beat of his heart while he took a mental inventory of his injuries.

His left arm hung dead at his side, limp and throbbing. Probably dislocated. He hissed through his teeth as he reached over with his good arm, gripping just below the joint to keep it from shifting. Warm, sticky blood oozed from the gashes across the right side of his rib cage. And his face...? It felt unnaturally cold. He was pretty sure he no longer had a left ear, and that may have been the least life threatening of his injuries. His ribs screamed with every ragged breath he took. Probably had a couple of broken ones along with the flesh wounds. *Damn-it!*

But even with the long list of injuries, he desperately clung to the fact that he wasn't completely FUBAR. His legs still worked, and God willing, his stubborn will to continue on wouldn't falter either.

Amber's worried voice echoed in his mind again, *But I really feel like you should stay—*

"Stupid. Idiot," he hissed through clenched teeth. She'd known something was off and had tried to get him to stay, and like a fool, he'd brushed her concern away.

Stupid-stupid-stupid! He groaned as his head swam and he nearly fell, the pain in his shoulder and ribs making it hard to see straight.

He needed to stop. He needed to fashion a makeshift sling for his arm and bind his wounds, but with that red-eyed demon creature still at large, he could not risk slowing down, not even for a moment.

What was that thing? It looked like a cross between a cougar and a dog, but it had been huge and hairless; black skin stretched tight over protruding bones. Even as emaciated as the creature was, it had still handled his big ass like a rag doll. He stumbled on down the road holding to his consciousness like a life preserver. He was losing too much blood.

With every step, he could feel that consciousness draining from him, a fuzzy ring around his vision and dullness in his mind. If he passed out before he made it to the camp store, he was a dead man, so he pushed on through the pain and disorientation.

The rain continued to hammer at him while his strength continued to dwindle, but finally, the camp store bobbed into view like a dumpy beacon of hope. Only about two hundred yards left. He was going to make it. He had to make it.

Hope surged in Dan's chest and he nearly sighed but with his next breath, came the scent of sulfur and rot. The creature came at him from the side this time, slinking out of the shadowed forest, a single malevolent, glowing eye fixed on his stumbling and broken body. He prepared to make his final stand, the air thick with the creatures' stench.

The beast circled him, as if it were looking for a weak spot in his defenses, only a slight limp evident in its fluid stride. How had the thing healed up so quickly? It wasn't even bleeding anymore.

Locking its remaining eye on Dan's dislocated shoulder, the creature screeched and leapt. Dan watched, his world moving in slow motion, as the beast sailed for his throat. With the last vestiges of his strength, he swept the survival knife up and deep into the soft spot below the creature's jaw. They crumpled to the ground in a heap where the creature continued to flop around like a dying fish before finally laying still.

Dan dragged himself over to retrieve his knife from the monster's jaw, but the moment his fingers closed around the handle, the creature screamed again, writhing and struggling to get to its feet.

With a primal roar, Dan wrenched the blade out of the stinking shadow's jaw and buried it deep into the side of its head. Without a sound, the beast burst into flames.

That was it. It was finally over.

As his consciousness began to fade, he chuckled to himself, "Thought I was...ready for anything," he said between coughing gasps. "Turns out I wasn't ready for shit." Dan rolled onto his back and let the cool embrace of darkness consume him.

Delirious and overcome by a fever-dreamlike state, images floated through Dan's mind while physical sensation was something distant. He knew that he lay face up on the ground simply because the falling rain slicked his face and stung his eyes. He blinked hard, trying to clear his vision as the echo of a low moan bounced around in his head.

The face of a dark-haired man floated into his line of sight and he spoke, but Dan's disjointed mind couldn't make any sense of the words. Pain shot through his entire body and another echoing groan cut through his delirium. Were those horrible noises coming from him? Was he floating? The treetops swayed at the edges of his vision then everything went dark once more.

Dan faded in and out of consciousness catching tiny bits of information as he did. He was indoors and there were two people tending to his injuries; a flame haired woman held him fast and stabilized his shoulder, while the dark-haired man steadily and firmly tugged on his bent arm. With a soft click, his shoulder popped back into place. Dan groaned in relief and tried to thank them, but the darkness claimed him again.

When some semblance of consciousness returned, all Dan could feel was burning. The left side of his face felt like it was on fire, and the sensation was mirrored in the wounds across his ribs and shoulder. He was thrashing uncontrollably and the two people struggled to keep him still while placing a cool dressing over his wounds.

He'd thought he was going to die out there on the road. His injuries were so severe that he should be a dead man already, but while his body was completely out of his control, his mind was growing sharper by the second. The metallic scent of blood mingled with the common smells of a cozy home after a hot breakfast. Panic bloomed at the sudden mental clarity. He'd heard about this; the brain going into overdrive right before the body gives up.

How had this happened? He was supposed to have been ready for the apocalypse. He'd trained for it. Planned for it. Yet he was flat on his back, being tended to by strangers in his final moments like a rookie. Only, he didn't feel like he was dying. Everything hurt, true, but something in his mind was telling him that this was not his end. Agony was the only physical sensation he knew, but in his mind, a void filled with nothing but hate began to form.

What was going on?

"Please," Dan croaked, "What is ha-happening to m-me? God, make it stop. It burns."

Neither one of the people holding him down answered and their voices sounded far away and thick with worry when they spoke to each other.

"That was a darkling spawn, Erik. When was the last time you saw even a trace of them in these forests?" the woman said.

"I can't remember, it's been a long time. A very long time," the dark-haired man responded.

"You know we're too isolated out here, even with the light dome," the red-haired woman said. "If the darkling have returned, and all the electronics are down, then it's *time*. We need to get to The Snow Forest, or to Evergreen at the very least, and there are precious few outposts between here and there. We need to move now before things get chaotic. You know we do."

The Snow Forest? What is an outpost? And what did they call that shadow with teeth? Darkling spawn? What the Hell was going on? Dan's thoughts thrashed as wildly as his body. *Why am I shaking so badly?*

"Wh-what is g-going on?" Dan demanded with a snarl, hoping the pair would take notice this time. "I have a wife and k-kid. I just want to g-go h-home. They need m-me." He reached out and a strong hand clasped his own.

"We're here, friend. We've got you," Erik, the dark-haired man, said. His face floated into Dan's view, and he smiled reassuringly before turning his attention to the woman. "We can't let him die, Alma. It's not right. He killed that spawn. He deserves better than this."

"It might be too late," Alma replied. "He's strong, true, but look at him—he may be too strong to simply give up the spark, and yet not strong enough to survive the remedy."

What were these people talking about?

The hateful darkness grew in his mind and a deep sense of wrongness filled his heart. Whatever that darkness was, it was to be avoided at all costs. He pushed back at the hate and swallowed. He wanted to live. He *needed* to live. Memories of his wife and their daughter flashed in his mind's eye, and he could have wept as the darkness retreated a bit.

Erik looked deeply into Dan's eyes and in that moment, Dan knew his very existence was being weighed by the man with the dark hair. Try as he might, words refused to form. All he could manage was what he hoped came across as a pleading look.

With a sharp nod, Erik turned away. "I think we can save him. I know there's a risk, but if we do nothing, it'll be worse," he said, eyes boring into Alma's. There was a long pause, but even through the pain haze, Dan could tell there was an unspoken battle of wills burning between the man and woman beside him. Erik gritted his teeth and continued in a huff, "Well, if you won't do it, I will. Hold him down. I'll be right back."

Erik released Dan's hand and left the room.

Alma sighed and took up Dan's hand in her own. "Lucky for you, that male has a stubborn streak wider than the Columbia River." Shaking her head, she smoothed his sweat-damp hair back from his forehead. "You're going to be alright, friend."

"D-Dan. My name is Dan."

Alma smiled down at him, "You're gonna make it, Dan. Just hold on."

Dan nodded and squeezed his eyes shut against the pain. His tremors continued for several minutes while they waited for Erik to return, all the while, a silent war raged between Dan and the hateful void in his mind.

When Erik's heavy footfalls sounded again, Dan opened his eyes to see the other man leaning over him holding a mason jar filled with a thick, dark liquid. "This is going to taste horrible and will probably give you a bit of a bellyache, but it won't last long. Just drink it all."

"Wh-what is it?" Dan croaked.

"An old family remedy for spawn poison," Erik said. The corner of his mouth quirked into a wry smile. "The poison is draining your spark—killing you. This is like an anti-venom."

So, he really was dying. Maybe he would be better off dead? The thought passed through Dan's mind with a chill. After all the study and practice and preparing, he didn't even make it through day one of the apocalypse.

The hateful void surged, threatening to black out all thought.

No*, no!* He couldn't allow it.

What would happen to his wife and kid? Were there more of those creatures in his town already wreaking havoc? God, were they dead already? He had to know. He couldn't die here in a room with strangers. He had a duty and responsibility to his family and community. *He couldn't just die here!*

Dan struggled to gain control of his shaking body to sit up and tell these people he wanted to live, but all he could manage was a frustrated groan as he tried to lift his head.

"I've got you, friend," Erik said as he gently lifted Dan's head and pressed the jar to his lips.

This was it. Either he'd die, or whatever was in that mason jar would save his life.

The void in his mind screamed. It didn't want whatever the remedy was.

His choice was clear.

Dan sucked back a mouthful of the viscous fluid. It coated his mouth and dropped into his gut like a nine-pound sledgehammer. His body revolted and the substance nearly came back up.

"Just breathe, Dan. Breathe. The first drink is the worst part," Alma said while smoothing back his hair. "Swallow hard and keep it down."

Dan did as he was told, his throat working over and over as his stomach roiled and the burning sensation in his body grew worse. The void in his mind railed against the substance like a wild, injured beast. The moments passed like hours. Had he made a terrible mistake? Gradually though, the scorching pain in his wounds cooled and his tremors began to subside. He swallowed hard again and then groaned as relieved tears slipped from his eyes.

"There ya go," Erik said, sounding relieved. "That's it. Feeling a little better now?"

Dan nodded weakly and Erik pressed the jar to his lips once more. "One more drink,"

The smell of the stuff hit his nose and the thought of swallowing it again turned his stomach so badly, he retched. Why did it smell like wine vinegar and...was that blood? What the hell had he just swallowed?

"I know. It's foul, but this last bit won't be nearly as bad if you can get past the smell. Trust me," Erik said. "Drink up. You've got this."

Whatever the stuff was, it seemed to be helping, so summoning some courage and strength, Dan raised a shaky hand to the other side of the jar and together he and Erik tipped it back. He sucked down the rest of whatever was in the jar and hardly tasted it. Erik was a man of his word. As it landed in his belly, a relaxing warmth began to spread through his body. Within moments, his tremors ceased altogether, and he sighed, relaxing back onto the hard surface he was laying on.

"I don't know what that stuff is," Dan breathed, "But thank God for it. And thank God for you folks."

"Don't thank us, thank the Goddess. We're just Her messengers," Alma said solemnly. "Now try and rest, you'll be feeling better soon." She laid a comforting hand on his chest. "Sleep, Seed Child. You are protected by The Light."

As Dan closed his eyes, he tried to wrap his mind around what had just happened. *Seed child? Goddess?* Had he stumbled into some random cult? Who were these people and how did they know so much about a creature that, by all rights, shouldn't even exist? He supposed he could think more on that later. His mind was foggy, and sleep was quickly creeping in to claim his consciousness. The last thing he remembered before he slipped off to sleep was Erik gently laying his head back on a rolled-up towel. Cult members or not, if he ever woke up again, he'd owe them his life.

Dan woke as the gray, early morning light peeked through the windows of the camp store and he gingerly took stock of himself and his surroundings.

He had been laid out on a pile of sleeping bags near the register. Miraculously, his head was clear and he felt strong, almost invigorated. He slowly sat up, waiting for his body to protest or his world to start spinning, but when nothing happened, he rolled his shoulder and ran cautious hands over his bare arms, chest, and face. He had been washed, all remnants of that shadow's black blood and his own were gone, while clean, white dressings covered his ribs and shoulder. Surprisingly, he felt no pain at all other than a lingering, dull ache in his ribs and left ear. He must have been out for weeks.

Wait just a damn minute.

His brows climbed up toward his receding hairline and his hand shot back to the side of his head.

Holy *shit.*

He had an ear!

58

4

An Impossible Choice

Dan

DAN WOULD HAVE NEVER CALLED himself a man of great faith, but as he sat numbly on his pallet of sleep sacks, virtually pain free and running calloused fingers across a newly formed ear, one phrase kept running through his mind: *Goddamn Miraculous.*

The only thing able to bring miracles, in his limited experience, was a higher power. He'd called that higher power God, just like most people did, even if he didn't personally believe in the average, Christian description of what God was. But his saviors, Erik and Alma, had told him to 'thank the *Goddess*' and that they were 'simply *Her* messengers'. That one statement had singlehandedly thrown his entire belief system in a blender.

He shook his head. How? How was it possible? Gathering his legs beneath himself, he carefully rose to his full height and stretched, looking around the camp store. Fresh clothes had been laid out in a pile on the counter beside the register, socks and underwear included. He glanced down to discover that he was as naked as the day he was born.

"Shit," he hissed, as he moved to cover himself, frantically glancing around the store. But if the folks that lived there had doctored and cleaned him, they'd already seen him naked, so he supposed there was really no need to panic.

He grunted to himself then chuckled, as he snapped up the pair of boxer shorts. It felt strange to not have any recollection of what had happened after he'd drank that remedy, but was he really expected to remember every detail of his ordeal when he had been torn apart and on death's doorstep?

He supposed then that his state of undress should be the least of his concerns at the moment and wondered where his guardian angels, Erik and Alma, were hiding. He quickly swiped the pants off the counter and tugged them on, then reached for the long-sleeved shirt and jacket. Clothes in hand, he padded barefoot around the counter and through an open door that led to the building's living quarters.

The space looked comfortable and lived in with worn, overstuffed furniture, a wood stove, and enormous built-in bookshelves. The kitchen appeared well appointed with a large dining table set in the center of the space.

Images from the night before flashed through his mind—Erik and Alma, the stench of that creature, its glowing eye. His heart leapt into his throat. He'd been laid out on that table. That's where Erik and Alma had reset his shoulder, where they had cleaned his wounds...where he had drunk that liquid.

His gut lurched and he dropped the clothes, rushing to the sink. *Keep it down.*

Alma's voice echoed in his mind, and he swallowed thickly at the memory. Shaking, burning with fever.

Breathing deeply, in through his nose and out through his mouth, Dan gripped the edge of the old farmhouse sink and closed his eyes, waiting for the flashback and wave of nausea to pass.

A curse slipped from his lips, low and sharp as a fine sheen of sweat prickled across his skin. His heart pounded in his ears and his throat tightened, breath coming in shallow, useless gasps.

No, no. Not again. It had been years since—suddenly he was somewhere else. His ears rang and his mind swam, vision foggy. Sand filled his mouth, nose, and eyes. He couldn't see...couldn't breathe...someone was screaming in the distance. No. It wasn't real. He wasn't overseas. It was just a bad memory...just a memory.

Recognizing the pattern of a panic attack, he flailed for a mental anchor to ground himself in the here and now. What had the therapist told him? Inhale slowly for five seconds. Exhale for five seconds. Recite your mantra and focus on your breathing. He did just that, but it was having little effect.

"It's over. There's no sand. I'm safe." The words slipped from whispered, sand-coated lips. "It's over. There's no sand. I'm safe," he repeated. "There's no sand, there's no sand, there's no—"

He coughed and spit into the sink. He needed water. Cranking the faucet on full blast, he nearly cried when nothing came out. Turning, he jerked the refrigerator open and grabbed a bottle of water. He just needed to rinse away the sand and the smell and the memory, but it refused to let him go, digging its claws into him, pinning him down, just like the demon creature had.

The familiar pattern of paralyzing fear slowly morphing into rage ran through him. This...this he knew. And it scared him. Back to fear. He slowly sank to the floor and struggled to twist the cap of the bottle. He just needed water. He just needed to breathe. He was safe. It was over. There was no sand. He just needed some fucking *water!*

The rage swept in again. Why couldn't he open the damn bottle? He felt like a growling, caged bear. The room was closing in. He couldn't breathe. The sand, the stench of that creature, it lay over him like a suffocating blanket. He needed water.

He squeezed his eyes shut and tried to focus on his breathing. "It's over, there is no sand, I'm safe," he managed to croak out.

"Dan? Are you alright?" a deep voice sounded from across the room as heavy boots pounded toward him.

"It's over, there is no sand, I'm safe," Dan croaked again; eyes still closed.

"Shit," Erik hissed, as he cranked the cap off the bottle in Dan's trembling hands. "Here-here-here, take a sip. Slowly now."

"There is no sand. I'm safe."

Erik gently pressed the bottle to Dan's lips. The moment the water touched his mouth, Dan's eyes flew open. He drank like a man that hadn't seen water in days then coughed and spat and dumped the remaining contents of the bottle on his face.

Water. He'd just needed *water.*

He closed his eyes and scrubbed his damp face with a calloused palm as his breathing began to slow. Finally, he let his head fall back to bounce against the cupboard with a dull thud.

Erik still crouched before him looking terribly concerned when Dan finally opened his eyes. "I'm sorry. Sorry you had to see that." Dan glanced around himself taking in the mess he'd made.

"No need to apologize. You've been through hell." Erik stood and offered a hand to Dan. "I'm sorry I wasn't here when you woke."

Still feeling off kilter, Dan took a moment to reorient himself. He was in the kitchen of the camp store. The dark-haired man extending his hand was Erik. One of the people he owed his life to. One of his guardian angels. Finally seeing the man through eyes unclouded by pain or panic, Dan noticed that Erik's face was almost too beautiful to be considered masculine, but his deep-set eyes, straight nose and strong jaw could have graced any number of his wife's large collection of romance novels. With a sigh, Dan raised his own hand, and Erik helped him to his feet then clapped him on the shoulder.

"Thanks," Dan said, offering a small smile. Once on his feet, he couldn't help but notice that he had to look up slightly to meet Erik's eyes. At six feet and four inches tall, looking up at anyone was a rarity for him. That easily put Erik over six and a half feet tall. *Damn.*

Erik pulled a chair out and motioned for Dan to sit. "You're going to need some food. Hang tight, I'll go get some meat." He handed Dan another bottle of water before heading out of the kitchen.

All Dan could do was nod as he slumped into the wooden dining chair. He didn't feel like eating, especially after that panic attack, but he couldn't deny that his body *needed* the food. If people were offering to feed him, especially during the apocalypse, he should take advantage. His stomach growled at the thought. Yes, food would be good. And candy. Maybe some fruit too?

The last of the shakes from the panic attack faded and he sighed in relief. He hadn't had one that bad since he was just out of the service, and he silently hoped that his experience with that stinking shadow with teeth wouldn't compound the PTSD that he'd already been struggling with. He ran a hand through his hair and brought the water bottle to his lips.

Just then, Erik returned with sausage and a carton of eggs. Alma trailed into the kitchen behind him, and Dan nearly choked on the last swallow of water left in the bottle. She was *gorgeous*. How had he not remembered just how pretty she was from the day before? Well, he had been dying. She was a good head shorter than Erik but that still made her close to six feet tall. Her deep red hair was tied back into a long ponytail and her green eyes raked him from head to toe as she walked into the room.

"Where are the rest of the clothes I laid out for you, *Seed Child?*" she asked, full lips tilting into a small smile.

Dan glanced around quickly, wondering where he'd dropped them and found them laying in a small pile near to the doorway that led into the market section of the building. He began to rise and retrieve them, but Alma was already making her way there.

She gathered them up off the floor and handed them back to Dan. "The bathroom is down the hall, second door on the right. I filled the sink with warm water for washing and there is a bucket of water in the shower to use to flush the toilet with. Just refill it when you're done. The hand pump is out back."

Dan nodded in thanks and shuffled to the bathroom. After closing the door behind him, he let out a sharp breath as his thoughts traveled to places they hadn't been in years. Had he been a younger man and single—he shook his head. What had gotten into him? Reaching out to grab the shirt Alma had left him, he snapped it up and tugged it over his head. Did it smell like her?

Violently shoving that train of thought out of his mind, he glanced in the mirror to smooth his tousled hair and his mouth fell open.

Not only did he miraculously have an ear, but he looked *younger.* At least ten years younger. He gasped, leaning closer to the mirror and inspected his face. The worry lines on his forehead and smile lines around his eyes and mouth were gone while his hair had somehow regained most of its natural, deep brown color. And it was thicker than it had been in years; his receding hairline and thin spot at the crown of his head had filled in.

Cautious hands traveled to the hem of the shirt he'd just pulled on and lifted it. To his shock, rippled muscle now sat where a slight beer belly had lived for the better part of a decade. He hadn't been in that kind of shape since he was in the service participating in morning PT on top of hitting the gym five days out of the week.

Stripping the shirt off, he gingerly peeled the bandages away from his wounds. Smooth, completely healed skin, not stitches greeted him. The only evidence that he'd been filleted like a fish was a faint spidering of red marks across his shoulder, ribs, and face. How? How was it possible?

He turned, nearly ripping the door off its hinges as he sprinted from the bathroom and back to the kitchen. "*How?*" he all but yelled at Alma and Erik.

They shot one another a knowing glance and gestured to the table.

"Here we go," Erik said under his breath, then louder, "Have a seat my friend, we have a lot to talk about and not much time to do it in."

Dan strode to the table and sat, leaning forward, elbows on his knees, while Erik finished frying the eggs and sausage and Alma toasted the bread in a pan. His stomach rumbled at the scents of food and he sighed, leaning back again in the chair.

When he had first awoken on that pile of sleeping bags, he had felt invigorated, better than he had in years, and now he took a moment to really feel into his body for the myriad of old injuries that had come back to haunt him over the past decade. He inspected his bare arms and torso. From his arthritic elbow and shoulder to his aching knees and constantly sore back, he felt absolutely none of the pain that normally infiltrated every aspect of his life.

Invigorated was too soft a word. He felt ten feet tall and bulletproof, like he could have maxed out a PT test. Practically overflowing with energy, he shifted in his seat. He wanted to blow something up. Wanted to do a keg stand. Wanted to hit the bar with his buddies and get some tail.

"What in God's name is going on?" He buried his face in his hands, voice strained and muffled through his fingers.

"Goddess," Alma corrected as she set a heaping plate on the table before him.

Dan glanced up at her, eyes darting around her face before settling on her mouth. "Jesus H. Christ, you're beautiful," he said in a daze as he reached out to take her hand.

What in the actual fuck was going on with his head? He'd just been an anxiety ridden mess not twenty minutes ago and now? Now he felt like a kid in his early twenties with only one thing on his mind.

"Yeah-yeah-yeah. I know," she replied, gently smacking his hand away. "Now eat your food. You don't even mean it. You're just buzzing from the remedy."

"What was *in* that?" he asked, squirming in his chair, while Alma turned back to the stove. He completely ignored the plate of food in front of him. "I feel like a candy kid at a rave—don't ask how I know what that feels like," his palms returned to his face then his fingers raked through his hair, "I can't sit still and I wanna touch *everything*." Even his hair tingled. "You guys are my friends, right?"

What was he even saying? He was equal parts excited, aroused, terrified, and mortified.

Alma glanced at Erik and tried not to snicker. When her eyes returned to Dan, she at least had the decency to look a little chagrined for laughing at his expense.

"You need to fill yourself with something pleasurable," she said, pointing at the plate of food he had yet to touch. "Food is a good place to start. If that doesn't work," she trailed off for a moment and glanced back at Erik, quirking a perfectly shaped brow. He nodded slightly and she finished, "There are...*other* things we can try to take the edge off."

What could she be suggesting? "Define 'other things'." Dan's voice dropped an octave.

"We'll cross that bridge if we must," she said while the corner of her mouth curled into a smile that had Dan's heart rate skyrocketing. His eyes widened and he leaned toward her expectantly.

"Cut him a break, Alma. Jeez," Erik breathed, a gently chiding tone to his voice.

Alma's brows knit together as she hit Erik with a mock scowl, "Oh, like you'd be any better if the roles were reversed." She turned her attention back to Dan and rolled her eyes, "He's such a killjoy. Just eat the food and we'll see where that gets you."

Dan eyed Alma and reluctantly picked up his fork, still struggling to make sense of what was really going on with these people. His eyes flashed between Alma and Erik, and he stabbed a sausage patty, then shoved it into his mouth whole.

The flavors exploded in his mouth, nothing he had eaten in his life had ever tasted so good and he groaned, scooping up a lump of scrambled eggs. He shoved those into his mouth and could do nothing to hold back the grin spreading across his face.

"This is delicious." His words muffled around the food. He ate like he hadn't seen food in months.

Erik and Alma both smiled and nodded, then fixed themselves a plate and sat down, studying the man shoveling food into his face with no regard for table manners. When his plate was nearly clean, Dan glanced up at them.

They looked back expectantly.

"Are you feeling more yourself?" Erik asked while pushing some eggs around his plate.

"Well, I feel less," he paused, searching for the right words, "Agitated." That didn't fully encompass how he was feeling, but it would have to do. Truthfully, he felt like he could have run a marathon and had energy to spare.

"I'm not sure if I'm relieved or disappointed to hear you say that," Alma sighed.

Erik shot her a warning glance, and she raised a delicate hand in surrender.

Unsure of what to say, but still buzzy enough to not care, Dan took a deep breath and asked, "So, how long was I out? It had to have been weeks. And how did this," he gestured to the red marks on his face and torso. "Heal up so well? I'm hardly going to have a scar, and that thing carved me up like a Thanksgiving turkey."

Alma's face turned serious. She gently laid her fork on her plate and placed her elbows on the table, fingertips steepled. "It's only been about eleven hours since you drank the remedy."

"There's no way," Dan said flatly. It made absolutely no logical sense.

"We found you in the road at about noon yesterday. Erik carried you inside." Alma's eyes held his gaze, unblinking.

"Yesterday? No, that's impossible," Dan argued.

"We swear on The Light Mother's Throne; she speaks the truth." Erik's stare pierced Dan's very soul and something seemed to jolt inside of him. A thrill ran through his body and his eyes went wide, a bone-deep *knowing* settling in his chest.

A self-satisfied smile spread across Erik's face, and he leaned back in his chair, crossing well-muscled arms over his chest. "You feel that don't you?"

Dan's mouth went dry, every cell in his body singing as the world around him snapped into crystal clear focus; a long-dead sixth sense springing to life.

"My God, I do," he breathed. "I don't know how, but I do."

"Our Sparks commune," Erik said.

"What do you mean by that?"

"We don't have time to go into all the details right now. We have a lot to tell you before we need to leave this place as it is," Alma said.

Dan nodded numbly and she continued while quickly eating her breakfast. "When we brought you inside, I was sure that you were going to die, but you just kept on breathing," she explained between mouthfuls. "Erik bound your wounds, and we set your shoulder then we waited. We—um... argued a bit on what we should do with you."

"I think I remember bits and pieces of that," Dan added. Blistering pain shot through his mind and he winced. "What convinced you to give me that drink?"

"Well, lucky for you, Erik is a softhearted being, despite his crusty outer shell,"

"I am not crusty." Erik hit Alma with a glare.

She continued as if he hadn't even spoken, "And no matter what I could have said or done, he had made up his mind to try to save you the moment he scooped you up off the road." Alma had the decency to look more than a little chagrinned. "For what it's worth, I'm glad that he gave you the remedy." Her eyes seemed to smolder. "Seems like you're a rare type of man," she trailed off but held Dan's gaze.

"Alma, what the hell?" Erik snapped at the same moment Dan's knee crashed into the table.

"You can't be suggesting what I think you are. Aren't you two...together?" Dan asked in a stammering rush.

Erik nearly choked on a mouthful of food. "Goddess, no. We're long-time friends. Business partners. Nothing more. Anyway, once you come down from the healing buzz, she'll probably lay off. You're oozing virility right now and she has no self-control."

Dan stifled a cough. So, he wasn't mistaken! Alma *was* coming on to him. Nobody but his wife had even given him a second look in years. And what did Erik mean by 'oozing virility'? He shook his head trying not to allow his overactive mind to travel down the path it was on and asked, "Okay then, how exactly does the healing work?"

"The short answer is that it's a gift from The Light Mother and a family secret."

"How bout the long answer?" Dan quirked an eyebrow. "Because I haven't looked or felt this good in a decade at least."

Erik hesitated a moment as if struggling with himself. "Oh, what does it matter now?" he mumbled, then shifted in his seat. "Your science does not know of its existence, and we'd like to keep it that way, if you don't mind, but I will tell you this; right now, your cells are going through a massive reconstruction. Your body, your *whole* body is healing, not just your injuries—All of your organs, even your brain."

"But there is nothing in the known world that can stop aging let alone reverse it," Dan snorted.

"Like I said, it's a family secret, and we'd like to keep it that way. You've seen what it's doing in the mirror. You can feel it from your head to your toes."

Dan couldn't deny what he was experiencing. *Something* was definitely going on.

"When I was...dying," he paused, rolling the unspoken words around in his mouth, "I heard Alma say that I might be too strong to simply give up the spark, then you said that our sparks commune. What does that mean?"

Before Erik could answer, Alma took over. "Every being on this planet has a spark. Hume—er, humans call it a soul. Your soul is, quite literally, a tiny piece of The Goddess. When one of her creations is injured by a darkling or one of its spawn, the creation usually dies. However, there are some that are strong enough to hold to life. When that happens, the darkness takes over and the spark is swallowed by the spawn's influence."

Life wasn't a science fiction movie. The shit he was going through just did *not* happen. Yet, there he sat, mind reeling. "I don't understand."

"Fortunately, you don't have to understand how or why it happens. You can keep away from the spawn just the same either way. The important takeaway here is that if someone you love gets attacked by a spawn, it's best to put them out of their misery." Erik spoke clearly and firmly.

Dan started making connections that he was afraid to give voice to, but he spoke the words into the ether anyway. "When all the attacks and disappearances happened last summer, it was those creatures, wasn't it?"

Erik and Alma nodded in unison.

"But no one had a clue what was going on last year, and here you two sit with a magic heal-all potion and more knowledge than seems natural." Dan waved his hand and leaned forward, bringing his elbows to rest on the table. "How do you know so much?"

Alma spoke this time, quiet and low, "Our family has been protecting this area from those creatures for more than thirty generations and there were others before us, all over the continent. There is much that humans today do not understand about this world, and things are about to get very, very messy."

Dan gaped as that thrill, that shock of energy, ran through him again and his heart settled somewhere in his gut. These people were not lying to him. His eyes flicked from Alma's to Erik's and then back again. Those eyes held a depth that he hadn't noticed before, full of ancient knowledge and power.

Even as that thrill coursed through him, Dan's stomach clenched, and cold dread settled into his chest.

"I need to get back to my family," Dan croaked, "but there's a girl a few miles up the road stranded in her car." Amber's worried face flashed in his mind. "I've got to go get her."

"Absolutely out of the question," Erik said, his tone flat and final.

"But she's just a kid," Dan said, his voice breaking with disbelief. "We can't just leave her up there. She wouldn't stand a chance against one of those creatures."

"There is never just one spawn," Alma said quietly, "and if, by some miracle the one you killed was alone, it wouldn't have been for long. I hate to be the bearer of bad news, but if you left her there yesterday, you've already signed her death warrant. There isn't a chance under the stars that she's still alive."

"Shit." Dan's entire soul withered. "But what if she is? I know her chances of survival get lower every second we spend here. And I made her a promise. I told her I would send up a flare if there was still food here...if it was still safe."

"Dan, if you send up a flare now and she is still alive, she won't be if she leaves her car." Erik's voice was gentle and sympathetic.

"We have to go get her," Dan abruptly moved to stand, "and if I have to go alone, so be it."

"The darkling and their spawn can only move in darkness," Erik's voice was urgent. "The thick cloud cover here makes this area a paradise for them. If she goes out in the rain—if *we* go out in the rain..." He trailed off a moment before beginning again, "If she has the good sense to stay put and the spawn don't manage to find her, the only chance she has is to wait for a sunny day to make the walk on her own."

The floor seemed to sink beneath Dan's chair and he wished it would swallow him up. What had he *done?*

"We can't go deeper into the forest now. We need to head down the mountain, away from the forest. The spawn will be weak, like the one that attacked you, for a few more days at most, but as they grow in strength and number, we'll end up stuck here. Even though it's raining now, our best chance is to head out as soon as possible, before they get too strong," Alma explained.

Dan shook his head violently. Oh, he'd fucked up. He'd fucked up bad. "W-what if we waited for a sunny day?" His voice came out choked and pleading. He had left a defenseless kid in the mountains like a complete idiot, and *he* was the one that had gotten a second chance at life? No, he had to fix this somehow.

"Yeah, we wait for a sunny day, then we go up there and bring her back? We could just wait for the sun again, then leave here. All of us, together." Dan tried reasoning with them but again he was met with resistance.

"Dan," Alma's voice was gentle, but her eyes were intense, "If we don't leave now, the spawn could make their way down out of the mountains and to your home before you do." Her firm gaze held Dan's. "You said you had a wife and kids. Would you leave them to face those things alone? Without you?"

Dan's gut twisted. He didn't want to admit it—he couldn't—but she was right. It was too late to fix his mistake, and if this really was the apocalypse, then this was war, albeit a completely different kind of war than he had ever experienced, but a war none the less. It would be every man for himself. And if some ancient creature was here to facilitate the end of times, he needed to be with his family. He needed his community to survive. Unfortunately, in war, sometimes the few were sacrificed to save the many.

The third rule to survive the apocalypse popped into his mind.

Don't ever be a hero. That's a one-way ticket to getting yourself killed.

"Damn-it!" he growled and pounded a fist against the table. Alma flinched at his outburst, but Erik only let out a deep, impatient breath, leaning back in his chair, clenching his teeth.

Chair legs scratched across the vinyl floor as Alma stood and cleared their plates. "I'm just going to take care of these." She disappeared through the wide doorway and down the hallway, leaving the two men alone.

"I know this is a hard decision—" Erik started but Dan cut him off.

"It's not hard, it's impossible. She's just a kid and I made her a promise. But my family needs me." Dan scoffed, pissed as hell at himself and the situation he'd unwittingly put himself in. "She told me she lives at home with her single mom and brother. If I leave her up there, it's my fault that they'll never know what happened to her."

"I know this is hard. I really do, but you strike me as a very prepared man with a solid amount of common sense."

Dan nodded.

"Did you do any research on what would happen to the population in the event of a nationwide power outage?" Erik raised a dark brow.

Dan's second nod was stiffer than the first. The estimates were dire. Some studies stated that half the population would be gone in less than three months. More than eighty percent of the population wouldn't last six months.

"Now imagine a horde of darkling spawn doing their damnedest to annihilate the remainder of the folks that survived," Erik said as Dan's shoulders sagged. "This is an extinction level event but my family and many others like it will be gathering far to the north to fight this darkness. We've been waiting for this our whole lives. We've *trained* for this our whole lives, and The Snow Forest is going to need all the help it can get. What I'm trying to say is that we need strong people like you in the community to help hold things together and I didn't give you my bloo—that bloody remedy for you to go wasting your second chance at life."

Dan just shook his head not wanting to admit that Erik was right. His eyes welled up and he blinked away the tears. "This fucking sucks." He sniffed and scrubbed at his eyes.

Erik stood slowly and moved to Dan's side. "It does. And there isn't anything we can do about it...yet." He laid a gentle hand on Dan's shoulder. "Get some water and get dressed. Meet us out back when you're ready. We leave at mid-day."

Eyes on the table, Dan listened to Erik's retreating steps and sighed as Alma's words echoed in his mind, *'Would you leave them to face those things alone?'* No matter what he did, no matter what he chose, someone innocent was going to die. It just wasn't fair.

Dressed and ready for the journey, Dan stepped out the back door and closed it quietly behind him. Glancing around, the dark forest looked sinister, the shadows seeming to scowl down at him. Were the creatures out there watching him already? A faint rattling and low voices caught his attention and pulled him toward a shed. His saviors were in there tinkering with three old mountain bikes.

"Aren't you worried those things are going to hear you?" Dan asked, poking his head into the shed door.

"Relax, seed child," Alma teased. "This place is protected by The Light."

"What is The Light exactly? And why do you keep calling me seed child?"

"This place is protected by The Mother's Light. No creature of darkness can step within its protective dome. It's around a quarter mile in diameter. And I call you *seed child* because that's what you are." She smiled up at Dan then said, "We'll have more time for explanations later. Help me with this." She turned one of the bicycles upside down and handed him a wrench.

"What are we doing with these?" he asked, trying not to pay attention to his raging libido.

"Well, we don't have horses," Alma chuckled lightly. "We're going to ride these instead."

Dan huffed a small laugh as he knelt and checked all the nuts and bolts on his bike then reached for a can of chain lubricant. The lengthy silence between them was beginning to feel awkward, as were the utterly filthy images flashing through his mind.

He broke the silence with a frustrated sigh, "Do either of you know how long I'm going to feel like this?"

"Still feeling a little riled up?" Erik asked while Alma breathed a deep, almost apologetic sigh.

"Yeah."

"Well, I gave you a larger dose of the remedy than I normally would have because your injuries were so extensive. The buzz could hang around for a few days." Erik grimaced, "Sorry about that."

"*Days?* How am I supposed to function?"

"Well, being around her isn't helping," Erik said, pointing a thumb in Alma's direction while rising from a crouch, "But once we get going, most of the extra...*energy* you're feeling should dissipate with exercise. Any activity that normally releases endorphins will take the edge off, but once you're home, I would suggest bedding your wife. Immediately." He winked and chuckled as if he had been in a similar situation sometime in the past.

Dan snorted and pinched the bridge of his nose between thumb and forefinger. "Seriously, I don't think I've ever felt this out of control. You could make millions selling that remedy as an aphrodisiac."

"It's more than just the remedy that's got you in a twist, friend. It took me years of living in the same house as her to learn how to tune it out. One of her Goddess given gifts is amplifying emotions and desires. Seed children tend to have a fairly standard desire, especially the males," Erik said with a small, crooked smile. "If it's any consolation, you appear to have much more self-control than most men would in your position."

Dan pursed his lips not fully understanding but mostly catching the drift. He was beginning to really believe that he was caught in the middle of something much bigger than he could have possibly imagined.

Goddess given gifts. Sparks communing. Demon creatures on the loose. No electricity. And these people talked like their goddess was actually present in their lives, not just some wizard sky-daddy that gave people commandments to live by and was never heard from again. He had to know if his hunch was correct.

"The Goddess, this Light Mother, is she here? On earth?" Dan asked, feeling foolish but wanting the answer too badly to care how he came off.

"She is," Erik answered.

The implications crashed into Dan, pushing all preconceived notions of what or who God was right out of his head. Instead of some invisible force in the sky that left humanity to sort itself out, their goddess was on the earth somewhere. It would have been an unbelievable statement, but with that thrill coursing through him again, the truth of Erik's words was impossible to deny.

"So, when you say that you're heading to the north, how far are you going?" he asked.

"Far," Erik said flatly, seeming to deliberately avoid eye contact with Dan.

With a sigh, Alma chimed in, "We'll try to make it all the way to The Snow Forest, to The Light Mother herself, but we may not have enough time. If that ends up being the case, we'll make for the village of Evergreen."

"Where is that?" Dan's hands stilled. Maybe she was going to actually give him some answers?

Just as Alma opened her mouth to speak, Erik spoke again, voice clipped. "To the north. Hidden near the sea."

Dan waited for Erik to elaborate, but the silent set of his jaw and shoulders spoke so loud, Dan knew the other man would say no more about it.

"Okay," Dan stretched the word out in a hushed tone and turned back to working on his bicycle, letting all the information he'd just heard marinate.

Suddenly, his eyes went wide with realization. "Wait, The Light Mother is *in* the Snow Forest? Physically?"

It was Alma who answered, her voice dreamy and light, "She is. Flesh and bone and light. She lives and breathes, just as we all do."

Dan's mind reeled as Alma shot a glare at Erik's broad back. Her tone turned serious as she spoke again, "There are a great many truths in this world that have been twisted to suit the needs of evil men. The tale of creation is first among them. Stars willing, you may live long enough to learn them all. But that's a conversation for another time, should we meet again. Right now, we need to get on the road."

With their means of transportation solidified, Alma disappeared into the house to grab their supplies while Erik pulled Dan toward the basement. Most of the tension plaguing Dan's body eased as the flame haired woman disappeared from his sight and he breathed a ragged sigh of relief.

Erik chuckled lightly and shook his head as he descended the wooden stairs ahead of Dan.

"Is it that obvious?" Dan asked, feeling ashamed and still not fully understanding why his body was reacting to Alma's presence so strongly. He had absolutely no real desire for anyone but his beloved wife. She was a wonderful mother, smart, beautiful, strong-willed, and stubborn.

"If you're feeling some sort of way about your feelings toward Alma right now, don't. Like I said earlier, it's part of her nature, her gift, if you could call it that. With the remedy in your system, you're just more aware of your body and its growing strength...as well as Alma's *gift*. You aren't going to feel so randy forever, I assure you, but the physical changes you're going through will be lasting."

They stepped off the stairs and entered the basement proper. Erik flicked on a flashlight.

"You're kidding me," Dan squeaked. Erik grinned over his shoulder at him, raising the flashlight to scan the room. "Like a permanent age reset?"

Erik nodded silently and wagged his eyebrows before continuing deeper into the basement.

Once again, Dan's mind reeled at the thought. *How was all this happening?* "Care to elaborate?"

"Consider it a gift of The Light. And if you make it out of what's to come still breathing, you'll eventually learn all you need to know."

Dan shrugged, deciding not to look a gift horse in the mouth, and followed Erik deeper into the basement. It was dank and musty, all the contents covered in a layer of fine dust, but despite the dust, the space was orderly and dry. Erik moved to a large crate, covered by a length of thick canvas.

"Help me move this." Together they lifted it and placed it in the middle of the room, beside an old weight bench, metal clanked on metal.

"Golf clubs?" Dan raised an eyebrow.

"Far from it, friend." Erik lifted the dusty canvas to reveal a pair of short swords and a recurve bow with quiver and arrows.

"Holy shit," Dan gaped. First miraculous healing and now weapons that looked like they were straight out of Middle Earth. What was happening? Should he even ask? "Why not a big-ass gun?"

"Guns are almost useless against the spawn. The only way to kill them is brain trauma, beheading or burning. When they're at their full strength, they heal too fast. Bullets won't even slow them down unless the caliber is large enough. Even then, unless you're lucky enough to get a headshot, they won't die. Getting in close, lopping off limbs is the best way to cripple them. Then"—he made a quick swiping motion with his arm— "off with their heads. Or, if you're good with a bow, you could put an arrow right through one of their beady little eyes."

"Are you telling me that the rest of our lives are going to be spent risking life and limb against those things?" Dan asked.

"Unfortunately, for the foreseeable future, yes." Erik nodded. "If you thought the daily grind and nine to five was harrowing, you're in for some brutal times, friend. Just surviving without all the comforts you're accustomed to is going to be a challenge."

Dan sighed. Just like his time in the sand box, except now, it was his family on the line, not just his own ass.

A thoughtful look crossed Erik's face, "Unless you can get your family back up here. This is the only outpost within a hundred-mile radius. You'd be isolated but completely safe under the light dome.

Our family has existed here for generations, so it's possible to survive here, even for you, but it would be a hard life, though not so hard as it would be without the protection of the dome."

Dan mulled the idea over in his mind. What lengths would he go to protect his family? He would suck shit through a straw if that's what it took. He supposed that he would have plenty of time to mull over their situation later, but for now, he needed to focus on getting back to his wife and daughter. He was pulled away from his thoughts by a feminine shout.

"Ok, guys, are we ready?" Alma called down the basement stairs.

"Just about," Erik called back to her as he strapped on his sword belt and slung the bow and quiver over his shoulder. He reached deeper into the crate and removed a matched pair of sheathed daggers, one rested in a cross-body chest scabbard, the other sat in a belt designed to carry the wicked blade at the back of the waist. The hilts shone even in the dim light of the basement, the craftsmanship like nothing Dan had ever seen. He handed them to Dan. "My gift to you, friend. It isn't much, but they're a far sight better than that crude blade you have."

Erik had already given him the gift of life and now the man was offering him daggers? It suddenly felt more like a peace offering.

"You've got that right." Dan accepted the daggers with a reverent nod hoping the other man wouldn't notice the tension in his shoulders. Erik turned to leave.

"Wait. I have to believe that Amber will make it here when the sun comes out," Dan said, regret and longing warring in his tone. He couldn't allow himself to dwell on the cold hard fact that her chances of survival out there in the woods was slim to none. Instead, he chose to delude himself with a dream of her survival. "We should leave something for her, something to help her out," Dan said.

Erik looked at him, eyes studying, seeing deeper than any human eyes should. Several heartbeats later he said, "She can have the whole store. I'll leave a window unlocked."

Dan knew Erik was simply pacifying him, saying whatever Dan needed to hear to get his boots moving and Dan was strangely ok with it.

"Thank you." His throat constricted and he coughed, fighting the urge to cry out at the injustice of it all.

Erik nodded then turned to go but Dan paused in following him. He should give Amber something specifically from him, some sign that he'd made it out, even if it was foolish to hope for such a thing. Even if she was already dead. He had to do something to ease the self-hatred that was building in his chest.

Turning quickly, he used his finger to write in the dust covered vinyl of the weight bench.

Be safe, girl. I'm sorry.

He gave the basement one last look, set his old combat knife on a shelf, then squared his shoulders and stepped out. The world he'd known was gone along with the decisions he'd made in that world. Now all he could do was march on into the unknown, one breath, one step, one mile at a time, back to his family.

5

Orchardville

Melissa

MELISSA WOKE TO THE SOUND OF shattering glass and her house lurching violently on its foundation. For a few disorienting seconds, she sat paralyzed in the predawn darkness of her room, heart thundering in her chest, while books and picture frames were flung to the floor. Earthquakes were not a rare occurrence in the Pacific Northwest, but this one felt different—angrier somehow. The windows rattled and she gasped as a crack appeared in the drywall.

Was this *The Big One* that the scientists had been warning about for decades? Bolting out of bed, she scrambled to her bedroom doorway and clung to the door jams. Family photos bounced then slid off the walls as the house groaned and shuddered around her.

"Joey!" she yelled down the hallway towards her son's room. Moments later, his door flew open. He stood, wide eyed and gaping in the doorway. "Stay there! Hold on to the door frame." Thankfully, he did as he was told. She could hear items elsewhere in the house falling, crashing. The house groaned and she squeezed her eyes closed. The quake rumbled on and on. Would it ever end? With a final heave, the house went still. Silent, except for her ragged breathing.

"Are you okay, Mom?" her son called out to her, his voice shaky and groggy.

"Yeah. Yeah, I'm ok. Are you?"

"Just a little shaken up," he said with a nervous chuckle. "What the Hell?" He looked around the dim hallway and blew out a breath taking a small step out of his doorway.

Glass and small, broken figurines littered the floor and Melissa instantly switched to mom mode. "Put some shoes on before you come out here and be careful of the glass."

Joey nodded and disappeared back into his room. Melissa did the same, pulling on her slippers and a sweatshirt. They met in the hallway and descended the stairs to inspect the damage through the rest of the house. Books had shimmied off the shelves and table lamps lay on their sides. Surprisingly, not much was broken. The portraits in the hall seemed to have fared the worst and she sighed in relief. Picture frames were easily replaced. Gathering some cleaning supplies, she made her way back up the stairs.

"I'm really worried about Amber, Mom," Joey said, the quiet concern in his voice broke Melissa's heart. She was worried sick for her daughter. The last time Melissa had checked Amber's location the day before, she was already well within the national forest, far from the city and reliable help. Then the power went out, somehow rendering every piece of electronics in her home and across the town completely useless. Nothing was working.

"I am too, but we just have to keep hoping that she's safe up there in the mountains and will try and make her way back here as soon as she can."

Melissa tried to convince herself as much as her son with her words. Amber was strong, independent, and capable. She always had extra food and drinks with her when she went camping and she had turned her car into a very comfortable temporary home over the years. When the power came back on, Amber would be able to call for help and then they would all be back together again.

Joey murmured something inaudible before going into his room to tidy what the earthquake had disturbed. As Melissa swept up the scattered shards of glass and placed the intact picture frames back onto the wall, her gaze lingered on one of her favorite pictures of her daughter. Amber had gotten her Jeep stuck in a mud pit only weeks after she'd bought it. Melissa had taken the photo herself, laughing so hard she could barely see through the viewfinder of her old camera as her daughter crawled out of the driver side window and up onto the roof.

It's officially mine now! I got it stuck! The memory of Amber's excited voice and triumphant grin as she stood there laughing, arms in the air clenched at Melissa's heart. The picture belonged downstairs where she could see it all day long. Perhaps she could hang it in the entryway until her daughter walked back through the front door?

Melissa nodded, the decision final, then allowed her thoughts to stray to the day before.

Her neighborhood was generally a safe one, but she had been shocked at how quickly some of the people that lived there had turned ugly, spouting all manner of doomsday garbage.

There was no way that what those neighbors were saying could happen. The government wasn't secretly screwing with the masses and the chances of a cyber-attack damaging the cars as well as the power grid...well, it just didn't make sense. Even with so many of her neighbors being supportive of each other, the few that were making waves had really upset her. More than that, they had made her begin to think, what if?

What if this really was the end times? She had no food stores or survival skills. She'd been a stay-at-home mom when her ex-husband had told her that he was leaving them, that he'd had a whole other family on the east coast and was choosing them over her.

Amber had only been seven years old then, little Joey had been just five, and they had never seen their father again. Part of her was glad of that fact, but it still rankled almost seventeen years later. She had basically been the side-chick and not even known it.

"Pilots," she mumbled, silently hoping that he'd been flying yesterday when the power went out. She quickly chided herself, gritting her teeth. It was absolutely criminal that she still thought of him, even all these years later.

But he had crushed her, and she vowed to never be so vulnerable again. She'd worked her tail off to provide for herself and her children, using his stupid face as motivation. He'd never loved her or their children, so she made sure her kids had more love and stability than they could possibly need from her and her alone. She took a course in medical transcription and was able to work from home, caring for her kids like a good mother should, while working full time hours. As the years wore on, she scrimped and saved, pinching pennies whenever and wherever she could, and finally, she was able to purchase their home.

The home that had just survived a horrible earthquake. As soon as the power came back on, she was going to have to call the insurance company and get someone out to check the foundation. A myriad of chores ran through her mind as she pushed the gathered shards of glass into the dustpan and carefully walked to the trash to dump it.

As the glass fell, she wondered how long it would take for the household trash to begin piling up. If this was indeed a total, grid-down situation, like some of her neighbors believed it to be, what if there were no more repair services and insurance claims? No more mail or garbage service? A hunk of lead settled in Melissa's gut. They'd be *screwed.*

Heavy footfalls sounded on the stairs, breaking her spiraling train of thought, and Joey appeared in his grocery store uniform. Melissa's eyes went wide. "You aren't going in to work today, are you?"

"Yeah, of course I am. The manager said that we would open for cash only purchases if the power was still out."

"I don't think that's a good idea, honey," she started but Joey brushed her off.

"It's fine, Ma. If I get there and it's crazy, I'll come back home. I should probably get some food while I'm there anyway, just in case."

"We just made a Costco run, we've got plenty," she sighed, pressing fingertips to forehead. She didn't know why she wasted her breath sometimes. That boy would simply do whatever it was that he wanted to do, and there was nothing that she could say or do to change that. "Be safe, damn it. And if you aren't home by 3 o'clock, I'm coming down there to get you."

Joey rolled his eyes and pulled open the door that led into the garage. "I'll be *fine.*"

She followed him into the garage feeling stiff and heavy. "Don't take any chances...with anything, Joey. I mean it." Something bad was going to happen. She couldn't explain it, but she could feel it in her gut.

The big aluminum door clanged as he disconnected the automatic garage door opener and pulled it open by hand. "You should keep the doors locked while I'm gone, just in case. And lock this behind me," he said pointing at the large garage door. He pulled his old BMX bike down off the hook that it was hanging from and set it on the floor. "I'll be back this afternoon."

He hadn't ridden that old thing since he saved up enough money to buy that ridiculous car of his, and Melissa smiled to herself at how young he still looked swinging a leg over it. How he had always wanted to follow his big sister around when they were young. It didn't matter where Amber had gone, Joey had been her little shadow. They were such good friends and hardly fought, one taking the heat for the other when they had been caught doing something they knew they weren't supposed to be doing. He was a good kid. They were both *great* kids. It still baffled her that they were so grown. She'd had Amber and was expecting Joey when she had been Joey's age.

As her son pedaled down the driveway, she tried to ignore the sick feeling in her gut. "Bring back a big bag of sea salt!" she called out to him and he raised his hand in silent acknowledgement. Once he was out of sight, she closed the garage door, twisted its manual lock, and returned to the kitchen.

Opening the freezer, she found the meat was still frozen but beginning to thaw out. If the power didn't come back on in a day or so, the meat would go bad. Turning to the pantry, she pulled the door open and reached for a tattered cookbook. It had been her grandmother's and then her own mother's after, both of the older women's distinct handwriting littered the pages, altering and improving the recipes within. She flipped to the back section, looking for the pages on canning. It was a dying art, but her mother had canned jam and vegetables every summer when she was alive, and along with this cookbook, Melissa had inherited all her mother's canning supplies after she had passed on. Now, it seemed they might finally come in handy.

The book held instructions for drying and salt curing meat as well, and she hugged the old tome to her chest. "I hope this isn't where we're heading," she whispered to the silent room.

∞

Just after noon, Joey returned from the grocery store rattling a shopping cart along behind his bike. She'd heard the racket from the cart all the way back in the kitchen and sprinted to the front door to see what all the noise was. It was full of canned food, rice, flour, sugar, yeast, coffee, more canning jars, pectin, dry goods, and the like. Melissa gaped at him. How had he known what to bring home? As he neared, she blinked in shock at his disheveled appearance. His uniform was torn, and red scratches and welts marred the skin on his hands, arms, and face.

"My god, what happened?" she cried out, running to meet him at the bottom of the driveway. She grabbed the handle of the cart and together, they pushed it toward the garage door.

"It's a madhouse out there, Ma. Old Mrs. Nancy from around the corner was there trying to buy supplies. Some guy took a loaf of bread right out of her hands then people just started pulling things out of her cart and pushing her out of the way. She was crying, Ma. *Crying.*" He panted and shook his head. "I helped her get what she needed and get out of the store. She's the one that told me what stuff to take and to get home. So, I ran back in and ditched my apron. People were fighting and tipping over shelves like one of those disaster movies. Mrs. Nancy even told me to get soap, vitamins, cold medicine, and pain relievers. That's all in the bottom." He ran a hand through his dark hair with a deep sigh.

"Jesus." Melissa paled visibly at his words. "Let's get you inside. Are you ok?"

"Yeah, I'm good. Just tired."

With a deep breath, she turned and ran back up to the front door and through the house cursing as she went. Once in the garage, she absently pressed the garage door opener and swore when nothing happened.

"The power's out, remember?" she muttered to herself as she continued on to the large, roll-up door and cranked the lock then grasped the handle and hauled it upward. Joey rolled the grocery cart and then his bike into the safety of the garage, then closed and locked the large door behind him.

"What a nightmare," he breathed as he sagged against the fender of her car. His entire demeanor screamed that he was overwhelmed and even though she knew a hug was probably the last thing he wanted at the moment, he definitely needed one...and so did she.

Melissa wrapped her arms around his shoulders and squeezed her son fiercely, fighting tears. Pulling back, she held his face in her hands and gazed up at him. "Are you sure you're okay? You aren't hurt anywhere?"

Joey had the nerve to roll his eyes at her and she squeezed his cheeks a little harder. "Just bruises, I'm fine. I promise."

Still, she ran her hands over his face and down his arms needing to feel for herself. Finding nothing, she hugged him tightly again. "I swear to god, if you ever scare me like that again..." she trailed off.

Joey groaned impatiently, "Ma. I'm fine."

Melissa's heart pounded behind her ribs. What if he'd been hurt badly? What would she do if he had not come home? She shook her head and finally let him go. Best to not think about those sorts of things. He was home and safe now. That's all that mattered.

Together, they emptied the shopping cart and prepared to preserve what perishable food they had.

6

Walking Out

WITH DAN GONE, THE DAYS passed on in a slow blur of endless rain and restless anticipation as I searched the sky for some sign of the flare he had promised to send up. Gazing out the back window of the Jeep with my eyes on the sky, I never saw a thing aside from the brooding, ever-present clouds, but the shadows in the forest seemed to twist and writhe around me. I couldn't shake the sickening feeling of unseen eyes watching me.

At first, I thought the moving shadows were simply a trick of the eyes or my imagination running away with me, but the longer I stared out of the rain-streaked windows, the more certain I became. The shadows didn't simply shift, they seemed to loom, clinging to the edge of the trees, darker than they had any right to be. And when they moved, it was too fast and fleeting to pin down. During the few times I opened the door of the Jeep, thinking I would relieve myself outside instead of using my camping toilet, the stench of rot and a sickening sense of dread had me immediately shutting myself back inside the safety of the car. There was indeed something lurking in the shadows of the forest, waiting for the opportunity to strike. I knew it, even if I couldn't see it

At the end of my third day stranded, I ate my last bits of solid food as the sun set. Streaks of red, orange and pink colored the sky, and as I took stock of what I had left, I hoped with all I was that the next day would be clear and dry. I still had a bag of candy bars, some trail mix, a bottle of water and a bottle of juice. That would hold me for another day at most, so despite my fears and the things I just knew were lurking in the shadows, I was going to have to walk to the camp store in the morning. I laid my head down, shimmying into my sleeping bag and began silently bidding the Jeep farewell.

I awoke the next morning to the cheery songs of birds outside my window. The sky was bright, and the damp trees glistened in the pale rays of early morning sun. I breathed a sigh of relief and rolled out of my sleeping bag to peer out of the windows. The forest looked oddly welcoming, and I canted my head to one side in confusion. After so many days of darkness, the twisting shadows and sense of foreboding seemed to have blown away on the wind with the clouds. I opened the car door, cautiously at first, and took in my surroundings. A light breeze whispered through the treetops carrying with it the sweet scent of clean, damp earth and early budding life. The air was fresh and devoid of the sulfurous rot that had surrounded me for days.

Had I imagined the entire thing? Had I really let my anxiety keep me stuck for three solid days?

My heart beat strong with excitement and relief. I was going to be able to get out of there. I could save myself.

Carefully, I packed my things and closed the doors of the Jeep but left them unlocked. If anyone else was stuck in the forest, maybe my vehicle could give them a dry place to rest until I was able to come back and rescue it. I gently ran a sentimental hand over the fender as memories flooded my mind, but there would be time for sentiment later, survival needed to be first and foremost in my mind, so I grit my teeth and set out down the road at a determined pace, chin held high.

Casting one last look back at the Jeep, I swallowed a lump in my throat at the sight of it shrinking in the distance surrounded by fallen debris. I blinked away the tears that threatened and rubbed my face, concentrating instead on the obstructions in the road ahead of me. The last thing I needed was to fall and hurt myself because I was getting all sentimental about a piece of machinery. But the Jeep was more than that. It was an old friend that had carried me through countless adventures and mishaps—mud pits, mountain trails and peaceful, stargazing nights. So many miles, so many years together, and now I felt like I was abandoning a piece of myself. Perhaps I was? But I pushed all of it to the back of my mind. I needed to make a plan to get myself home. If the phones worked at the camp store, I could get a hold of a tow company to retrieve my car and then finally call my mom to let her know I was alright. This wouldn't be the last time I saw it.

Besides, the sun was shining, and the birds were singing again. I could do this. Even though I was still up shit creek without a paddle, it didn't seem so bad. I could get myself out of the forest.

I continued down the road, scrambling over downed trees and branches, whistling to myself to pass the time, one foot in front of the other, making my way to safety. I'd been walking for what seemed like hours, watching birds dart from tree to tree, when I nearly stepped in a large puddle.

No, not a puddle.

I looked closer.

It was a blood smear, watered down to a sickly brownish pink from the rain. Just beside it, a long drag mark of a black, gelatinous substance led across the road and disappeared into the ditch, the edges of it seeming to melt into the pavement with an oily sheen, as if the rain couldn't quite wash it away. The unnatural way it glistened churned my stomach. Could it have been from roadkill?

No. Not a chance.

My heartbeat picked up, pounding as if trying to escape my chest. The blood smear was curiously close to a discarded bottle of juice.

What in the actual—?

Moving closer, I crouched to inspect a plastic bag speckled with more of the black substance. My hand reached out instinctively then jerked back as the scent of sulfur and rotting flesh brushed my nose.

It was a half-eaten bag of jerky.

My eyes went wide, swinging to the bushes and grass that crowded the roadside and my blood ran cold.

"Dan?" I called out, my eyes darting from the bushes to the deep shadows in the forest.

"*Dan!*" Panic bloomed in my chest and my heart leapt into my throat.

Had I actually seen a shadow in the bushes when Dan had left? No, my eyes had to have been playing tricks on me. I had smelled something too though...and that—that was definitely the bag of jerky I had given to Dan.

"Christ," I whispered as I took off down the road at a dead run, my heavy pack bouncing awkwardly on my back.

I ran like the devil himself was after me. My lungs burned, my legs felt like jello, my pack began rubbing blisters on my shoulders and back, but still, I ran. And when I finally stumbled up to the front door of the camp store, it was locked up tight like no one had been there in days.

"Oh, no." I whispered. There was a good reason I had never seen a flare.

Dan had never made it. *He'd never made it.*

I circled the building frantically calling out to anyone who might still be around, but my own voice echoing off the trees was the only response. Looking around, I found a large shed nearby (also locked), and a carport with two cars in it. Around the back side of the camp store building there was what appeared to be living quarters. After pounding on every door and window again, I decided to break in.

I'm no thief, but my brother and I had climbed in through an unlocked window a time or two over the years. Scanning the other buildings, I spotted a small stack of empty, five-gallon buckets and using one as a makeshift stepladder, I peered into every window I could reach. Finally, I came to one that was unlocked. Carefully as I could, I removed the screen and pulled the window open.

"Hello?" I called into the room one more time, just in case someone hadn't heard all the pounding and yelling before, but who was I kidding? The house was silent. Empty. So, I retrieved my pack and tossed it through the window then climbed in after it, closing the window behind me.

A dim bedroom with an en-suite bathroom greeted me. The furniture was sparse while the bedding and decor appeared untouched. It didn't appear to be one that was used often. I opened the door to find that I was at the end of a long hallway. A linen closet door to my right and a half-open bedroom door sat directly in front of me. I peered around the door and into a dim room filled with masculine décor. The closet and dresser drawers hung open as if they had been hastily rummaged through.

I turned and crept down the hallway, tense in a stranger's home. A bathroom and third bedroom passed to my left. Both were empty but also showed signs that they had been occupied recently. Dresser drawers had been pulled out and many empty hangers hung in the open closet. I continued on, feeling like an intruder but still too afraid to leave. A wide doorway on my right opened to a great room. Kitchen cabinets hung open on their hinges and the dining table looked as if it had been hastily cleared, crumbs of food still littered the smooth, wooden surface. The living room was simple but cozy, the couch and overstuffed chairs all facing a large wood stove fireplace.

It appeared that the folks that lived and worked here had left in a hurry.

Continuing on, I reached for a light switch and flicked it. Nothing happened so I made my way into the camp store proper. Silent aisles and rows of refrigerators and freezers full of food and supplies greeted me. All the labels faced out, so neat and tidy, it felt like the whole place was holding its breath, waiting for someone to return.

The aisles sat, eerie and dark, so I walked behind the front desk and into the deli kitchen. The industrial freezer was closed and still cold, but it wasn't running. Turning back to the front desk, I ran to the land line phone and yanked the receiver up, carefully pressing it to my ear.

Silence. The land lines were down too.

"I'll be damned," I muttered shaking my head. Dan had been right. This really was a total grid-down situation.

I paled at the notion that I was now considered an apocalypse survivor...for the time being anyway, and I wracked my brain for movie and television examples of what to do in this sort of situation, but my mind was blank.

Exhausted, hungry, and afraid, I knew I wouldn't be able to think straight until I got some food in my belly and some quality sleep. After perusing the store, I settled down at the table for a dinner of crispy rice treats and corn chips, washed down with a blue sports drink.

When I was finished, I wandered my temporary home, familiarizing myself with it. The whole place felt safe in a way I couldn't put into words. For the first time in days, my heart rate returned to normal as I studied the living space.

There was no television which immediately struck me as odd, but in what would have been the perfect place for a flat screen or entertainment center, sat an enormous built-in bookshelf. Hundreds of books occupied the space in neat rows and I smiled to myself. A television would be a waste anyway seeing as there was no electricity.

The kitchen was well stocked with cooking utensils, and the food pantry was filled with canned and shelf stable foods. The refrigerator had been mostly emptied save for condiments and food storage containers filled with leftovers. I would have to deal with those eventually. Puzzled by the sudden sense of feeling at home, I shook my head with a wry smile. This was *not* my home, but given the situation, I imagined that the owners would be forgiving as long as I took care of the place and didn't stay too long.

As far as places that I could have been stuck went, I counted myself extremely lucky to have ended up at the camp store. It was set up like a small-town market, a grocery store, complete with a little deli counter and grill. Hunting and fishing gear, along with ammunition, basic camping supplies and Pacific Northwest swag in the form of jackets, shirts, shot glasses, magnets, stickers, and stationery occupied the back corner. Some of that could be very useful. Then it dawned on me that the reason I felt so at home was due to the fact that the store was a familiar place. After all, I'd stopped there a countless number of times over the years since it was just up the road from my favorite place in the world.

I picked up a stout, leather journal and pen from the gift shop area, turning it over in my hands, pondering. Maybe keeping a diary would help me process the situation I had found myself in? At the bare minimum, it could help pass the time.

I walked back into the living quarters and to the spare room. It didn't feel right taking one of the beds that belonged to the people that called this place home before me. I removed my soiled clothes and changed into my sweatpants and night shirt.

Settling onto the bed, journal in my lap, I began to write: *"I just spent three days hiding in my car and I'm pretty sure that Dan is dead."*

The words poured out of me; all of my fear, my confusion and wondering spilling out onto the page in cheap ballpoint pen. The daylight faded quickly and I stared blankly at my handwriting until I couldn't see the page anymore. It was impossible to sum up the roller coaster of gut churning emotions I had been riding for the past three days, not when I knew that Dan was dead.

Dan was *dead.* And I sat inside on a bed, warm, dry, and safe. If a man like Dan—strong, capable, and prepared—could die on day one of the apocalypse, what chance did *I* have? I had no plan or *real* survival skills. What chance did my family have? They were so far away. How would I ever make it back to them? I closed the journal and lay my head down as my mind whirled, latching onto one name after another: Mom. Joey. Were they alright? My heart clenched at the thought. I didn't know what I would ever do without them—they were my life. And what about my few scattered friends? And DJ?

Alone and in the dark, I felt impossibly small. Tears threatened again but I stubbornly refused to let them fall. Crying about my situation wouldn't help a thing. I needed a plan.

No, I needed rest. Tomorrow I would figure out where to go from here.

7

Settling In

THE CRACK OF DISTANT GUNFIRE shattered the morning silence. My body bolted upright, heart hammering behind my ribs. Several shots in quick succession followed. I threw the covers off my legs and sprinted to the front doors of the store and peered out the window with a shaking breath.

The small parking lot was empty and the fog hung low in the conifers, their tops seeming to disappear into the mist. The sky was gray, sun blotted out by the thick clouds, and I absently wondered what time it was. Glancing around the store, I found a small, analog clock hanging on the wall behind the register. Just after 10 o'clock. I'd slept much later than I had meant to.

The gunfire continued, each shot echoing the thunderous beating of my heart. Where was it coming from?

Unable to open the store doors, I wound my way through the building to the rear of the house, where a regular residential door separated me from the outdoors. I unlocked the deadbolt and twisted the brass doorknob with a trembling hand. The door opened easily, and I was greeted with the sweet smells of mountain air and rain as I stepped out on to the small, covered patio. Tip toeing to the edge of the concrete pad, I peered around the side of the building, toward the parking lot. The narrow road disappeared into the mist, and I strained my eyes to try and see into the shadows. More shots rang out, seeming to echo off the fog itself, followed by deafening silence.

I darted inside, back to the store and snatched a paper map out of its slot on the magazine rack. Kneeling down on the chilly linoleum, I spread it open and quickly scanned it for my location. I found the chain of reservoirs I'd driven past, then followed the road to where it crossed over the river. More gunfire broke the near silence.

North. The shots were coming from the north. The tiny town of Riverside wasn't far—maybe two or three miles to the northeast as the crow flies—but by road? Five miles, maybe more. My lips peeled back off my teeth in a grimace.

The sound of sporadic gunfire continued, and my stomach sank as Dan's words echoed through my mind: *There are only nine meals between peace and anarchy.*

I knew that my family only had about a week's worth of food in the house at any given time, and assuming most families were like my own, people would be starting to run low on supplies any day now. Were the people in Riverside fighting amongst themselves already? Or was it other people, living on large properties in the forest, gone raiding in town? Either way, I did *not* want to stick around and find out.

I had to get back home.

Frustrated and half sick with worry for my mom and brother, I stood in a huff, leaving the map on the floor and marched back to the room I had slept in. I dressed quickly and filled my pack with food from the store. Throwing the heavy bag over my shoulders, I marched to the back door and pulled it open. I grit my teeth and grappled with the thought of walking all the way back home to Orchardville. It was far, true, but I knew the way by road like I knew the lines of my own face. It would be tough, but not impossible.

I can do this.

I closed the door firmly behind myself and started walking. The gravel of the parking lot crunched under my feet, loud in my ears compared to the silent, dripping forest. When my feet hit the pavement of the road, I paused, suddenly feeling uneasy about my rash decision to leave the store. The air was deathly still. No birds sang in the trees. The forest itself seemed to be holding its breath. Even the distant gunfire had ceased. Bone deep unease radiated outward from the pit of my stomach, but I forced my feet forward. Just one step. Then another.

Even in the rain, the forest normally sang; the birds, wind, rivers, and trees all harmonizing to create the forest melody I loved so much, but as I marched down the road, the only sound that met my ears was the steady squish of my shoes on the wet asphalt and my own, ragged breath.

An unearthly shriek shattered the silence and I whirled. It had come from behind me. Every hair on my head prickled as my eyes frantically scanned the bushes. A twig snapping pulled my attention to the leafless underbrush to my right, and I froze in terror. My breath hissed too loudly in my ears, and I willed my frantic heart to slow so that I could listen more closely, muscles tense, ready to flee. More crashing sounded to my right, and I forced my feet to start moving back to the safety of the camp store.

All at once, a deer leapt from the forest fifty paces ahead of me, crossing the road in a single bound and I sagged.

"Just a deer," I whispered to myself, leaning forward, placing my hands on my knees. I croaked out a shaky laugh.

Never in my life had a deer terrified me so completely. I stood back up and rubbed my face like I was trying to wash away the panic, then started walking again. I'd never make it home panicking like that—letting a deer bounding through the woods scare me stiff.

I. Could. Do. This.

Just then, three more deer burst from the cover of the forest. Being closer to them than I was to the first deer, I could see their eyes—wide with fear and ringed with white—when they crossed the road, their ears pointed back, tails in the air.

My heart hit the pit of my stomach.

Something was chasing them. What could it be? An animal? Or people? Maybe the people with the guns?

Cold fear lanced through my body and my limbs refused to listen to my silent command.

Don't just stand there, move.

But I was frozen in place, fear holding me immobile. Then the grating sound of a strangled cry cut the air, shaking me from my stupor. I turned to see another deer struggling at the edge of the road, half its body hidden in the undergrowth of large ferns. It cried out again, warm breath rising into the chill air while its front hooves scraped across the pavement.

Its eyes bulged, tongue lolling out of its mouth. Its terrified gaze connected with mine, as if it were begging for help—as if it knew it was dying.

At that moment, my body broke free.

Just one shaky step backward. Then another.

The deer screamed; one last keening sound, its eyes blinking then glazing over before something jerked it back into the shadows of the forest. The wet sound of rending flesh and a low rumbling hiss rose out of the forest in its wake, souring my stomach.

Move, damn it. *Move!*

Something in me snapped. Instincts took over and I sprinted back toward the camp store even though I knew in my soul that running from whatever predator could have made that noise was the stupidest thing I could have done.

I tore back through the gravel lot and around the back of the building to the patio, charging through the door and slamming it closed behind me. I threw the deadbolt back into place with clammy, shaking hands.

What the hell had I just witnessed? My palms scrubbed at my face and I huffed, "What is going on?"

I sank to the floor in a heap, heart hammering, chest heaving, ears straining for any sound outside.

Silence.

My eyes squeezed shut and all I could see was the round, terrified eyes of the deer. Slowly, my huffing breaths morphed into sobs, and I let the tears fall, curling my knees to my chest. Gasping, snotty, drooling, I let myself go. I screamed through palms clamped across my mouth.

I cried for Dan, cried for myself, cried for my mom and brother. I cried for the helplessness I felt, for being stranded, for not knowing what to do, for whatever terror was stalking the forests. I cried because I knew I was stuck, and I truly didn't know how to take care of myself. I cried because, in that moment, I knew that nothing was ever going to be okay again.

Eventually, I stripped off my shoes and made my way back to the bed and lay down. Tears continued to fall, but I wasn't as hysterical as I had been sitting with my back to the door. Still, it felt like I was trapped in a nightmare that I couldn't wake from. How had I been so unlucky to be going through this all alone? I wanted to be home. Safe. With my mom and brother. Or even sharing a drink with DJ like a normal, twenty-four-year-old...like I had said I would just a few days ago. It just wasn't fair.

After what seemed like hours, I knew that I couldn't wallow in my own self-pity forever, so I hauled myself up off the bed and went in search of food, stopping in the bathroom on my way.

The sink had been plugged and was filled with water, and there was a five-gallon bucket in the shower, also full of water. Canting my head to one side, I wondered why, but I turned to the toilet to relieve myself anyway.

As I pressed the lever down, the toilet flushed but did not fill back up. I jiggled the handle hoping that would help. When it didn't, realization dawned. No running water. Someone had filled the bucket on purpose. I retrieved the bucket from the shower and filled the tank with it, then with fingers crossed, I pressed the lever. I'd never been so happy to see a toilet flush in my life, but if there was no running water, how had the bucket been filled?

Pursing my lips, I made my way to the back door and peered out through the leaded, diamond-paned glass. Not twenty feet from the back patio, there stood a cast iron hand pump. Not as easy as turning on a faucet, but at least there was fresh water...as long as whatever had killed that deer wasn't outside waiting in the ferns at the edge of the yard.

But to get the water, I had to go outside.

It wasn't the inconvenience that twisted my stomach in knots—it was the forest. The fear of what might be lurking there. I was going to have to get used to it sooner rather than later.

"Well, it's now or never," I whispered to myself.

I opened the back door and listened hard, eyes scanning the tree line for movement. The breeze had picked up, bringing the pleasant swishing sound of wind through the conifers. A murder of crows cawed to each other as they flew over the store. It sounded almost peaceful. I stepped outside and walked to the hand pump. It clanked and squeaked as I worked the lever, then the cool water poured into the bucket. It was too loud. I was too exposed. Scrambling for the bucket's handle, I picked it up and ran back inside, locking the door behind me. With a sigh, I returned the full bucket back to the bathroom before finally going in search of food.

When I got to the kitchen, I paused. How was I supposed to cook? Walking to the stove, I sighed in relief. It was gas, not electric like the stove at home. I had run out of fuel for my jet boil the day before I left the Jeep and rather than waste space in my pack with equipment that I couldn't use, I had left it behind.

I rummaged through the pantry and found a can of chili. Dumping it into a small pot, I set it on the stove and cranked on the gas. Nothing happened.

"No," I sighed, cranking the knob back to the off position. My shoulders sagged and my head fell forward. "I just need a break," I said through gritted teeth.

The smell of propane filled my nostrils and I brightened. The gas was flowing, but the electric igniter was dead. I rummaged through drawers searching for matches or a lighter. "Come on, I know you guys kept a junk drawer somewhere."

Finally, I found a drawer filled with random knick knacks and spotted a box of long handled stick matches.

Jackpot.

The burner roared to life and as I stirred the chili, I mulled over the particulars of surviving here. The store was filled with food, sure, but eventually, I was going to have to venture out. Plus, I couldn't stay at the camp store forever. I needed to make a plan, see what resources I had at hand, gather more supplies, and then go *home*. I ate the chili right out of the pot while standing at the stove, staring into nothingness, completely overwhelmed.

When I was finished, I set the pan in the sink and turned the faucet on out of habit. When no water emerged, I groaned and took the pot to the back door, but I hesitated after I slipped my shoes on. It was getting dark outside and my stomach knotted remembering the deer. Was that movement just beyond the tree line? No, it had to be just the wind, right?

When I'd filled the bucket, nothing had felt amiss, just raw nerves and exhaustion. But as I made my way to the pump, the air felt different—off somehow. The hairs on my arms lifted, and it wasn't from the cold.

Was something watching me? My eyes flicked to the shadows between the trees as I lifted the handle and pressed down, the water flowing from the well and into the dirty pot. My gut clenched and an icy shiver crawled down my spine.

Something was definitely watching me. I snatched up the pot and power walked back inside, cranking the deadbolt home with a shudder.

After washing and drying the dishes, I made my way to the bookshelf in the living room. The daylight was fading fast, and it was getting hard to read the spines of the books. Heading back to the junk drawer, I found a mini flashlight and used it to quickly scan the titles. Though I would have normally preferred sci-fi or fantasy, with everything going on, I felt like something a bit less harrowing was in order. I settled on a worn romance novel—a classic bodice ripper from the late '80s with the legend himself, Fabio, on the cover.

I giggled and plopped onto the couch wrapped snug in a blanket, book in my lap. A fire would have made the moment perfect—warm and safe—but there was no way I was going outside for firewood. Not now. That would be a chore for tomorrow.

My eyes flicked over the pages, but the story never really reached me. I was too distracted. The pop of gunfire echoed in my mind, that thing in the woods...that poor deer. Sighing, I set the book aside and went to my room.

I wondered for a moment about why I had thought of the guest bedroom as 'my room' but brushed the thought away and picked up my journal and a pen. Maybe if I wrote it all down, I could make some sense out of this whole, impossible situation.

The next morning, I dragged myself out of bed. As I made myself some instant oatmeal, curtesy of the camp store, I decided that since I was going to be there for a little while, I should probably start poking around the out-buildings to see if there was anything I could use to make my life easier for the time being.

I dressed and stepped quietly outside, listening hard for anything that sounded out of the ordinary. After a few tense moments, I took a deep breath and walked toward the tool shed. My steps sounded loud in my ears, and I considered going back inside, but I stuck my chin out and kept walking. I would never make it back home if I couldn't suck it up and get to work. The deer incident from the day before sat heavy on my mind. The forest was full of animals—some of which could kill me if they wanted to. I'd always known that truth, but it hit much harder up in the mountains, alone as I was. I did have a new stash of bear spray and a good selection of hunting knives at my disposal; again, curtesy of the camp store, and as worried as I was about being outside, I didn't have any deep gut feelings telling me that it wasn't safe, so I marched up to the door of the shed.

It was locked.

Of course it was locked. Would nothing be just easy here?

I sighed and looked around for something to use to pry the lock, then remembered catching a glimpse of a screwdriver and a pair of pliers in the junk drawer the day before. Twenty minutes later my aching hands and sore arms had done nothing more than bend the metal, raising dozens of sharp, jagged edges while the lock held firm. Frustration burned in my chest, and I grit my teeth. With an angry grunt, I jammed the screwdriver behind the lever and yanked down hard. It slipped from my grasp and pain lanced through my hand, a gasp erupting from my throat.

I looked down to find a deep, jagged gash running diagonally from the base of my pointer finger and across my entire palm. For a few tense moments, the cold kept it from bleeding and all I could do was stare at it in shock. I knew immediately it needed stitches. Blood began seeping in to fill the cut then dripped through my fingers.

"Damn it," I groaned as I rushed to the water pump to rinse it.

After several minutes with my hand under the cold water, it wouldn't stop bleeding, so I went back into the house and scrounged through a first aid kit. After disinfecting the wound, I tried with shaky hands to close the cut with butterfly bandages, but they wouldn't stick. I huffed and tried not to let my frustrated tears fall. I needed help but I had no choice other than to figure this out on my own.

A fuzzy memory formed in my mind—Joey and I on summer break, binge watching sci-fi television. A man, terrified and on the run, closed his wounds with a tube of super glue so the zombies that were chasing him wouldn't be able to smell his blood. A bitter laugh escaped my lips. It was a stupid movie, but the idea wasn't.

Retrieving a new tube of superglue from the camp store, I struggled to open the package one handed then held the thin dropper over my palm. I lightly cupped my injured hand to close the wound, then with a deep breath, I squeezed the tube.

"Jesus-H." My voice grated through clenched teeth. Liquid fire scorched into the wound, the pain like hot iron, and I hissed as I tried not to flinch. My fingers trembled and my head felt giddy as I blew across the wound, willing the glue to dry faster. The sharp scent of the glue filled my nose and after a few minutes, I gingerly opened my palm. The glue held. Relief sagged my shoulders, and I quickly wrapped my hand in gauze then an elastic bandage. It wasn't pretty but it would have to do. I could only hope that it wouldn't get infected.

I could have stopped there, could have called it a day and laid down to rest, but the damp chill crept into my bones, making my fingers stiff. If I couldn't get into the shed, at the very least I could bring in some wood and get a fire going. Behind the carport, under the low eave, I found a large stock of split wood and a battered wheelbarrow. I filled it to nearly overflowing then struggled to roll it to the back patio.

By the time I finished with that task, it was well after noon. My hand ached, my body was stiff and sore, and I was painfully aware at how much time I had wasted because of a stupid mistake. I leaned against the side of the building staring blankly at the wheelbarrow. Out here, alone, one small mistake could cost me my life. The realization hit like a kick to the gut. I *had* to be more careful. I had to be smarter. I had to be better. Because the next time I slipped up, I might not be so lucky.

An hour later the wood stove began chasing the chill out of the air and I melted into the couch with a sigh. After having been cold for so many days, my icicle toes and fingertips began to thaw, and my muscles began to really relax. My hand still hurt like the devil, but I had a belly full of hot soup and a warm fire to relax by. Within minutes, my eyelids fluttered closed, and I didn't wake until dawn.

When I pulled myself up off the fluffy couch, I decided that it was going to be a productive and safe day. No injuries, no frustration. Think smart, act smart.

First, I needed something bigger to pry the latch off the tool shed and the first thing my clear, well-rested brain thought up was a crowbar. There were none laying around, so I investigated one of the two cars parked under the carport. The keys were inside on the seat. It was a sedan that looked straight out of the 80's with a front bench seat, ash trays in every door, and a cracking vinyl top. Just to be sure, I tried to start it. Nothing happened, so I took the keys and opened the trunk. Removing the spare tire, I pulled out the tire iron and hefted it in my hand. It would do perfectly.

Back at the shed door, with a better tool in hand, I had the latch pried off in a matter of minutes and swung the door open. The shed was filled with hand and gardening tools, lawn equipment and loads of things I had no idea how to use. While rummaging around through one of many metal toolboxes, I found a magnetic hide-a-key box with three keys inside. Scurrying to the back door, I tried one that looked like a house key. It unlatched the deadbolt. The other key was stamped *'MASTER – Do Not Duplicate'*, so I knew that had to belong to the front, camp store doors. The last key fit the heavy basement door.

I carefully opened it, and it groaned on its hinges. Rickety wooden steps appeared to descend into a black pit, and I fought back a shudder.

Everyone has an irrational fear of basements, right? I thought to myself while I stood, paralyzed at the entrance staring into the darkness. Turning on my heel, I went back into the house and slid my new prizes onto the keychain with my own house keys. My lips curled slightly with the ghost of a smile. I suddenly felt a lot less like a squatter. Leaving my bundle of keys hanging on a hook beside the back door, I grabbed my flashlight then returned to the basement.

"You can do this. There's probably nothing down there but dust and cobwebs." I gave myself a short pep talk before placing my foot on the first step.

It creaked as I settled my weight on it, but the step was solid, so I continued down the stairs. At the bottom, I scanned the room with the flashlight. It was a cavernous space, and despite all the dust and cobwebs, it was extremely well organized. Shelving filled more than half the space making aisles of a sort. The shelves were filled with boxes of what appeared to be back-stock for the store. The other shelved section of the space looked to be filled with neatly arranged personal items. Large furniture pieces, boxes of clothes and miscellaneous household items, and seasonal decorations.

In a wide space toward the middle of the basement sat a home gym that looked like it came straight out of the 80's. A wooden crate was sat just beside the weight bench, looking very out of place compared to the meticulous organization of the rest of the space. My curiosity piqued; I began making my way over to it when an old camping lantern caught my eye.

Now that could be useful.

I detoured and lifted the lantern off the shelf to inspect it. It appeared to be operational, so I leaned in to see what else was on that shelf. Several older tents, sleeping bags and outdoor gear greeted my eager eyes. I almost cheered when I found a camp stove with a set of cast iron cookware beside it and plenty of those little green propane tanks. I knew that no matter how much propane was left in the giant white tank by the carport, it wouldn't last forever, and the little camp stove could help stretch that out for a bit longer while I learned how to cook outdoors over a fire.

I shook myself a bit. I needed to get home, not get settled and completely comfortable here. But, still, the set of cast iron cookware deserved to be in the kitchen. It was all my mom cooked with for years. If I used them, I could feel closer to her in a way.

Glancing around quickly, I spotted an empty plastic storage tote and filled it with a couple pieces of the cookware, the camp stove, and the lantern. Tiny flashlight in my mouth, I hefted the tote with a grunt and awkwardly moved it to the open space near the home gym. I knew I would have a hard time lifting it back up off the floor, so I waddled to the weight bench, hoping I wouldn't trip over anything, and set it down heavily. Dust curled up in the beam of the flashlight as I removed it from my mouth and glanced down. Something had been written in the dust on the weight bench.

"Damn-it," I whispered to myself.

Having had no contact with anyone in a week, I was getting desperate for any type of communication. I lifted the tote once again and peered down at the bench. The center of whatever had been written had been smudged away by the tote, but on either side of the smeared square of dust that it left behind, I could make out a handful of letters.

'Be sa— —roy', I frowned at the half-erased letters.

What the hell did that mean? Be savage? Be sorry? I leaned closer, brushing my fingers over the dusty letters as if I could somehow make the lost words reappear. The writing must have been recent; even with the dust I had stirred up, the letters still looked fresh. That meant someone had to have been here after the power went out, which I had already figured out days ago by how hastily cleared out two of the closets had been. But why would they have written some cryptic note on a dusty weight bench instead of writing a normal note like a functional human being? I rolled my eyes and let out a deep sigh. It was probably nothing anyway.

With a grunt, I picked up the tote and set it back on the bench again. Whatever had been written was lost and there wasn't anything I could do about it. Turning, I pointed the flashlight into the wooden crate I had spied earlier. It was empty save for packing material, so I dragged it closer to the rows of shelves and continued my search for useful things. In a corner, I found a square mark on the floor that was curiously devoid of dust. It was about the same size as the crate that had been sitting beside the weight bench. Judging by the amount of dust in the corner, that crate had to have been sitting there for decades before it was moved. There were so many other heirloom quality things in the basement, the crate must have held something either very important or very sentimental if the folks that lived here had taken it with them when they left.

Continuing on, I came upon an ornately carved hardwood pedestal, nearly hidden between a large bookshelf and an ancient armoire. The wood grain gleamed like golden silk in the glow of the flashlight. It was the only thing in the basement that was completely devoid of dust or cobwebs. On top of it sat an equally ornate stone box. The seam where the lid met the bottom was nothing more than a thin line, no thicker than a human hair.

As if of their own accord, my fingertips traced the swirling, carved lines of an infinity symbol encircled by an oval ouroboros on the lid; two snakes, each one consuming the tail of the other. I'd seen the symbol somewhere before, but where?

A strange awareness charged the space, tickling down the back of my neck, like the moment before lightning strikes, the air crackled with power. Beneath my unease, a deep recognition stirred, whispering just beyond hearing, tickling the edge of memory. Then under my fingers, the box warmed as if responding to my touch— thrumming, pulsing with power, beating in time with some unknown rhythm. The energy curled about my fingertips like a caress filling me with love, strength, and a sense of belonging.

I snatched my hand away, heart leaping into my throat. "What the hell." I took a step backward, shaking my hand, unnerved down to my bones.

The moment I retreated, the pulsing power faded, but something in me resisted the distance, like I had just stepped away from something safe. Something that *knew* me. In the dim glow of the flashlight, the box seemed to blur at the edges like I wasn't seeing it properly.

Probably should *not* have touched that. Had I learned *nothing* from my incident the day before? Caution was a must. Self-preservation over curiosity, *always*.

Gooseflesh tickled up my spine and across my scalp as I backed further away from the box and pedestal. Whatever was inside that box wasn't just idly sitting there, it was waiting. I could feel it in the depths of my soul. Heart still pounding, I gathered up the tote and scurried out of the basement, shutting the door solidly behind me. The last thing I needed to be doing in this new, strange world, was to be messing with something I didn't understand.

Back in the house, I cleaned and oiled the cast iron cookware, then placed all the items in the oven and baked them, wondering what Mom would say if she could see me. I quickly heated another can of soup on the stovetop and carried the pan with me to the bookshelf, slurping the hot broth out of a giant wooden spoon. I could still feel the energy of the stone box in the basement, could almost say with a certainty that it was about ten paces to my left and straight down.

What was that about?

I shook my head and returned to perusing the bookshelf. My eyes passed over a book about Pacific Northwest wild edibles. Right beside it was a tall, hardcover book with no title on its spine. Sitting the spoon back into the pot, I gingerly reached out with my injured hand and wiggled the book off the shelf. In worn, gold print, the cover read *Primitive Survival*. I tossed it and the wild edibles book on the couch to read later. Even if I didn't stay here at the camp store forever, the contents of those books could be pivotal. I knew nothing about surviving for extended periods without power or infrastructure and I hoped that those books could help me out. Only time would tell.

After finishing my meal and cleaning the dishes, I sat down to read and learn while I waited for my cast iron pans to finish seasoning. Mom would definitely be proud if she could see me now.

8

Creature in the Woods

THE NEXT SEVERAL DAYS PASSED easily and without incident. The cut on my hand ached but the pain faded with each passing day without any signs of infection. I'd gotten lucky in that regard, and I made myself a vow to never be so sloppy again.

Because my hand had been so painful, I'd spent most of the daylight hours devouring the Primitive Survival book while cozy and warm on the couch. Initially, I dismissed its contents as a bunch of long winded, mumbo-jumbo, but it seems that the people that lived here took stock in it, making notes in the page margins on specific topics. They even added entire pages about processes and recipes they had perfected that where slightly different from what was printed in the book. In addition to the survival book and the one on wild edibles, the large bookshelf held several books on natural medicine and herbs. Some were completely devoted to what could be found growing wild in the local area, while others focused more on planting one's own medicinal herb garden and how to preserve the subsequent harvest. I also found several current year farmer's almanacs in the store on the magazine rack and brought one to the bookshelf as well.

My grandmother always studied the almanacs to decide when it would be best to plant her garden and since the only way I had to forecast the weather was by simply looking up at the sky, I figured any help I could get—even if it wasn't exactly scientific—would be better than nothing. The information was all utterly fascinating and because the skies had done nothing but drip since I'd arrived at the camp store, I had all the time in the world to study up.

Just as I was beginning to feel the first twinges of cabin fever begin to take hold, I awoke to the first bright morning in more than a week. Stepping outside in my pajamas, I looked up and studied the sky. The clouds were high, thin, and wispy with several gaps open to the stark blue of the sky. The birds were singing and for the first time since I had arrived, the road and gravel lot were drying out with the light breeze. A genuine smile slowly spread across my face as I inhaled the cool, mountain air. It was about time the sun finally showed its face.

I slipped my chilly feet into a pair of men's slippers that I had found in the closet of my room and shuffled carefully out into the parking lot, eyeing the forest around me while listening not only to my surroundings, but to that quiet, inner voice. My gut.

The forest sounded bright and cheerful, the air resonating with hopefulness, like the morning I had left the Jeep. All the wrongness I had felt on the dark, rainy days, now rightened by the rays of the sun.

Not wanting to waste what little clear weather I might have; I decided that I should get some chores done outside. I returned to my room and dressed then hastily stuffed a granola bar into my pocket and headed back out the door.

I moved several days' worth of wood from the large pile to the patio then got to work fabricating a meat drying rack over a ring of stones. The meat in the industrial freezer was continuing to thaw out and I wanted to save as much of it as I could. The survival book detailed several different ways to cure meat for long term storage without refrigeration. Cold smoking thin cut meat appeared to be fairly straight forward while salt curing seemed the best way to preserve the larger cuts of whole muscle.

Building the drying rack and fire pit was much easier than I had imagined it would be, and with that done, I headed back inside to preserve the large cuts of meat I had pulled out of the freezer.

I followed the instructions in the book to a T, coating the large hunks of meat with sea salt and placed them on a cooling rack inside a storage bin to cure. It would take at least five days, emptying the drawn-off liquid every morning, before I would know if I had done it right. If it worked, I'd have enough meat to keep me fed for years, not just months. It would be a lifeline. And if it didn't work? I didn't want to think about it.

A little thrill shot through me as I closed the primitive survival book and placed it back on the bookshelf. I was doing more than simply existing, I was surviving. Planning ahead. A small spark of pride lit in my chest but was quickly dampened by the thought of my family. They should have been there with me. I knew Mom would be beaming if she could see what I was doing, and if Joey were here, I could make *him* split the wood. I chuckled lightly, trying to clear the tightness in my throat as I shuffled to the front windows of the camp store and looked out.

DJ's face flitted into my mind's eye for the first time in days. I'd texted him from here not ten minutes before the power had gone out. I might very well have been the last person he'd messaged before communications went dark. Would I ever see him again? And if I did, would he even remember me? Could he be looking up at the sky right now wondering if I was still alive up here? Sighing at the thought, I shook my head and brushed the sweet daydream away.

The skies were still light and dry even though the gaps in the clouds had closed up, so I decided to take a quick walk up the road to a view point I knew of that overlooked the quaint town of Riverside. I wanted to see if I could get an idea of what might have been going on in the town a few days ago when I'd heard the gunshots. That little bit of knowledge would help me decide how much longer I could stay put.

Birds singing in the budding trees, their voices muted through the glass, met my ears and I took that as a sign that the rain would hold off a bit longer. Hopefully long enough for me to get to where I was headed and then back again. Not wanting to delay a moment longer, I laced up my trail runners and headed out the door.

The further I walked from the camp store, the more unease crept into my bones. Then, about 150 yards out, I walked right into something invisible but undeniable—a shift so stark I could have sworn I had just stepped from a sun-warmed porch and into a crypt. An icy chill prickled from my scalp to my toes, and I shivered, though the actual temperature surrounding me hadn't changed at all. Everything around me still looked, smelled, and sounded the same, but the comfortable, easy energy I had grown accustomed to while in and around the camp store was gone, replaced by an eerie awareness that I needed to stay sharp.

Should I go back?

I turned, gazing back at the log building in the distance. It looked so unassuming, so insignificant and small, tucked away under the towering conifers, but some sort of power radiated from it, warm, safe, and inviting, like the sweet sensation of a mother's embrace. I could feel it in my bones.

Turning my feelings inward, I really listened to my gut, just like Mom had taught me. All I could feel was a desperate need to not let my guard down, which was understandable. The last time I had been on this section of road, I had been sprinting away from a watery blood smear. And when I had walked the opposite direction only a few days ago, I'd watched a deer—I shook my head, not wanting to recall the sight...or sound.

With a determined breath and my eyes on the road ahead, I forced my feet to carry me farther away from the camp store. The warm sensation clung to me, hesitant; like so many unseen hands reluctant to let me go. Then, with a whisper-soft touch, it faded away, like a puff of warm breath on an icy day, leaving only the damp cold in its wake, a silent farewell before fully releasing me into the world.

Nothing seemed amiss as my eyes scanned the budding underbrush that crowded the roadside, so I kept walking, continually searching for any shadows that seemed out of place.

About a mile up the road, the small pull-out of the viewpoint appeared around a corner. I broke into a jog, but as I neared the rock wall imbedded with information plaques about the view, my heart sank. The beautiful town of Riverside, surrounded by hills with a sparkling river winding around its edge, was on fire. A thick column of smoke rose into the sky to blend with the high clouds. Fortunately, much of the town and surrounding areas didn't look to be burning, but what appeared to be the heart of the town itself was fully engulfed in black smoke.

My mind raced. Were people down there rioting? Looting? Would that sort of thing even happen in a small town like that? Were the fires related to the gunshots I'd heard days ago? Would the fire spread?

There are only nine meals between peace and anarchy.

What if people tried to leave their destroyed town and headed up into the hills? Would I be safe alone at the camp store if they did? I knew from first-hand experience that it wouldn't take much for a determined person to break into the store to take what they wanted. I had done it myself.

The thought of trying to talk or reason with other survivors turned my stomach in knots. All I could do was stare down at the chaos below me and wonder. A tear slid down my cheek leaving a chilly stripe in its wake and I smudged it away with a fist. Tears would not help me, but I simply couldn't turn my back on the tragic scene.

I sat up at the lookout for what felt like hours, feeling sorry for myself and missing my family and home. Was Orchardville burning like Riverside? Was my house still standing? God, were Mom and Joey alright?

DJ's dimpled smile flashed into my mind's eye. What was he going through right now? Was he wondering what had happened to me? I snorted at the childish thought. Of course he wasn't thinking about me. Why would he be? We'd only just met. He was probably neck deep in survival, just as I was, but unlike me, he would have others to work with. Others to bounce ideas off of. The only reason I was thinking of him at all was because I was lonely, sad, scared, and he was the last person I had talked to before my world went to shit.

With a sigh and tears brimming my eyes, I continued watching the picturesque town burn. The clouds kept rolling in, piling up against the hills, shrouding the mountaintops in thick mist. Then, with the denser clouds came the rain, a sprinkle that quickly turned to a solid rain shower. I reluctantly turned away from the view and headed back to the camp store, moping and listening to the droplets patter the asphalt and the fresh, spring leaves, hoping that the rain would drown the fires.

As the sky darkened further, the rain fell heavier on my hunched shoulders, and I picked up my pace not wanting to end up soaked to the bone. The camp store was still at least a quarter mile off. Eyes on the road at my feet, I trudged onward, but a prickle of unease crawled up my back and spread out across my scalp. My stomach dropped and a deep sense of wrongness took root in my chest, like the day Dan had taken off alone toward the camp store.

I slowed and held my breath, ears straining to hear something other than the rain pattering the road and trees.

114

Something shifted behind me—a thin scraping against the pavement. I whirled, mid-step.

A shadow, too large to be a deer and to fluid to be a bear, slithered off the pavement and into the underbrush several hundred feet away. A sense of wrongness bloomed in my chest. That movement was wrong. Too smooth. Too fast. Could my eyes have been playing tricks on me?

No, my gut urged. *This is real.*

The air around me shifted, thick and pressing, as my legs carried me into a frantic power walk. A predator was near. Stalking. Hunting. The trees took on the sinister look I remembered from my days spent hiding in the Jeep, shadows seeming to twist and writhe at the edges of my vision.

Always trust your gut, Amber. It'll never lead you astray. My mom's sweet voice sounded in my mind.

Even though I was moving, the feeling of being followed didn't fade. It grew more powerful, a thorny vine of fear winding its way around my ribs, squeezing. Traumatic memories of my first long walk to the camp store flashed in my mind and my entire body began to tremble, heart pounding in my ears as I scurried across the pavement in the rain.

The blood smear.

The bag of Jerky.

Dan.

What had happened to him? Something had to have gotten him. Something terrible. What living thing could have hauled off a grown man that was over six feet tall without a trace?

I risked a glance over my shoulder. The foliage rippled as something large stalked through it. It had closed the distance between us by half! My stomach dropped, adrenaline searing through my veins, and I bolted.

Wide eyed and terrified, I couldn't feel my feet as they pounded the pavement. The swishing of the bushes got louder. Closer. I pushed myself to run harder.

Faster. I had to run *faster.*

Don't look back, Amber.

Just run.

Run!

I rounded a bend in the road and the camp store bobbed into view. Instantly, that feeling of warmth and relief washed over me and I sped the last hundred yards toward the door. Once inside, I cranked the lock home behind myself and peered out the front windows, puffing from exertion while my limbs trembled. I could see nothing out on the road. No movement, no shadows. Just rain.

"What the hell was that?" I whispered to myself. Something had been stalking me. Hunting me. There was no denying it. My gut told me it didn't matter what on earth it was, it was all bad and I needed to avoid it at all costs. I had felt fine before it had started raining though, and for some reason, I felt completely safe once I had made it to the parking lot of the camp store.

But why? What was the feeling of peace that surrounded this place?

I sighed deeply and my palms found my face. "What on earth is going on?" I groaned.

The forest, rain or shine, had always been my sanctuary, the one place aside from my own home, where I felt completely safe, and now, it terrified me. I grappled with the situation, trying to make some sense out of it. Trying to find a pattern in all the madness.

The only time I felt that sickening twist in my gut was when it was dark or raining. Even from the safety of the camp store, the forest felt and even appeared different when the rain came.

A frustrated sound escaped my throat as I paced back and forth in front of the camp store windows, feeling like a child again, scared of the dark and wanting her mother's comfort. I wrapped my arms tight around myself and let my head fall back.

My gaze drifted to the yellowed ceiling tiles and I forced my feet to still. "Okay. There has to be a reasonable explanation to all this." I spoke firmly into the empty room. "Last summer...the attacks at Yellowstone...Grand Teton, they happened almost exclusively during the dark hours of night."

Only a handful of them had occurred during daylight hours, and those all happened on cloudy or rainy days. Like today.

A chill prickled through me. Could that be the key? Keeping indoors unless the sun was out? I would have to test that theory.

But what was it about the camp store and the surrounding area that seemed to hold whatever that creature in the forest was at bay? My mind drifted to the stone box in the basement. I could feel it there below my feet, a safe and grounding energy. What was inside of it? Did I dare try and find out? My fingers seemed to itch with the need to touch the stone again, but no, I had more pressing things to worry about.

Pushing thoughts of the strange box out of my mind, I focused on more practical things. If my hunch about sunlight was correct, I was going to be stuck at the camp store much longer than I had intended. I *needed* to keep studying that survival book.

Every morning, I rose with the dawn. Surviving was serious business, and since I was alone at the camp store, my days were filled with work from sunup to sundown. Evenings were for writing in my journal and studying the survival book. Between it and the handful of other useful books I'd scavenged, there was so much to learn.

One philosophy, repeated in all of them, stood out: *Strength is survival. Stay fit. Stay sharp. Stay alive.*

Dying was obviously low on my to-do list, so I took the advice that was both printed and scrawled in the margins, and I made it my mantra: *Keep Your Strength Up.*

At the top of the basement stairs, I scratched a fresh tally mark into the wooden beam with a large nail. It had been twenty-one days since my car broke down. Three whole weeks, and I was still standing. My thoughts drifted to Dan. I would not allow myself to fall.

I made my way down the creaking steps, doing my best to ignore the faint, thrumming power emanating from the stone box. The old weight bench, now devoid of dust, welcomed me, and I groaned. This was the worst part of my routine, so I got it out of the way first. "Just an hour," I told myself as I knelt and lit one of the camping lanterns, its cool glow flickering against the basement walls. "One hour, then you're done."

Even in high school, I'd hated PE. Hated sweating. Hated exerting myself. Hated every single moment of gym class. I'd always been a twig—a weakling.

But the weak didn't survive out here.

117

Dynamic stretches. Light lifting. Push-ups, seated v-ups, leg lifts. My mind never strayed from my family as I grit my teeth through every set. I was doing it all to get back to them. Every day, the exercises got easier. Every day, my body felt less like a liability and more like something capable. Lifting firewood, hauling supplies, moving efficiently—it all took strength. And I needed to be strong.

The stronger I grew, the more determined I became. I would make it home, come hell or high water.

Nothing would stop me.

Not the rain.

Not the cold.

Not that *thing* in the woods.

Out in the gravel parking lot, I ran sprints. The morning was dry, but the sky was thick with clouds. The creature hadn't shown itself in days—no movement in the trees, no scent of rot on the chilly breeze, no prickling at the back of my neck.

Had it moved on? Or was it simply waiting? Watching. I still didn't know exactly why the camp store was different, but I knew in my heart that it had something to do with that stone box, and I believed with every cell in my body that the safe, protective energy surrounding this place was real. And I hoped that someday I'd find someone who could explain it all to me.

After my workout, I returned to the house, washed up, ate breakfast, and checked on my food stores. The salt-cured meat was progressing well. Most of it, anyway. One of the larger cuts had begun to grow a thin, powdery, white fuzz.

I stared at it, stomach twisting.

The book had mentioned this. Penicillin mold. Perfectly normal and beneficial to the drying process. Humans had preserved meat this way for centuries before refrigeration.

But every twenty-first-century instinct in my body screamed at me to throw it out.

What if I was wrong? What if I gave myself food poisoning? Or ended up with some gut-rotting bacterial infection or a parasite? What if I got an infected cut? What if I caught pneumonia?

A heavy weight settled in my stomach.

I needed medicine, and not just the mild, over the counter basics that were here at the camp store.

118

I needed real painkillers, antibiotics, anything that could keep me from dying from something stupid. The pharmacy in Riverside... if it hadn't been completely raided already, it might have something left.

On the next sunny day, I would find out.

9

From Bad to Worse

Melissa

THREE WEEKS. That was all the time it had taken for the world to turn upside down. Melissa stood at the front window, arms wrapped around her middle, staring out onto the street. They had food and water for now, but every day, the unease in her heart grew harder to ignore.

Two weeks ago, a small detachment from the national guard arrived—separate from the main force deployed to Portland—bringing food, supplies, and the promise of a path back to normalcy. But that promise rang hollow; normal felt further away with each passing day.

The military somehow still had some working vehicles, a fact that chafed some members of her community, but despite the periodic outbursts, people in general remained civil, especially after everyone was notified that the military was attempting to repair the infrastructure in the city. Unfortunately, nothing had been successful as of yet, but everyone was told that repairs of that nature take time.

The ration lines in the park were tense from the beginning. The first time a man tried to shove past the line to take extra supplies, the soldiers handled it quickly. Barking orders, stiff postures, and rifles raised just high enough to instill a sliver of fear. It had quieted the mob, but now, instead of crying out, the people glared while clenching fist and jaw. Melissa knew in that moment that the community ceased to see the soldiers as protectors and peacekeepers. They had become an obstacle.

After another serious scuffle at the ration lines, many of her neighbors made the decision to leave the area for some other place they thought would be safer; some even had second homes in lesser populated areas. Melissa scoffed at that. It must be nice to have options in a situation as dire as the one they were all in at the moment.

As a whole, the local community had come together to try and figure out what could be done to make their situation easier. The lack of easy and fast communication was the largest hurdle initially, and Joey, bless his heart, had volunteered to begin a bicycle messenger service along with several other youths in the neighborhood. They'd become a liaison between the military and the civilians. In exchange for their efforts, they were given additional rations for their families.

They worked in shifts around the clock not only carrying messages but also delivering supplies and food to the members of the community who were unable to visit the ration lines themselves. Then, like a bloody harbinger of things to come, the first bike messenger was found dead in the street on a chilly morning, his messages and deliveries stolen. No arrests had been made, and while the military claimed to be 'investigating', Joey had his suspicions about who had done it.

Melissa sagged and let out a relieved sigh as she spotted her son returning home from his shift. He always told her not to worry, that he'd be fine out there, but every day when he walked out that door, she feared it would be his last.

As he swung his leg off his bike and locked it to the post of the front patio, Melissa opened the front door for him. His face looked more drawn than usual as he met her with a tired smile.

"What happened, Son?" Melissa reached out to him then thought better of it. Instead, she gave him space to come in from the damp cold and remove his wet shoes. He'd talk when he was ready.

After setting his shoes on the rug beside the door and taking off his jacket, Joey finally spoke. "There's a group of people out there that are bad news, Mom," he explained to her. "They've been getting into it with the soldiers set up down by the mall. And some of the other couriers, that live in and deliver to the tougher neighborhoods, say that the same group has been breaking into houses and just taking what they want."

"Ok, you're done with this messenger thing, young man. I will not have you disappear on me too," Melissa stated, voice firm, allowing no room for argument.

Her son would argue and push and try to get his own way, but damn it, she couldn't lose him too. They had not seen nor heard from Amber in over three weeks and Melissa knew that if her daughter had been physically able, she should have made it home by now—*would* have made it home. Although Melissa's whole soul held out hope that Amber would eventually come walking through that front door, a little piece of her hope died every time she locked the house up for the evening and her daughter wasn't safe inside where she belonged.

"I can't just *not* show up there tomorrow. I have my route, and people are counting on me for their food and water," Joey said earnestly.

"I don't want to say it, but you remember what happened the last time I suggested that you stay home from work?" She would not allow another close call, like his last day at the grocery store, happen again.

That day had been simple looting. But just two days ago, a young man had been killed in cold blood. If people were getting desperate enough to kill a kid on a bicycle for the food or messages he was carrying, the situation truly had gotten worse than she could have ever imagined.

"That was different, Mom." Joey turned his back on her and strode from the entryway and into the kitchen, emptying several pieces of non-perishable food items from his large backpack and placed them on the countertop. "You've seen the people at the ration lines. Do you really think that they're all just gonna quietly starve while they wait for the government to figure things out?" His voice was raw and thick, edged with frustration. "Delivering messages is keeping us more well fed than most of the other people in the community. Plus, I can't just stop my deliveries. People need their food. Their medicines. And I know you don't want to go back to waiting in those lines for scraps."

Melissa stomach twisted as she followed her son into the kitchen and sat down heavily on her kitchen chair. He wasn't wrong, but she'd already lost her daughter. Could she really risk losing her son too?

"You're right, I don't. But I would much rather stand in that line and live on scraps, than have you end up dead, like that poor kid. I can't imagine what his parents must be going through." Melissa ran a hand through her dark hair and looked up at her son.

His face was so much like his father's, but he had inherited his body type from her side of the family tree. Her older brother, father, uncles, and grandfather had all been tough, wiry fellows. Said that those features had come from her great grandmother. And the apple hadn't fallen far from the tree where Joey was concerned. He was just above average height and built like a string bean, sharing the same dark hair that was so common in their family. His eyes were brown though, like his fathers.

"Did you know him well?" she asked, trying to steer the conversation away from confrontation.

Her son's eyes softened, "I only met him a few times, but he was cool. His name was Brad."

"I'm sorry, hun."

They shared the space in silence for several minutes before Joey spoke again. "Is anything ever going to be normal again, Ma?"

The note of pain in his voice nearly broke her heart. She stood and wrapped her arms around him half expecting him to brush her off or squirm away with a tense laugh. He didn't though. He returned her embrace with a sigh, resting his chin on the top of her head.

He's scared, Melissa realized, *scared to death and trying his hardest not to show it.*

Suddenly she wasn't holding her grown son, she was holding her baby boy, just like she had when he was small, and needed comfort. Only now she couldn't hug away the fear like she had when he'd woken from a nightmare. Couldn't kiss his forehead and tell him everything was going to be okay. Because life had turned into a nightmare neither one of them could wake from.

She struggled to find the encouraging words that she knew he needed to hear, but she was scared too. Terrified.

"I hope so," she whispered, hating how hollow the words sounded.

If she had learned only one thing from all her years as a single parent, it was that her children needed guidance and love above all else. In any other situation, she would have had the right words for him, but in this case, she was just as out of her depth as he was.

Nothing she had ever experienced in her forty-four years of life could have prepared her for what they were experiencing. The only thing she knew for certain was that she had to protect her children.

Joey stayed home the next morning and the morning after that. Melissa was silently grateful. If Amber was truly lost to them, she couldn't risk her son too. He may be twenty-two years old, a fact that made her wonder where all the years had gone, but he was still her baby...her very *grown* baby.

The deep rumbling of vehicles pulled Melissa to the curtained windows at the far end of the living room, and she cracked the fabric just enough to peer out into the gray morning light. Several large, canvas covered trucks from the National Guard rolled past on their way to the community park to set up the ration lines. She checked her watch. It was just after 10:30AM. They usually opened the lines around noon, so she and Joey would need to leave soon to get ahead of the crowds.

"Hey, Joey?" Melissa called up the stairs.

"Yeah, I heard them. I'll get dressed. Gimme five minutes."

Melissa moved to the hall closet and wrapped herself in a warm, shapeless jacket then tugged on a pair of Amber's old, leather hiking boots. Rolling her shoulder length, brown hair into a low bun, she sighed and pulled on a dark stocking cap. She even wore her son's loose-fitting jeans.

Joey worried that even at her age, someone could still try and take advantage. Word had gone around that several women who had gone out alone had been accosted, harassed and one nearly assaulted near the park where the ration lines were located.

Some undesirable types of people were taking advantage of the lack of law enforcement and limited communication to stir up trouble. At that news, neighboring women had taken to dressing in men's clothing and only going out in groups of three or more to make themselves less of a potential target.

Melissa herself was a petite woman that had never really grown out of the 'knees and elbows' stage of youth. At just over five feet tall and barely 110 pounds, she could easily be mistaken, at a distance, for a boy just entering his teenage years—as long as she made sure to walk and stand the right way. So, she practiced standing in the manner that Joey had shown her, hands in her pockets, to hide her delicate fingers, and shoulders turned in to mask any hint of breasts that weren't fully camouflaged beneath the snug sports bra and oversized jacket she wore.

She never thought that she would be forced to hide who she was out of fear of bodily harm. The fact made her stomach churn, but worse was the fear she felt for her daughter. She had been gone almost a month. Even if Amber could have only walked five miles per day, she should have made it home already. What if she had tried to make it home and had met with foul play? Or what if she was lost in the forest?

Melissa had notified the authorities the first time they had rolled through her neighborhood but there was little they could do. Communication was difficult to say the least, and what electronic equipment the military could get to work was tied up with 'more important things' than a wayward adult. When she had asked what she could do, their response was simply, "Pray."

She scoffed at the memory. *Pray? To who, exactly?* She'd wanted to strangle that man. Instead, she'd forced a smile, gritted her teeth, and muttered curses under her breath as he'd walked away.

Heavy footsteps thudded down the stairs, pulling Melissa from her thoughts. Joey stepped into view. He was wearing his shoes in the house, that little turd.

"You ready?" Joey asked as he appeared around the edge of the banister.

"How many times do I have to tell you, no shoes in the house?"

Joey glanced down at his worn sneakers and shrugged. *Shrugged.*

"We've never worn shoes in this house, and all of a sudden you decide that marking my clean floors up is acceptable when you *know* we only have so much floor cleaner left? So, help me kid." She smiled despite her firm tone. "You're cleaning the floors when we get back then."

Joey chuckled, shaking his head, and opened the front door for her, "After you, Ma."

Melissa pursed her lips at her son then turned to gently touch the picture she'd hung in the entryway of Amber and her Jeep. Together she and Joey exited the house, locking the door behind them, and joined the other neighbors already making their way toward the ration lines.

The community park was teeming with people when they arrived. The crowd of people milled impatiently, tense voices raised in shouts. In general, most of the people around her appeared indifferent to the sporadic outbursts around them, but the number of military personnel had tripled since she and Joey's last visit. A tense knot formed in Melissa's chest. Not only were there more soldiers, but they were armed to the teeth.

Her stomach clenched as she turned to Joey, gripping his forearm. "Wait. I don't like this."

"This is just how it is now, Ma. People are getting hungry and there is less and less to go around," Joey said matter-of-factly and Melissa paled.

Was this really her only option? To fight the aggravated crowds at the ration lines, staring down the barrels of high caliber rifles, or send her son off to carry messages with the risk that he could be hurt or killed? What had their world come to?

Her feet slowed of their own accord, a creeping dread crawling from her chest to her limbs.

Joey looked down at her. "What is it? What's wrong?" His brows knit over concerned eyes, and he took her hand in his.

"I—I don't know. Something feels off." She pulled her eyes from her son's face and scanned the crowd. The misty rain seemed to hang like a damp cloth all around them. Everyone looked chilled, hungry, and irritable.

"No, we need to go." She could feel the energy shifting from that of irritated discontent to something akin to a frenzy, like she was standing in the midst of a cache of powder kegs, and someone was holding a lit match.

Some soldiers were quickly handing out packages of food and bottles of water, while others assisted in crowd management, but they weren't the ones that had Melissa concerned. It was the ones perched atop the vehicles with their eyes on the surrounding trees, guns at the ready, that made her pause. Others walked the perimeter of the park in pairs, heads on the swivel. What could they be looking for?

"Before you left the courier hub the other day, did you hear about anything besides the boy that was killed?" she asked Joey quickly and quietly as they slowly shuffled along with the herd of people filing toward the trucks.

"Just some stuff about the group that was causing trouble, but that's it," he replied, voice low as he looked around, following the path Melissa's own eyes had taken moments before. "Ya know, this does seem like a lot of fire power if all they're worried about is a small gang. Maybe it's worse than what they've been letting on?"

Just then a shriek sounded from across the crowd. Heads turned and a wave of sharp movement pulsed through the mass of people a second before panicked screaming split the air. The sentries all raised their weapons, aiming toward the center of the commotion while the ones on foot moved quickly into the panicked masses.

"Everybody, down!" a soldier's barking voice called out over the commotion.

Melissa and Joey ducked low as shots rang out over their heads and a screech that sounded like it came straight from the depths of hell itself cut through the rain, tearing up Melissa's spine. The crowd broke, people scattered, running for their lives. She and Joey scrambled to their feet to follow suit. In the chaos, Melissa caught glimpses of people falling; from bullets or something else, she was unable to tell, but bodies were dropping by the dozens.

"Run, Mom! C'mon!" Joey pulled at her arm then shoved her along in front of him.

A growling hiss sounded to their left and she turned her head just in time to see a screaming man pulled feet first into the shrubby trees that marked the edge of the park. The bushes shook violently before a shower of blood sprinkled the fresh green leaves in crimson. Her heart hammered in her throat, drowned by the madness surging in every direction.

People everywhere screamed and fell. The soldiers fired round after round straight into the roiling crowd at something large and dark, shrouded in shadow. She willed her feet to move faster while Joey grasped her hand and pulled her along. They splashed through puddles and cut around slower people, the stench of rotting flesh and sulfur assaulting her senses. Melissa chanced a glance behind her; at the mayhem they were leaving behind and was met with a sight that made her blood run cold.

A black-skinned, bear-like creature charged across the green lawn of the park, straight for a soldier. The man in uniform stood firm and took aim, bullets flying from the rifle in quick succession. The sound of the rifle cracked the air, but the creature barely missed a step. It stumbled once and kept charging. The soldier fired round after round at the beast but in seconds, it was on him, tackling him to the ground, his scream cut short by the fangs of the creature closing around his throat.

As the soldier's arms fell out to his sides, his rifle fired in a sweeping arc, bullets flying straight toward them.

Melissa moved on instinct, lunging for Joey to drag him down, but her world moved in slow motion. She couldn't move fast enough. Her arm wrapped across his back, but before she could yank him off his feet, something snapped through the air beside her. A sharp pop tore through her sleeve, a spray of white goose down bursting into the air.

At first, she felt nothing, just the rush of adrenaline through her veins, then he jerked. His breath hitched and they tumbled down into the soggy grass.

"Joey?" His name came out strangled and small.

His eyes were wide, chest rising in short, uneven gasps. Blood darkened his sweatshirt.

"No—no, *Joey!*" Melissa gathered him into her arms, palm pressing into the wound as if she could hold him together. Goose down drifted through the air then settled in his hair like snowflakes. He managed one shuddering breath, then another. Then...stillness.

A scream ripped through her throat, raw and broken. Not Joey. Please, God, not Joey too!

Her heart shattered into a thousand pieces as she cupped is sweet face. Vacant brown eyes stared back into hers of green as her world unraveled. She gathered his limp body into her arms and screamed. She screamed until she thought she would vomit.

Her son. Her baby. Gone.

A screeching hiss nearly stopped her heart, eyes going wide. She looked up to find the creature stalking toward her. Without a thought, she clamored over Joey's body protectively, locking eyes with the beast. The orbs glowed red as they bore into hers and it snarled, its blood-soaked muzzle pulling back to reveal long, sharp, yellowed teeth.

In a grief-filled rage, Melissa snarled back, tears streaming down her face, spittle flying from her lips.

It would not take him. It would have to go through her first.

The creature moved from a slinking walk to a ground-covering trot, focused only on Melissa. She rose to a crouch, still cradling Joey's head in her arms, every cell in her body screaming to tear the abomination before her to shreds with her bare hands even though she knew she stared her own death in the eye. It was closing the distance. She would not look away, *could* not look away.

A shot rang out. The creature stumbled; a gaping bullet hole torn through its flank. It whipped its head to the right, searching for what had injured it, its eyes locked on another soldier. A shrill scream tore from its throat, its teeth bared with rage, eyes glowing with malice as it coiled its body to spring, but the sound was cut short by a second shot. This one cracked straight through the creature's skull, and it collapsed, silently bursting into flame. Melissa watched in stunned horror as the flames died quickly, leaving the ashen husk of the creature smoking and disintegrating in the rain.

The soldier quickly made his way to her side and tried to lift her to her feet, "Ma'am, we need to leave. *Now.*"

"But my son," she croaked, fighting his hold on her, refusing to let go of her son's limp form.

The soldier glanced at Joey's body and then back to her. "He's gone—"

"I won't leave him!" she cried. Grief rising in her throat to choke her.

With only a moment's hesitation, the soldier lowered his rifle and gathered Joey's body over his shoulder with a grunt. Melissa reached out, hands closing on nothing but empty air. A hollow wail crawled its way up her throat as she staggered forward, desperate to hold onto him just a little bit longer.

"Let's go." The soldier extended his free hand toward her, his pained, hazel eyes locking onto hers.

Melissa swallowed hard, grasping his hand while she stumbled numbly to her feet. He gently but firmly placed her hand over a strap on the side of his vest and nodded. Melissa nodded back, tears still streaming down her face, and they were off, quickly making their way out of the park. Gunfire and screams still sounded behind her, but she refused to look back. And the world just kept screaming.

10

Nightmares

Dan

DRENCHED IN A TERRIFIED SWEAT, heart pounding, sheets trapping his legs, Dan lurched awake from the nightmare with a strangled breath. The scent of the darkling spawn still stung his nostrils, acrid and wrong, while Amber's terrified screams echoed in his ears. He panted, struggling to shake off the smells and sounds that clung to his mind. He wasn't in the forest. He was home. He was safe. Home with his wife, Emily, and their daughter, Kate.

Emily bolted upright beside him, pulled from sleep by his thrashing. She reached out gingerly, not knowing if he was fully awake yet, gun shy after his first nightmare and rightly so. He'd still been half asleep and when she'd touched his arm, he'd flailed and almost hit her before flinging himself off the bed, upsetting the nightstand and breaking his bedside lamp.

His gaze found hers, soft, steady, concerned. Moonlight caught in the golden strands of her hair, messy from sleep, and lit her high cheekbones in silver. Even half asleep she was like an angelic lifeline, and he reached for her like a drowning man reaches for a life preserver in a torrential sea. Her arms wrapped tight around his shoulders, and he leaned into her swallowing a sob.

He was safe. His family was safe. Soft and reassuring fingers ran through his hair while she gently rocked him until the shaking ceased.

"Wanna talk about it?" she whispered into his hair then pressed a kiss to his forehead.

"No, but I probably should." He sighed, not wanting to burden her with his trauma.

"Whenever you're ready, I'm here to listen."

So strong. So sure. She had carried him for years after he had returned from overseas, a broken shell of the man he was before he'd been deployed. He'd wanted to give up. Wanted to end it all. And her stubborn, relentless love refused to let him go. She'd even pried the gun out of his trembling hands once. Soft words and firm hands, begging him to stay. Christ, he owed her his life so many times over.

Through all the bad times and the good, she was the glue that held their little family together. And here she was again, the only thing keeping him from shattering. God, he loved her. *Goddess*, he corrected himself, pulling back from her a bit. He ran calloused hands over his face then let them fall to his lap and turned to face her.

"I just—" he hesitated, not sure where to begin. "I just can't get her face out of my head. She's terrified and I just walked away." He sagged as Amber's worried face flashed into his mind. Her wringing hands, her furrowed brow.

She was dead because of him.

Emily reached over and took up his hand, quietly holding space for him.

"I keep having this dream that I'm walking away from her. Leaving her alone in the forest and she calls out to me asking me to stay, but I leave anyway. Then I hear it—that creature."

His breath caught in is throat and he looked away, but the words continued to spill out. "She's inside her car trying to hide but the creature is there beside it just looking at me. I'm so far away but I can see it's only got one eye. One, single, red eye. And then it launches itself through the window. I can see her face through the glass and she's screaming, pounding on it. Then it's just blood. Blood everywhere. Her hands—" Dan winced at the memory of the recurring dream, at the vision of Amber's limp hands sliding down the glass leaving streaks through the gore.

Emily squeezed his hand, scooting closer, leaning in until her forehead met his, a quiet, steady anchor.

"Then that thing crashes through the back window and runs straight for me. I can't move. Can't breathe. I'm screaming at myself to do something, *anything*, but I just...stand there, frozen. And then—" a tight sob forced its way up his throat.

Emily let out a slow breath and pulled him into her arms again.

"What if—what if Kate was just a few years older and in her position?" His voice cracked. "What if some overconfident idiot left her up there to try and fend for herself? And she—" his throat clenched, the mere thought of it made him nauseous. "I fucked up, Emily. I fucked up bad, and now that girl is dead. How am I supposed to keep going knowing that? Knowing it's my fault?" His voice was barely above a whisper, but the weight of his decisions crushed down on him like a gut shot he could see coming but was powerless to stop.

Emily cupped his face, thumbs brushing along is cheekbones, smudging away the tears dampening his face. "Honey, there is no way that you could have known what was going to happen. If you would have convinced her to walk with you, she probably would have been the one attacked, not you. And if you would have waited with her, you may not be here."

Dan clenched his jaw. He knew she was right, but it didn't matter. "First it was my team in the desert, now it's her. And I'm the one that gets to walk away." Again, *he* had been the one to survive another wretchedly traumatizing event, except with this situation, the one who died was a complete innocent. Amber hadn't joined the military knowing that her job might one day claim her life. No, she was just a kid trying to get in touch with nature on the wrong damn day. And he'd completely failed her.

Emily didn't argue. She just held him. For a long time they simply sat in silence, drawing strength from each other. His arms tightened around her, anchoring himself to the present.

Finally, she pulled back just far enough to meet his gaze. "You can't beat yourself up about this forever, my love. I'm not saying that you have to stop now, but eventually, you're going to have to start moving forward."

He exhaled, nodding, but the guilt sat so heavy in his chest he was having a tough time breathing.

Emily leaned in and kissed him gently. "You are a good man, Dan. You always do what you think is right."

Dan scoffed at that notion. "What I thought was right got an innocent girl killed."

She laid a delicate hand on the center of his chest. "What you thought was right would have been the best decision if the world still made sense, but it doesn't. No one could have predicted that thing was out there. Not you. Not those two folks that brought you down the mountain. Even they didn't know those things were out there. You said that they couldn't remember the last time they had seen one in the area."

Dan raked a hand through his hair, frustration warring with his guilt. "There are just so many 'what-if's'."

"Life is full of them, you know that. And if you let them consume you, you'll never move past this. You won't be living in the present."

All Dan could do was nod as he ruminated on what his therapist—and now his wife—had told him many times: Living in the past nurtures depression, while living in the future produces anxiety. The only place that one can live and experience true peace is the present. He tried to bring that bit of advice to the forefront of his mind.

He was home.

His wife and daughter were safe.

Erik and Alma had shown them how to barricade the area and the town itself from the darkling spawn, it wasn't perfect, but it would slow them down. They had told them what kinds of plants to grow in their garden and that working together every day with their small community would be the only way they would be able to survive.

The two had moved on to the north saying that they were going to join in the battle to fight the plague of darkness and if they made it through what was to come, they would return to their home in the forest, to the light dome that kept them and their family safe for generations. But first, they had to make it through each moment—each singular heartbeat. They had saved his life. More than that, they had literally given him a new one, a stronger body and more years with his wife and daughter. He couldn't dishonor that gift by wallowing in despair.

"But she was a good kid, I could tell. She deserved better than that." His voice sounded small in the dim light of their bedroom.

"Then make sure someone else gets what you couldn't give to her."

Emily's words hit him like a hammer to the chest and a thought took root. Something inside him locked into place, fierce and unshakable.

No more walking away. No more standing by. "If I ever have a chance to break Rule #3 and be the hero, I'm going to do it. No matter what. I'll do it for Amber."

"I think she would be grinning from ear to ear if she could hear you say that." Emily smiled up at him, brushing his knuckles with her thumbs.

With a sigh, he dragged his wife into a bone-crushing hug, then thread his fingers through her long, golden hair.

He would carry the weight of his failure for the rest of his life but that didn't mean he couldn't make the pain count. He would find a way to set things right.

11

Eyes in the Shadows

CLOUDS, MIST AND RAIN. The days kept passing in bleak and dreary shades of muted gray, but I kept up my routine. The busy schedule I had set up for myself was the only thing that was keeping me sane. I started working out more, training harder and lifting heavier. In nearly a month I had gained weight and muscle and confidence in myself and my ability to survive, but I longed for human interaction. I almost missed the crappy drivers in the city and the inconsiderate neighbors out mowing their lawns at seven o'clock in the morning on a Saturday.

The forest creatures that frequented the area around the camp store were my only companions and although the family of crows that spent most of their time in the trees at the edge of the parking lot would caw at me when I talked to them, I hadn't spoken to anyone but myself since Dan left. I did find comfort in my own company, but I worried that if I didn't run into another human being soon, I would fall into the steady, mental decline that begins the moment someone truly starts talking to themselves.

Keeping myself busy seemed like the best way to maintain my sanity, so I made my way out to the woodshed.

A steeply slanted shed roof covered the dwindling pile of already split firewood, while a large lean-to, enclosed on three sides and connected to the back side of the car port, housed all the large, un-split rounds.

I ventured into the shed, loading the wheelbarrow full of rounds to move to the splitting area beside the lean-to. After my third load, I had revealed the back wall of the woodshed, and in doing so, discovered that the back wall of the shed and the back wall of the carport were not the same wall, even though it was all technically the same building. Upon closer inspection, I discovered a large, sliding door behind the cars parked in the carport.

I couldn't believe that I had missed something so obvious for so long. Shaking my head, I grasped the small handle and slid the door open. Inside were dozens of older mountain bikes and I realized that they had to be the rental bikes Dan had mentioned when we spoke. I felt like I had hit the jackpot even as my heart sank a bit at the memory. Dan had been right though, riding a bike would be so much easier than walking.

After rifling through the bike storage, I settled on a graphite gray and forest green mountain bike. It looked to be in decent shape and it had what appeared to be a fairly comfortable seat. I rolled it out of the storage and onto the back patio. With a huff, I flipped it upside down and balanced it carefully on its handlebars and seat.

After retrieving a handful of tools from the shed, and a can of chain lubricant, I set about checking all the nuts and bolts, making sure everything was solid, just like Joey and I used to do when we were younger. Once I was satisfied, I turned the bike back over on its tires and lowered the seat then pressed the heel of my hand into the tires. They were low.

I returned to the bike shed and found several air pumps stored just inside the entrance along with shelves of replacement parts. Pump in hand, I returned to the porch.

Suddenly, my crow friends cawed in the trees just as a buzzy, prickly feeling skittered across my scalp and down my spine.

I wheeled, instantly alert, eyes scanning the tree line. The crows' insistent cawing brought my eyes higher up into the trees. They were all gathered on an ancient, broadleaf maple, beaks pointed to the south, flapping their wings and bobbing with each shrill call. My eyes followed their intent gaze to a narrow gap in the foliage at the back side of the property. It was a long way off, and I was certain that their higher vantage point offered a much better view of whatever had their feathers ruffled.

The bushes, now full of fresh leaves, rustled while the buzzing sensation crept across my scalp again. I could think of only one thing that would have my feathered friends in such a frenzy. I shivered at the memory of the large, black shadow that had stalked me on my return from the viewpoint, and for the first time since I had been stranded, I thought of my camera.

Maybe I could get a picture of it?

Turning on my heel, I set the pump down and rushed inside the house, not bothering to remove my shoes. My camera sat on the dresser in my bedroom, and I scooped it up, quickly returning to the patio. Wrapping the strap twice around my wrist, I silently moved toward the edge of the building. The buzz ran through me again and I knew, with every fiber of my being, that the creature was looking right at me while hidden somewhere in the shadows of the ferns and underbrush.

With lightly shaking hands, I brought the viewfinder to my eye and twisted the telephoto lens, then quickly refocused. I panned the forest's edge, from left to right and then back again, but all I could see were new leaves rustling in the light breeze. I puffed out a breath and lowered the camera.

I couldn't see anything in the trees myself, but perhaps the film might pick something up? Bringing the viewfinder back to my eye, my stomach fluttered. I twisted the focusing ring and pressed the shutter. My thumb found the wind lever and I advanced the film then pressed the shutter button again. Three more times, I pointed and shot blindly into the forest.

There were still eleven frames left on the roll I had started at that park in town. It seemed like a lifetime ago already and I was suddenly gripped by an intense need for normalcy and a reminder of my *real* home.

A restlessness settled on my shoulders and my gut twisted again. There was definitely something out there watching me, I could feel it's gaze crawling over my skin, but with that sense of unease came the calming presence of protection and the sense of home. I knew in my bones that whatever the creature was, it could not get to me. Not here beside the camp store. The gentle awareness of the stone box in the basement settled on my shoulders like a warm, comforting set of hands. I was safe.

The raucous calls of the crows began to subside, and I raised my voice to the forest. "That's right, keep it pushin'." My slight scowl turned into a small smile as I looked up at my friends, settled in the maple tree. "Thanks guys. Good looking out. I'll go get you some nuts."

Heading into the house, I placed my camera on the countertop and dug through the kitchen pantry to a large bag of roasted peanuts. Back outside, I placed a handful of the nuts on a rotting stump a few dozen paces away from the house. "These are for you guys whenever you're ready."

Several of the large birds looked at me quizzically, heads tilting this way and that, their black eyes studying. I returned to the bike under the patio roof and stooped to air up the tires. If I could befriend the crows, they could be a great early warning system. I was gonna need more nuts.

After a bit more fussing, I climbed on the bike to test it out. It rode well enough, gears shifting smoothly as I made a few loops through the gravel parking lot. Satisfied with the bike as a whole, I parked it on the patio and went back inside. All I needed was a sunny day to make my way into Riverside town.

Two days later, I would get my chance.

The morning dawned bright, not a cloud in sight, and I hastily pulled on my clothes. I packed some snacks and water, tucking them carefully in my backpack beside my camera, then headed out the door. Swinging my leg over the bike, butterflies flitted in my stomach; not with horrible, gut-twisting fear, but with excitement. I was finally going to test my sunlight theory.

Before leaving, I staged my bike and pack in front of the camp store doors and snapped a couple pictures of it and the outbuildings. I rode through the parking lot and pulled out onto the narrow road. The birds chirped and the crows cawed. Although the air was still chilly, the sun was warm on my face, a sure sign that better weather was finally on its way. The map I had stuffed into my jacket showed about a five-mile ride to Riverside and I hoped with my whole soul that there were still kind people there.

I looked back at the camp store fading into the distance and a twinge of concern settled in my chest a heartbeat before I passed through the warm, comforting barrier. It felt like stepping away from the radiant warmth of a glowing bed of coals, except there was no real heat to it; only the feeling of the safety one feels when gathered with a group of friends around a glowing campfire.

I waited for the concern to blossom into something bigger, something harsher, and when it didn't, I breathed a sigh of relief.

"The Glow. That's what I'm going to call it," I said to myself, referring to the barrier of safety I was sure encircled the camp store.

The ride to Riverside was mostly downhill and I cursed inwardly, already dreading how difficult the ride back to the camp store would be. As I pedaled down the road, my thoughts wandered to my mom and brother. I hoped they were safe and well...and that those shadowy creatures weren't in Orchardville too. I wondered about my distant circle of friends, which in turn had my mind wandering to my poor Jeep, abandoned and lost in the mountains, just as I was.

I wondered about DJ, playing out a happy scenario in my mind of what would have happened had my trip into the mountains gone as planned. We shared drinks, and laughs. He met my mom and instantly got along with my annoying little brother. Even my friends liked him when we all met for the first group camping trip of the season on Memorial Day weekend, and we all laughed and drank and ate around the fire.

Fire. The sharp scent of damp, smoldering ash stung my nose as I approached the town of Riverside and rolled to a stop in front of the moss-covered town sign.

The Town of Riverside Welcomes You
EST. 1932
Population: 1100

What I could see of the town appeared to be about as far from welcoming as a town could get. The once quaint, old-timey buildings were mostly burned and the ones that had escaped the fires were fronted by broken windows. Several buildings still smoldered, but thankfully, I could see no active flames. The streets were damp from all the rain but drying quickly in the sun, steam rising from the pavement while a deep silence permeated the air.

Riverside was a ghost town.

Debris littered the streets. Discarded shoes, pieces of clothing, a purse with the contents still inside, burned out cars, chairs, shards of glass, a half-burned mattress, trash, pieces of wood and twisted metal.

What happened here?

I snapped a few photos of the street, finishing off my roll of film. Many of the buildings had burned to the ground but quite a few had survived.

"Hello?" I called out into the deafening silence. The rustling of a paper in the breeze was the only response.

I began slowly making my way down Main Street, studying the rubble and busted store fronts, calling out to anyone who might still be around. Maybe people were afraid and hiding, but as I rolled past several large blood smears, any hope I had of finding survivors vanished. Near many of the blood smears were streaks and puddles of the same black stuff I had found on the road after leaving my Jeep.

I coasted to a stop beside a particularly large smear of the thick, dark fluid and knelt down to inspect it. It was slightly iridescent in the sun and appeared to have the consistency of clumpy, black motor oil. It was steaming lightly in the sun like the puddles of water on the road. I swallowed a nervous lump in my throat and grimaced as I reached a finger out to touch the black substance then thought better of it. What if it was caustic? Glancing around, I found a charred twig and poked it into the substance. It jiggled and stretched like coagulated blood.

Slowly, I brought the stick to my nose and retched at the pungent odor of week-old roadkill in August. "Oh, what in the actual—" Tossing the stick aside, I backed away from the puddle and swung a leg over my bike again.

What is *that stuff? Could it actually be blood? From that creature? It did usually seem to bring the smell of death with it...*

I closed my eyes, trying to conjure up a mental picture of the road when I had found the bag of jerky and juice bottle I'd given to Dan. Beside what I could only assume was Dan's own watery blood smear, there had been a puddle and a long, drag mark of the black substance that led all the way off the road and into the ditch. If the black stuff had been that creature's blood, then Dan had to have injured it before it killed him.

Opening my eyes again, I studied the empty street. Amidst the scattered debris, I could make out brass and shotgun shell casings flashing in the sun, the buildings themselves were littered with bullet holes.

My blood ran cold. The gunshots I'd heard my first morning in the camp store—had the people in this town been shooting at that creature? But there were *way* too many bullet holes for all those shots to have been for a single, solitary creature. There must be more than one. It was the only explanation.

"Shit," I whispered to myself, suddenly feeling very small. Could all of the people in this town have met the same fate as Dan? My hand went to my mouth.

No. Someone had to have survived. Maybe they were holed up somewhere, hiding, waiting, just like I was?

But the silence of the burned-out town told me differently. For better or for worse, I was alone.

With no one around, I went searching for any place that might have food supplies, clothes and what I needed to develop my negatives. The burned shops in town leaned at odd angles or had fallen in on themselves, but the ones that remained standing were still fairly well stocked.

Poking my head inside the hardware store, I made a mental note to come back, perhaps another day, for all sorts of outdoor supplies. I continued on past a building that looked like it could have been the local burger joint before it burned down. Another couple of buildings on the block had collapsed into unrecognizable piles of rubble, but as I crossed through an intersection, I saw that the general market had survived. Thank goodness.

I walked my bike up to the front doors and set the kick stand down before cautiously approaching the shattered doors. Glass crunched under my shoes as I peered inside. The shelves had been raided, that was for certain, but there was still a fair amount of food items, toiletries and the like on the shelves.

Beggars can't be choosers, I thought to myself.

As I made my way into the store, I paused to allow my eyes a moment to adjust to the dim lighting. Several skylights in the old building's ceiling let in enough light to see by, so I continued deeper inside, scanning the aisles and listening closely for anything out of the ordinary. I rounded the corner of the last aisle and there, in the back of the store, sat the pharmacy.

The windows were open.

After deciding that I needed medicine supplies, I had imagined trying for days to break in through a heavy, locked door or struggling with a rolling security grille. I couldn't believe my luck!

Quickly hopping the counter, I rummaged through shelf after shelf of prescription medications scanning for antibiotics and anything that sounded familiar. I wasn't an expert, but I recognized a few names. Amoxicillin, azithromycin, other drugs I'd taken for past illnesses, and even a couple that I remembered our old dog taking. I filled my pack with anything that seemed useful then hopped back over the counter and headed for the cold and flu aisle.

Before I made it there though, a small photo department caught my eye. The automatic film processor sat highlighted by a tiny shaft of sunlight. Hurrying over to it, I took a closer look, hoping it was indeed an actual film processor and not a large, digital photo printer. If it was a real processor, then actual photo chemicals would be stored somewhere nearby.

After a few moments, I'd found them. A veritable treasure trove of 'hard-to-find outside the internet' photography supplies. I couldn't contain my excited giggle, and I rushed out the door to check the other shops for things I could use to scab together a developing tank and negative spool. I wandered for about an hour before stumbling upon a very small but well-appointed hobby shop. It held almost everything that I needed, and I rushed back to the General Market to get started, my pack near to bursting.

Hidden in a dark corner of the pharmacy, I rigged up a makeshift dark room and began the process of developing the negatives. Mixing chemicals with bottled water, I felt like a mad scientist, truly enjoying myself for the first time in a solid month. My mom had always loved that I had taken an interest in photography like she had when she was younger. The camera I had brought with me was actually the same camera she used in her own photography class when she was in high school. My heart beat strong in my chest knowing that I had a piece of her with me.

Once the negatives were finished, I hung them to dry and wandered around town to see what other things I might be able to bring back up to the camp store with me. In a quaint antiques and consignments store, I found a few pairs of sturdy shoes, pants and an Instagram-worthy, brown felt hat. There were beautiful furniture pieces that I knew my mom would have gone crazy over, right beside or even housing 1990's era baby toys and clothes. The shop was chocked full of bric-a-brac and every sort of thing a person didn't really need, but would want, all the same.

On my way out, I nearly tripped over what I initially took for a large doggy stroller, but on closer inspection, I found it was a tow behind bike cart.

Now, *that* would be useful.

Walking it and my bike over to the hardware store, I borrowed some tools and attached the wagon to the back of the bike.

Back at the general market, I loaded the wagon with food and supplies before heading to the back of the store to check on my negatives. Finding them dry, I walked out into the midday sun and held them up to the sky.

They had developed well, crisp black and gray shapes greeted me, and I instantly recognized the shots I snapped of DJ. A sad smile quirked the corners of my mouth and I sighed. Continuing on, my eyes slid over a shot of the river and small bridge in the park, then a picture of my Jeep where it had stalled on the side of the road. Beside that were several shots of the tree line near the camp store. Squinting at the tiny negative, I could just make out a pair of black specks. Thinking it had to be an issue with the developer, I checked all of the frames on the roll. The black specks only appeared in the shots of the tree line.

"Oh, my God," I whispered to myself as I ran back inside the store and set to work.

The printing process involved a little bit of trial and error and a lot of cursing, but eventually I put together a serviceable enlarger out of cardboard and duct tape.

As I set the photo into the shallow tub of developer, a sliver of ice began to settle in my gut. The print slowly darkened to reveal a slightly out of focus shot of the forest, but when I looked closer, my stomach clenched. Even though the print was blurry I could easily make out a pair of white, glowing orbs surrounded by shadow, peering out of the bushes and staring right into the camera. The top of the shrubby bush, beside what I could only assume were glowing *eyes,* was well over five feet tall and those sinister looking peepers were fairly close to the top of it.

"Holy shit," I whispered as I lifted the print from the developer and dropped it into the tub of stop solution. There was more than one set of eyes.

I turned, snapping up my stack of negatives and ran out into the full sun, holding the negatives up into the light. The dark pinpoints in an otherwise muddy gray negative seemed to stare straight into my soul. A shiver crawled up my spine as my eyes moved to the next frame, then the next. First it was one pair of eyes, then two. My heart pounded and my stomach churned. Three...or four maybe?

What are they and where had they freaking come from?

"Goddamn," I mumbled before scanning the wrecked street before me. Even though I had been in town all morning and hadn't seen nor heard any other signs of life, I had to try again, even if it was foolish. "Hello? Anybody! Hello!" I yelled. Silence answered once again.

Was everybody *really* gone? Or were they all dead? This was a small town, true, but there were over a thousand people that called this town and the surrounding area home. Someone should have survived. My gut told me otherwise.

I stood on the sidewalk in indecision knowing I should take a look around the small neighborhood too. But the ride back up the mountain to the camp store would be a long and hard one...and I absolutely had to make it there before dark. So, I quickly loaded all the photography supplies into the wagon and left.

12

A Reason to Live

Melissa

THE UNENDING SWATH OF HIGH, grey clouds dampened the sunlight above as Melissa stared down at the freshly turned earth of her son's grave. There had been no real service, hardly a word had been spoken between her and the stoic but kind young soldier who had carried her son's body home from the park that day. They had simply dug the grave in silence, wrapped his body in a sheet, and laid him to rest.

"He's a good kid. He didn't deserve this," was all she had managed to say before she had broken down. The soldier had gently helped her into the house and laid her down on the worn sofa.

She didn't care that she was a mess or that they had tracked mud all through her clean house. Nothing had mattered in that moment.

He covered her with a throw blanket, crouched down beside her and asked, "Is there anything else that I can do for you ma'am?"

Melissa simply shook her head and croaked out, "Thank you."

"I'll see myself out then." He nodded and rose smoothly then made his way to the front door pausing at the stairwell to study their family photos. An unsteady finger lifted slowly toward the picture of Amber standing on the roof rack of her Jeep laughing, the SUV buried up past the hubs in a mud pit.

He turned back toward Melissa. "Is this...your daughter?" he asked, his voice just above a shaky whisper.

Melissa nodded, "Amber."

The soldier rushed back to her side, eyes wide. "Did she ever make it home? From that camping trip?"

Melissa's heart stopped. "You know Amber?" she squeaked, sitting up quickly and reaching for the young man's gloved hand.

"I'd only just met her. She helped me jumpstart my car the day the grid went down." The soldier said in a rush, hope touching the edge of his words. "Did she make it home though?"

Melissa lowered her eyes then shook her head, letting out a slow, sad sigh.

His shoulders sagged, a bit of the light going out of his eyes. "She took my picture with an old camera, and I invited her out for a drink." A touch of sadness edged his words, but then he brightened. "But I texted her about ten minutes before the grid went down. She sent me a selfie...she was parked in front of a log cabin store."

Melissa's heart soared at his words. Her eyes met his and she gripped his hand tighter. "Do you think she could still be up there? At the store?"

"I—I don't know. She told me that it was closed, but she couldn't have gotten far before the power went out. Maybe she was able to get someone to come to the door and let her in?"

Melissa nodded quickly, wanting to hold to that hope, but it slipped through her fingers like fine dry sand. It had been weeks. *Weeks.*

The soldier reached for Melissa's other hand, "Don't give up hope, Ma'am. If we lose hope, the creatures win."

All she could do was nod as fresh tears began to fall.

"We don't know much about them, but we do know that they have an aversion to sunlight. We didn't think they could come out during the day at all, but..." He trailed off.

Slowly he got to his feet. "Don't go out on cloudy days and keep your curtains closed. I'll do my best to check back soon."

She stood with him. "Thank you. I don't know what I would have done...I think the universe brought us together for a reason."

"I'm glad I was there to help, and I'm sorry we couldn't have met under better circumstances." He nodded and started toward the door again. This time Melissa followed him. "And lock the door behind me...don't answer it for anyone other than military personnel."

"Why?"

"You're alone here and we've been having some problems with hostile civilians trying to take advantage of the situation."

She nodded numbly, "Thank you," her eyes flicked toward the name on his uniform, "Cooper?"

"You can call me DJ," he said glancing down at his last name then back to Melissa.

"I'm Melissa—er, Mel. My friends and family always called me Mel."

DJ nodded and they exchanged sad smiles before he turned and walked out onto the porch.

She gently closed the door behind him and only heard the sound of his boots retreating after she had turned the deadbolt and slid the chain into place.

Melissa clenched her eyes shut against the memory as well as the tears that never seemed to run dry. Her son in the ground and her daughter missing, presumed dead. What more did she have to live for?

A silent sob shook her shoulders. Sinking to the ground, one hand wrapped across her middle, while the other covered her mouth. She wanted to scream. She wanted to wail out her pain and loss, but the skies were gray, the clouds thick and threatening rain, which meant those creatures would be out. Hunting. So, she cried in silence.

Why? Why was all of this happening? Moisture soaked through the layers of her dirty, bloodstained clothes as she laid out in the damp grass of the back yard. Joey had been gone a week, and she still hadn't changed. Hadn't bathed, hadn't eaten anything other than scraps. From sun-up to sundown, she sat beside Joey's grave, rehashing what had happened at the ration lines. What could she have done differently? What small thing could she have changed, and her son would still be with her?

Round and round her thoughts swirled, and she sank deeper and deeper into despair. But her thoughts always returned to the soldier that had saved her life. DJ had never come back like he'd said he would, and she feared the worst for him as well. Was the entire world dying all around her?

Suddenly, a piercing, panicked scream split the gray silence pulling Melissa from her spiraling thoughts. She froze in the damp grass, lungs locked, ears straining. Another terrified human scream sounded, accompanied by a hissing snarl. Her heart leapt into her throat as she rolled to her feet and crept toward the sliding glass door then silently slipped into the house.

Sliding off her worn shoes and leaving them by the door, she tiptoed toward the sunken living room. Her stomach twisted and she tried to steady her breathing as she reached a trembling hand out to peer around the curtain.

Bile rose in her throat at the sight before her.

The poor man who lived next door lay in the street surrounded by a growing puddle of blood and innards as two of those nightmarish creatures tore at him—eating him alive—clothes and all. He made a feeble attempt to drag himself away, arms flailing weakly, before he went limp, but he wasn't dead yet. The man's faint groans, muffled through the glass, reached Melissa's ears, the sound tapping into a distant and primal instinct. She needed to hide. Needed to escape. But her modern mind couldn't force her feet to move. His head lolled back and forth as the creatures ripped him apart like a pair of starving wolves playing tug-of-war over a carcass.

Finally, mercifully, he went silent, eyes blinking slowly once before the vacant look of death relaxed his contorted features. Something within her snapped as a strangled cry escaped her lips. She clapped hands over her mouth as she realized what she had done, but it was too late. The sound had given her away.

One of the creatures, large, cat-like and well-muscled, whipped its head in her direction, glowing red eyes peering through the window and straight into her soul. She couldn't move. Couldn't breathe. Cold terror held her fast in its grip as she watched her own death playing out before her.

The creature prowled toward her, shoulders rolling beneath leathery, black skin, its long tail twitching. This was it. She was going to die, suffering the same fate of her neighbor. It would leap straight through her beautiful picture windows and rend her to pieces right there on her cream-colored carpet.

Not sixty seconds ago she had laid in the damp grass wanting nothing more than to join her son in death knowing she had nothing left to live for. But as that creature took another tense step in her direction, something within her soul solidified. She was not ready. This was not her time! Amber was still out there...somewhere. She knew it in her bones. Felt it in her soul. Amber had to be alive...and her daughter needed her. But now, with the gaze of that creature tearing through her, she knew that these were her last moments.

She silently begged the universe not to spare her own life, but to watch over her daughter and grant her the strength to survive the nightmare that their lives had become. And she could have laughed at the bitter irony: it had taken staring death in the face for a second time to realize she wasn't truly ready to leave this world.

Just then, the second creature, that had been hauling in mouthfuls of flesh, grasped what was left of her neighbor in its too large maw, and took off running down the street. The one still stalking her direction paused for the briefest moment then broke their eye contact, turning to watch its companion's retreat. It turned back toward her with a fiery glare and hissed before bounding away as well.

It took a few moments for Melissa to realize that she was, in fact, still among the living. She breathed a sigh of relief and thanked the stars above that she had been spared. But why? Why had that thing run off when it clearly had seen her standing there?

Perhaps there really was a God?

Shaking herself, she let the curtain fall and bolted upstairs to the large linen closet. Her kids had always given her hell about all the extra blankets she collected over the years, saying that every bed, chair, and couch didn't need half a dozen throw blankets on it. But as she grabbed the first pile of dark fleece, she couldn't have felt more vindicated in her collection. Once back downstairs, she fished a box of pushpins out of the junk drawer in the kitchen and set to work.

Boarding up the windows on the lower level would be better, safer, but the blankets would have to do until the sun came out and she could try to gather supplies.

Two days later, Melissa woke to a bright ray of sunlight streaming through the small garden window above the kitchen sink. From where she lay, wrapped in a comforter on the couch, she could just make out the dust motes floating in the slanting, yellow light. Memories of Amber and Joey trying to catch the tiny particles of dust as children, danced like ghosts in her mind's eye and she swallowed a lump in her throat.

A single tear slipped from the corner of her eye, tracing a slow path across the bridge of her nose before soaking into the pillow beneath her cheek. Oh, how she ached to see her children again.

With a stubborn sigh, she sat up and made her way into the kitchen and pulled a granola bar from the pantry then turned to head outside.

She had work to do.

13

The Glow

THE NEXT SEVERAL DAYS WERE dry but thickly overcast, the constant threat of rain and the prickling awareness of those creatures out beyond the safety of The Glow was my constant reminder to stay put. The devastation in Riverside sat heavy on my mind every moment of every day, threatening to push me headlong into despair. If a town as small as that could be virtually wiped-out only *days* after the power went out, what could be happening in an actual large city or metropolitan area?

My home was situated in an area where several small communities had grown and merged into one sprawling swath of suburban bullshit; strip malls and highways, big box stores and housing developments built right up into the foothills of the forest. If more of those creatures spread and made their way down into Orchardville, it truly would be doomsday, and my mom and brother and friends were smack dab in the middle of it.

Was it possible that the military might come in to assist since Orchardville was so close to Portland? If they had, then maybe it was possible that the cities were safer than the forest? That thought didn't last long. If there was one thing that could never be guaranteed, it was public safety. In an emergency, there would always be at least one group, crazy and organized enough, to make life hell for the peaceful members of the community that just wanted to survive.

I had to get home. Sooner rather than later. But the only thing I had to help me predict the weather was my limited knowledge of the clouds and a Farmer's Almanac. I was definitely up shit creek.

According to the Almanac, the month of April was supposed to be much wetter than average, while most of May was predicted to be sunny and dry. Seeing as how that was the only information I had to go off of, I decided to try and make it home in May, as soon as the first hint of fair weather presented itself. If I didn't make it home by then, the Almanac stated that the rain would return and would not improve until the end of June. *June!*

I could feel my tenuous grip on sanity beginning to unravel at the thought of being stuck at the camp store. Alone. For another two months.

In an attempt to ease my cabin fever, I commandeered the community cork board in the store to use as a conspiracy board, focusing my angst and anxiety on solving the mystery of the creatures stalking the forest. Neon note cards, sticky tabs, and full sheets of printer paper all mingled. At the center, *What are the shadow creatures?* was scrawled on a sheet of plain white printer paper in black marker.

Above the central question, several sticky tabs pinned in a crooked arc, held all known information: *Aversion to sunlight? Killing machines. Black blood? Stinks of death. Black in color to blend in with the shadows? What do they look like?*

Beside the central question, a note card was tacked, the question on its surface: *What makes the camp store special? What is The Glow?*

I stood back, one arm crossed over my chest, while the other supported my puzzled face. Scribbling frantically on a sticky tab, I peeled it off the stack and slapped it onto the cork board then speared it with a push pin.

Why do the creatures not cross into The Glow?

I scribbled on two more tabs and pinned them to the board.

Where does The Glow come from?

Do the owners of the store know this place is special?

My gut kept urging that the stone box in the basement had something to do with it, but I didn't have any solid evidence to support the feeling.

Stepping back again, I studied the board. Mom would have told me to simply trust my gut, but I had a burning desire to work the problem out with facts and tangible evidence.

My eyes roamed the store and settled on a framed newspaper article just beside the front door. The paper was yellowed with age, the frame and plaque below it covered in a fine layer of dust. My fingers reached out to run across the brass placard, wiping the letters clean. The store had been added to the national register of historic places in 1976; the building itself having stood there since 1895.

The store was remote now, but it had to have been downright isolated in the late1800's. Its original owners had to have known of the area's significance. The article stated that the store had been run by the same family for over sixty years, but the house had been there for much, much longer, and, according to the ancient newspaper clipping, had survived record breaking snowfalls, a major fire the summer of 1942, and massive spring flooding the year the building was granted its historical status.

I shook my head, an amused huff escaping me. And now it was surviving the apocalypse. Keeping me safe.

"There's probably been *something* here for way longer than that." I set my pen and pad down beside the register and sighed as my mind once again drifted to that stone box in the basement. "There better be some sun coming soon or I'm going to go insane."

Two days of sun. That was all I got before the rain left me trapped inside again, but I took full advantage of those bright, cloudless days. I made four trips into Riverside to gather more supplies and in doing so, discovered that there is a fine and sharp line one walks between doomsday prepping and hoarding. Everything I brought back up to the store was brought with purpose and a planned use. I was still sorely tempted to just grab everything I could carry but resisted the urge. Barely. I found a couple of cute outfits at the thrift store and couldn't resist keeping them even though the chances of my wearing them were basically zero. I needed a sense of normalcy.

One of the many reasons for all the trips into town was rodent activity. A few bags of potatoes and a bag of flour in the store had been chewed on, and I didn't want to set out poison for fear that my crow friends would find a body, dead from the poison, and end up dead themselves. So, I grabbed several mouse and rat traps.

The main reason I hustled to and from the town four times in two days was the farmer's almanac planting guide. It stated that April would be the best time to begin sowing seed for gardens in this region of the country, so I snagged every seed packet I could find at the hardware store and the general market. The garden section of the hardware store even had several live vegetable starts that needed rescuing and rehabbing, so I brought them back to the camp store as well.

Behind the building, beyond the patio, I could see where there once had been a large garden plot, mostly taken over by grass and stringy weeds. A row of ancient looking fruit trees sat to one side of the plot, while several blueberry bushes and a half wild row of raspberry vines were nearly hidden in the tall grass nearby. I focused most of my energy toward getting the ground ready for planting and when I tired of digging through sod and turning the earth, I pivoted towards building raised garden beds.

The more I labored and sweat, scabbing together a life and purpose out of scraps, the more determined I became. If I worked diligently over the next few weeks, I would be able to turn this place into a haven. I knew I could convince Mom and Joey to come back up here with me, especially with the added safety of The Glow. This place would be perfect for us.

And if the people that owned the store ever did come back, maybe they would be pleased enough at how well we had taken care of their home that they would allow us to stay? I would just have to keep stocking the place with food and supplies, then cross that bridge if I ever came to it.

My crow friends carried on, screaming at one another in the trees above me, while I knelt in the dark earth, throwing large tufts of grass into the wheelbarrow. As I cleared the weeds from the last section of the garden, I glanced up at the sky. Slate gray clouds blotted out the sun but didn't seem to be threatening to rain. After a bit more raking, as long as the weather held, I would plant a few rows of corn.

The large, black birds that would have normally kept their distance, safely in the trees, were getting braver by the day. Several members of their family would fly down to waddle around the yard, waiting for me to throw a peanut their way. I always carried the bag with me when I was out in the garden now and they were learning quickly.

"What do you guys think? Will the owners let me and my family stay here if they ever come back?" I asked the crows.

Several of the big birds waddling nearby chortled, while one twitched its head to the side and blinked at me. I reached into the peanut bag and tossed a small handful towards my feathered friends. Wasting no time, they swooped in, picked up the peanuts and flew away to enjoy them. I paused to consider the fact that they were so smart, they were actually training me and not the other way around.

Chuckling to myself, I sat back on my haunches and let my eyes wander over the garden plot. Things were really starting to come together. In addition to all the seeds that I had planted, I managed to get several old heads of lettuce and cabbage to root. I planted handfuls of sprouted baby red, gold, and white potatoes along with dozens of giant russet potatoes. Between my salt cured meat storage and the potatoes, I would have a great supply of protein and carbohydrates—I just hoped that the fruits and vegetables would grow well.

I allowed myself a moment to just sit and take in my surroundings. The weather was still a bit chilly, but the breeze that sifted through the trees no longer held the icy bite that it had a month ago. The day of my eventual departure was fast approaching and as I listened to the forest breathe around me, I ruminated on the logistics of my journey back to Orchardville.

I had already chosen a route, one that kept me away from large freeways, but it did take me directly down the Columbia River Gorge. My other option would have been to take a more direct route, but I would have been surrounded by dense forest until I made it to within fifteen miles of my house.

With my chosen route, once I was down out of the mountains, it was a mostly straight shot down The Gorge with only a few small towns to pass through until I reached the outskirts of Orchardville. Even though I was confident in my ability to physically handle the ride home, I was worried about overnighting outside of The Glow.

If Riverside was any indication, every town along the way had probably met the same fate. I just hoped with all my heart that my mom and brother were alright.

I stood with a huff and stretched, then brushed the damp earth from my pants. My stomach gnawed at itself, and I absently wondered what time it was...not that time really meant anything anymore. Only the daylight mattered. Still, I had neglected to eat lunch, and my guts were chastising me. I needed to dump the wheelbarrow and put away the gardening tools before I fed myself though.

As I made my way over to the debris pile I had started, I thought about starting a compost pile to help feed the garden. But that would be a project for another day. With all the tools and wheelbarrow stowed in the shed, I washed my hands at the pump outside and made my way back into the house, humming a tuneless song. Oh, how I missed music.

Once in the kitchen, I slapped a peanut butter and honey sandwich together and made my way into the camp store. My conspiracy theory board stared back at me, now completely covered in sticky notes. A small corner, dedicated to my trip home, was the only organized section.

I read aloud, around a mouthful of bread and peanut butter. "Stick to the route. Trust no one. Hustle home. Sleep in trees or abandoned vehicles. Stay silent. Expect the worst. Hope for the best."

I chewed and swallowed, then took another bite of the sandwich. "There's no way I'm going to make it home in one day. I'm at least seventy miles from home. Probably more than that. I should pack extra food for Mom and Joey too, and I'll need a couple gallons of water too. I'm not going to need a tent, but a sleeping bag would be better than just a blanket. I'll need to bring stuff to barter with too...just in case I do run into anybody. Coffee. Booze. A bottle of antibiotics, maybe some pain pills too. Those could be high value items for people. Maybe even enough to buy my passing if the people are hostile."

I shuddered at the thought. If only I had wings to fly...like the woman from that video last summer. I lost myself in the memory for a moment. My mom's strained voice at the realization that the woman, or angel, or whatever she was, was pregnant. My brother laughing at our reaction. The smell of our house.

My shoulders sagged a bit, and tears stung the back of my eyes.

If only I had wings to fly. But I didn't.

Thinking back to the news stories about everything that happened near Yellowstone last year, and everything I had experienced in the last month, I went over everything I knew about the creatures stalking the forest...for probably the hundredth time. Nothing aligned with anything science had ever made sense of.

Many people had thought that what had happened was a plague of biblical proportions; a sign of the second coming of Jesus Christ. Last summer I had scoffed at that, but standing in the camp store, alone, surrounded by mountains of supplies, while chewing on a peanut butter sandwich, I started to wonder.

Was that winged human of God and the shadow creatures of the Devil? I had never been to church a day in my life, but Christianity was everywhere. I knew the basics and from what I could tell, the biblical explanations seemed to fit the closest. But still, the situation nagged at me. It was the not knowing. Up until thirty-five days ago, I had lived in a world of instant information; any question I could conceive could be answered in a matter of moments with just a tiny device that we carried in our pockets. That seemed almost absurd now.

My mind attempted to wander further but I shook myself and shoved the rest of my sandwich into my mouth muttering, "I gotta get outta here, or I'm gonna go crazy."

I was prepared. Had all my ducks in a row, so to speak. The only thing I hadn't been able to do was to spend the night outside the safety of the camp store. It was the last thing I wanted to attempt knowing that those shadowy creatures were always just outside of the safe zone that The Glow provided, but I had to start somewhere.

Sometimes at night, I would be jarred from sleep, a half-remembered screech still ringing in my head, while a low, warning hum vibrated in my chest. My gut told me that it had to have been the creatures, possibly testing the strength of The Glow, and somehow it was warning me, telling me to stay alert. Those nights I was never able to fall back asleep. Those nights are what told me that I absolutely needed to make it out of the forest and to the Columbia River Gorge my first day on the road, because if I didn't, my chances of survival were next to nothing.

The fear of my own death clenched my chest, and I spun on my heel, marching away from my conspiracy board. I needed to suck it up. Face this fear. Or else I would be here alone for the rest of my miserable, lonely life.

I strode out the back door and made my way into the basement, gathering a small pup tent and a sleeping bag, slowing only a moment to lay eyes on the stone box and wooden pedestal before marching back toward the basement stairs.

They used to say that exposure therapy was the best way to cure a fear or phobia, but most people involved in exposure therapy sessions weren't actually risking their lives, no matter what the trauma centers of their brains told them. My life, however, had been in danger every second of every day since I'd been stranded on this damn mountain, and if I was being honest with myself, I had never truly felt more alive than I had the past several weeks. I was growing comfortable with stress. Not just comfortable—I was thriving in it.

Maybe I could become a better, stronger person without the comforts of the modern world? Maybe that was why I loved roughing it out in the forest so much? Maybe this was how humans were supposed to exist? The only thing fueling our desire to wake up being the need to feed, shelter, and clothe ourselves. Our need to survive, against all odds giving us the motivation to rise each day and fight.

I grunted as I took the stairs two at a time up out of the basement, slamming the door behind myself. Tears, hot with anger, frustration and loneliness stung the backs of my eyes but I blinked them away as I strode into the parking lot of the camp store. I let the tent and sleeping bag drop to the ground as I gazed out beyond the boundary of The Glow.

"I'm here, mother fuckers! Come get me!" I screamed at the top of my lungs.

I wouldn't stay there alone a second longer than I needed to, and I refused to let the fear of those creatures hold me prisoner here anymore. Dying in that moment would have been a better fate than trying to face the rest of my life, stuck at the camp store all alone.

I needed to know exactly what I was up against, so I was going to get a look at those things. And I was going to use a couple of dead rats and *myself* as bait.

14

The Writing on the Wall

Melissa

CRINGING AT THE SHARP SOUND of the hammer, Melissa set the last few nails in the plywood that now covered her front windows. She would miss the afternoon sun bathing the entire great room in golden light, but the added security was necessary. Glancing over her shoulder for what felt like the hundredth time, the street behind her was clear, save for the brown-red bloodstain—the only thing that remained of her neighbor.

The road through her neighborhood was quiet and as the spring season slowly marched toward summer, the lawns and flower beds had begun to take on a decidedly wild appearance. Weeds sprouted in the grass and from between cracks in the sidewalks. All the beautiful flowering trees had lost their petals, leaving the wilted remnants gathering in piles at the road's edge. The place looked and felt truly abandoned.

In all her searching for supplies, every door she knocked on had remained closed. Whether or not anyone was actually home, she was unsure, but so many of her neighbors had been in the park at the ration lines when the creatures had first attacked. She shuddered at the memory and shook her head. She was a survivor, she had to think like a survivor.

Her next-door neighbor's house had turned out to be fairly well stocked with supplies when she had finally ventured in. After commandeering the plywood for a half built shed in his back yard, Melissa set about removing several fence boards between their back yards. If she was quiet, she would be able to move supplies completely unnoticed, even in the rain.

Part of her heart felt nothing but guilt for raiding her neighbor's home, but he no longer counted himself among the living. Given the situation, his things were fair game, and she would use all she could...even his yard space. She moved his non-perishable food items to her own pantry and cupboards, and when she began to tire, she locked the front of his house up tight and exited through the back sliding door. Carefully closing it behind herself, she made her way through the open section of fence and back into her own yard, pausing for a moment beside Joey's grave.

Tears stung her eyes, and she sighed. He would want her to survive, so survive she would.

The clouds returned the following day. No surprise there. Late spring was always very wet with wild swings in temperature in her corner of the Pacific Northwest. When the sun was out, she could almost smell the summer heat returning, but when the clouds rolled back in, the damp, bone-chilling cold followed. The temperature hovering ten degrees above freezing day and night. It was awful. Luckily, the skies were only partly cloudy at the moment, and the intermittent sun warmed the front side of her house.

As she sat in her dark living room wondering about Amber, she had nearly dozed off when the sound of a large vehicle approaching pulled her back to alertness. Sprinting up the stairs, she ran to Amber's bedroom window that overlooked the street and peeked out from behind the blanket hanging over the window.

Midway down the road, a large military truck rolled to a stop, and a dozen soldiers poured out the back. One stayed behind, settled into position behind the mounted gun above the cab. Melissa watched with curiosity, wondering if they were scanning for the creatures or the opportunistic raiders that had begun seizing control of entire neighborhoods before the monsters had arrived. The rest of the soldiers fanned out in pairs, some heading her direction, others moving to the far end of the street. They knocked on doors and waited.

All of the houses on her street were empty. She knew this because she herself had knocked on every door multiple times before breaking in to gather resources. When no one came to the doors, the soldiers forced them open and went inside, presumably searching each house. Once finished, they boarded up the doors and spray-painted peculiar markings on the front of the house or garage door.

Melissa's brows drew together. What did the markings mean? She would have to ask...and she wouldn't need to wait long. A pair of soldiers were headed toward her house. She ran down the stairs and paused several feet away from the front door. The knock came and she nearly jumped out of her skin. Her hand shook as she crept forward and reached for the deadbolt. DJ had told her military personnel could be trusted, but what if these men weren't military personnel at all? What if they were nothing but scavengers in stolen uniforms?

A nervous sweat broke out across her top lip. She'd been alone for so long, but what if this was her only chance at some real information?

A second knock came followed by the muffled voice of a young man, "Wellness check! Anybody inside?"

What if DJ was with this group? She had to know. With a determined set to her jaw, she cranked the deadbolt and slowly opened the door as far as the chain would allow. Her eyes locked onto the face of a young man that couldn't have been more than twenty years old, the one beside him might have been a year or two older. Babies. They're just *babies.*

"Can I help you?" she asked, trying to keep her voice from quavering. Was it nerves or the fact that either one of these boys could have been Joey if he wasn't—

They glanced at one another in obvious shock before the younger man nodded and spoke. "I'm Private Jones, this is Mathieson. We're out with our unit doing wellness checks in the neighborhood. Are you in need of any assistance?"

A kind voice. Concerned faces. Melissa sighed and closed her eyes, fighting back the sting of tears. "I—I just need to talk to someone other than myself," she stammered then cleared her throat, trying to dislodge the lump that had taken up residence there. She closed the door a bit then pulled back the chain and opened the door wide. "Is DJ with you?"

162

The soldiers looked at each other then Jones turned back towards her, "What's DJ's last name, Ma'am?"

"Cooper," Melissa said. She could have sworn she saw Jones stiffen, nostrils flaring slightly. A flash of something—concern? Or was it shock? —widened Jones' eyes a moment before he settled his features into a well-trained mask of neutrality.

Too late.

"You know him, don't you? Where is he?" Mathieson turned and whistled, waving another soldier over. Her gaze tracked the third man, who was walking briskly in their direction, for a short moment before she turned her eyes back to the two young men before her.

"We don't—" Jones started then clamped his mouth shut so fast his teeth clicked. Mathieson shot him a hard look.

Melissa's pulse spiked. *They knew something. Something they weren't supposed to mention.* The third soldier arrived, and the two Privates stepped back from her door.

This man, for he was indeed several years older than Jones or Mathieson, introduced himself as a Lieutenant, but the moment his last name was spoken, Melissa immediately forgot it. Her mind was too busy reeling.

Why were these men so shocked to find her there? Were they really just doing welfare checks? What did the ominous spray-painted markings mean? Should she have even answered her door? *Where was DJ?!*

"Ma'am?" The Lieutenant leaned in like it wasn't the first time he'd tried to get her attention.

Melissa blinked and shook her head, bringing herself fully present. "Yes, I'm sorry. I just haven't seen anyone in weeks, and I've been waiting for word from DJ...er—Cooper. Is he with you? Do you know him?"

"When was the last time you saw him?" the Lieutenant asked, raising dark brows at her.

Have they lost him? The lump in Melissa's throat returned and her heart pounded for a new reason. *Is he gone too?* Not another loss. Her heart couldn't take another loss. She barely knew DJ, but he was a good, strong, kind, and considerate man. They had met for a reason, she just knew it, and the thought of him not making it hurt almost as much as losing her own children...because DJ knew

Amber. He knew where Amber might be. He was Melissa's last connection to her daughter and now he might be dead too.

She clenched her teeth and swallowed through the tightness in her throat. She would not lose her composure in front of these people. She had to be strong. "I was in the park the day those creatures attacked the ration lines. He helped me escape and get back home." Her chin kicked up a notch and she met the Lieutenant's hard gaze.

He nodded and paused a moment as if searching for the right words. "How well did you know Cooper?"

He's speaking in the past tense...oh, God. "He and my daughter are friends." These men didn't need to know that Amber and DJ had only just met. After he was so kind and even helped bury Joey, Melissa considered DJ as good as family. "She obviously knows him better than I do,"

"Is your daughter here?" the Lieutenant pressed and Melissa shook her head.

"She was camping when the grid went down. I haven't seen her since." The dull ache in her chest grew to a piercing stab as she said those words aloud. "Is DJ dead?" She had to know.

"He is missing, presumed deceased, or—" the Lieutenant's mouth drew into a thin line. "He hasn't been seen since the attack at the ration lines. No body found. We've been unable to locate his next of kin; do you know them, by chance?"

"Oh, God. No." Melissa's hand found her mouth and her knees wobbled but she managed to stay upright, leaning on the door frame for support. Just because he had never returned, didn't mean that he had suffered the same fate as her neighbor. She clenched her eyes shut at the memory. DJ was trained and he was obviously an excellent shot. He'd hit that creature right between the eyes before it had even had a chance to charge him. He had to have survived. "No, I'm sorry. I don't know them." Tears welled in her eyes.

"I'm sorry, Ma'am. I know it's terrible news. Of course there is a chance that he's still alive, hiding out somewhere, but we assume that he would have made his way back to headquarters weeks ago if that were the case," the Lieutenant said with all the fuzzy warmth of a flagpole in January.

Melissa blinked hard and ground her teeth. "There's no way. He said he'd come back to help..." Her voice trailed off.

"If he does show up in the next twenty-four hours, keep him with you. We're setting up a secure community of survivors at the Orchardville Mall. Tomorrow afternoon, weather permitting, another unit will be coming through this area, gathering people and supplies. Chances of survival are much higher if we are all together." The Lieutenant's voice was matter of fact, like he was reading from a manual. This was an order.

The park. The ration lines. All Melissa could hear was the echo of screams and the rattle of gunfire. Her friends and neighbors being picked off like fish in a barrel. A safe zone? Absolutely not. Her gut twisted violently, screaming at her to stay hunkered down in her own home.

That attack on the ration lines had been coordinated, no matter how outlandish it seemed to her very logical mind, and the way that creature had stared at her through the living room window...she could almost see the gears turning in its mind. Those creatures could think and strategize just as well as any human, she was sure of it. And if this obstinate oaf of a soldier couldn't see that, then there was no way she would be going to any *'community'* the government was trying to set up. And on top of everything, perhaps the most important reason of all for her to stay put, was Amber. She needed to be there for her daughter. Even if the odds were next to nothing that Amber would make it home...she couldn't give up hope.

"Well, I—I don't have much here...maybe a weeks' worth of food and water for myself," she said softly, looking at the ground, *lying through her teeth.* "How much am I allowed to bring to the mall with me?"

"Individual space is limited, but we are allowing two medium sized suitcases of personal items. Be sure to pack your identification, a passport or birth certificate if you have it, a list of medications and any medical equipment you use. We will supply beds, toiletries, and rations." The Lieutenant rattled off the list like he was reading a textbook. He'd obviously lost his sense of compassion ages ago. Melissa couldn't really blame him though. He'd probably seen more death than any one person should in a single lifetime.

She nodded stiffly and finally allowed the threatening tears to roll down her cheeks. She scrubbed them away with a fist and sniffed. The soldiers began excusing themselves and as they turned to leave, she caught Jones' eye. Lines furrowed his brow, and his mouth twitched into a grimace. The young man looked like he wanted to scream.

"Wait, Jones?" Melissa reached out, laying a hand on his elbow. The other two glanced back, hesitant to leave the young man. She spoke just loudly enough for the departing pair to hear, "You remind me so much of my son. Those creatures killed him at the ration lines..." She trailed off and let more tears fall—*lying through her teeth again.*

Jones turned to Mathieson and the Lieutenant, "Gimme a minute, I'll catch up."

Melissa only had moments to speak, and she pulled the young man into a tight, awkward hug, speaking in a low, steady voice. "I know you think this mall community is a bad idea. I can tell by the look on your face." The young man stiffened. "Tell me what you think I should do."

Jones moved closer into the hug, really returning it, and whispered, "Don't go. My parents were killed in the first community they tried to set up over in Portland. Those things are too smart, and they coordinate their attacks. They always go for places where people are congregating. I think you'd be safer here." He paused, dragging in a ragged breath. "You're the only person we've come across in days."

Melissa's blood ran cold. The only one? She pulled back from the hug to look at his face then glanced over his shoulder to make sure the other two soldiers were well out of earshot. "What else do you know about them? What do I need to know to survive?"

Jones shuffled back a bit more, inner conflict deepening every crease on his young face. "It's classified," he glanced over his shoulder then back to her, "Oh, fuck it." He sighed then spoke low and fast. "We stopped receiving transmissions from every major city on the western seaboard shortly after the attack at the ration lines. Those creatures hit every station in the area at the same time."

The boards of her front porch seemed to tumble out from under her feet, her world dropping into a free fall.

"Thousands of the creatures somehow coordinated an attack on every major city, town and gathering of people over the course of three days and nights. We got word from our contact in The Rockies that they were absolutely annihilating every command center across the country...most likely the continent...and then communications went completely dark. We have no idea what's going on, but this feels like a last stand to me. It's a shit show."

Melissa blanched. A small part of her had held out hope that somewhere, a city or community was still standing—that the military still had some control in all the chaos. But it was not so. The entire western seaboard had fallen—possibly even the entire country. Her ears rang as she reached out, steadying herself on the doorframe. Millions of people, thousands of cities, just gone. While she lay in her back yard, silently mourning the loss of her son, those creatures had been systematically dismantling civilization, ending hundreds of years of development in a single week.

"Just, don't go to the mall. They'll take it down no matter how fortified these idiots think it is. It's a death trap. They're too fast. Too strong. And every time we see a pack of them, the numbers just keep growing. We don't even know where they're coming from, they're just multiplying." Jones' shoulders sagged.

"What in God's name," Melissa trailed off.

"These things have to be coming straight out of Hell...and they're going to destroy the human race."

A sharp whistle turned both their heads toward the large truck. The soldiers were loading up to leave. Melissa pulled Jones into another tight hug. "I'm so sorry about your parents," she whispered.

"Yeah, me too." He straightened and turned to leave but Melissa stopped him again.

"What do the markings on the houses mean?" she asked quickly.

"They're a variation of FEMA markings." He gestured toward the fresh spray paint on her garage door. "How many people," he said, pointing to the top number, "The number of survivors and the number of deceased," he continued, pointing to a second set of numbers below the first. "And this is for resources found in the residence ranked from zero through five." His arm dropped to his side. "If everything is a zero, we board the front door and paint an 'X'."

"Jones! Let's move!" the Lieutenant hollered from outside the now loaded truck.

"I gotta go. If DJ ever shows up, tell him Kyle says 'Hey. I knew he'd make it.'" Jones said in a rush before jogging to the truck.

The driver fired up the motor and with a lurch, the truck rumbled past her house and down the street. Kyle Jones raised a hand from the back of the truck as it passed then pointed to where the truck had been parked. Melissa raised a hand in return then glanced to where Jones had pointed.

A single can of spray paint sat in the middle of the road. Once the truck disappeared around the corner, she retrieved the can then inspected the markings on her garage. No doubt, the unit deployed to pick up survivors and supplies would roll through each neighborhood checking the markings from the street, stopping only when the markings showed something valuable inside. The markings on her garage broadcast a single person, a single survivor, zero deceased. The 'Resources' section was left blank.

She could still hear the truck rumbling further away from her neighborhood in the eerie quiet that had taken over the world. The familiar hum of electricity, the drone of traffic from the main road, horn blasts, music, dogs barking, children laughing...the sounds of human life in the suburbs. It was all gone, replaced by the sweet songs of birds and the wind hissing through the conifers and new spring leaves of the deciduous trees. She was alone again, her house like an oasis in the sweeping desert.

Staring down at the can of spray paint in her hand, she put together a mental list of things that needed to be done. She needed to create a hidden way to enter and exit her home, so it appeared to be just as abandoned as every other house on her street. But first, before she could do anything else, she would paint over and replace the modified FEMA markings.

Her fate was not up to them.

She wasn't going anywhere.

15

Training for the Journey Home

I PLACED THE LAST ROCK INTO the ring of stones that would serve as my fire pit in the parking lot of the camp store and surveyed my makeshift camp. The small tent stood behind me and beyond that, the camp store sat, slowly fading into the long shadows of the afternoon. Across from the fire pit, I had laid out an old area rug to serve as my sitting area, and beyond that, way out past the border of The Glow, sat two dead rats beside two baited rat traps. It was my hope that the small corpses would bring the shadowy creatures close enough that I would finally be able to get a good look at one of them.

I set about building a fire. I wanted it bright and crackling by the time the sun went down, but just in case that failed, I had a large flashlight on the rug. As the sun dipped lower, my nerves inched higher. I hadn't spent more than seconds outside in the dark since I had been stranded at the camp store, I was too afraid of those creatures. But now that I was confident in the unseen barrier that protected the area, I knew I needed to start practicing spending the night outdoors again. Conquering my fear of the dark; learning to steady my nerves and think through my fear was my only chance at surviving my trip home. The survival book had a passage dedicated to learning how to keep thinking through emergency situations, not panicking.

Don't Lose Your Head – *Survival in the wilds, away from civilization was just a regular Tuesday for our ancestors. Every step they took, they carefully weighed their options for safety and survival. For the modern man, it is exceedingly rare that we need to devote more than a second to such thoughts. Why would we when we have immediate access to clean water, food, heat, shelter, and infrastructure dedicated to keeping us all safe? If anything goes wrong when we are alone, we have a device in our pockets that we can use to signal for help, but more often than not, we're close to hundreds of other people, most of which would also be happy to call for help in an emergency.*

But if you are alone, cut off from contact with the modern world, what do you do then?

You develop a plan, then a back-up plan, and a third plan should the back-up plan fail. Be aware of your surroundings. What do you hear? What do you smell? What can you see? What can you taste? And let us not forget the most important of all, what do you feel? Both what you can touch and what you feel in the depth of your bones. Listening to this sixth sense is becoming a dying art, but our ancestors relied on this sense often. When our five basic senses fail us, we look to our intuition to fill the gaps. And if all our senses fail, the last thing you can do is remain calm and think clearly. If you develop those skills, there will not be a single situation that you can't get yourself out of or better yet, avoid completely.

My intuition, my gut as Mom called it, was screaming at me to get indoors before it was dark, but I wouldn't be able to get back to her if I didn't find a way to safely exist outside of The Glow, so my best chance was to teach myself not to panic.

As the sun disappeared behind the trees and eventually behind the mountains that separated me from my home, the forest seemed to come alive around me. Crickets and frogs began their night songs, and the small, nocturnal creatures scurried out of their hiding spots to forage through the dark hours.

I pulled my journal from my coat and wrote:

April 14ᵗʰ: *I don't know what time it is right now but I'm sitting out by the fire and just heard something in the bushes. I can't see*

much past the fire, but I think if I sit with my back to it, my eyes will
adjust to the dark. I can just make out the rat traps sitting on the road
out there but don't see anything yet. I'll just keep waiting.

The gentle rustling of the wind through the trees along with the
crickets began to lull me to sleep and I stretched out on the rug, laying
on my side with my back to the fire, and pulled an old blanket over
myself for a bit of added warmth. I must have dozed off because when
my eyes flew open again the forest had gone deathly silent. I didn't
move when I woke, but I mentally took note of what my senses were
telling me in the moment.

My body began to tingle as my heart pounded in my chest. I
could hear the fire gently crackling behind me as something slid out
of the bushes that bordered the road, far beyond the light of my low
fire. The sound of claws scratching on the pavement echoed off the
tall trees. My eyes strained to focus, willing the shadows to part so I
could see what was in the road. I could barely make out the shadowed
shape of the traps just beyond the edge of The Glow. The breeze had
died, so I couldn't smell anything other than campfire smoke and the
dank rug beneath me.

As I lay there, out in the open, pretending to sleep, I began to
think that this whole thing had been a terrible idea, but I took a slow,
steadying breath and tried to convince myself not to panic. I couldn't
lose my head...really, I had no reason to. I was safe within the
boundaries of The Glow.

But as the sound of claws on the road grew closer, two pairs of
glowing red eyes emerged from the night. The slightly darker,
shadowed outline of two creatures materialized a moment later. They
made their way to the rat traps, their enormous bulk like nothing I
had ever seen before. I held my breath. Had it been light out, I could
have seen them in detail easily, but shrouded by the night as they
were, I couldn't tell what they looked like at all. They appeared to be
nothing more than a large shape with glowing eyes.

One of them lowered its head toward one of the rat traps, and it
snapped closed with a crack that rang loud as a gunshot in the silent
dark. That snap was nothing compared to the sound the creature
made. Its scream like tearing sheet metal blended with a high-pitched
animal cry. It was a screech that seemed to harmonize with itself, like
it had two voices. One that could have been a somewhat normal yip
for a canine of any sort, but the louder screech was something else

entirely. It echoed, the sound slicing through my body and down my spine, my back twitched, and my teeth ached.

I clapped my hands over my ears trying to block out the sound but never took my eyes away from the large, shadowed forms. As soon as I moved, the creatures bounded back toward the trees. I scrambled to grab my flashlight and turned it on just in time to see a dark form disappear into the tall grass.

One moment, their presence filled the darkness—and the next, they were just...gone, swallowed by the forest. The grass rippled lightly in their wake, then all went still. I panned the edge of the road and the bushes beyond but couldn't make out anything beyond the edge of the road. A heartbeat later, another scream cut through the still night air, distant and echoing.

How the hell did they move so fast?

I shivered, the goosebumps skittering down my neck having nothing at all to do with the cold air. I threw some more wood on the fire and crawled into the little tent to try and sleep the rest of the night away. Sleep never came though, and as soon as night yielded to the first weak light of early morning, I bounded out of the tent and walked down the road to where I had left the baited traps. As I approached The Glow, I slowed my pace, listening hard.

The forest was silent. Too late for crickets and frogs, but too early for the first birds. With a deep breath, I stepped through the warm barrier. There was no sign of the creatures, and my gut wasn't sending any warnings, so I squared my shoulders and strode the ten or so paces to the area that I had left the rat traps.

The rats were gone and so was one of the traps. In its place were several droplets of the black stuff that smelled like death. If the trap had injured one of them, then it confirmed two of my theories. The black stuff was indeed their blood and if they could be injured, that meant they could also be killed. But it also raised another question: Why on earth would blood of any sort be black and smell like a rotting corpse?

I stood, my eyes scanning the surrounding area. Just across the road, I spied a broken leaf on a large fern. That must have been the path the creatures took to enter the forest. As I made my way over to the fern, I passed more droplets of the black blood. They had definitely come this way.

The forest was still cloaked in shadow, casting everything under the thick canopy in eerie, sinister shapes. Just beside the broken fern, a single paw print pressed deep into the damp earth. Cold air bit at my cheeks, sharp as needles, and my breath curled out in a pale cloud while the acrid tang of sulfur lingered on the air, faint, but unmistakable.

The hairs on the back of my neck bristled as I knelt to inspect the track. Heart hammering, I reached out, my hand trembling as I laid it inside the print. My outstretched fingers didn't even reach the claw-tipped indentations of its toes. It was massive—easily the largest paw print I'd ever seen—like a cross between a big cat's pugmark and a wolf's track.

I straightened and chanced another step into the forest. Just beyond the shrubby bushes and ferns at the roadside, the underbrush in the forest proper thinned considerably. It would be easy to traverse once the sun actually came up, so I turned and jogged back to the camp store, praying for clear skies.

Once back in the house, I slammed my morning coffee and oatmeal, threw some sturdy pants and shoes on, strapped my pack across my shoulders, and headed back outside. I paced the parking lot cursing the foggy, lingering clouds and hoped they would give way to sunny skies soon.

In my hand, I fidgeted with an old knife I'd found in the basement. It looked like some military surplus thing—it even had *USMC* stamped onto the blade. I paused in my pacing to really look at it. The knife was well-used, the leather on the handle worn smooth and gleaming like polished wood, but the blade itself was razor sharp. Someone had loved this knife.

Seemingly without cause, an image of Dan flashed into my mind's eye; smiling to himself while he sharpened the blade. The knife really did look like something he would carry, and a sad sigh escaped me at the thought. For someone who had seemed so prepared and knowledgeable, it was a shame that he had never made it out of the forest that day.

Not just a shame...it was downright unfair. Unfair that someone with a wife and kid waiting for him at home, would die out here in the forest, while someone like me had managed to survive.

I shook my head and slid the knife back into its sheath and snapped it onto my belt. The morning fog was slowly burning off, bits of golden sun beaming through the breaks in the mist. With the birds now singing a sweet morning melody, I started off toward the edge of the road. Once I'd located the giant paw print, I took a deep, determined breath and stepped into the forest. It was utterly silent, like the trees themselves were holding their breath, waiting for me to take that first step.

In just a half dozen paces, I turned back looking for the small gap I'd used to enter the forest, and I had a hard time locating it. The last thing I needed to do was end up lost in the woods, so I turned back to the tree line, searching for just the right stick. A supple, broad leaf maple branch caught my eye, just a few feet long with plenty of leaves. Pulling the knife from my belt, I cut the thin branch and perched it awkwardly on top of a large fern, so it laid across the small opening I had stepped through. It would be impossible to miss.

Satisfied with my trail marker, and taking note of the steller's jay singing its raucous song in the canopy above, I continued into the forest, following the faint trail left by one of the creatures. Before long, the first set of tracks was joined by another. The new set was larger by half and looked like some sort of bear print, but it wasn't quite right.

"What the hell?" I mumbled to myself as I knelt down to take a closer look at it.

I might not have known much about animals, but it was plain, even to my very untrained eye, that these creatures were definitely not natural. I had argued with myself before that they had to be regular animals and that my imagination was playing tricks on me, but that moment truly settled it for me. They bleed black blood that smells like death, the sound they make doesn't sound like any living creature I had ever heard, and their tracks didn't look like any animal I had ever seen either.

As I continued following the trail, leaving markers in my wake, I thought again about how sleeping in the trees could be the best way to keep myself alive overnight when away from the safety of The Glow. The creatures seemed to stick to the ground.

I was so deep in thought that I practically tripped over the missing rat trap. It had been chewed on, several deep gouges in the wood were evidence to that fact, and it was lying face down on the mossy ground.

I stooped to pick it up then squeaked in shock and dropped it again. Heart pounding in my ears, I leaned over to inspect the trap more closely. A flap of black, leathery skin lay trapped under the metal bar. Hand to my chest, I picked up the trap again with two fingers and examined it. The skin was hairless and black blood smeared across the wood of the trap like grease. I didn't dare touch it. As I moved it into a patch of sunlight to get a better look, the skin began to blister then smolder, tendrils of rank smoke curling into the air.

I gasped, "The sunlight actually hurts them."

Quickly turning the trap so the skin was facing down, protected by shadow, I began making my way out of the trees. Before I stepped out onto the road and into the blaring sun, I chanced another glance at the flap of skin. As soon as the light touched it, it started smoldering again. Cursing under my breath, I tucked it under the bottom edge of my hoodie and scurried back down the road to the camp store.

I didn't notice at first, but as I grew nearer to The Glow, the trap began to hum and when I crossed into the protective barrier, it was buzzing like a cell phone on vibrate. I dropped it and as it hit the ground, the flap of flesh caught fire, burning away like paper.

I stood there gaping as the wood of the trap caught fire as well. So, the sunlight hurts these creatures...and The Glow? Well, it appeared to set them on fire. No wonder they never came anywhere near the camp store!

I left the trap to burn away in the parking lot then marched back into the camp store and straight to my conspiracy board. Permanent marker in hand, I edited some of the sticky notes.

Sunlight hurts the creatures.

The Glow sets the creatures on fire.

The black stuff really is their blood.

I grabbed a new stack of sticky notes and started writing, *Where do they go when the sun is out?*

I slapped it on the board and stabbed it with a tack, then began scribbling on a second piece, *Do they only stay in the forest for better protection from the sun?*

I ruminated on that thought for a moment. Judging by how sensitive they had to be to sunlight, I reasoned that they would have to be cautious going out in open areas like fields when the skies were clear. If the sun rose and they didn't have cover, they would probably burn up like the flap of skin did. I knew then that if I could get out of the forest and into the open, my chances of survival might go way up.

My plan of making it out of these woods by sunset on the first day on of my journey seemed to be a solid one. Ride like hell out of the mountains and just make sure I'm well-hidden before the sun sets.

A thrill shot through me, new knowledge making me bold. I was going to get out of here. I was going to finally get back home. I just had to hold out until the first clear day in May.

16

The Journey Begins

MY BREATH CLOUDED IN THE COLD, morning air, curling skyward before being whisked away on the breeze. The cold stung my cheeks and nose, but I barely noticed it. Today I was going *home*.

The damp gravel of the camp store parking lot crunched beneath my feet as I swung my leg over my bike and took in my surroundings like it might be the last time I ever saw this place—this oasis of safety in a new savage world. The blue-gray light of early morning crept along the conifers and the moon still hung, pale and distant in the brightening sky. The night had been cold and a light layer of frost shimmered like powdered diamonds everywhere the sun touched. But even through the frost, the smell of warming earth brushed my nose, and I sighed. The frost would be gone within an hour. Even though it was just the end of April, true spring was finally in the air.

I had awoken before sunrise with a terrible sense of urgency, something deep inside telling me—*ordering* me—to leave right away. I hadn't hesitated a second. The feeling had grown steadily over the past several days. My backpack and the bike wagon had been packed for over a week, I had just been waiting for the first sunny day in May. My gut told me that today was that day, and it didn't matter what month it was.

Just go already, will you?

With a determined breath, I pushed off and began pedaling, the heavy load on the wagon adding some strain to my legs. I'd loaded it down with food and supplies for Mom and Joey plus a couple gallons of water for me while I rode. My pack also sat heavy on my shoulders, loaded with a change of clothes, an extra pair of shoes, medication, small booze bottles and other things for possible trading.

As I rolled out of the parking lot, I carried a plea of sorts in my heart. *Please let me make it home in one piece and find my mom and brother well.* I kept repeating it until I passed through The Glow.

Suddenly tears stung the back of my eyes as a lump formed in my throat. I slammed on the brakes and turned to look back at the log cabin. The old store had kept me safe, warm, and dry for over a month, and it felt like a home that was all my own. I would miss it and the safety it provided dearly, but I would be back, come hell or high water (like my mom always said).

"Thank you," I whispered, placing a hand over my heart. "I'll be back soon."

The invisible barrier of The Glow seemed to pulse with power, shimmering for a moment, slightly blurring everything within it, and then the camp store seemed to shiver out of existence. The parking lot, the outbuildings, *everything* faded, then disappeared.

My breath caught and a cold jolt shot through my chest. It had to be a trick of the light or my own tears. I blinked and rubbed my eyes. But, no—the store, the outbuildings—it all vanished, leaving behind nothing but an overgrown clearing beside the road.

Heart pounding, I set my bike's kickstand and ran back toward the edge of The Glow. I could still feel it there, but something was different. The moment I passed through the barrier, the camp store reappeared.

"Holy shit," I whispered as my heart pounded in my ears. Just when I'd thought I'd had it all figured out...

I could see my bike and wagon several paces away just like normal but as I exited The Glow once more, the camp store blurred and flickered back out of existence.

Cloaking abilities? Well, I'll be damned.

The camouflage was so effective, I knew I would miss the area without some kind of marker. My eyes swept the roadside until I spotted several large rocks near the ditch. I gathered them in a neat pile a few feet away from the edge of The Glow, like a cairn trail marker.

Pleased with my marker, I thanked the area again then turned and rode away not looking back for fear of losing my nerve. My path now was forward. Only forward. All the way to Orchardville. I would ride hard, pushing myself to the limit physically all day. I had to make it to the river. I had to make it out of the forest. I *had* to get home.

The narrow road curved and hills rose and fell. I had to get off and push the bike and wagon up a long, steep climb, but I had traveled this road by car before and although it wasn't the same route I had taken to get up to the forest back in early March, I knew that that was the last big hill before the elevation steadily dropped to the Columbia River Gorge. I sweat despite the chill in the air, puffing with exertion, and was grateful for the miles of downhill and flat road ahead of me. The forest continued to thin as the morning wore on. I was making good time in my estimation. I had left at dawn and even though I was still several miles from the river, the sun still hadn't reached its zenith.

The temperature steadily climbed the lower I dropped in elevation. The winter chill still clung to the mountains, but closer to the flat lands, spring was in full force. By the time I hit the foothills, the chill in the air was completely gone, replaced with the sweet smell of warm, damp grass. I sneezed. And wildflowers...so many wildflowers. It was like I had just jumped weeks forward in time. The nights, and most days for that matter, still hovered just above freezing in the mountains, but down in the foothills, the air felt almost balmy. It had to be over sixty degrees.

The truly warm air brought a wide grin to my face, and I hummed as I pedaled along. Then, a shape began to take form in the distance. Buildings lining the road.

People? As I pedaled closer, the truth hit me like a punch to the gut. The small town of Riverdale, sister city to Riverside in the mountains, was dead. Burned buildings stood like hollowed-out corpses, their blackened skeletons leaning and reaching at odd angles. The ones that remained intact were silent, windows either broken or dark and empty. I called out as I drifted down the road, but the only response was my own echoing voice.

A prickling awareness tingled across my scalp, and I picked up my pace. There was no reason to spend a second longer in this town than I had to.

Worry took up residence somewhere between my heart and my stomach. Was every town I passed through going to be dead or abandoned? I tried to push the thought aside and focus on more positive things, like my mom's sweet smile and Joey's raucous laugh, but not even those beloved images could shake the deep concern that vibrated within me. That concern quickly morphed into cold dread. Something about the empty town set my nerves on edge, even the wind felt like it was watching me, so I dropped a couple gears and pedaled harder, leaving the ruins of Riverdale behind me.

Finally, the road I was on met with Washington State Highway 14. The hard wind tugged at my hair, and I breathed in the smell of the river. In the summer months, the Columbia teemed with boats, jet skis and windsurfers. Even in the spring, fishermen and sailboats were a common sight—but as I stood on the silent railroad tracks that ran between the highway and the nearly mile-wide body of water, the only thing moving across that massive expanse of blue-gray was a grain barge, turning slowly as it drifted downriver...clearly unmanned. I found myself wondering what would happen when it ran into the dam a few miles away. Abandoned cars littered the highway in both directions. The only living things in sight were birds.

I felt small...and completely alone.

With a sigh, I carefully made my way down the railroad embankment and back to my bike. The towns would slowly grow to cities the closer I got to home, which meant more abandoned cars and a higher chance of running into people, a thought that made my gut churn.

The shadows of trees, rocks and broken-down cars stretched as the day wore on. There was no way I would be able to make it to Orchardville before the sun set no matter how hard I pushed myself, so I pondered on what would be the safest way to spend the night while I rode, leg muscles beginning to burn.

A car, either an SUV or a pickup truck with a canopy would probably be my best bet, but I still had several hours before dark, so I pushed on.

Before too long, I neared another town but some sort of structure completely obstructed the road. As I rolled closer, I could make out cars. At least half a dozen of them, all pushed together bumper to bumper. Wooden posts formed a sort of makeshift fence at least ten feet high, and the whole thing, cars and fence, was covered with razor wire. The barrier ran toward a side-street, effectively walling off the main road through town, funneling anyone who traveled the highway down a pre-determined route. Alarm bells went off in my mind. This could be very bad. I looked around for an alternate route, but I couldn't find anywhere I could get my bike and wagon through.

Pulling out my map, I tried to find a backroad that avoided the town altogether. To my dismay, the only road that bypassed the town was all the way back in Riverdale...and it took a meandering route through the forest before it entered Orchardville on the far east side, near the Plum Mountain community. That was a complete no go. I was familiar with that road; it was remote and almost entirely forested. I would have to take my chances with the razor wire route.

My heart hammered in my chest as I pedaled down the side street, feeling like some type of livestock being forced through a chute. I passed an old gas station and a diner, both appeared to be abandoned, then I was forced into a residential area. Every first story window was boarded up and every cross street was barricaded in the same fashion the highway was. I imagined that the folks that lived here had to have done this to keep themselves safe. The barricades probably did a fantastic job of keeping the creatures out of certain areas of town. The same could have been said for wandering people as well.

The people of this town obviously just wanted to stay safe and alive.

I kept my head on the swivel as I continued down the road. The town was quiet. Too quiet.

As I rounded a corner, the unmistakable clack of a shotgun being cocked sounded over my right shoulder. That was *obviously* meant to be heard.

My heart landed somewhere in my toes as I slowed to a stop and raised my hands, still straddling my bike. I had no weapon aside from the combat knife strapped to my belt. I had no choice but to stop and comply with whatever this person demanded.

Damn it! But maybe if they saw I was no threat, they would let me go?

"I'm just trying to get to Orchardville. I don't want any trouble. I just need to pass through," I called out, trying to keep my voice from cracking. No response was forthcoming, so I cleared my throat and continued, "I was in the forest when it happened, and I've been hiding in an old store this entire time. I just want to get home to my mom and brother." My voice failed me, breaking in a pitiful sort of way.

"Your family's dead, kid. Best just leave that bike and crawl back into whatever hole you've been hiding in." The voice came from a doorway to my right, and it sounded like a woman, perhaps my mother's age, but with a smoker's rasp.

"Is there anything I can give you to buy my passing? I need the bike to get home," I pleaded. "I'm unarmed. You wouldn't shoot an unarmed girl, would you?"

There was a pause before the woman answered, "I don't want to shoot you, but I will if I have to."

"Please—" my voice wavered, throat tight, on the verge of tears. "I just need to get home."

A child's voice, muffled like it was coming from inside the building said, "Momma, don't shoot her. She's scared."

The woman hissed at the kid, "You shut up and git your ass back away from this door." Then to me she said, "I've got babies that are hungry in here and their lives mean more to me than yours does."

Of course.

My mind spun, trying to think of a way out of this predicament. I could do without the wagon if I had to. Mom wouldn't want me risking my life for some food and supplies.

"Take the wagon. It's full of food—enough to last you weeks. Just let me go." I was about to continue my pleading when I heard the click of another gun to my left.

No!

A sob tried to work its way free of my throat and I swallowed, a tear trailing down my face as I turned to my left. There, a man leveled a rifle at me as well.

"We're taking that bike. I heard Orchardville is a ghost town. Too close to the forests. It's overrun with those things that come in the dark. You should go back to where you came from," he said flatly. "Step off the bike and we'll let you live."

182

I had no other choice. I set the kickstand down and stepped away from the bike—my lifeline. All my food and water taken just like that. More frustrated tears ran down my cheeks.

How could they? In a world filled with things that just want to kill and most likely eat us, it galled me that humans were still willing to kill one another instead of just working together. I was disgusted and hurt. I should have just stayed in the damn forest.

"What about her backpack, Jim?" Smoker's Rasp called from across the street. My head whipped back in her direction as a kid, not more than five years old pushed past her and looked at me before grasping his mother's leg.

"Don't shoot her, Momma. She's just like Jeni. Jeni is probably still trying to get back to us. You wouldn't want someone to shoot *her*, would you?" the little boy pleaded with his mother.

Oh, the wisdom and kindness that could come pouring out of the mouths of children.

Please listen to your kid, lady.

The woman faltered and looked past me to Jim. My eyes did the same, studying his face. He had to be the child's father. They had the same sandy hair and sad eyes.

Jim lowered his gun, and the woman did the same, then Jim said, "If we send her off without anything, she's as good as dead. I have to believe that there is some good left. Then maybe Jeni will find her way back to us." He walked toward me, rifle in hand, and peered into the bike wagon. "She wasn't lying. There's a shit-ton of food in here." He looked hard at me, then asked, "Where did you say you were holed up?"

"At the store near River—" my voice cracked as I tried to cover a sob. Then it dawned on me; I could not, under any circumstances, tell these people where I had been hiding. If they were willing to rob an unarmed girl blind during the midst of the apocalypse, they would have no problems at all making their way to my camp store and taking everything I had built there...that was, if they could even find it. Still, I wouldn't tell them a thing.

I angrily rubbed at the tears on my face and sputtered out the name of the empty town I had passed earlier that day. "R-Riverdale."

The man looked down at me and seemed to actually see me for the first time. "Aw, Shit, honey," he called to Smoker's Rasp. "She's just a kid. We've gotta leave her with something."

183

"You're too damn soft, Jim. Walk her out of town and send her on her way. And take that backpack," the woman barked at him.

This *bitch!* I hated her. How dare she!

Jim shook his head in what looked like near disgust and reached into the wagon pulling out some canned goods and meal bars then handed them to me to put in my pack. I cringed at the light sound of a pill bottle rattling in my bag and hoped that Jim hadn't heard it too.

"I will shoot you too, Jim!" Smoker's Rasp yelled. "Everything you give her takes food out of our mouths."

"Well, I guess I'll be the one going hungry for a few more days then," Jim retorted, sounding more than a little irritated.

The woman huffed and retreated back into the building dragging the child behind her and slammed the door.

Jim shook his head. "I'm really sorry we have to do this, but we've got four littleun's in there that haven't eaten good in days."

I remained silent, fighting the tears that ran down my face. To his credit, Jim really did *look* sorry. Whether he was actually sorry though was up for debate.

"Can you at least leave me with the bike? There has to be another one somewhere in this town." I resorted to begging. "I don't know if I'll make it without wheels."

"You may actually be better off without them." Jim pulled a bottle of water out of the wagon and handed it to me as well. "I bet if you didn't have this bike, you would have found another way around that block on the highway."

No, if I didn't have the bike, I would have never made it down off the mountain, but he didn't need to know that. Guess he wasn't really sorry after all. He did have a point though. I just hadn't counted on people being as large of a threat as the shadow creatures were. I naïvely thought people would be like I was, lonely and close to desperate for human contact, for friends, or a community, or an extra set of hands to help the group survive. I was wrong.

He solemnly handed me a few more food items then gestured down the road with the barrel of the gun. I started walking.

While Jim escorted me down the road, I scanned the houses and buildings as we passed. Curtains moved in second story windows, and a few people peered out from around the side of buildings. Once, I made pleading eye contact with a blonde, teenage girl, but the barrel of Jim's rifle between my shoulder blades stopped me from saying anything. Clearly, he had some pull in the community because no one even came out to gawk openly.

We walked the predetermined route through town and when we made it to what appeared to be a dead end, he ushered me into an empty concrete building with heavy steel doors. Jim switched on a flashlight, and we continued through a series of winding alleyways made up of grocery store shelves before coming to the rear door, also made of heavy steel with an industrial deadbolt and a steel bar latch. No one and no*thing* would get through that door without being let in. The door groaned on its hinges as it swung open, and he pointed me toward a trail that led back up to the highway.

Without a word, I walked away, angry tears streaming down my cheeks, absolutely irate with myself and the town of cowardly people that refused to help. At the same time, I was beyond grateful to have escaped with my life, either one of them could have shot me and been done with it, but I should have planned for something like that. I should have *known* that people would be desperate...and desperate people are capable of terrible things.

There are only nine meals between peace and anarchy.

Dan's voice echoed in my mind again. My bike wagon held much more than nine meals...all those supplies had most likely saved my life, but now I had next to nothing to bring home.

Drying my tears with my sleeve, I put boots to pavement and trudged along, thinking that this new world I was living in was a lot more like the Wild West than I ever could have imagined. I walked until the sky glowed orange and my shadow stretched out long behind me before I started trying doors on abandoned vehicles. An old, red sedan that still smelled like cheap cologne and stale cigarettes finally opened for me. Aside from the smell, it looked like it would be pleasant enough to overnight in, and the large bench seat in back looked clean and comfortable.

I sat on the hood of the big old sedan watching the sun set over the Columbia River and tried not to feel sorry for myself. Jim had let me keep my backpack, at least. The most important things I could need on the road—water, antibiotics, painkillers, and my journal—all tucked safely inside. In the waning light of evening, I wrote it all down. The robbery, the guns, the kid with too much kindness for the world he was being brought up in...it all ran out of my head and onto the pages of my journal in stark, black ink.

When twilight approached, I locked myself into the old sedan, listening to the wind sweep across the river. I hoped for sunny skies in the morning and an uneventful night as I curled up on the back seat. There was no way I could handle any more surprises.

Tomorrow, I had to keep moving. No matter what.

17

Followed

GOLDEN SHAFTS OF LIGHT SPILLED through the sedan windows painting the cracked dash in warm rays. The morning sky was clear, and I exhaled in relief. I had survived the night. No monsters came knocking and even without The Glow, I'd slept like the dead.

My feet throbbed, my legs ached, my head pounded, and my heart...my heart hurt worst of all.

The crushing realization that yesterday hadn't been a bad dream settled on my shoulders, and I groaned as my hips protested any movement. I shifted slowly, sitting up to peer out the windows at the wide, glassy river and the mountains beyond. The sun had just crested the cliff of the river gorge to the east, creating a perfect mirrored reflection on the water's surface. It was a rare morning when the wind wasn't howling through The Gorge.

I opened my pack to retrieve a meal bar and ate it without tasting it then chased it with an 800-milligram tablet of ibuprofen. No matter how badly my body or my feelings hurt, I had to put some miles behind me. I had to get home.

I quickly traded my hiking boots for my lightweight trail runners and hit the road.

The first mile was rough, and I moved slowly but as my muscles warmed up and the anti-inflammatory kicked in, I started feeling better. It was a chilly but beautiful morning and despite having been robbed at gunpoint the day before, hope and determination smoldered within me. If anything, my experience in that town had lit a fire in my soul.

I was a survivor. I was going to make it. And once I was with my mom and brother again, we would make a plan to get back to the camp store together.

As the morning edged toward midday, an uneasy prickling crawled beneath my skin. It was faint at first, just a tickle at the base of my skull, then a whisper of pressure between my shoulder blades— the burning sensation of being watched. I tried to tell myself it was nothing, just nerves resurfacing after the trauma from the day before, but as I neared the middle of a long stretch of straight road, I chanced a glance over my shoulder.

In the distance, half-hidden by the dappled sunlight on the road—moving when I moved, pausing when I paused—a shape. No, a *person.* Maybe more than one. How long had they been following me? Did it really matter? I had the sneaking suspicion they had been sent by Smoker's Rasp, and they were after my pack. She had wanted Jim to take literally everything I carried and boot me out of town to die. The idea that she would send people out after me the very next day wasn't a far stretch.

Shit. I had to think.

A line from the survival book took up residence in my mind: *Don't lose your head. Develop a plan, then a back-up plan, and a third plan in case the back-up plan fails.*

I increased my pace, knowing another town was close, but it was still at least a mile off. The people following me couldn't have been more than fifteen minutes behind, and I couldn't let them know I had spotted them. I would bet good money that they were armed, and if they were as awful as Smoker's Rasp, I had no doubts about them taking a shot at me if I took off.

Up ahead, the road curved, a bend just sharp enough that it would hide me from sight for a moment. Once they couldn't see me, I could pick up my pace even more.

As my sneakers padded silently across the pavement, I weighed the worth of what I was carrying. The knife at my hip stayed, no question. In my pack, the meal bars and medication were light, the bottles of water and my boots were absolutely necessary, which meant the canned food would have to go. The road began to curve and after several paces, I chanced another glance behind me. Thankfully, I was hidden from view. I quickly repositioned my backpack across my chest and opened it. Rummaging past the bottles of water on top, I dug for the cans of food without slowing my pace. One by one, I tossed them into the drainage ditch beside the road while my heart rate climbed. My pack had lost around ten pounds. That would help.

Slinging my pack back onto my back, I cinched down the straps and broke into an easy jog. If the people were indeed about fifteen minutes behind me, I could almost double that lead if I ran. That would put me into the next town before they'd be able to set eyes on me again. If they decided to run as well? I didn't want to think about it.

Thanking myself for choosing to run sprints in front of the camp store every morning for the past month, I pushed myself into a flat run. My joints protested, but I grit through the discomfort, periodically glancing behind myself to be sure I was still out of sight.

When I neared the first buildings of the town of Whitecap, I knew in an instant that this town had suffered the same fate as Riverdale and Riverside. The acrid odor of damp ash still hung in the air, heavy and pungent. I slowed to a jog and turned left at the first street that looked passable.

I could only imagine that the people following me would bank on the fact that I was young and would simply keep following the main road because it was the easiest and most direct route I could take. If I could just shake them...but I didn't want to get myself lost in the process. I could head toward the river and walk on the other side of the embankment that the train tracks ran on. That would give me some cover and hopefully a clear path to follow all the way into Orchardville.

My plan solidified.

I continued down the residential street, hopping over debris, doing my best not to disturb anything around me. I had to stay calm. I had to think clearly.

The river shimmered in the distance, barely visible through the trees that lined the street of the neighborhood around me. A wide swath of completely exposed marshland occupied the space between the neighborhood and the train tracks. It was too far.

Shit.

I'd never make it to the other side of that marsh on foot, and if I kept going straight down the street I was on, I knew the people would see me.

My plan evaporated.

I had no time. No real choices. I had to hide. *Now.*

I ducked into an overgrown yard not far from the turn I had made. The house's raised porch, enclosed on all sides with lattice, had a crawl space underneath. Beside the worn steps sat a short, crooked gate propped halfway open by a rusty can of paint. That was my way in. Judging by the cobwebs and dry leafy debris crowding the edges of the house, no one had been there in ages. It may have even been empty before the electricity went out. I could barely make out the outline of a lawnmower in the darkness of the small storage area. It sat right beside the lattice and anything beyond it was hidden by shadow. I prayed that the storage would be too exposed for one of the creatures to seek refuge from the sun, then crept down into the shadowy space. It was empty, save for an unsettling number of spiders, so I squeezed myself in among the yard tools and cobwebs, trying to calm my breathing and racing heart.

Only minutes later, the sound of raised voices met my ear.

"Well, where the fuck did she go?" a deep voice cursed.

It was a good thing I had stopped; they would have caught me out in the open, for sure.

"I friggin' told you that she saw us on that straightaway," another male voice retorted. Both huffed, trying to catch their breath. "Maybe we should split up? If we come back without that backpack, Tanya's gonna be pissed."

So, Smoker's Rasp had a name. I *knew* it was her behind this. That *bitch.* Why couldn't she just leave me alone? I grit my teeth.

"Alright," the steady voice of a woman spoke this time. "You two head down that way. Craig, you're with me. We canvas, block by block. If you find her, take the backpack and fire two shots, we'll come to you."

There were four of them. *Four.* And it sounded like all of them were armed.

"Tanya doesn't care about the girl, but she wants whatever pills she has in that pack. I, however, am *ordering* you to let her go unharmed." The woman's voice was firm.

So, Jim *had* heard the pills rattling in my pack. He hadn't really been sorry at all, the asshole.

"What if she runs again?" the first voice I had heard spoke again. "It'd just be easier to shoot her."

Sweet Jesus, is it really so easy for some people to take a life?

"Then you take your lazy ass and you *run* after her. If you kill her, so help me, I will shoot out your fucking kneecaps and leave you in the dark for the creatures." The woman sounded deadly serious.

I wished I could see them. Their disembodied voices sent a sliver of ice down my spine, but after a moment, the sound of shuffling feet met my ears.

"Alright, fine. You don't have to be such a hard ass," the first man said sounding thoroughly chastised. "We'll let her go."

"Good, let's go."

Moments later, the woman and the man I assumed was Craig, stalked down the center of the road, rifles in hand, scanning the houses and yards to the left and right. I held my breath and tried to sink into the ground against the foundation of the house. Spiderwebs clung to my arms, face and hair and I barely resisted the urge to wipe them away. Just then, a faint crawling sensation tickled across the side of my neck and without thinking, I swat at it, flailing in the cramped space and knocking into the tines of a metal lawn rake.

Damn it.

A large spider hit the dirt and crawled beneath the dusty old lawnmower a moment before Craig walked into the yard.

"You good?" the woman called out to him.

"Thought I heard something."

"Alright, make it quick."

I held my breath and hoped he wouldn't be able to hear my frantic heartbeat. Worn leather boots crunched over the dead debris heading right toward my hiding place. Just then, another spider tickled across my hand, but I managed to keep still, my fingers digging into the dirt below me, stomach clenching.

Craig's boots paused just on the other side of the lattice, not five feet from my face. I went rigid, not even daring to breathe, eyes clenched shut, wishing I could cloak myself in invisibility like the glow had done to the camp store.

A shift. A breath. Boots scuffing against dead leaves. Waiting. He was waiting.

Please, just keep moving. Please.

After what felt like an eternity, he continued on, moving along the side of the house before leaving the yard and continuing down the street, the sound of his boots fading with every step. Breath left my lungs in a whoosh, and I tried to rid myself of spiderwebs and creepy-crawlies without having a complete meltdown.

Don't lose your head.

My body wanted to crawl out from under the porch and run in the opposite direction, but I knew that I needed to wait. I had no idea which way they had gone. My best bet was to stay put and wait them out. Just me and the spiders.

The minutes crawled by and slowly melted into hours. What I could see of the sky was beginning to glow with the coming sunset and I still hadn't seen or heard any of the people again. I was going to have to make my move. I either needed to find a place to hide for the night in this town, or I needed to try and put as much distance between myself and the town as I could before nightfall...and I only had a couple of hours before dusk.

With a determined grunt, I slowly crept out from under the old porch and listened hard. The songs of birds and the wind rippling through the trees were the only sounds I could make out, so I hunched through some bushes and peered around the side of the house.

The road looked clear, so I scurried across the street and through another yard, hopping over a low chain link fence between two backyards, and silently made my way to the front corner of another house. Checking that all was clear again, I jogged as quietly as possible down the sidewalk trying to avoid the old bloodstains that littered the concrete. I passed through several neighborhoods this way and when I finally made it to the other side of town, I worked my way through a small patch of trees to the edge of the marshy area.

The train tracks were much closer. A short gravel road and parking lot that bordered the edge of the protected marsh was littered with abandoned cars, while an unpaved nature trail ran through the marsh and toward the river where it crossed over the railroad tracks and continued for miles near the water's edge.

I had never walked this particular section of the waterfront trail, but I did know that it ran all the way into downtown Orchardville, joining with the main Waterfront Park walking path just over two miles from my house. It was a slightly different route than I had planned on taking to begin with, but it would still take me in the general direction that I needed to go. Plus, the walking path wound through some of the richest neighborhoods in all of Orchardville. Some of the houses there even had their own private river access and boat dock.

Following the train tracks would take me to within a quarter mile of my house, but there may not be anywhere for me to take cover in the dark...besides up a tree. There would surely be plenty of abandoned cars in the neighborhoods along the walking path route for me to overnight in though.

I stood in indecision for a short moment. No matter which route I chose, I needed to get to the other side of the train tracks, and there was still a large open area and parking lot I needed to get through. I checked my surroundings again and seeing nothing of note, I jogged straight toward the parking lot and paused between two cars, crouching low and listening hard. I wound my way between cars to the edge of the lot then took another good look around me. No one was heading my direction; all I had to do was sprint the hundred or so yards to the train tracks and I was home free. I edged around the side of an old pick-up truck and readied myself for the run. I could make it.

Suddenly, something grabbed my ankle, yanking me off my feet. I hit the ground with a grunt, but before I could scream, a large hand clapped over my mouth and dragged me under the truck. Panic surged within me, I grunted, kicked, and flailed like a wild animal caught in a trap. My elbow slammed into the gut of my captor and my heel found a shin or a knee. He muttered curses and I fought like my life depended on it.

"Hush, girl," his hard voice commanded in a loud whisper, "And be still."

No. No it couldn't be. My breath stilled, heart hammering in my chest, every muscle in my body locking tight.

I *knew* that voice.

"Joanne and Craig are on the other side of the train tracks waiting for you," he murmured into my ear. Calm. Steady. Safe. "I'm going to let you go but we've gotta go back the way you came. Find a place to hide for the night."

My throat clenched, relief surging through me so fast it hurt. I nodded against the hand covering my mouth. His grip on me loosened and I craned my head around to stare right into Dan's kind face.

He was *alive.*

18

Second Chances

"**S**ORRY ABOUT THE BRUISES." I said sheepishly as Dan and I settled into the corner of an old auto shop building to wait out the dark hours. The building was made of cinderblocks and steel, the doors were heavy and easily barricaded, and there were many cars inside to bed down in.

He shot me a crooked smile as he sat down and leaned back against the wall, "You've got some sharp elbows, Girl. And I accept the bruises," he paused, running a hand through his hair. His face and voice turned serious, "I still can't believe you're alive. I thought I was seeing a ghost when Jim was walking you out of town."

"You're telling me," I couldn't keep the excited tone out of my voice. Dan looked like he was equal parts relieved and upset, but I continued. "When I found that bottle of juice and bag of jerky next to a puddle of blood, I just knew something horrible had happened to you and when I got to the camp store and it was empty...that meant you had to be dead."

He nodded solemnly.

"But you're not. You're ok," I continued. "More than ok, seems like." I gave him a good once over. He looked like he'd lost ten years and gained ten pounds of muscle at least. Even his hair was darker and thicker. "Have you been working out or something?" I cocked an eyebrow at him.

"It's a long story," he sighed. "But I'd rather hear about how you managed to survive out there. How did you make it to the camp store?"

Why was he dodging the question? I squinted at him, making a mental note to press him about it another time, then continued, "Remember when I told you that I had a bad feeling?"

He cringed and squeezed his eyes shut. "All too well."

Something was definitely not right with him, but I figured I should keep talking.

"Well, I just got back in the Jeep and stayed there, scared half to death for three days," I said slowly. "I got lucky and the day I ran out of food, the sun came out. So, I walked to the camp store, climbed through a bedroom window, and set up shop." I gave him the quick version. "But you're not getting out of telling me what happened to you. Spill it, man."

I could tell he didn't really want to talk about it, but I'd just spent about six weeks completely alone. I needed to hear someone other than myself (or someone who wanted to rob or kill me) talk for a while. And since I had been certain that Dan was dead, it was an extra special treat to hear his voice.

"Well," he sighed, "I don't really know where to begin."

I studied him while his gaze bounced around the shop seeming to want to land anywhere but on me. He looked tired or stressed, and he definitely seemed unsure, which gave me pause. Dan had been so confident when we'd met the day the grid went down but now—now he was struggling for words, hedging around my questions and wouldn't even look at me.

"Dan. Are you alright?" I asked, truly worried for him.

It was a while before he answered. "No. No, I'm not alright." His eyes went to the floor and stayed there.

I didn't know what to say, so I let his words hang in the silent, chilly air. He fidgeted a bit, and I could almost see the wheels turning in his head as he tried to start talking, hesitating twice before he was able to force a few words out.

"I've been having recurring nightmares since I got back home. You're in them. And you die—killed by a one-eyed darkling spawn. And it's my fault."

Oh, no.

He sighed and then his words tumbled out in a rush, "I made a choice, to leave you up there. Not just once but twice. I walked away from you in the forest, completely dismissing your concern. I see that concern over and over again in my dreams, and I just walked away. And then, after the spawn attacked me and I was healed, Erik and Alma told me that because I left you, you were already dead. I wanted to go back the next day to get you but—" His voice faltered and he cleared his throat before starting again, "They were heading down the mountain, and they knew so much about the darkling and what was going on in general...even though they said you were dead, I had to believe that you would survive, so Erik left that bedroom window unlocked on the off chance that you would live through the rainy days. And I left with them. I could have stayed but I was so worried about my family that I left you a second time, even when I knew those creatures were out there."

He finally looked at me then, soul-crushing guilt lined his face and watery eyes. I scooted closer to him and gingerly took one of his broad hands in both of my own. "I'm alive. I've never even gotten a good look at one of those things. I've been warm and fed and completely safe up at the camp store. You really did the only thing you could have done. I would have done the same in your position." Dan shrugged and shook his head, guilt rolling off of him in waves. I squeezed his hand tighter. "Dan. I'm gonna need you to stop kicking yourself over this. I need the funny, strong, self-assured Dan that I met in the forest to help me out again."

He snorted, "You sound like my wife."

"Well, your wife must be a smart lady then," I said, canting my head to one side and smiling at him. "I think things happened just as they were meant to." I swung his hand side to side like I had done as a little girl with my own father before he left us. Tears stung my eyes as I realized what I was doing. How I was feeling. "Ya know, your family is so lucky to have you. I wish I knew what it was like to have a dad that would literally fight monsters to keep me safe." I paused and thought about what I had just said. "I guess I sort of do now, though."

Tears were rolling freely down Dan's cheeks, and he scrubbed them away with his free hand. I wasn't ready to let go of the one I was holding yet.

"I'm so sorry, Amber."

"There is nothing to apologize for," I told him, truly meaning the statement down to my bones.

He pulled me into a quick, awkward hug and I squeezed him around the waist.

"I don't know why I keep getting all these second chances," he whispered, his chin resting on the top of my head for a moment before he pulled away.

"What do you mean?"

"Well, I've lived through a lot; when I came home from overseas, my wife forced me to not give up on myself. Then I survived the darkling spawn attack, and now you forgive me for abandoning you. I don't deserve it," he said.

"Everyone deserves a second chance, Dan," I said, my voice low and firm. "Heck, my mom would say that the universe is saving you for something great. I'd say she would be correct."

Dan let out a noncommittal huff, "Maybe."

I could tell that it was going to take much longer than a five-minute conversation for Dan to really believe me, but he seemed to be on his way toward forgiving himself. "Now, you've gotta tell me about what happened on your way to the camp store...and what do you call the creatures? Darkling spawn?" I prompted again.

Dan began reluctantly at first, but once he started talking, the words just poured out of him...and his storytelling abilities amazed me. He painted vivid pictures with his words and when he finished his account of everything that happened at the camp store, many of my questions about the creatures were answered and I felt like I knew Eric and Alma almost as well as he did.

"On the way down the mountain, Alma filled me in on what they thought was going on. They wouldn't give me all the details, only just enough to stay alive," Dan said, sounding a bit irritated and slightly skeptical. "Everything they did tell me has checked out though, plus whatever that spawn poison remedy was, it turned me into a staunch believer." He looked down at his lap then back to me. "There is no other explanation."

I sat for a moment and let everything he had shared with me sink in. The story Dan told did seem far-fetched, but after staying at the camp store all those weeks, feeling the energy of The Glow—er, Light Magic, as Erik and Alma had called it, I could no more doubt the truth of his story than I could my own experience; especially after watching the camp store *disappear* when I left. And I could plainly see the physical changes in Dan. He looked like a man in his early thirties that hit the gym on a regular basis, not the beer-bellied dad pushing fifty years old that I had first met on the forestry road all those weeks ago. I had to believe him.

"Erik and Alma said that they were going to try and make it to some place called The Snow Forest to see if the Aeon were rising again and that they were going to fight The Darkness alongside them," Dan said, leaning over to rummage through his pack. What he showed me nearly took my breath. Two silvery daggers with ornate, clear moonstone hilts flashed in the dim lamp light. "Erik told me that these were made in the palace forge at the center of The Snow Forest." Dan held one out to me, hilt first.

"My God," I breathed as I held the dagger. "It's like something out of a faerie tale."

"Goddess," Dan corrected with a smile. "That's exactly what I thought. You've met Erik and Alma before, right?"

"Erik. Super tall. Devastatingly handsome. Makes the best milkshakes in the world."

Dan barked out a laugh, "I suppose that would describe him."

My mouth quirked into a sly smile. "Oh, I made sure I saw him every time I went to the camp store. I didn't know his name or anything, but I did spend close to a hundred bucks on milkshakes last summer just so I could look at him." He had to be the most perfect specimen of a man I'd ever seen in my life. "And I chatted with Alma once when she was at the register. You know, I told her that if the world ever ended that I would go straight to their store just so I could have one last huckleberry milkshake before I died." I palmed my face and had to laugh at the sheer irony of it all.

Dan was wheezing with a quiet, choking sort of laughter, eyes squinted shut.

"It's ridiculously unfair how good looking they both are," I said as I handed the dagger back to Dan. "Erik winked at me once and I forgot how to talk." I sighed at the memory. "And I always thought they should both be working as cover models instead of running an ancient store in the middle of nowhere."

"I'm convinced that they aren't human," Dan said, still chuckling lightly.

"Well, they are inhumanly beautiful, so I can see that," I said jokingly as I glanced back at Dan's face. He was definitely *not* joking. "Oh, shit, you're *serious?*"

"When you add it all up, it's the only thing that makes sense."

"So, they came from outer space or something?" I asked, trying not to sound skeptical and failing.

"No, I think they've been around for a very long time. Like earth has an ancient past that humans don't know about...or maybe it has been deliberately suppressed? Alma kept calling me Seed Child and referring to people as Hume, not human. That alone implies that she views herself as different from us," Dan said.

I could tell he'd had this discussion with himself many times over, so I sat quietly and motioned for him to continue.

"Erik also mentioned 'Goddess-given gifts' that they both possess, and when I talked to him—*really* talked to him—a strange energy ran through me. I'm telling you, he's seen some shit. He might look a certain age, but he felt ancient to me." Dan tapped fingers to his chest, right over his heart, "In here."

I'd never really seen past Erik's good looks, but for some reason I could not explain, I believed Dan. I believed him on a soul deep level. "Well, they did say that their Goddess is living and breathing, here on this planet, right?"

"Yes, *and* they called her 'Creation', like the Goddess of Creation. She created all living things, so I suppose that she is our Goddess too, we just didn't know about her." He leaned toward me. "It's like they've been engaged in an eons long battle with the darkling. They knew just how to kill them and how to cure their poison. They knew their habits and typical behaviors. And they even knew exactly where to go to be of service. There is something big going on here. Something really big."

"Do you think," I started and then paused. This was going to sound absolutely insane. *Oh, screw it.* "Do you think the stories about the Yellowstone attacks and that 'Angel' from last summer are related to this somehow?"

"I think its *all* connected, girl. We just have to live long enough to figure it out." He leaned back against the wall again and closed his eyes.

I did the same, finding my body heavy. I stretched and yawned, scooting a little lower and reached into my pack. I removed a few items, digging down towards my journal. When I pulled it and my pen out, Dan was looking at my stash of things, head still resting on the wall.

"You found my old knife," he said with a tired, half smile.

"This is actually yours?" I held the knife up. No wonder I kept getting the feeling it was something Dan would carry.

He closed his eyes again and nodded. "I killed the spawn that attacked me with it. Left it in the basement when Erik gave me the daggers. It suits you." His eyes flew open, and he bolted forward. "Did you see my writing on the weight bench?"

"That was you too?" I laughed. "You couldn't have written me a note and left it on the kitchen table or something?"

A sheepish smile crossed his face. "Yeah, that probably would have been best, but in my defense, I had been attacked, almost died, was brought back from the brink, *and* I was having some *really* strange feelings after drinking that remedy. I wasn't thinking clearly, not by a long shot."

"I set a storage bin down on the bench and smudged the center of the words away before I even realized that they were there. Didn't have a clue what it said." I shook my head at him. "You are such a man-brain." I reached over and jostled his shoulder.

He smiled then pointed his chin at my journal. "Whatcha got there?"

"A journal. I found it in the camp store. Been trying to write my feelings...and things I think might be important."

Dan grunted. "Are you gonna put all this in there?"

"Yeah, and a few other things."

"Would you write something for me?" he asked.

That's an odd request. "Uh...sure. What do you want me to write?"

"It's something that Erik told me right before he and Alma left. He told it to me in secret, and it keeps playing over and over in my head like a movie. I remember exactly what he said. Verbatim. It's...bizarre." Dan made a face I couldn't interpret.

"Alright, let's hear it," I said, pen in hand, ready to write.

Keep this knowledge close and guard it from the unsavory hume in your community. I have encountered several and I'm certain that you will know who they are soon enough. Erik breathed deep and looked toward the high clouds before beginning again. *I'm afraid your world is about to get very dark, my friend.*

"What do you mean?" Dan asked.

Just be silent and listen. Hear me and remember these words. Erik said, grimly. *My family and I have been waiting for hundreds of years for this day to come. We are spread thin all over the globe but The Dark One—The Dark Mother,* he corrected with an absent shake of his head, *was imprisoned on this continent, so most of us have been waiting here.*

"What—who is The Dark Mother?" Dan interrupted. Erik placed a firm hand on his shoulder and looked deep into Dan's eyes.

Listen. Quickly. There was something ancient in the way he said it, something that pulled rank—sharp, authoritative, and unshakable. Dan shut his mouth and listened. *The camp store is an Outpost and is protected by The Light. The darkling and their spawn cannot penetrate the dome of Light Magic; nothing possessed by The Dark Mother's taint can. This entire situation will deteriorate in the coming months. Spawn will spread like wildfire. The animals and hume that survive their bite will join their ranks. You will see this happen at greater and greater frequencies. It nearly happened to you already.*

Dan nodded and continued listening, committing all of Erik's words to memory.

In time, your community will also begin to unravel. Only the true of heart and mind can survive in times like these. The weak-minded will fall apart at the seams. Before that happens, if you can, take your family and go back to the camp store. The journey could be extremely dangerous so be sure to be prepared. You are one of the good ones, Dan. Our sparks commune. You know that I speak the truth.

Dan nodded solemnly as a tiny piece of his soul warmed. Erik nodded back with a knowing smile and shook Dan's hand.

Be safe and walk in light and truth, my friend. Until we meet again.

"Well, that's frikkin' heavy," I said as gooseflesh prickled my skin.

"And I can't get it out of my head." Dan rubbed his temples.

"Erik never told you who or what The Dark Mother is?" I asked.

"No," Dan huffed, "But I'm guessing that she is the antithesis of The Light Mother."

I nodded. "That makes sense. I mean, if The Light Mother is the Goddess of Creation, then The Dark Mother would be, what? The Goddess of Destruction or Chaos maybe?"

"I've been trying to fully wrap my mind around it since they told me. It's hard to change a lifetime of assumptions and habits when it comes to a higher power, but if you compare what's going on to the Bible, I think we've been living through the Revelations. The Four Horsemen of the Apocalypse have arrived. The Dark Mother being Death and the darkling spawn, The Hosts of Hell."

I grimaced, "I dunno...that's a *lot*, Dan. Especially for someone like me who has never set a foot in a church for a Sunday service. I mean, Christianity is woven into our culture, but I've never read the Bible and I'm nowhere *near* a believer."

Dan raised his brows, "But you definitely believe what's going on around us right now?"

"Yeah, obviously. We're living it."

"Then maybe," Dan quirked a smile, "The reason you didn't believe before is because—"

I suddenly felt dizzy, my world spinning as my mind, no, my whole self, was finally understanding a truth I had never even considered.

"—Somewhere deep down, I knew the truth had been twisted to suit the needs of the tyrannical leaders who used religious texts for fear and control." I interrupted him as my heart hit the pit of my stomach, words flowing from my mind to my mouth as if they had been put there by someone else. But as I sat with the buzzy feeling filling my body, I knew, beyond the shadow of a doubt, that he had just spoken truth. That all of it was real.

Holy Shit, this *was* big. *Huge* even. Did the leaders of all the churches know the truth, choosing to perpetuate the lie? Or were they kept in the dark just like the rest of the masses? Religion in general drove so much conflict. Conflict drove wars. Wars, whether or not people called them Holy Wars, kept people living in fear. Wars even pushed the world economy. And most of the world's leaders were corrupt old men, unwilling to give up control.

My mind raced to all the 'pseudo scientists' and conspiracy theorists who believed with all their souls that some sort of cataclysmic event nearly wiped the human race off the planet thousands of years ago; to the people that believed in ancient aliens and a super advanced global civilization. And what about the pyramids and the truly ancient stone structures and ruins all across the world?

Machu Picchu. The Sphinx. The Eye of the Sahara. Göbekli Tepe.

Shit, the burning of the Library of Alexandria!? What ancient knowledge could have been preserved there? Could it have held unequivocal proof that the rulers, who won the old wars and wrote the histories, were *liars?* That they made sure only texts that furthered their agenda survived? Could this have happened more than once?

"Oh, my God—er, Goddess," I breathed.

Dan's small smile grew. I must have looked like a rabbit in the headlights because he said, "Emily got the same look when I told her that."

"We really are living through another cataclysm, aren't we?" I breathed, "And Erik and Alma—the people they know—they have the tools to survive it."

"Exactly. It was Erik that showed us how to barricade parts of the town from the darkling spawn," Dan nodded. "But it was all Tanya and Jim's idea to rob the humans that passed through."

He shook his head. "Erik warned me about the unsavory people in the community." Dan sighed and ran a hand through his hair again. "But they were my friends and neighbors...I thought they were good people, I just couldn't believe him. I should have. He tried to tell me—showed me all the evidence—but I didn't want to see it. Now, no one in the community is willing to stand up to Jim and Tanya. They've organized and have enforcers like Joanne and Craig to do their dirty work." His shoulders slumped. "I might have to be the one to make a stand come tomorrow."

At his words, my mind settled back to our immediate issue. "What makes you say that?" My brows knit together.

"As soon as I saw you, I wanted to head out of town to give you a hand, but Jim wasn't letting anybody out. That evening, I went to the tavern where they meet and overheard Joanne talking to Craig and Bruce about being sent to recover your pack. I volunteered to go with them. They were all too happy to bring me into the fold since

I'd been resistant when they'd first approached me about it weeks ago."

"So, what does that have to do with you standing up to Jim and Tanya?" I shrugged. "You could just sneak your family out when you get back and then head up to the camp store. Let the community unravel without you being there."

Dan took in a heavy breath. "I killed Bruce."

My chin hit the concrete floor. "You what—? Wait, who's Bruce?"

"We spotted you crossing a street. You were a couple blocks down and didn't see us through the bushes. I moved out to follow you, but he shoved me back and lifted his rifle. I—I didn't even think. The dagger was in my hand and then he was on the ground, choking to death on his own blood." Dan gritted his teeth and swallowed hard. "I couldn't let him just—not after—"

I could feel the blood draining from my face. Bruce had to have been the one that wanted to kill me from the get-go. "Oh, shit."

"He was trash—no conscience at all, and I will never regret ending his life to save yours, but I—" He leaned toward me and reached out but hesitated. His mouth turned down, eyes pleading, "Please don't be afraid of me now."

Without realizing it, I had leaned back and scooted farther away from him. "Just gimme a minute." I raised a hand and tried to keep my voice neutral as I looked inwardly and tried to justify Dan's actions. I was sitting right beside a literal *murderer*...had hugged and cried with him. But was it still murder if he'd killed to protect the life of an innocent? Could I just let something like that go?

After a long moment Dan spoke again, his voice just above a whisper, "Well, now you see my predicament." He leaned back against the wall. "When Craig and Joanne get back, they're going to report that they lost you, the backpack, and the other half of their team. Then, when I come waltzing back into town alone, without you or your pack, and without Bruce, they're gonna put two and two together."

My mind reeled then skidded to a halt. You know what? To Hell with Bruce. To Hell with *all* those people. Dan's wife and kid were still in that town. Sure, I didn't know them, but if they were important to Dan, then they were important to me. Would those horrible people do something to them in retaliation? What would they do to Dan? The thought turned my stomach.

"Take my pack!" I blurted. "I just need some water and a couple meal bars to make it home; it's not far at all." My mind whirled, "Make up a story about how Bruce died. You took my pack and let me go. Or tell them that you killed me and left my body for the darkling spawn."

Relief spread across Dan's face, but it was still lined with concern. "I wish it was that simple."

"Well, it can be. It is. It has to be!" I climbed to my feet and began pacing in the dim space. "You stuck your neck out for me, and you don't even really know me, the least I can do is try and..." I trailed off. No matter which way I looked at the situation, I couldn't figure out a good plan. "We can figure this out. I know we can. Even if we have to stay up all night."

Dan looked doubtful but nodded.

"Tell me everything you know about Tanya and Jim."

The next morning, I jostled Dan awake. "Wakey-wakey, sleepy-doo. Sun's coming up."

He grunted and started to roll back over but then his eyes flew open. "Shit, what time is it?"

"Not a clue but the sky is getting brighter. It's full of horsetail clouds though. Bad weather is probably coming soon."

He sat up, bleary-eyed and rubbed his face. "Where'd ya learn that?"

"The Farmer's Almanac." I smiled in the muted light and rubbed the sleep out of my eyes. We were up for hours past dark talking and trying to figure out what to do. When we finally laid down to sleep, we were no closer to a solid plan than we had been hours before. We were both just going to have to wing it. The one thing we did decide on though was that Dan was taking my pack back to Tanya.

We silently gathered our things and stepped out into the early morning light.

"Well, this is it," I said as I handed him my pack. It was much lighter than it had been the day before, most of its contents transferred into Dan's pack, which he held out towards me. "I hope she's happy with a few anti-inflammatories and some cephalexin."

"I hope so too. And I'll look in the ditch for those cans of food you dumped." He shot me a smile that didn't quite reach his eyes.

I nodded. "We're gonna make it. We have to," I said as I slung his backpack over my shoulders and cinched the straps down. I looked up at him.

"C'mere, bring it in." He opened his arms wide.

I crinkled my nose, "You're not going all soft on me now, are ya?"

He laughed and dragged me into a bone-crushing hug. "You're a damn sight tougher than you look, girl. Tougher than I ever thought you could be back up on that mountain."

All I could do was sigh. I suppose I had toughened up a bit after being on my own for so long. "We're both tough. And smart. And good people. That's why we're gonna survive."

"Your mom raised you right. I hope you find her soon," Dan said. "What part of Orchardville did you say you lived in again?"

"How familiar are you with the southeast side of town?" I asked, trying to decide how specific I could be.

"I know it like the back of my hand."

"We're in the Kingfisher Terrace neighborhood just a couple of blocks west of the main entrance near the corner of Robin Avenue and Middleton," I said, tucking a stray hair behind my ear.

"I know exactly where that's at. You're not too far from an old coworker of mine," he said, then added absently, "I wonder if he's still around?" He made a noncommittal sound in his throat then stepped back and placed a heavy hand on my shoulder. "Don't forget, if you find yourself followed again, you can start a false trail or double back,"

I nodded and went over the particulars of how to do that in my mind. He'd also told me how to cover my tracks and tie myself into a tree so I could sleep without worrying about falling.

"Keep that knife sharp and on your belt, and I know I don't have to say it but I'm going to anyway," he paused, "Take care of yourself, girl." A broad, genuine smile split his handsome face, and I noticed for the first time that he had a dimple on his left cheek. It faintly reminded me of someone, but I couldn't place it.

"You too, Dan." I smiled and turned to walk away. "I can't wait to meet your family up at the camp store," I said over my shoulder. "I left the back door unlocked."

"We'll see you there. Walk in Light and Truth." Dan raised a hand, and we parted ways.

As I strode away from that empty town, I couldn't help but feel a deep connection with Dan. If the world had kept going as it had been, Dan and I would have never met. We would have gone on living our lives oblivious to the others presence in the world, but after spending less than twenty-four hours with him, I couldn't imagine life without Dan in it. He really was a good dude...even if he was a complete man-brain.

19

No Safe Harbor

AS I MADE MY WAY DUE WEST on the cluttered roadway, walking around an ever-increasing number of abandoned vehicles, a large highway sign loomed in the distance. The road had gradually widened, and I came upon the first of three large roundabouts I would encounter before the two-lane road morphed into a six-lane freeway.

As I approached the sign, a riot of butterflies took flight in my stomach. Downtown Orchardville was only nine miles away, but the sign had been defaced. Large, red, spray-painted eyes glowered down at me. Beneath the eyes, in bold, black letters, the word 'DEADVILLE' had been painted directly over Orchardville, and below that, 'KEEP OUT!'. The paint had dripped in several places giving the entire sign a decidedly sinister look.

Sinister sign be damned. I kept walking.

Past the third roundabout, the train tracks ran close to the highway. Those same tracks ran along the edge of my neighborhood then continued into downtown Orchardville, where they split to run directly north-south along the interstate between Portland and Seattle. I wondered what the big cities might have looked like as I made my way through an empty lot and toward the tracks. I would likely never know and was curiously okay with that fact. If the outskirts of Orchardville were any indication as to how every city had fared, which was to say the entire area looked like it had been ransacked...I shook my head. I didn't even want to think about it. I had to stay positive. But as I took in the buildings around me and the eerie silence that permeated the area, a seed of doubt took root in my gut.

The sweet quiet of the mountains was one thing, but when that same quiet blanketed what should have been a bustling suburban city, the effect was beyond unnerving. My scalp prickled as I stepped onto the railroad tracks. A tunnel of trees lay ahead of me, the dappled sunlight shining on the steel rails. I glanced up at the sky taking note of the high, wispy clouds moving slowly across the otherwise blue expanse. They were thicker toward the west. I had to make it home tonight.

I pushed myself to a jog, keeping an eye on my feet to make sure each step I took landed on the wooden railroad ties. The chortling of the birds and the air passing in and out of my lungs were the only things I could hear. My feet ate up the miles and even as my lungs burned, I pushed myself forward. I was suddenly reminded of DJ and quickly came to the conclusion that he had to have been nuts to do this for fun. At the same time, I could understand why he would have pushed himself to run for miles every day. Every breath that burned through my lungs let me know I was alive, and the pain in my limbs at every stride told me that I was one step closer to where I needed to be.

The forest began to thin as I neared the edge of my neighborhood on the southeast side of Orchardville, and I could make out large houses through the green space between the train tracks and the road. In the distance, a wide-open space caught my eye. That had to be the intersection with the road that led straight toward the entrance to my neighborhood. My heart soared. I frikkin' made it. I was so close I could almost smell the comforting scents of home—candles, lemon scented floor cleaner, and Mom's perfume. I slowed to a walk to catch my breath and pulled a bottle of water out of the pack Dan gave me. The water was warm but still refreshing after running for so long. Sunset had warmed the cool blue of the sky, transforming the gathering clouds to the west into a riot of color. I suddenly wished I had brought my camera with me instead of leaving it safe in my room at the camp store. I let my heart take a picture instead.

If I hadn't been walking, I may not have heard the sound of a vehicle approaching the railroad crossing until it was too late. Without a second thought, I dove off the train tracks, the coarse gravel crunching beneath my trail runners as I sprinted for the green space to my right. Just as I settled down into the bushes, an ancient looking pickup truck with a lumber rack on top rumbled slowly through the railroad crossing.

A man, clad in dark clothing with a rifle aimed over the cab, stood in the bed of the truck, while three more armed individuals covered the left, right and rear. It rolled to a stop on the tracks, and I could hear the driver speaking to the people in the back but was too far away to make out their words. The truck rolled forward before completing a three-point turn, heading back in the direction it had come from. The same direction that I needed to go.

Damn it.

The truck quickly made a right-hand turn, heading down the street that ran along the other side of the green space I was crouching in. I stayed low and motionless, barely daring to breathe as I listened to the truck rumble away. As the sound of the motor faded into the distance, I breathed a sigh of relief and slowly crept through the green space to the edge of the road. I knelt in the bushes for a long while just listening and trying to muster the courage to cross the narrow road.

The houses that bordered it had been built decades before the cookie cutter homes of my neighborhood had popped up. The yards were large and un-fenced with plenty of native vegetation for me to hide in should I need to, but the sun was going down, and although most of these houses appeared to be abandoned, I couldn't be sure any of them would be safe to overnight in.

As I took a closer look at the few I could see clearly, I noticed spray painted markings near the front doors or on the garages if one was present. The houses that had an "X" painted on them also had the front door boarded up. That had to mean they were empty, right? Or did it mean that there was something dangerous trapped inside? As I crouched in the undergrowth puzzling over the markings, I heard a twig snap across the street and to my left. I stayed as low as possible while trying to get a look at what could have made the sound.

Slowly, almost so slowly I thought my eyes were playing tricks on me, a person emerged from the bushes near to where I thought the snapping sound had come from. Judging by the width of the shoulders, they had to be male. His head was covered by a stocking cap and his face was obscured by safety glasses and what appeared to be a neck gaiter pulled up over his nose and mouth. His clothes were dark in color, close-fitting, and gloved hands grasped a handgun while a rifle hung by a strap at his back.

What the heck could he be looking for?

I glanced around myself quickly and took a slow breath. About fifty yards up the street to my right, another figure stalked up out of the greenery. This man appeared to be fully outfitted in the same manner as the first. I gently—*silently*—eased myself back into the foliage as the two figures acknowledged one another. One made some hand signals, gesturing to the green space where I was hiding.

A cold chill ran down my back and I suppressed a shudder. They were looking for *me*. And they definitely couldn't have been from Dan's town. These people came off as disciplined in a way that Joanne and her cronies couldn't ever dream of matching. Their movements reminded me of special ops soldiers in movies. What I could see of their gear didn't look as tactical, they weren't wearing helmets or body armor and the like, but their smooth, crouched walk and the way they held the weapons sure fit the bill.

My heart pounded in my ears as I looked up through the canopy of trees at the darkening sky. Dusk was fully upon us. I was so close to home and yet I could have been a million miles away. The two figures slipped off the road and into the green space—one distantly to my right, the other closer to my left. The quiet, rasping sound of their movement through the bushes blended almost perfectly with the hiss of the wind through the trees. What was it about a lone female traveling that seemed to bring out the hounds?

I swallowed the panic rising in my throat. They were either murderous, thieving, or another 'unsavory type' I didn't want to think about. Either way, I knew it would be disastrous if they caught me.

If I moved toward the road they would see me. I could hear them getting closer with every step. I huddled down beside a decomposing, mossy log, the ground curiously soft beneath me.

Lower, I had to get lower. As quietly as I could manage, I shimmied beneath a clump of sword ferns and fallen limbs and tried to control my ragged breathing. Even if I managed to evade capture or death by these people, it was almost dark! And night falls fastest under the trees. At some point, the men would have to head to safety, but where would that leave me then? Stuck in the green space. Less than half a mile from my home. In the dark. Surrounded by red-eyed monsters.

I understood then why the highway sign had been defaced, calling the city 'Deadville' instead of Orchardville. Either the darkling or the humans that were still surviving would make short work of anyone making their way through town.

Jim had been right all along.

Shit.

The clouds in the sky, once painted bright orange and pink by the setting sun, were growing dimmer by the second, but in the green space, it was already nearly as dark as night. I opened my eyes wide, trying to see through the shadows while listening to the sounds of footsteps growing nearer.

Something moved below me, the slightest shift in the ground and I reasoned it away. It was only a stick sinking into the soft ground. Maybe I'd just laid down on top of a mole hill or something? I needed to be still. Silent. But the ground moved again.

What the—

A low, guttural growl rumbled the soil directly beneath me. My heart lodged in my throat. I couldn't breathe. If I had been afraid of the men just moments ago, the sound of that growl rocketed me straight into abject terror. The loose, damp soil shifted below me, and I threw myself to the side just as the stench of death and sulfur permeated the air around me.

Jesus Christ, they sleep in the ground!

Glowing red eyes blinked up from the depths then focused, pinning me where I lay. The darkling spawn slowly rose to its full height, towering over me, shaking the loose soil from its patchy fur and black skin. Its lips drew back from a dog-like snout to reveal large, yellowed teeth as it took a single prowling step toward me.

This was it. This was how my life ended. After I'd come so far. Not even a ten-minute walk from my front door. I'd never see my mom or brother again.

"Holy fuck!" a male voice barked to my left a split second before the gun he held broke the near silence with a resounding crack.

I clenched my eyes shut as darkling blood rained down on me. The creature launched itself over my prone form, like the bullet wound was nothing more than a bug bite and plowed into the man with the gun. He didn't even have the chance to scream before the creature tore his throat out.

In the chaos of the attack, I scrambled to my feet and sprinted toward the road, hopping ferns and bushes as I went, the sloppy sounds of rending flesh and cracking bone fading behind me. More shots sounded in the green space and as I flailed out of the trees, tripping and falling into the shallow ditch at the road's edge, the old pickup truck came barreling down the road toward me. I half ran-half stumbled across the street and toward a house with an ancient maple tree standing sentinel at the corner of the yard. Its branches spread wide, reaching toward the roof.

The truck skid to a stop behind me and I glanced back to see the two remaining gunmen leap from the vehicle and charge into the bushes. Apparently, they were more worried about their comrades than me.

I lurched to my feet and sprinted to the tree. The nearest branch was at least twelve feet above my head. *Damn it!* I wheeled around as an unearthly screech erupted from the trees behind me, followed by male screams and more gunfire. The man in the truck yelled into the green space, but I couldn't understand what he was saying. How was I ever going to get up into the tree? My eyes shot around the yard in a panic.

The screeching and screaming continued across the street as I ran to the front door of the house and tried the handle. Locked.

Shit.

I turned and climbed up onto the railing of the front porch then grasped the rain gutter. With a strength I didn't know I possessed, I pushed off the railing with my feet and pulled myself up. My chin crested the gutter, and I grunted, throwing an elbow up into the roof. My feet dangled and I kicked and shimmied for all I was worth.

The gutter buckled, separating from the roof.

Shit.

Across the street, the screaming had died, and an unearthly hiss floated from the trees. The driver of the truck put the pedal to the metal, tires squealing away from the scene and around a corner. Adrenaline surging like acid in my veins, I struggled for purchase on the roof, the gutter groaning beneath my weight, then finally, *blessedly,* I scrambled up onto the first story roof. Above me were what looked like three, short attic windows. Maybe I could crawl all the way to the top and hide on the other side of the roof? Or maybe a window would be unlocked?

Panting, I scurried on hands and feet to the first window. Locked. The second window. Also locked.

Just then a howl cut the air, and I whipped my head around to see the darkling spawn emerge from the shadowy depths of the green space and step onto the road. It scented the air a moment before its glowing red eyes zeroed in on me.

Shit!

Every muscle in my body locked up, frozen in terror. I couldn't breathe. The creature took two smooth steps, then leapt toward the house. I was going to die.

You're a damn sight tougher than you look, girl. Dan's voice echoed in my mind.

I had to do something. I couldn't die here. I *wouldn't* die here! But what was there for me to do?

I scrambled to the edge of the roof where the branches of the maple tree just tickled the side of the house. There was no way the ends of the branches would hold my weight. I looked down. The beast was in the yard beneath me, pacing, growling, and hissing. I took a step away from the edge as it glared up at me. Maybe I was safe up on the roof? Sure, the darkling spawn was big, but maybe it couldn't jump that high? Its footsteps moved around to the front of the house, and I followed its movement, watching as it glanced around the yard then back to me on the roof. In the waning light it was nothing more than a shadow with red eyes ghosting across the ground, but I knew it was thinking, trying to reason out a way to get up onto the roof, just like I had. It paused for a moment then turned as if it was going to leave.

I breathed a sigh of relief and closed my eyes, mumbling as I sank to my knees. That was too close. I wanted to cry. I needed to puke.

A crash directly in front of me brought my eyes wide. Instead of leaving, the creature had taken a running leap and was struggling, just as I had, to get up onto the roof. I launched myself backwards and scrambled higher as the darkling spawn's claws scraped, then gripped the shingles. It inched itself higher and higher onto the roof. One back leg found purchase on the loose gutter, and it snarled in what sounded oddly like triumph, red eyes burning into me.

I rolled, scrambling to my feet then ran the few steps to the edge of the roof and leapt off, blind with terror, into the branches of the maple tree. My arms pinwheeled and out of sheer dumb luck, my hands closed around a branch. Rough bark tore into my palms as I fell but I held on. The branch bowed and cracked as it took the whole of my weight. I reached for another branch and missed but my feet brushed a limb below me. It was no thicker than a baseball bat and as the branch I was holding snapped above me, my trail runners slipped off the limb and I tumbled. For a sickening second, I plummeted toward the ground, but somehow my knee hooked the limb, and I managed to catch the crook of my elbow over it as well.

Dangling like a sloth on a branch that could barely hold my weight, I chanced a quick glance toward the house. I could just make out the shadow of the creature slinking along the edge of the roof. I grunted and shimmied toward the trunk of the tree, crying out in pain as my torn hands grasped the branch. It seemed that luck was still on my side as I came to a fork in the tree limb. Reaching upwards, I was able to scoot and wiggle myself back to the top of the narrow limb.

It was nearly too dark to see, but I could *feel* the night coming alive around me, the air itself dangerously charged with a frenzied, wild energy.

The darkling spawn barked—three piercing chuffs that rattled the air—part bear, part dog, all nightmare. A cacophony of shrieks and howls responded in the distance and my blood ran cold.

There had to be *dozens* of them out there.

I dared to stand up on the limb and worked my way even closer to the trunk of the tree where the branches would be the strongest. In the darkness it was difficult to tell how far above the ground I was, but my gut was screaming at me to climb. I reached up and grit my teeth as my shredded palms closed around the branch above me. Fingers slick with blood, I struggled to hold on as more darkling spawn converged on the yard beneath me. Pain lanced through my hands as I pulled myself up. If I didn't get higher, well out of reach of the creatures on the ground, it would be my last night among the living.

I continued upward until I could just make out the horizon line in the distance. Shadowed rooftops interspersed with the tops of fir trees set grim, black silhouettes against the dark navy sky while in the shadows below me, creatures shrieked and hissed and growled.

With a hollow thump, the tree shook, the violent, jarring movement nearly dislodging me. I clutched the trunk like my life depended on it. Again, and again, and again, the tree shook, and I clung to it with all my strength. Finally, the night went eerily silent. No frogs or crickets sang in the dark...even the wind seemed to be passing through the trees without even rustling a leaf...and there was no sound from the creatures either.

There in the total darkness, my heart finally began to slow, and as I dragged in lung-fulls of the crisp night air, the nausea I had felt earlier finally overwhelmed me. I leaned over and retched. Below me, the shadows undulated and growled. A sea of glowing red orbs gazed up at me, silent as the grave. Somehow, the silence was worse than their screams had been.

I rested my forehead against the rough bark of the tree and whispered something like a prayer to The Light Mother for protection to survive the night.

It would seem that in my darkest hour, even though I had never entertained the idea of a higher power, I had put my faith into something other than myself.

When dawn finally cracked the horizon, I was still breathing. I was also shocked that the clouds I had seen to the west the day before had pushed east overnight without much more than a sprinkling of rain. The sun rose through thick, cumulus clouds to the east, but directly above me was nothing but stark blue sky. I cried in relief.

The night had been a long one. Not only had I not slept for fear that I would slip out of the tree and into the sea of darkling spawn below me, but every inch of my skin that had come in contact with the creature's black blood stung like the worst sunburn I'd ever had in my life. I used a bottle of water to wash my wounded hands then wrapped them in strips of a tee-shirt I had in my pack. After my hands were wrapped, I used the rest of the shirt and water to clean the black blood from my exposed skin. That eased the sting a bit, but it didn't come anywhere close to relieving it completely. And on top of it all, I stank like four-day old roadkill in August.

The sun moved higher in the sky and when the yard below me was bathed in light, I steeled myself and looked down. What had been lush grass the night before was now muddy, churned earth. The trunk of the tree had sustained a myriad of scratches, presumably from the creatures trying to climb it in the dark. They were gone now, crawled back into whatever hole they'd chosen to spend the day in, thank God—er, The Goddess...but I shivered with the knowledge of how close I had come to dying.

I looked around then gingerly shifted my weight on the branch. My body ached all over. Even my teeth seemed to protest as I yawned and tried to stretch. I had to get down from the tree somehow and my hands were in no shape to be grasping anything more than a bottle of water...and even that was excruciating.

With a determined grunt, I hooked my elbow over the nearest branch and lowered myself down. The process was slow and painful, but eventually, I made it to the lowest branch. I knew I would break my leg if I jumped from that height. I would have to hang and then drop. My poor hands screamed as the full weight of my body pressed into the raw cuts. My vision swam and I let go, dropping the six or seven feet to the ground. I landed with a grunt, ankles tingling from the impact, but I was whole.

I thanked the ancient maple tree and The Light Mother for saving my neck then stumbled out of the yard and onto the street. I couldn't have given a single, solitary shit about being stealthy in that moment. I just needed to be home. I needed my mom's warm comforting embrace and my brother's obnoxious laugh. I needed familiar surroundings and love.

Less than ten minutes later I stood in the road gazing at my house, the old welcome mat still lying in front of the door. But the windows and front door were covered in plywood and a giant 'X' marred the garage.

I was too late.

My family was gone.

20

No Mercy

"**M**OM?" I POUNDED ON THE BOARDS over the front door. "Joey? Where are you?" The pain in my hands was nothing compared to the agony blooming in my heart.

They were supposed to be here. We were supposed to have a loving, tear-filled reunion. We were supposed to be hugging, Mom and Joey helping me into the house, Joey telling me what a badass I was for making it all the way home and Mom fussing over my injuries, saying that she was worried sick, but she always knew I'd make it.

But the house was empty.

Were they just gone, moved somewhere safe, or were they dead? Did that old blood stain on the road belong to one of them?

"Mom!" My voice cracked as I moved to the garage and pounded with all the strength I had. I pushed up on the big, aluminum door, blood seeping through the wraps on my hands to streak across the cream-colored paint. It didn't budge.

Dropping to the ground in a heap, I wailed, "No. No!"

After all the weeks, all the struggle, all the near-death moments, the distance, and the longing for a familiar, safe place to lay my head and burdens down, I finally, against all the odds, made it back home—and they were gone. My heart cracked, bleeding out the hope I had held so tightly to. Hope was the only thing that kept me focused, the only thing that kept me from absolutely losing my mind. And now my hope was gone; dashed to pieces on the concrete of my driveway.

I screamed. *Screamed.*

My tenuous grip on sanity slipping out of my ruined hands. Why should I exist if the people I loved most in the world were gone? This house and everything in it didn't matter without them. It was nothing—*I* was nothing without them—just another lost soul with nowhere to go and no one to turn to. I'd fought so hard to survive. Not just to simply survive, but to thrive, all because I had a vision of my family with me. All of us surviving together. Now that they were gone, what did I have to live for?

Exhausted and broken, I lurched to my feet and shuffled out of the driveway, throwing one last look over my shoulder at the house that built me. With a few pieces of plywood and a spray painted 'X', it *broke* me.

Tears blurred my vision as I wandered aimlessly out of my neighborhood, my feet carrying me where they would. I scrubbed at the salty streaks on my face, the wraps on my hands growing more damp by the minute. The sun was directly overhead by the time my feet stopped, and I looked around.

An empty parking lot greeted me, the sounds of a creek in the distance met my ears as I turned to gaze down a winding path. The grass along the path, normally mowed and edged to landscaping perfection, grew long and wild, dotted with dandelions. I could barely make out the little wooden bridge that spanned the creek through the tall weeds.

The ghost of a memory drifted to mind; my Jeep parked beside an aging, forest green Subaru, jumper cables spanned between the two batteries.

Of course, my feet would have taken me back to this place after everything I loved had disappeared. Back to the last place I could remember where life was just normal. I sat down on the asphalt and wallowed in my own self-pity. Why was I still alive? What was the point of it all? It wasn't even worth trying to make the trek back to the camp store to live with Dan and his family. I'd just be the odd one out. The poor kid whose own family didn't make it, lost and alone in the world, a pitiful burden. I wanted my own family. I *needed* my own family.

The shadows on the ground stretched as the sun began its descent toward the horizon. Dusk was still several hours away giving me plenty of time to make peace with how my life was going to end.

I pulled Dan's knife out of its sheath at my hip and placed the tip of the blade against my wrist, pressing lightly. Tears welled in my eyes once again. I didn't want to live without my family, but as I sat there staring at the muted glint of steel against my pale skin, my hand faltered.

"Come on." I grit my teeth, tightening my grip on the knife handle and pressed harder.

A single drop of crimson welled into a trembling pool on my skin before rolling toward the crook of my elbow. I closed my eyes, and a sob hissed through my clenched teeth carrying spittle with it.

I don't want to do this anymore!

I tried to press harder, to drag the blade down and back, but simply could not move my hand. It was as if some outside force held Dan's knife, physically stopping me from ending my struggle right then and there.

My knife hand shook and with a defeated groan, I let the blade fall away from my wrist. I was simply too weak to take my own life. Perhaps I should just sit out in the open...in this stupid parking lot, until the darkling spawn came to finish what they started last night?

Sliding the knife back into its sheath, my shoulders sagged, and I sat, despondent and numb. I didn't know what else to do. When the distant rumble of a vehicle approaching reached my ears, my gut twisted, telling me to run, but I ignored it, resigned to whatever fate I was about to be dragged into.

I turned to see the same truck from the night before rolling towards the parking lot and I closed my eyes in utter defeat. I should have taken off down the walking trail when I'd first heard the truck heading my way. But what did it matter anyway? If they were going to kill me, that would be an easier death than getting eaten alive by darkling spawn.

A watery smile took up residence on my face and I waved limply as the truck rolled to a stop in the road. My eyes drifted to the treetops swaying in the light breeze and I took in the beauty of new, green life like I would never see it again.

Four men leapt out of the truck bed, the sound of their boots hitting the pavement pulling my gaze back in their direction. They were all clad in the same dark clothing as the men from the night before, faces covered, rifles drawn.

The driver shot out of the cab and marched straight toward me, tearing off his stocking cap and pulling down his neck gaiter as he came. The gunmen formed a semi-circle while the driver hauled me to my feet by the straps of my pack.

"You little piece of shit," he growled, shaking me so violently, my head snapped back and forth with the motion. "You got four good men killed last night!" His left eye twitched with barely controlled rage and his breath rolled over my face in sour waves of coffee and stale cigarettes.

In a disjointed sort of way, I realized that he could have been a handsome man had he not been looking at me with murder in his eyes. He was just above average height, clean shaven, with short-cropped dark blonde hair, pale blue eyes, a sharp nose, and a stubborn set to his jaw.

I blinked up at him, unsure of what to say.

He shook me again, "Don't you have anything to say for yourself? Four men died trying to save you from the demons!"

They were trying to save *me? Oh, Bull. Shit.*

Where resignation sat in my chest just moments ago, rage flared to life, hot and nearly suffocating. This man had no idea what I had just been through. I was tired. *Sick* and tired. Tired of being hunted. Tired of running like nothing more than prey. Sick to death of being accosted, threatened, robbed, and terrified. And the fact that I had nothing left to live for completely eliminated any inhibitions I might have had left.

I scoffed, "Well, maybe if they'd said something like, oh, I don't know, *'we're here to help you'* the whole thing could've been avoided." I pinned him with an equally hostile glare.

He smirked as his eyes roamed my face, "You think so?" He clapped my ear—hard—before I could even utter a single word.

"Ow, what the Hell?" I instinctively brought a wrapped hand up to cover my throbbing ear.

"It's your fault they're dead!" He stabbed a blunt finger into the center of my chest. "Tell me why we shouldn't execute you right here."

"Are you kidding me?" I yelled back at the driver. Consequences be damned, all self-preservation flown straight out the proverbial window. "Are you the one that told them to search the trees?"

His eyes narrowed but he said nothing.

"Then you're the one who got them killed, not me." I spit in his face.

His fist came from nowhere. One moment I was on my feet and the next I was splayed face-down on the asphalt, vision blurred, cheek and eye throbbing. I'd never even been slapped, let alone punched by a full-grown, fucking man.

You're a damn sight tougher than you look, girl.

Oh, Dan. Why did his words have to pop into my head now?

A lump formed in my throat. He'd killed a man to ensure that I stayed alive. He'd hugged me, showed me he cared, told me that he was proud of me, that he believed in me, and I was just giving up.

A sound that began as a cross between a groan and a sob morphed into a strained laugh as it tumbled past my lips. If I was going down, I was going to go down swinging, and if all I had to fight with was a smart-ass comment, then that was exactly what this jerk was going to get.

I mumbled then, my words slurred together, "S'that—all you got?" I shook my head trying to clear the fog.

"The fuck you say to me?" the driver growled as he loomed over me.

Breathing deep, I pushed myself to hands and knees, eyeing the people arrayed around us. The gunmen all had their weapons trained on me, but as my eyes panned the semi-circle, one of them seemed to waver, the barrel of his rifle dipping as his finger dropped away from the trigger altogether. My gaze returned to the driver, and I glared at him through my swelling eye.

"I said," I cleared my throat, making sure I was loud enough for all of them to hear, "You hit like a *bitch.*"

The toe of his boot connected with my stomach with so much force, I was airborne for a sickening second before I landed flat on my back, trying to suck air into lungs that refused to inflate. All I knew was burning pain as I finally dragged in a few ragged breaths. "Just kill me already," I croaked.

The driver ignored me completely. "Put her in the Goddamn truck," he barked.

One of the gunmen removed my pack and knife before my wrists were bound behind my back with zip ties. Then, I was unceremoniously lifted and shoved face down into the bed of the old pickup, my injured cheek scraping across the gritty metal of the truck bed. I tried to breathe through the daggers of pain lancing through my ribs but even breathing hurt like hell.

"Driver Three to HQ," the driver spoke curtly.

Seconds later, a tinny voice sounded, "Go, Driver Three." The unmistakable chirp of a walkie-talkie followed.

"The troublemaker from last night has been secured. Returning to HQ now. Travel time from Miller Park."

"See you in ten," the voice on the walkie-talkie responded, and the truck rumbled down the road.

I tried to sit up, but a booted foot pressed into my back between my shoulder blades. I winced and didn't resist. I couldn't have if I tried.

Several minutes later, the truck rolled to a stop and boots hit the ground in a chorus of dull thuds, the sharp clacking of rifles rang in my head as all the gunmen leapt out—all except for the one that still had his boot resting between my shoulder blades.

The driver's door squeaked open then slammed shut with a metallic clang. Heavy footsteps circled to the rear of the truck and the tailgate came down. All at once, rough hands grasped my ankles and yanked. Before I could even breathe, the driver fisted the back of my hoodie and hauled me upright as if I weighed nothing at all.

Pain screamed through my ribs and gut as I fought to keep my knees from buckling. I held my breath, refusing to cry out. The driver grasped my left arm with a jerk, and I hissed out a breath through clenched teeth while the last gunman hopped down off the tailgate after me and carefully took hold of my right arm. Together they walked me into what used to be the sporting and outdoor store—now fortified against the creatures; the outside looked more like a prison, all cinderblock, steel, and wire.

The inside had barely changed though, reminding me of the simple, easy life I used to live. A bitter laugh nearly escaped, catching in my throat as we passed the aisle stocked with my favorite backpacker meals. My sore middle and face protested, and the would-be laugh came out as a strangled groan. My knees wobbled and I missed a step.

224

The gunman on my right took my weight gently, supporting me while I tried to get my feet back under me, but the driver jerked me back to my feet and cursed under his breath, "Fucking waste of oxygen."

We continued toward the back, where construction lights washed everything in a harsh, white light. A generator rumbled somewhere in the distance, and I wondered absently how they had gotten it running. Halfway down a long hallway, we walked into an office with the door propped open.

A scent cloud of cheap cologne singed my nostrils, pulling my attention back to my current situation. I looked up and focused on a man sitting behind a desk. Something about the slightly amused look on his face soured my stomach and the hair on my neck prickled. The driver and gunmen might have been violent and mean, but this man felt truly wicked. I blanched and tried to retreat, taking a step backward. The men on either side of me held fast, fingers digging into the flesh of my upper arms. An oily, half-smile tugged at the corner of his wide mouth, and the glint of ruthless anticipation lit his dark eyes at my immediate revulsion.

He studied me for what seemed like an age, eyes raking me from filthy head to tattered sneaker. The silence stretched so long it felt like his eyes were peeling back my skin, just to see what was underneath. What I was made of.

Finally, he spoke, "*This* is what got your entire crew killed last night?"

"Yes, Sir," the driver responded with a slight jerk of his head.

The man behind the desk scoffed, "We need more women, but this one should have been left to the demons. Too scrawny."

"With all due respect, you did say any stray female should be brought in," the driver said.

"Correct. I did. With the population decimated, we'll need as many as possible to insure the continuation of the human race. But this," he lifted his arm, waving a non-committal hand in my direction and let his words hang in the air as he sneered.

The words popped out of my mouth before I could catch them. "I've had enough of being talked about like I'm not here. What the hell could you possibly want with me?" I really did have a death wish.

The gunman to my right stiffened slightly while the driver cursed at me. I glared at the driver then turned back to the man behind the desk. He rose slowly from his worn office chair and made his way around the table.

Bile rose in my throat as he came to stand directly in front of me, every cell in my body screaming at me to flee. He wasn't tall but he was broad and his black eyes held nothing but morbid fascination. My eyes went straight to the floor. There was something *wrong* about him. Something deep-rooted and unwell. This was a very dangerous man. A nervous sweat broke out across my brow, and I wet my lips.

He reached out gently—too gently—and took my chin between his thumb and forefinger, forcing my head up. "Look at me," he commanded.

Bile rose in my throat, but I did as I was told...and regretted it immediately. His dark hair was receding but cut so short it was barely noticeable. His brows were thick and low, nearly connected at the bridge of his crooked nose, and he wore enough cologne or aftershave to deodorize a landfill in a heatwave.

Despite his clean-cut appearance, something about this man tapped into my survival instincts. I needed to get away. I wanted to thrash, fight with everything I had against these men holding me. I needed to run—to get far, *far* away—but I knew I could not allow him to see just how frightened I was of him. I suppressed a shudder.

His eyes roamed my face, taking in what was sure to be a split cheek and a blackening eye, one that I was having trouble holding open. "Do you know who I am?" he asked in a smooth, sinister voice.

I couldn't stand to look at him a moment longer, "I don't give a shit who you are," I hissed and jerked my face away from his thick hand. If I couldn't utilize my flight response, then fight response it was.

He barked a laugh and glanced at the driver. "At least she's got bite." They shared a brief belly laugh before his eyes locked onto mine again.

My nostrils flared and I grit my teeth. *Screw this guy!* "Get fucked," I ground out.

A feverish expression shadowed his face a second before his meaty hand closed around my throat and squeezed. Panic surged through me and my entire body stiffened. I tried to move backward but was held fast by the driver and gunman. Black spots dotted my vision, I tried to swallow, tried to breathe, but even through the panic and pain, I never took my eyes off him. A dull rumble began to fill my head making his voice sound distant.

"I'm going to thoroughly enjoy giving you a little attitude adjustment. The harder you fight, the more fun it's going to be for me." His words slithered their way to my ears, and I tried to imagine kicking his teeth in even as I struggled to remain conscious.

He released me with a sharp jerk that had my gut and ribs screaming all over again. As I coughed and choked, he returned to his seat behind the desk and sighed as he sat down.

"I want her fully healed then brought to my home before she's put into rotation," he ordered.

"Yes, Sir," the driver replied, tightening his grip on my upper arm. The two men turned me to exit the room.

"I need a few more words with you, Frank," the man said.

The driver dropped my arm and nodded to the gunman, who continued marching me out of the room. Once we were out of the hallway, the gunman slowed his pace and relaxed his hold on my arm. He supported and walked *with* me rather than simply dragging me along.

"Where are you taking me?" I asked. My voice rasped and I swallowed hard then tried to clear my throat. All that did was make the scratching, burning sensation worse. He glanced down at me briefly and shook his head. His tinted safety glasses sat atop his stocking-capped head and a neck gaiter still covered his nose and mouth. His eyes, tired and sad, lingered on my face a moment before returning to the path we walked.

At the other side of the store sat an enormous, army green canvas tent. We ducked inside through a door flap covering the small entryway and he shifted slightly behind me, cutting the zip-ties and freeing my wrists.

The interior was lit only by a long strand of hanging solar powered lights. Narrow cots lined the walls to my left and right while the back side of the tent housed medical, and first aid supplies organized on tall shelves. A kitchenette occupied a small corner and beside it sat a small dining table with four chairs. A lounge area dominated the center of the space; several tattered chairs circling a low coffee table littered with books and magazines.

A brown skinned woman, who appeared to be in her thirties, sat in a shabby lobby chair. She shot to her feet as we entered and flicked on a bright exam light, her dark, curly hair, rolled up into a tight bun, face grim.

"Set her down over there," she pointed to a cot then turned to drag a small rolling cart over to where I had been deposited, "and bring me that stool." She pointed and the gunman did her bidding without question, also dragging over a folding chair for himself.

I numbly allowed the woman to examine me while tears dried on my cheeks. What did the man behind the desk mean by 'rotation'? And why were they gathering any women they could find? What the heck were these people doing? I had so many questions but none of the energy to ask them.

The woman sucked in a breath as she took a good look at me. "Why the hell do you guys have to beat on them so badly? Look at her face...and her neck? My God." She turned to the gunman who was setting his rifle down by the entrance and glared.

"I've never hurt any of them and I never would, you know that," the gunman said slowly as he removed his stocking cap and made his way over to the chair he'd set up for himself. He sat down heavily, head low, shoulders sagging and passed a hand through his dark, wavy hair then steepled his gloved fingers at his chin.

"Lay back, baby girl," the woman said to me.

I did as I was told and closed my eyes with a groan, wrapping my arms across my middle. My ribs and stomach were killing me.

"Can I take a look at your belly?"

I nodded. She gently poked and prodded. I winced. She shifted on her stool and gathered something off the rolling cart. "They may be just badly bruised, but I think you probably have a couple of cracked ribs. I can't say for certain without imaging. And you don't seem to have any internal bleeding, thank God." She sighed and shifted on the stool again.

"You don't do a damn thing to stop the others from knocking them around, though." There was venom in her sweet voice as she spoke again to the gunman, "Guilty by association." She made a disgusted noise. "And take that stupid mask off. You ain't hiding from anybody in here."

I could barely make out the sound of fabric sliding down off his face.

"Sweet Jesus, honey, what happened to your hands?" she breathed after freeing my palms from the makeshift wraps. The fabric stuck to the deepest cuts.

"I-I climbed a tree," I stuttered and coughed.

The woman gasped.

"Actually, I jumped off a roof and into a tree...in the dark."

She clucked her tongue. "Survived the night in a tree just to get caught by these assholes? Just don't seem fair to me." After turning my hand this way and that, she said flatly, "The cuts aren't deep enough for stitches but it's like your palms are completely covered in road-rash. Hurts like hell, doesn't it?"

I nodded, my eyes still clenched shut.

"How much do you weigh, honey?"

"About one-fifteen," my voice rasped, throat feeling like I swallowed a hot coal.

"I'll get you some pain meds and some lidocaine gel so I can clean your palms. And don't talk more than you need to. Your throat is really bruised too."

I nodded again and my heart collapsed. If crying hadn't hurt so much, I would have been in absolute hysterics, but as it was, tears began to seep from my closed eyes again. The woman returned shortly and helped me to sit up. I swallowed whatever pills she handed me with a wince and laid back down. The lidocaine gel stung like crazy at first, but then my hands went blessedly numb, and I sighed in relief. I couldn't bring myself to open my eyes. I couldn't stomach the feeling of settling into my shit situation.

Nothing had gone according to plan since I had left the camp store. I'd been robbed at gunpoint, then stalked and almost killed by some people from Dan's town. Then I'd almost been killed by a pack of darkling spawn. My family was gone; whether they left or had been killed, I didn't know. Then I'd been beaten, kidnapped, and taken to this place—a community full of armed and dangerous people. Dan was the sole bright spot in a sea of darkness that was now my life.

I never should have left the damn camp store.

As the nurse soaked one of my hands in a tub of sudsy, warm water, I began to relax despite myself. At least I was receiving some medical care and was safe from the darkling spawn. I sighed and almost didn't hear when the woman spoke again.

"You gonna try and help this one get out too?" she whispered to the gunman.

"Absolutely," he ground out, voice low.

Get out? Like escape? What?

My eyes flew open, and my head snapped to the side as the woman stood and made her way over to the shelves of medical supplies.

My heart hit the pit of my stomach.

It couldn't be.

My head swam and I blinked hard, thinking my addled brain and teary eyes had to be playing tricks on me. My logical mind fought against what my eyes were seeing. His hair was longer, and beard stubble covered his jaw, but...I knew that face. What was he doing here with these people?

His sad, hazel gaze held mine for a moment before he sniffed and wiped unshed tears from his eyes with the back of his gloved hands. An equally sad smile tugged at the corner of his mouth.

"DJ?" I croaked.

"Hey...Just Amber," he whispered.

21

The Cost of Survival

Dan

AS DAN APPROACHED THE RAZOR WIRE topped barrier that led into his hometown his heart sank. Rifle barrels appeared out of two narrow slits in the large rolling gate, while Jim, the town's self-appointed leader and two-faced bastard extraordinaire, appeared in the lookout tower just to the left of the gate with a dark scowl on his weathered face.

"The prodigal son returns," he called over the gate, voice dripping with sarcasm.

Dan removed Amber's backpack from his shoulders and held it up for Jim to see, hoping that it would be enough to convince the man to let him back into town. "I caught her, took the backpack and turned her loose, just like Joanne ordered."

"What happened to your partner? Where's Bruce?" Jim raised his own weapon, aiming the barrel at Dan's chest.

Damn it.

"I lost him in Whitecap," Dan called out, "But we *all* lost the girl in Whitecap. Joanne split us into teams. He thought the girl had gone one way, I thought she went another. We couldn't agree so we split up and planned to meet up on the opposite side of the neighborhood once we were finished canvassing."

It wasn't a *total* lie. He and Bruce did have a disagreement about Amber and he *had* lost Bruce in town...in a way. In a 'stashed a body in the bushes' sort of way.

Dan grimaced internally but put on his best cocky demeanor, hoping that Jim would buy it. "I caught the girl close to sunset and sent her packing then fired off two shots so Craig, Joanne and Bruce would know I had the bag. None of them ever showed so I hid out in an old garage and waited out the night."

Jim's brows knit together a moment, as if he were terribly disappointed in Dan's made-up story, then he sneered, "That's a lie."

"It's the gods honest truth," Dan yelled back. Hopefully, the Goddess would forgive him for that lie. Then again, maybe she didn't even care about telling untruths. For he and his family's sake, he hoped he would be forgiven for doing what he'd had to do. He'd been given a second chance to *be the hero* and in the name of all things holy, he hoped he could get one more second chance before his luck or grace ran out. He had to get his wife and daughter out of this town and away from these people.

"You wanna know how I know you're a dirty liar?" Jim spat over the wall.

Not particularly, Dan thought as his heart frantically slammed against his ribs. He shrugged hoping he looked nonchalant. He could still salvage this. He had to.

"Because we found Bruce's body well before sunset, with his throat gaping from ear to ear," Joanne said through one of the gun slits.

"And?" Dan forced a sneer, "You think *I* would do something like that?"

"You really think any of us believe that scrawny kid could've done it?" Joanne spat back at him.

"If she had a sharp enough knife, she could have," Dan growled as Jim turned to descend the watch tower platform.

"Could she drag a two-hundred and twenty-five-pound dead body thirty feet through the dirt and stash it under a hedge?" The last few words out of Joanne's mouth were close to a scream.

Damn it! This was about to go to shit.

Alarm bells rang out in Dan's head as he shifted in his hiking boots. "Adrenaline and determination are a wonder drug," he said through clenched teeth.

"You shut your lyin' pie hole, Dan," the rasp of Tanya's voice sounded from behind the gate. "Drop the backpack and your weapon."

He was caught.

Lifting the rifle strap off his shoulder, he tossed it and the backpack on the ground in front of him then took several large steps backward, hands in the air. He heard the large latch being disengaged and the big gate rolled open revealing Tanya and Jim, who strode toward him, guns aimed at his chest.

Jim stopped at the rifle and backpack while Tanya continued to his side. Shotgun at the ready, she stepped behind him. "On your knees, hands behind your head."

Dan obeyed with a sigh while Jim picked up the backpack and opened it. "It's definitely her bag. Pill bottles, canned food, water bottles, clothes."

"Why'd you kill him?" Tanya demanded as she jammed the shotgun barrel between Dan's shoulder blades.

He pitched forward but caught his balance, mind reeling. If lying couldn't get him out of this mess, maybe the truth would?

"He was about to disobey Joanne's direct orders and shoot the girl," Dan said through clenched teeth.

"Death seems like a steep price to pay for trying to shoot a girl that *I* told all of you didn't matter." Tanya's voice cut through the afternoon air like a serrated knife. She stepped out from behind him so she could look him in the face. "Bruce was a valuable asset, and since you took something I value, I'll be taking something *you* value."

What?!

The heavy gate rolled open a few more feet to reveal Joanne and Craig who held handguns to his wife and daughter's heads. His wife, Emily, was quiet and stoic, glaring at Jim and Tanya in turn, while his daughter, Kate, cried and struggled against Joanne's grip on her upper arm. Dan's heart cracked in two.

No, please, no...

Tanya leaned in close, "But I'll be nice and let you choose which one lives and which one dies." She sneered, her sour, boozy, ash tray breath washing over him.

"Me! An eye for an eye. I killed him, you kill me!" Dan's voice was strained, raw, broken. Just like his heart.

"That's not how this works, big guy." Tanya's raspy voice was low and evil as she gestured to Kate and Emily. "After this is all over, I'll need a little bit of leverage to keep you in line. These two are just a resource suck. They consume and don't contribute enough to the town." She paused a moment before continuing, "You, on the other hand, have skills and knowledge that we can utilize."

"Damn-it, Tanya. You kill *me!*" Dan boomed.

Kate's small voice called out, "No Dad!" Then to her captors she said, "Please don't hurt him. *Please!*"

Tears stung Dan's eyes as his gaze found his wife's. She reached over to take Kate's hand in hers, squeezing tight.

It wasn't supposed to go this way. He was trying to set things right, to balance the wrong he had done in leaving Amber up on that mountain. He'd tried to do good again and now—

"You choose or we kill them both!" Tanya yelled while jabbing the barrel of her shotgun into Dan's temple.

Emily flinched, her grip tightening on Kate's hand who continued to sob and struggle in Joanne's grip. She mouthed the words *'I love you'* as she carefully widened her stance and squared her shoulders, releasing Kate's hand.

"It's ok, Katie-Bear. Everything is going to be ok," she said, using the nickname their daughter had been trying to get them to stop using since she was twelve.

Emily, don't do it...

Dan couldn't force the words from his throat. His mind flashed back to the evening after their first official date. He'd invited her over to his place and as a means of easing her mind, he'd taught her how to disarm a would-be assailant with a handgun, pointing it back at them. The flash of her triumphant grin when she'd finally disarmed him—he'd fallen head over heels that very second. Now, everything he held dear in the mess he now called his life, was threatened.

"Emily, don't," Dan rasped, barely finding his voice.

Her gaze flicked to his—just for a second, but it was long enough to say everything she didn't have time to put into words, *'If this doesn't work out, take care of our daughter.'*

"Mom, please," Kate sobbed.

Then Emily moved.

She bobbed and twisted, grabbing Craig's wrist and the gun at the same time. With a flick and another twist, she had the gun pointing back at Craig's head. Textbook perfection. Everyone froze in utter shock at the sudden change of events. Craig scowled but his hands rose to either side of his head.

How was she so strong in the face of so much danger? Her hand didn't even waiver. She was a lioness protecting her pride because her fool husband couldn't do it himself.

"Let him go, Tanya. We'll all leave right now; you can have everything. Just let us all go. You'll never see any of us again," Emily said, voice tense but measured.

Tanya gaped a moment looking toward Jim who was still holding Amber's backpack, stiff with shock. The barrel of her rifle swung toward Emily as redness crept up her neck and onto her cheeks. Pure hatred burned in her eyes, "Kill the kid."

"*No!*" Dan roared.

Joanne's hard face fell. "I'm not killing a kid, Tanya. Have you lost your damn mind?" Utter disgust sharpened the edge of her words.

"Do it, or I will!" Tanya ground out and took aim at Kate's chest.

Dan gathered himself to lunge toward Tanya at the same moment Emily swung her gun arm in Tanya's direction and fired. Dan froze, halfway to his feet as the bullet punched straight into Tanya's chest. She stumbled and gaped, mouth opening and closing like a fish out of water before her knees buckled and she fell. Emily hadn't even waited for Tanya's body to hit the ground before she aimed the gun back at Craig, while Jim, finally shaken from his stupor, raised his rifle toward her.

Dan's world moved in slow motion as three more gunshots rang out, one from Jim's rifle and two in quick succession from Joanne's handgun. Crimson bloomed across Emily's chest as she fell backward a heartbeat before two bullets slammed into Jim's chest. He toppled like an old oak tree, rifle clattering to the ground beside him.

Dan didn't feel his legs move but suddenly he was on his knees beside her. Emily's chest rose once, twice, then faltered. She coughed, blood spilling from her parted lips, bright red against white teeth.

"Emily, no. No—stay with me, honey. Stay with me—"

Her fingers twitched toward his but there was no strength left in them. Her lips parted as her eyes met his again. Dan could have sworn she tried to speak, but then she smiled softly, a single tear trailing from the corner of her eye. Then...nothing.

His world blurred. The screaming in his ears—was it Kate or himself?

Kate jerked free of a stunned looking Joanne and fell into Dan's arms. His ears rang, breaths short and shallow.

No. No!

Kate wailed into his chest, her arms crushing tight around his waist. "*Mom!*" she screamed.

Craig stood numbly over Emily's still body, her long, golden-blonde hair splayed out on the ground around her head like a halo. His gaze jerked toward Joanne, "What did you—why would you— what the hell, Joanne?"

Joanne looked as if she were about to be sick, eyes darting to the gun in her shaking hand, breath rushing in and out of her open mouth. She flipped the safety and threw the gun into the ditch.

"Get out of here," she whispered as her strained eyes focused on Dan.

He was too stunned to move.

Joanne took a wobbling step in Dan and Kate's direction, pointing at the backpack that started this whole horrifying mess. "Take it and go," she said, finality creeping into her voice.

Dan reached for Emily. He couldn't leave her there. His wife. His rock. His *everything.*

But with Kate still screaming and coughing into his chest, his training and instincts took over. "We gotta move, Katie. Come on." He unwound her arms from around his waist and grasped her hand then moved toward the backpack and rifle on the ground. Stooping to pick them up, he took one final look at the woman who had been the center of his universe for eighteen years. Hot tears streaked down his cheeks as he strapped the rifle to the backpack and slung it across his shoulders.

Kate continued to sob, murmuring, 'Mom...' over and over again.

Craig stooped to retrieve the gun Emily had taken from him, still held fast in her hand.

"Can I—" Dan's voice cracked around the lump in his throat. "Can I at least take her wedding ring?"

Craig glanced from Dan to Joanne who gave a quick nod. After tucking the gun into its holster, Craig took several steps back.

Dan's fingers trembled as he knelt and gently slid the ring off her still-warm finger. A choked sob wrenched its way out of his throat as he stood and stuffed the ring into his pocket then pulled his daughter tight to his side.

"Don't come back...or I'll kill you myself," Joanne said and turned her back on Dan and Kate.

He had no idea how the two enforcers were going to explain the deaths of their town leaders to the rest of the community, and he frankly didn't care, but Joanne had spared the life of his daughter and then killed the man who had murdered his wife. The woman must still have some good in her. He slowed his pace and called over his shoulder, "She wanted to be buried, not burned. You were our friend once, before all this shit. Please, Joanne...please."

After a long breath, she nodded curtly.

"Thank you," was all he could say before his emotions choked him.

With the hardest step of his entire life, he turned away. He had to be strong. Strong for Kate and even stronger for himself. Emily would want him to be...*need* him to be. She would have made sure he was strong as steel, tempering his own will to push on through the pain with her stiff-backed determination and unconditional love, but now, all he had was her spirit to guide him.

As Dan put boots to pavement, he swore he could still smell her, feel her warmth beside him. He swallowed hard, forcing himself to focus on the road ahead, but that fierce spirit of hers seemed to whisper to him with the wind.

Emily's voice pounded in his mind, cutting through his gut-wrenching guilt and sorrow, piercing his soul with an urgency that burned through his veins like acid, *Run. Run with Katie-Bear and don't look back.*

So, he did.

22

The Road to Light

Dan

DUSK WAS FAST APPROACHING AS Dan and Kate rummaged through empty buildings in Riverdale searching for supplies and warmer clothes. They were heading up country into the forest and although spring was in full swing on the flatlands near the Columbia, he was sure the night still held a bone-chilling cold in the upper elevations. Once they made it to the camp store, he would be free to wander and scavenge as he needed, but he knew that they had to prepare for the trek up the mountain.

Katie still sniffled by his side as she pulled a hideous but very warm looking long coat off the rack in a second-hand store and inspected it.

"I think this'll fit," she said as she shrugged the garment on and stuffed her hands into the pockets.

Its multicolored pattern and faux fur lined hood and wrist cuffs were straight out of the early 2000's and Dan smiled sadly at his daughter. She turned to examine herself in a cracked mirror and after a moment, her puffy red eyes welled up again.

"Mom would be laughing her face off at this thing." Her tear strained voice cracked and she scrubbed at her eyes with the pads of her fingers.

"It's a little big." Dan's own eyes welled.

"But it's warm," Kate nodded as she flipped the large hood over her dark blonde hair. "God, it's so ugly." Her nose wrinkled and she let out a choked laugh.

Dan stepped up beside her and placed what he hoped was a comforting hand on her shoulder. "Let's see if you can find some gloves and then we can hit the hardware store down the road. See if we can find some rope and a few other things."

Kate nodded and turned to the other side of the store where a wall of vintage fashion accessories sat and began rifling through the piles of scarves, hats, and belts. He needed to find her a bag of some sort, big enough to carry some snacks and water. After some digging, he came up with a baby pink, canvas, cross body messenger bag that would work well...but Kate *detested* pink. His brows furrowed at the idea of a sixteen-year-old girl hating the color, but then again, Emily hadn't liked it either. A blush peach was both of his girl's favorite color.

The lump in his throat returned and he cleared it away with a cough. "I found a solid bag for ya. It's about as ugly as that jacket but it'll work."

"As long as it isn't pink, I don't care what it looks like," Kate threw over her shoulder as she pulled on a pair of gray isotoner gloves.

"Well," Dan let his words hang in the air as he held up the very pink bag for Kate to see.

"Dad," she let her head fall to the side, "Seriously?"

"Maybe the hardware store will have some fabric paint or dye?"

"It better," she said as she marched over to him and snatched the bag with a crooked smile.

Between the oversized jacket, the gloves and the pink bag, Kate looked like a scowling little old lady that was late for bingo night. Emily would have loved to have seen this.

Her voice sounded in his mind then, so clear she could have been standing beside him, *I'm here, my love. I will always be by your side. Not even death can keep me away.* Dan held his hand out toward his daughter who took it and gave his a little squeeze.

"Let's find some paint and something to eat," she said and started walking toward the door, dragging him along behind her. Tough as nails, just like her mother.

Dan sighed and allowed himself to be led out of the small shop by his determined child. The street appeared to be empty, and the afternoon shadows stretched long.

"Let's be quick. We still have to find a safe place to hide for the night," he said as his free hand felt for the daggers that Erik had given him, still strapped safely in their scabbards across his chest and waist, hidden beneath his old puffy vest. He hoped he wouldn't have to use either of them again anytime soon.

Less than an hour later, Dan stood outside of an abandoned UPS truck watching Kate spray paint her new bag a dark gray color. When she was finished, she hung it over the limb of a tree in the overgrown yard of a rundown house. The neighborhood was old but had been one of the beautiful, well-kept types that were common to the area, and Dan wondered if spaces like neighborhoods would ever become commonly used again in his lifetime. He doubted it.

In the morning, assuming the sky was still clear, they would search the neighborhood for some serviceable bicycles then make their way up the mountain, but at the moment, he motioned to his daughter to hurry. They planned on sheltering for the night in the big brown truck and it was almost dark.

She climbed into the cab then ducked into the cargo space. Dan closed and latched both doors behind them and turned on a flashlight. They had put together a cozy sleeping space with blankets and foam from the shops in the area and sat down with prepackaged snacks and bottled water for their dinner.

After eating her fill, Kate turned to Dan with a thoughtful look, "I've been thinking about Danny."

Dan nearly choked on his granola bar. His estranged son from his first relationship hadn't really crossed his mind for more than a second or two since the world had gone to hell, and now he wondered why that was.

"Whatcha thinking about?" he asked, voice gentle even though his mind was whirling. Danny lived so far away from them and the chances of him even being alive were slim to none.

"Well, I know you guys haven't talked much lately, but he messaged me almost every day on Snapchat and Insta." She sighed. "I miss his jokes and all the funny stuff he'd send me."

Of all the possible conversations that could have come up, this was one he hadn't counted on. Dan grunted and tried not to gape at his daughter. His son never reached out to him unless it was a holiday or birthday. Of course, Dan wasn't big on social media or reaching out either. He was too busy for Facebook or anything of the sort and if he was being honest with himself, he thought that if his son wanted to talk, he would have reached out. They had been close once, but age and distance had pulled them apart.

Danny was almost twelve years older than his half-sister, and the two hadn't grown up together; but the years he had come to live with Dan, Emily, and Kate, while his own mother tried to get clean and sober, were some of the most stressful and happy years of Dan's life.

His son had been thirteen years old when the state took him from his mother and placed him with an aunt in San Diego. A couple of years later, Dan was notified that his ex-fiancé had passed away and Little Danny was asking to leave his aunt's care in California to live with his father.

Dan had been ecstatic. After years of short summer and holiday visits, he would finally be able to really raise the young man that carried his name. His son. He would finally have his *son*. Emily had been only mildly hesitant to blend the family at first, saying that their house was small, but he had seen right through the weak excuse. Her real concern was Dan's own mental health, and if he was well enough to take on a teenager—who was quite possibly troubled and traumatized—full time. But there was no way in hell that Dan would have or could have said no. Only a single option existed; bring his son home, where he belonged.

He had known that there was no telling what kind of treatment Danny had been enduring at the hands of his addict mom, her random boyfriends, and the entire alcoholic family, but during his short, summer visits, especially the summer that Kate was born, he vowed to be the best big brother in the world. He never made any mention of trouble or abuse, but he always cried when it was time for him to head back to his mom's care. He cried more saying goodbye to Kate than he ever did when saying his goodbyes to either Dan or Emily. He greatly respected his father and stepmother, but he loved his baby sister with his whole heart, and the two of them had a connection that warmed Dan's own damaged soul. Emily even had their favorite saying printed onto a pair of t-shirts for them one summer, 'Big Bro and Little Sis, Best Friends Till the End.'

Dan was jolted from his memories by Kate's deep sigh.

"Do you think he's still out there?" she asked.

"I don't know. I hope so. He's smart and pretty darn tough. If anyone could survive in So Cal, it would be your brother," Dan said with a solemn nod, even though he thought the odds were probably next to nothing. He couldn't bear the thought of dashing Kate's hopes like that, but he paused a beat to really consider if it was possible that Danny was still out there somewhere.

Even at just fifteen years old, Dan could see his son had developed a hard edge. An edge that also seemed fairly dark...dark enough that it planted a seed of worry in Dan's gut. He never worried that his son would hurt anyone, least of all his kid sister, but whatever coping mechanism he developed had put a hard look at the edge of his eyes and the way he carried himself. That alone told Dan that the boy was struggling with something deep—and he refused to confide in his father.

So, Dan had made sure his son was speaking to a therapist, scheduling their appointments on the same days. While Dan's own father had been a 'suck it up and self-medicate' type of man, Emily refused to allow Dan to pass his childhood trauma to their daughter...or his already damaged son. Vulnerability and speaking openly about everything was a requirement of Emily's; if that couldn't happen, then issues were worked out with a therapist. It helped the whole family. What was he ever going to do without her?

"Dad, I have something to tell you, but please don't be mad, ok?" Kate said, wringing her hands and shifting uncomfortably.

Oh, man. Now what? Dan thought, dread flooding his system. "Okay," he said, stretching the word.

"You can't be mad. Promise?"

Dan nodded. "I promise." What could she be so worried about telling him?

"He made me swear to secrecy. He wanted to surprise you," Kate said.

"Ok, spit it out, Katie-Bear."

Kate rolled her eyes, "Dad, I'm not twelve anymore. Katie is fine."

"Just tell me, Katie,"

Kate sighed and closed her eyes before she spoke, "Danny moved back to Orchardville late last summer."

Dan's heart hit the pit of his stomach. "He—what?" The words came out like a groan.

"You promised you wouldn't be mad!" she squeaked, then covered her mouth as if she'd just remembered that it was dusk outside, and the darkling spawn would be rising soon. "You promised," she whispered again.

"I'm not mad, sweetheart, I'm just shocked. Why would Danny not want you to tell me? He could have stayed with us."

"He was living with roommates and wanted to get settled in his own apartment before he told you and Mom, but rent is almost as crazy here as it is in California, and he was having a hard time getting approved for a place."

"But why wouldn't he just ask?" Dan said more to himself than to Kate.

"He said he didn't want to be living with his parents in a small town down The Gorge. Plus, you can be a little bit of a bulldozer, Dad."

"I'm not a bulldozer," Dan said defensively.

Kate pinned him with a level stare. It was the same *'quit bullshitting yourself'* stare that Emily would give him when he was being pigheaded or obstinate...which was more often than he'd like to admit. She'd always kept him honest, now it seemed that his daughter was there to take up the torch.

"Okay, okay." Dan raised his hands and chuckled. "You're right. So, how was he doing?"

Kate smiled at him in a triumphant sort of way then opened her mouth to speak but was cut short by a distant screech. Her eyes went round as saucers. Dan placed a finger to his lips then killed the flashlight, plunging the cargo bay of the UPS truck into total blackness. There would be no more chatting for the night.

"Try and get some sleep," Dan whispered. "We'll pick this back up in the morning." He could hear Kate moving to lay down and she sniffled. He reached out in the darkness and laid a gentle hand on her head, "It's gonna be alright, sweetheart."

"Love you, Daddy," she whispered.

Dan lay in the dark listening to his daughter's breathing slow as sleep crept up and claimed her, all the while he kept one ear on the night noises just outside the delivery truck. Once he was sure she was out, he rolled over and prayed that the next day would be clear, then he finally let go of his tough facade. The lump in his throat he'd been swallowing down all day rose again. With a silent sob, he let himself fall apart, shaking and crying silently in the darkness until sleep claimed him as well.

A thin shaft of light speared into the delivery truck through a gap at the rear door and Dan stretched, sitting up to look around the space. Kate still slept, her breathing slow and deep, as he climbed out from under the blankets and onto his feet. He made his way to the sliding door that led into the cab of the truck and squinted through the small, grimy window. The sun shone high over the treetops. They'd overslept. *Damn it.*

"Kate. Wake up, sweetheart. We gotta get going."

His daughter stirred, yawning. "Is it raining?" Her voice was rough with sleep.

"Nope. But who knows how long the weather will hold. Upsy-daisies, sweetheart."

Kate grumbled something unintelligible and covered her head with a blanket as Dan slid the door open. It rattled the entire truck and flooded their sleeping space with light. Dan sighed at what a shame it was that this truck wouldn't start, it would have been so much easier to drive up to the camp store than it was going to be to bike all the way up there—and they still had to actually locate a pair of bicycles before they could even start. He climbed out of the cab and into the late morning sun.

His daughter followed a few moments later, squinting and shading her eyes. "How far off is the camp store."

"Probably around twenty miles, but half of that is going to be mostly uphill."

"I'm gonna need more than a ten-speed then." She huffed and looked around.

Dan was just hoping they could find any bicycles at all let alone something with gears, but he didn't share that with Kate. She gathered her bag off the gnarled tree she had hung it from the night before and went back into the delivery truck to pack the few things they had gathered. Dan gazed up at the sky and noted the horsetail clouds that Amber had mentioned the day before had pushed off to the east and were followed by lower, heavier clouds that were beginning to pile up on the mountains.

A sick sense of dread filled his gut. "What are we going to do, Emily?" He whispered to himself.

You have to hurry, my love. Hurry. His wife's voice rattled his very bones, and he looked frantically around himself to be sure she wasn't really right there with him.

Was he finally losing his mind? Had all his trauma finally snowballed into a big enough problem that his mind was breaking? Scrubbing palms across his face, he forced a smile as Kate emerged from the truck with her bag packed.

"Who ya talking to?" She canted her head to one side, puzzled.

"Just myself," Dan sighed. "Come on, let's get outta here." He twitched his head toward the old neighborhood to their left.

Kate nodded silently and followed.

Within an hour they had found two serviceable bicycles in addition to a few more supplies and were headed north, into the forest. The sun was already high in the sky and Dan's stomach churned. Emily's voice kept on sounding in his mind, *Hurry. Hurry. Faster.* The urgency of her words pumping adrenaline into his veins.

Kate whizzed along at his side, puffing from exertion, with a determined set to her jaw, so much like her mother. She reached up to brush a tear from her cheek and wiped more unshed tears from her eyes, blinking hard.

"It's ok to cry, Katie," Dan said over the rush of wind in his ears.

"I know. It's just—I feel like," his daughter struggled to find the right words as she looked over at him, slowing her vigorous pedaling. She coasted to a stop. "Dad, I keep hearing her voice. Like she's just over my shoulder telling me not to be afraid." Tears were streaming freely down her cheeks and her chin quivered.

Dan set the kickstand down and stepped off his bike, then quickly wrapped his daughter in a tight hug. If Kate had been hearing Emily in the same way that he had, could it be that he wasn't losing his mind after all? Was it really possible that his wife's soul was actually there with them? Guiding them, urging them along, like a guardian angel?

"I know it sounds crazy, but—"

"I hear her too, Katie-Bear," Dan interrupted. He wouldn't allow his daughter to feel alone in her experience, especially since he was truly sharing it with her.

She looked up at him with shock in her red-rimmed eyes. "What?"

"It's like she's right here with us, giving us the push that we need."

Just then a gust of wind rammed into them, bringing the scent of rain with it.

Go. Go now!

Dan and Kate both jumped and sucked in a breath, staring in shock at each other's faces, eyes round as saucers. "You heard?" Kate whispered.

Dan nodded and without another word, they spun toward their bikes and continued on. The clouds grew thicker with each passing moment and as they neared what Dan hoped was the last steep climb before a short descent to the camp store, dread began leeching into his guts. He clenched his teeth and pushed harder at the pedals. His heart pounded and his legs shook as he climbed the mountain road. Kate's muscles gave out a heartbeat before Dan's own did, and they dismounted to shakily walk their bikes up the steepest portion of the road, all the while Emily's voice sounded on the wind between them.

Keep going. You can do this. Hurry. You have to hurry!

Near the top of the grade, Kate pushed herself to a jog, huffing and puffing.

"We're getting close. Only a couple more miles," Dan said through wheezing breaths. He really should have worked more on his cardio rather than simply dusting off his old weights after he'd returned home.

"Come on, Dad. I know you're old, but you can do this. Don't crap out on me now," Kate teased, like she knew that the little jab would make him double down on his efforts.

Dan picked up his pace then hopped onto his bike, Katie followed suit with a sly smile. Dan smiled back as they pushed on.

But their smiles, were short lived. As they crested the hill and began a short descent, the yellow of the sun-tinted atmosphere around them slowly faded to a muted gray. They looked to the sky to see the clouds quickly closing ranks, blocking out the blue that remained.

"Shit," Dan hissed.

They rise!

The urgency in his veins burned into gut-piercing panic.

You have to go faster, my love. Hurry!

"Dad?" Kate called over the wind.

"Keep pushing, sweetheart," he ground out without looking over at his daughter. And then the first drop of rain smacked him right in the forehead.

"Dad!" Kate yelled and pointed behind them.

Dan's head whipped around. Two shadows ran down the road far behind them.

"Damn it," he whispered to himself, then calling over the wind he said, "Shift up to the hardest gear and push!"

Katie's bike clanked as the lever pushed the chain to the next gear and then once more. Each pump on the pedals pulled her further ahead of him. Good, he thought. Keep going, sweetheart. Go. Go!

Rain began falling in earnest, soaking the road, blurring objects in the distance. He glanced over his shoulder again to see another shadow materialize out of the trees and onto the road, joining the two darkling spawn already on their tail. One of the creatures let out a screaming shriek and Dan felt the blood drain from his face. All around them, the distant echoes of other creatures calling back filled the air.

Kate's face was pale as a bedsheet when she looked back at him.

"Keep going! We're almost there. It should be right around this bend," Dan yelled. He glanced behind himself again. The creatures were gaining on them. How the hell did they move so fast?

To the left!

Dan cranked his head just in time to see a creature with sparse, brown fur and curled, goat-like horns leap from the cover of the forest and onto the road, landing gracefully on cloven hooves and spindly legs not twenty feet behind him. Its neck was too long and its face was all wrong. Goat eyes glowed red out of the creature's skull, but its mouth gaped wide, filled with a row of sharp teeth and a forked tongue. It skittered on the pavement a moment before launching after him.

"Faster, Katie!" Dan bellowed. His bike was already in the hardest gear, so he stood on the pedals and pumped for all he was worth.

The clack of the creature's hooves and panting breath sounded closer behind him as he gained on his daughter. As they zipped around the last bit of the curve, a stretch of straight road greeted them and right where he had known the camp store should be, lay an empty, overgrown lot. *What!?*

You're almost there, my love. Go!

"Go where?" Dan called into the ether a second before Kate disappeared right before his eyes. A shriek sounded behind him a heartbeat before the back tire of his bicycle was jerked to the side and he crashed to the ground, rolling across the asphalt. He grunted as he hit the pavement shoulder first, but as he tumbled, he passed through a wavering barrier, sliding to a stop on his back, Amber's backpack saving him from a serious case of road rash.

He looked up to see the creature leaping toward him, but as it passed through the barrier after him, it burst into flame. The darkling spawn disintegrated into nothing more than floating smoke and ash before it even hit the ground. Dan scrambled backward, eyes darting in all directions. He was in the camp store parking lot. All the outbuildings sitting just where they should be...where they *hadn't* been just a moment ago.

How—

"Dad! Watch out!" Kate cried out a second before the three other darkling spawn skidded to a halt just outside the barrier, snarling.

The light dome!

Get inside, quickly! Emily's urgent voice rattled in Dan's mind as he lurched to his feet.

"Go around the back!" he called out to his daughter, but she was already disappearing around the side of the building. Dan lunged after her, arms pumping, the backpack bouncing awkwardly. His boots slid in the loose gravel at the side of the building, and he darted to the back door where Kate waited, holding it open for him, wide eyed.

Once inside, he slammed the door shut and cranked the deadbolt, puffing a moment before pulling his daughter into a crushing hug.

"Are you okay, sweetheart?" He pulled back and held her face in his hands.

Katie nodded, her hair plastered to her forehead by the rain. "Yeah, I think so. But what about you?" She reached up to touch the shredded shoulder of his shirt and vest, then paused, "Road rash?"

Dan looked at the shoulder in question, "Probably, but it doesn't feel like anything else is wrong with it," he said as he tilted his head from side to side and rolled both his shoulders. He felt alright considering he'd just wrecked while going full tilt on a twelve-speed mountain bike.

They both stood in the back entryway of the camp store simply trying to catch their breath a moment.

Kate sank slowly to her knees then flopped onto her back. "We made it," she breathed. "We're alive."

Her voice sounded small as trembling fingers brushed damp hair out of her eyes, then palms covered her face while silent sobs wracked her body.

Dan knelt down beside her as she turned over on her side, curling into a ball.

"We're safe, sweetheart," he said as he lay a hand on her shoulder. "It's gonna be alright. Let it out."

Kate sat up and locked arms around her father's waist. "One more second and you wouldn't have made it. Mom knew," she spoke between huffs and sobs, "Mom knew you were getting too tired. She told me to tease you about being old," she laughed through her tears.

"Your mother always did know how to keep me motivated," Dan chuckled through his own flowing tears.

"What are we going to do without her, Dad?" Kate's voice cracked. "She was the glue that held us together."

"Definitely the boss in every way. She held us accountable and held us together. But look at us now," Dan said, sniffing and drying the tears on his cheeks with the back of his hand. "By some miracle, she got us here, now we have to keep going. We've got to survive and make her proud."

Kate nodded, her head still pressed to his chest.

I am already so proud of you,

Dan and Kate both stilled.

And I want nothing more than to wrap you both in my arms.

Dan turned to face the sound of his wife's voice and found a tiny orb floating beside him. It glowed with a sparkling white-blue light that pulsed in time with his own heartbeat. He stopped breathing.

Kate lifted her head from his chest and gasped at the sight. "Mom?"

Oh, my Katie-Bear, you are so strong and brave and beautiful. The orb bobbed. *Keep growing into the force I know you are meant to be.*

She nodded vigorously, and sniffled.

Listen to our daughter, my love. She may be young, but she knows what is good for you. She gets that from me.

Dan sputtered a broken laugh and continued to sob with a crooked smile at his lips.

I love you both so much and I would stay with you always...but...something pulls me. Calls me to come home. I don't think I can fight it much longer.

"How can I do this without you?" Dan said, choking on the words. He would never be able to protect and raise a teenager in the midst of all this chaos and death. Not on his own. Not without *her.* Sure, he put on a confident face for the world, but the only reason he was still breathing was because of his wife. She'd saved his life every single day with her easy smile and the stubborn way she loved him. She was his foundation; she grounded him in reality and held him there so he could try to be the man his family needed him to be. He was nothing without her. "You've always been my rock. I don't think I can even stand on my own two feet without you by my side."

You can and you will, my love. You won't be on your own for long and there will be many others for you to lean on. The sparkling orb began to drift and fade, and with it, the strength of Emily's connection to them both. *You cannot imagine it now, but you will soon. The peace and love I feel in this form is indescribable. You will feel it too. I promise.*

Dan shook his head, not believing the agony of loss would ever fade.

"But how are you always so strong? You always know just what to say and do...I could never—" Kate's voice cracked, "I could never be as strong as you."

You already are sweetheart. If only you could see what I see in you now. You are going to mature under the guidance of so many great beings. Better days are coming, and I wish I could be there to see your face when you learn all that I know in this form.

"I miss you so much." Dan reached a shaking hand toward the orb, but it drifted out of reach.

I will be missing you both until we are together again, united with The Goddess. *But do not mourn me.* Emily's words were barely a whisper in Dan's mind. *I'm happy and my eternal spark continues on. You'll see me in every sunrise, in the light that shines down on your face, and every time you hear the wind whisper through the trees, you'll know I'm there with you. Remember me in the love for life that burns in your soul. Release your sorrow and know that I am free and filled with joy for all the new experiences that await you both.*

The orb faded out of existence and with it, the loving embrace of the most important person in Dan's life. No, that person was Kate now, and she clung to him as if her life depended on it.

"We're gonna be ok Katie. We're gonna be ok," Dan whispered into his daughter's hair with a tight squeeze, trying to convince himself as much as his daughter.

This was the hardest thing he could have ever imagined having to endure. He had always thought that *he* was going to be the one to pass on first; learning to live without his wife had never even crossed his mind.

With a sigh, Kate began to relax in his arms, her sobs growing softer. Was it really possible to keep going? To continue without the love of his life? Nothing would ever be the same in his world, but his wife's last words still rang in his mind. *Release your sorrow and know that I am free.* Her energy still permeated the air, and he breathed deep, trying to hold to the remnants of her light, but the tighter he held to what was no longer there, the more his chest ached. He swallowed a sob. It was too hard. He couldn't do this.

"Dad, you have to let her go," Kate whispered into his chest.

But he didn't want to let her go. He needed her there with him. It hurt too much to imagine life without her.

"Please try."

His chest tightened, and he closed his eyes, struggling to release the pure anguish in his heart. Tentatively, he reached for the hope that Emily had left behind. Peace began to spread through his chest, radiating out through his limbs in waves of warmth and love.

Unbidden, an image appeared in his mind's eye: an orb slowly drifting toward a tall woman whose dark skin and coiled hair seemed to glow with the same shimmering light as the orb. The woman reached out an elegant hand, a dreamy smile dancing on her full lips. The orb settled in her palm, and she spoke—her voice low and resonant—as she brought the orb to her chest: *Welcome home, Seed Child.* The orb flashed brilliantly, and the scene faded.

Dan opened his eyes and gasped. More tears streamed down his face, but in the place of sorrow, his heart was filled with gratitude. Gratitude for having known such an extraordinary woman and for the knowledge he now possessed that her beautiful soul really existed with the Goddess. His heart still longed to beat in time with hers and probably always would, but he knew that with time, he really was going to be alright.

23

Monsters in Men

SIX DAYS LATER, I WAS GOING STIR CRAZY. My ribs still ached but not nearly as badly as they had, and although my neck still bore the bruised marks from the man behind the desk's meaty fingers, I could swallow and speak pain free. I was up and pacing the diameter of the canvas medical tent when the nurse, Gail, stepped inside with a plate of food.

She really was a kind woman, captured and trapped in the situation just as I was. Also, she wasn't really a nurse. She had been a CNA and after realizing that she didn't really like dealing with human patients, she went to school to become a veterinarian. Now, in a world where people with medical skills were extremely hard to come by, she made herself valuable to this group of heathens by stepping in as a field nurse.

My first night in the tent, when I had been unable to speak, after she had finally shooed DJ away, she told me all she knew about the group we had found ourselves a part of. Before the power had gone out, most of the high-ranking members had been part of the Emergency Preparedness Community. They called themselves 'Survivalists' or 'Preppers'. Several of them had in-ground shelters built into their homes or yards and all of them had food and supply storages to support them and their families for a solid year at minimum. All were avid gun owners, which partially explained the plethora of firearms and ammunition the group had access to, and for some reason, there weren't as many women involved in the community as there were men. The men outnumbered the women three to one, and when testosterone flows that thickly, terrible incidents could happen.

Enter Charles Williams, the man behind the desk. A man with a bad case of narcissism, paranoia, and a God complex. He'd placed himself at the head of the community and ruled with an iron fist, making it his life's mission to ensure humans survived this catastrophe by whatever means necessary, and since females were scarce, that meant finding as many as possible to bring into the fold and making sure these females were...fruitful. Meaning, he basically wanted every woman barefoot and pregnant for the rest of their lives. I felt like I had been tossed into the apocalyptic, Godless version of A Handmaid's Tale.

Gail explained to me that 'Rotation' required all women of childbearing age to spend their fertile days of the month with a male who was unattached. If she didn't conceive that cycle, she would be rotated to the next male in line for her next cycle, and the rotation would continue until she conceived. Then she would be placed with that male permanently. Her thoughts on the matter were not considered. At all. It was something Charles demanded of every woman in exchange for food, shelter and—relative—safety from the demons (what they called the darkling spawn).

Gail, however, was not part of the rotation. She'd had a hysterectomy a number of years prior, and if it weren't for her medical skills, there was an equal chance she would have been put out of the community or held in the whore house to be used at the will of whatever man needed release. A sickening shudder rolled down my spine at the thought.

Together with DJ and a friend of his, (whose name they kept to themselves) they had helped over a dozen women escape rotation and the whore house. But I absolutely did not trust DJ as far as I could have thrown him. It didn't matter to me whether or not he was helping women escape, he was part of this horrid group of people. He could have left, but he chose to stay. Gail was a prisoner, just like I was, but DJ was technically a free man. He could leave if he chose to...but he stayed despite how cruel these people were.

Even though Charles and his closest enforcers still had no idea how the women were escaping, they did know there was a hole in their security, and they were trying like hell to find it. It made me sick to think about what might happen to Gail if they found out she knew anything about it.

I smiled weakly as Gail handed me the plate. She smiled back and together we moved toward a small dining table in the kitchenette area of the tent.

"How's your throat feeling?" she asked with a sigh as she lowered herself into the chair across from me.

"The bruises are still tender but it's a little better every day," I said as I picked up my fork and scooped up a mouthful of bland chicken and rice. It was worse than hospital food. "This is horrible."

"White people cooking. What more did you expect?" Gail said as a smirk played across her full lips. "No offense."

"None taken," I chuckled around my mouthful of food. "It's like they don't even know what salt and pepper is."

She produced a handful of salt and pepper packets from her jacket pocket and set them in a pile at the center of the table.

"Thanks."

She nodded in response and examined me while I seasoned the food and ate. As a veterinarian, her clients couldn't tell her what was wrong, and even though I told her I was feeling better, she carefully watched how I chewed, swallowed, and moved in general. "Your ribs are still bothering you, huh?"

"A little bit. Only when I move a certain way or cough." A sarcastic note crept into my voice, "The bruises are turning all kinds of pretty colors," I said with a small smirk as I put my fork down to lift the edge of my shirt. The marks were fading from angry red and purple, to brown, green, and yellow.

"That's a good sign. How are your hands doing?"

I presented my healed, if slightly peeling palms to her for inspection.

Gail bobbed her head, "Quick healer," she remarked as she pushed herself to her feet. "DJ is asking to speak to you again." She casually threw the statement over her shoulder as she made her way to the exam corner where all the meds were kept.

It was a good thing she was halfway across the tent before she mentioned his name, or I may have socked her. "I don't have a thing to say to him. Just like yesterday. And it'll be the same tomorrow."

"He's trapped here, same as you and me. You know that."

"He's been out every clear day with a crew, looking for supplies and women since the beginning," I spat back at Gail. "And he could leave if he really wanted to, but he doesn't."

She turned around and pinned me with a glare that could have made a grown man wither as she cranked open a pill bottle. "And where would he go?" Her brows arched as she marched back toward me. "Not everyone here is a shit bag, you've got to understand that. Most of us are just doing what we need to do to survive." Her voice dropped to a tense whisper as she neared the table. "You know what we're doing here. Every woman taken against her will, every girl that would rather face the demons and starvation than live this way, he's helped escape."

"But he's *here*. He *chooses* to stay here. On some level he's got to agree with it."

"He has to keep up appearances. If Charles found out that DJ is the security breach, he'd be executed. Plain and simple. Besides, you seem to trust me—"

"Well, you aren't a man. And you aren't benefiting from the situation the same as they are," I interrupted with a harsh whisper.

She'd done this the last couple of days, telling me that good people can get mixed up in bad things much easier than I would expect, but to me it was black and white. Good people left bad situations or died trying because their conscience wouldn't allow anything else. It's what Dan was probably doing right now, and as far as I was concerned, he was the only good man I had met—aside from my little brother—my entire life.

First, my stupid father had up and left us. Second was my first boyfriend in middle school who decided that he'd rather hold hands with another girl than me. Then there was that time I tried the dating apps...which was a complete disaster. Every other guy was just looking for a way to get ahead or get laid and even though I had met DJ organically, I was convinced he fell into that group as well. Plus, who knew if he was really letting those women escape?

"You should at least hear him out," Gail said as she placed a pain killer and glass of water on the table in front of me.

I snapped up the pill and the glass with a glare. I didn't want to hear him out. I wanted to hold to all the anger I felt because if I didn't have the anger—the fury—at my situation, I knew I wouldn't survive rotation. I'd rather be dead than passed around like a sex doll until I got knocked up. Motherhood was never a role I'd wanted for myself either. I'd seen how hard my mom struggled to raise Joey and me. And for what? They were both probably dead now. All of her hard work for nothing. If this was the way the world was going to be, I didn't want to be in it, let alone bring another human into it. What if I gave birth to a girl? No. I refused to be a part of this mess. I'd rather walk out into the dark.

After swallowing the painkiller, I shoveled another bite of the bland chicken and rice into my mouth as Gail moved to the tent entrance and held it open.

DJ walked in.

I promptly lost my appetite.

Dropping my fork onto the plate with a clatter, I leaned back in the chair and folded my arms across my chest. My stomach churned at the memory of his sweet, confident smile the day we met in the park. It felt like a lifetime ago. How stupid was I to have dreamed up an entire Prince Charming persona for him while I was stuck at the camp store? While I was up there dreaming of a perfect life with my family and a perfectly handsome, kind, and caring DJ, he was down here capturing innocent and terrified women and forcing them into sexual servitude. I should have known better. Mom taught me better than to be a daydreaming, lovesick fool.

I hit him with a hard stare as he made his way across the tent. He was wearing regular clothes instead of the gear all the gunmen wore on patrol. A dark hoodie, some light jogging pants and running shoes. He'd shaved since I'd seen him last, only a small bit of beard stubble darkened his chin. He looked like a regular guy you could introduce your family to—make a life with.

He was a wolf in sheep's clothing.

I looked between him and Gail feeling more than a little bit trapped. My heart kicked up a notch as DJ settled himself into the chair opposite from me and Gail stepped out of the tent.

"What do you want?" I asked sullenly.

"I just want to talk," he said, voice low and soothing.

"So, talk. Doesn't mean that I have to listen."

He sighed and rubbed his face before letting his hands fall to his lap. "You're not going to make this easy, are you?"

"Why should I?" I waved an angry hand in his direction.

"Because I'm doing the best I can with this shit situation." His eyes roamed the tent then settled on his hands.

He couldn't even look me in the face and was obviously feeling guilty. About what exactly, I wasn't sure, because he did have a lot to feel guilty about.

"And you 'doing your best' is supposed to convince me that you aren't just as dangerous as the Driver that beats on women or the leader of this shit show that wants to 'give me an attitude adjustment'?"

He flinched at the venom in my voice and for an instant, I felt that maybe he really didn't deserve my anger. But I needed it, so I brushed away any sympathies or imagined feelings I might have once had for him and glared.

"I never imagined you could be this hateful and stubborn when I first met you back in the park," he said with a crooked smile.

"Well, I've been through some shit since then. And I could have never imagined that you would have taken up with a group of gun-toting rapists, so please excuse my piss poor attitude," I snapped at him.

"Would you at least listen to how I got mixed up with these people in the first place?" he sighed. "Then you can make whatever decision you want to about me. Regardless, Gail and I are going to do our damnedest to get you out of here before—" He stopped short, searching for the right words, "We're *going* to get you out of here." His gaze flashed toward mine then went back to his hands.

Damn it, was that real emotion behind his eyes? It would have been so much easier to hate him if it didn't actually seem like he was telling the truth. At the very least, he looked like he believed what he was saying.

A seed of hope took root in my chest despite my best efforts to lock anything he was saying out of my heart. It was then I understood the real reason for my anger and why I didn't want to see or speak to him. I had expected him to be different. And that had just set me up for disappointment—for feeling let down that he wasn't acting the way I thought he should.

All traces of my anger vanished, and I leaned toward him, eyes pleading. "Come with me," I whispered. "We could leave all this madness behind. You and me."

He blinked as if taken aback and paused a beat before answering, "I-I wish I could, but..."

"But, what?" I asked as the hope I had just felt began to drain away. Of course, there would be a *but.*

"If I left, the people they capture would be trapped here. No chance of escape," he whispered back at me, leaning forward, his eyes finally met mine. "This is an organization that needs to be unraveled from within."

I sat back with a heavy sigh and a bitter smile. "Of course. How convenient," I snorted. "You know, if you cut the head off a snake the body dies too."

"And Charles is the head of the snake?"

"Duh."

"That's where you're wrong, Amber. This snake has a dozen heads. There are too many people here that agree whole-heartedly with his vision. They won't stop. They're too well provisioned. Too well organized. These people have had a hard-on for the apocalypse for decades. They're literally living their wet dreams right now and making other people's lives a nightmare in the process."

I blinked. *Well, shit. I hadn't considered that.*

Just because DJ had a deeper knowledge of the inner workings of the budding Survivalist society didn't make him any more trustworthy. My lips pressed into a thin line, and I sighed heavily, really contemplating listening to him. My mind was angry, and my heart was sore, but my gut was gently prodding me to give him a chance...and in spite of everything, I wanted to believe him.

"Alright, I'll humor ya," I said.

DJ's entire body rose from deflated and resigned to cautiously optimistic in a single heartbeat.

"Thank you." He reached across the table toward me then let his hand drop when all I did was stare at it. I wasn't going to be that easily convinced.

I pointed at him with my chin in a silent command for him to continue.

He pursed his lips and began, "About a week after the power went out, the national guard rolled into town. They set up ration and water lines and when I went through the first time, I told the soldiers there that I was a former service member, and I knew that my current bartending job wouldn't be calling me back any time soon. There were several other people that had the same idea as me and we rode back into Portland with them. After a brutal briefing, and several chances to back out, I was processed and put back in uniform."

All that seemed plausible. I had seen remnants of military occupation around town as I wandered from my house to Miller Park. "Okay, but how did the military still have running vehicles after the power went out?" I asked.

"Military vehicles are hardened against EMP's. The electronic components are all easily replaced, and the motor pool keeps most spare parts in EMP proof storage containers, but that's not important." He huffed a bit before continuing, "We were told from the get-go that there was a connection between the earthquakes that had happened at Yellowstone last year and the big one we experienced here, but it was classified information we couldn't share with the public. Things were mostly calm, and command wanted it to stay that way."

"So, they knew about the dark—demon creatures," I stammered, barely catching myself before I said their true name, "before everyone else did and they did nothing to stop them?"

"I think so, but we weren't told about them until an attack happened out in Canby, Oregon. The creatures attacked a checkpoint at night and completely leveled it. We were on high alert after that, but the attacks kept happening every night. They were getting closer and closer to downtown. Command set up massive blockades on the interstate bridges, then we heard of other attacks in Seattle and all the way to the south of Tacoma. Reports of attacks were coming in from all over the country along with rumors that the creatures were everywhere from Canada to Mexico. Command switched tactics and every remaining battalion west of the Rockies was told to hunker down. We still had civilians to feed, so we continued the ration lines twice a week. Then, the creatures caught us all by surprise and attacked in broad daylight. Well, it was cloudy and raining when they attacked. We didn't know—" His voice broke off, but he shook his head and kept going, "I was added security for the ration lines at Ellsworth Park."

I shot forward in my chair, "That's right near my house."

A shadow passed over DJ's face, his eyes looking far away. "The creatures attacked the ration lines. There were so many people there...so many of my friends. It was a bloodbath." He shook his head and closed his eyes. "I ended up on a residential street and the creatures were closing in. I took a bunch of them down but—if you don't hit them in the head, they just keep coming. I ran out of ammo. They cornered me up on a porch. I was on my ass with my back against the door reciting The Lord's Prayer when the door behind me opened and I was dragged inside. I was so confused; I didn't even register what was going on until Charles pulled me up and told me to follow him. There were other people in the house, all of them moved like they had military training, and we made our way down to his basement while the demons came crashing in behind us. He had a bunker built right under the foundation of his house. We all piled in through a steel hatch."

My mouth hung open, "*Charles* saved you?"

"He did."

That meant that that sleazebag of a man probably lived somewhere in my neighborhood! I tried not to look shocked and disgusted.

"I really thought he was one of the good ones," DJ continued, "He had all sorts of functioning tech in the bunker, security cameras, monitors, a CB, and two-way radios all listening in to the military and police frequencies. The place was a fortress, stocked with food, supplies and water for months. Seeing them so prepared while listening to the military get obliterated, I decided I should stay with them." DJ slumped in his chair, head hanging, shame rolling off of him.

"You...deserted?"

He grimaced and nodded. "It sounds awful when you put it like that, but yeah, I guess I did. I'm not proud of it now, but in the moment, it was clear that the creatures had our number. I told myself I'd just hide with Charles and his crew until the sun came out, but a week later, we lost all contact with central command...radio silence across the country. What was left of the Orchardville detachment was planning to gather all the civilians they could and create a secure community at the Orchardville Mall, but by then Charles' guys had figured out that when people gathered in large groups, the creatures could find them easier somehow, or they just made a better target. Charles even tried to send a warning to the detachment that a gathering of that size was ill advised. Of course, the military isn't going to listen to a 'crazy doomsday prepper' that's hiding out in his basement, but he was right.

"The Mall community was wiped out. Once that happened, Charles and his crew commandeered the rest of the working military equipment and set up the command center here. They are the only force in the area and since he's figured out how to fly under the creatures' radar and several members of the group have bunkers on their properties, everyone that comes here on sunny days to meet and gather more supplies has a safe place to go after dark or when it's raining."

My mind reeled. Could Mom and Joey have gone with the military to the mall community? Is that why the house had an 'X' painted on it? Best not to think about that. They were gone either way.

I turned my thoughts back to the matter at hand. "We've been stuck here for, what—a week? I haven't heard the creatures at all, even at night." I said, "I know there are more people than just the three of us here. How has this place not been attacked like the mall?"

"It's a big building with thick, concrete walls and no windows. There is no way for them to get up on the roof and the security doors can't be opened from the outside. You remember seeing what these people did to secure the front of the store?" DJ asked, raising his eyebrows at me.

I had seen when I was being dragged into the building. Where automatic, sliding glass retail doors had once stood, a cinderblock and concrete wall had been erected. Heavy, steel doors had been installed and blocking it all from the outside world was an industrial strength, steel rolling security grate. I nodded at him.

"I've been here every night along with two other truck teams for security. Charles and his inner circle left, but it's been cloudy and raining since the day after we found you. So, the rest of us have been stuck here, waiting out the weather."

"That doesn't make me feel any better," I said with a shudder. Knowing that Gail and I were the only females locked in a building with about fifteen probable rapists made my stomach turn.

"I'm telling you this because I want you to know that you're safe here for the moment. There are rules in place, and no one is stupid enough to go against Charles' orders. But after you're healed up, hell, maybe even before that if the weather clears up, they're going to transfer you to Charles' place and I—"

"What?!"

DJ brought a panicked finger to his lips, head whipping to the entry of the tent. Gail popped her head in a moment later. "He's coming," was all she said before disappearing again.

"Son of a bitch," DJ cursed under his breath as he bounded to his feet almost upsetting his chair.

"What? Who's coming?" I hissed, my voice just above a whisper. I rose to my feet as well.

"Fucking Frank," DJ said in a low voice that made my blood run cold. Frank was the Driver that nearly broke my ribs and busted my face. Pure, unadulterated hatred twisted DJ's handsome face into a hard mask as he stalked towards me. I stepped backward as he advanced, my heart hammering in my chest. His demeanor had gone from zero to life-in-prison in a heartbeat.

What the hell?

"DJ, what's going on?" My voice came out weak and shaky. I brought my hands up to protect myself from him as I continued backing away, but then my back met the canvas of the tent and I froze, heart in my throat. I couldn't move. Couldn't breathe.

DJ gently wrapped an arm around my waist and pulled me toward him as his expression softened. "This guy is the worst of Charles' inner circle—helped him develop the entire system they run on, but he's a rule follower. Act afraid, push me, struggle, do whatever you have to do, just play along," he whispered just as the tent entrance flapped open and Frank stepped in. At the soft scraping sound, DJ's expression returned to that hardened mask while his hazel eyes bore into mine.

My vision blurred at the edges. Act afraid? I didn't have to act. He was too close. He shouldn't be touching me. And that look of hunger on his face? My gut tightened, adrenaline shot through my veins, and I shoved at the broad expanse of his chest but got nowhere.

"What are you doing?" My voice wavered just above a whisper as I clenched the front of his hoodie in my fists and pushed at him again. "Let me go."

He didn't though. His grip tightened as he wound his fingers into the hair at the nape of my neck and slowly pulled my head back, exposing my neck. I gasped as my neck and ribs protested to the movement. He lowered his face to mine and wet his lips. "I'm so sorry," he whispered.

For a moment, the world stopped. No sound. No words. Only DJ's hand tangled in my hair and the feeling of my own, hot blood roaring through my veins.

Frank cleared his throat and DJ stiffened. I kept shoving.

"Well, what do we have here?" Frank's slimy voice filled the tent, and I went rigid.

DJ threw a look over his shoulder and grunted, "None of your business. Just walk away. You didn't see anything."

"I wondered when one of these bitches would catch your eye. I never thought you'd have a thing for scrawny brunettes," Frank said, amusement touching his voice. "But then again—"

"Fuck off, Frank. I'm busy here," DJ growled as he loosened his hold on my waist to turn and glare fully at the other man. His jaw clenched as his hand, still tangled in my hair, squeezed lightly and my eyes went wide.

"Now that her face is healing up and she doesn't smell like demon blood, I s'pose she is pretty cute. I get it." Frank took a prowling step in our direction.

Something snapped within me, and I flailed. "Let go of me!" I hissed. DJ shook me gently by the head and I grit my teeth as the movement combined with my struggling strained my ribs and neck again. Tears stung the back of my eyes as I brought my hands up to my head to pry at his fingers.

"Still a little feisty, eh? You know Charles likes to deal with the spicy ones."

"Well, so do I and it's not fair that he gets to do all the breaking around here." DJ's voice didn't even sound like his own as he spoke.

Frank barked out a laugh, "Shit," he dragged the word out with a sneer, "all it took was a week locked in a building with some fresh meat and suddenly your hand ain't doin' it for you anymore?" He clucked his tongue and shook his head. "Well, if it was up to me, I'd say we get the rest of the boys in here and run a train on this bitch for what she did to my last crew," Frank drawled, voice dripping with venom. "But I've known Charles for years and he'd have our heads." Frank clapped DJ on the shoulder, "Besides, I hear you're first in rotation after Charles is done with her. You're moving up, kid."

"Sloppy seconds ain't my style," DJ drawled, "and they're too docile after he's done with them anyway. This little feral cat is mine to tame."

My stomach churned and I struggled harder, gritting through the pain in my ribs and neck.

"You know, that's something I would actually love to see," Frank's eyes raked me from head to toe, and he licked his lips hungrily before he turned back to DJ. "But she's not a whore, she's a breeder, and rules are rules. If we don't live by them, we die by them. Understand?"

DJ turned back towards me and our eyes met. A look of longing darkened his eyes as a greedy gaze took a slow tour of my body. My blood ran cold.

He turned back to Frank. "This is bullshit, and you know it. Just look at her. She's a perfectly sized plaything."

"Fuck you," I ground out, trying not to break down into a fit of tears. "Fuck you both."

They laughed as DJ turned his full attention back to me, his eyes dark and fevered. "I can't wait," he murmured, gaze dragging over my face like a brand, "to see you tied and bent over the side of my bed," he wet his lips—slow, deliberate—then flicked his eyes to my mouth and leaned in closer...so close I could taste the warmth of his breath on my parted lips as I sucked in a ragged breath.

His grip in my hair loosened and the heat of his palm settled on the back of my neck as his thumb grazed the hinge of my jaw. My heart pounded in my ears. Then his eyes locked onto mine, smoldering and possessive, "Panting, waiting," his eyes drifted back to my mouth, "Wet," he growled and pulled my face toward his.

My palm cracked across his cheek with all the strength I possessed. A look of amused shock danced across his face a heartbeat before a dark smile spread across his lips. My palm stung and my heart pounded, but the look in his eyes lit something deep within me. He was enjoying this. I knew it from my gut to my wobbling knees.

He hissed in a breath and growled, "A little rough too...just the way I like it. Good girl."

Warmth pooled in my belly. Why did I suddenly want to—no. No. Absolutely not.

He winked before letting me go then walked away, shoving and laughing with Frank like they were old pals. I stood shaking and panting, one hand on the canvas wall of the tent, the other covering my mouth. What was that all about?

"When the weather clears up, we'll get you out to the whore house to blow off some steam, eh?" Frank laughed as he and DJ left the tent together.

My ears rang. The warmth from his fingers still lingered on my skin. What had just *happened?* I sank to the floor trembling, bile rising in my throat, tears stinging my eyes.

Overwhelmed, helpless and confused, I dissolved into a sobbing mess. Moments later, Gail was at my side, helping me up and over to my cot.

"Are you hurt?" Gail asked as she took a hard look at my neck again.

"Of course I am," I sobbed. "He's a fucking monster." I knew it. I *knew* I shouldn't have trusted him.

Gail gave me a flat lipped look. "Did he hurt you or did you hurt yourself struggling?"

" *What*—why would you even ask that? Did you hear what he said to me?"

"Alright, just breathe," she tried to soothe while I tried to catch my breath. After a while she said, "DJ wouldn't hurt you. Not on purpose. Think about it. Since the beginning, has he ever actually hurt you?"

I thought back to when I was thrown in the truck. That wasn't him, but he had pushed me down with his boot when I tried to sit up. I relayed that to Gail.

"Did he kick you, stomp his foot down?"

"Well, no. I guess he didn't." The pressure on my back had been gentle and when they dragged me into the building, he'd supported me when my knees buckled. Even when he'd just shaken my head, he'd done so gently. Had my ribs and neck not been bruised, it wouldn't have hurt at all. He'd even apologized.

As I played it all back in my head, my heart rate began to slow, and Gail rubbed my back.

"He's got a good heart, I know you can see it," Gail whispered. "But these men are hard and cruel. The only thing they respect is brute strength and cunning. If Frank had walked in and caught you two just talking, he would have known something was up, and DJ didn't have enough time to get out of the tent without being seen. He did what was necessary to keep the secret."

I nodded knowing that she was right but still sick that DJ could code switch so quickly. One second, he'd been the open and kind person I'd met in the park and the next, he'd morphed into the monster these men expected him to be. But Gail hadn't seen the look in his eyes. She hadn't seen the hunger there. I had.

That had felt *very* real.

I'd been so excited to get to know him once when he'd just been a friendly stranger out for a jog on a sunny morning. He'd been charming and funny and handsome and easy to talk to. There had been so much potential for something more, but in our current situation he had truly scared the hell out of me. It made my stomach turn.

I swallowed as saliva flooded my mouth. I began shaking all over as the adrenaline leeched out of my system. "I think I'm gonna be sick."

The other woman snapped up a plastic tub and held my hair back as I lost what little food I'd eaten. "Oh—God, I'm sorry,"

"It's alright, baby." She set the tub out of the way on the floor and pulled me into a warm, comforting hug. "These times will make good people do horrible things just to survive. You're strong. You can do this. But you've got to keep your chin up. And you've got to trust him. He knows what he's doing."

"How am I supposed to ever trust him when he scares me so badly?" I croaked into her shoulder.

Gail didn't answer, only sighed, and stroked my hair.

Suddenly, Dan popped into my mind. He was caring, considerate and always tried to do what was right. He had a family that loved him, and he'd *murdered* a man just to keep me alive. But he was still a good person. Of course, Dan had never pretended to be something that he was not. Unlike DJ.

The whole situation was as murky and gray as a fog-shrouded swamp...and I was stuck in the middle, wading through the mire. Maybe things really weren't as black and white as I thought they should be?

24

The Everything Bath

SEVERAL MORE DAYS PASSED IN a blur. DJ never came back to the med tent, but his laugh echoed through the store, mingling with other voices, loud and careless as ever. Gail kept me filled in on the weather and what the survivalists were doing, but it did little to ease my mind.

All I could do was wait. I waited to heal, waited for my meds, waited for my supervised bathroom breaks, waited for my every other day bath. Waiting, waiting, *waiting.*

I lay, stretched out on my cot, sulking, and half-dozing when Gail strode into the tent with a grim look on her face.

"Now what?" I sighed, sitting up.

"The weather's clearing up. Frank told me to make sure you're ready to go by this evening."

"Go?" my heart stuttered. "Go where?"

"You know where."

I groaned and flopped back on the cot, "Fuhhhh..."

"Come on, we gotta get you cleaned up. It's an everything bath." She tugged me to my feet, and we shuffled out of the tent and into a long hallway.

The designated bathing area—an old employee restroom outfitted with a metal watering trough, shelves, and a few chairs— smelled faintly of mildew and lavender. On a shelf, someone had neatly laid out shampoo, conditioner, body wash, razor, tweezers, towel, body oil, clean clothes, and a new pair of trail runners.

I glanced at Gail. "What happens if I refuse?"

She opened her mouth to speak, but Frank's voice oozed through the doorway like oil. "Then I get to assist in making you ready for Charles." He sucked his teeth as he stepped into the doorway; the look in his eyes could have peeled the paint off the walls.

I shrank back and stepped behind Gail.

"Oh, get outta here, Frank. I don't need your help," Gail snapped, walking over to press a firm hand to the center of his chest, forcing him back a step.

A crooked, hungry smile curled his lips, but he allowed himself to be pushed out of the room. "Pity—" he drawled.

Gail slammed the door in his face before he could finish the thought and cranked the lock then turned back toward me.

"DJ told me he was working on something," she whispered as she walked over, "I don't know what it was—the less I know about his plans, the better—but he was trying to get you out of here before this happened. If Frank is the one that takes you to Charles, for the love of all things holy, do not fight either of them. About anything."

My blood ran cold.

"Come on, clothes off." She spoke loud and clearly then pointed at the door and mouthed: *He's still out there.*

Numb, I kicked off my shoes, peeled off my socks then slid my loose jeans down my legs. I'd rather die than let either of those scum bags touch me.

Dan's words echoed in my mind, as did the memory of his kind face, *You're a damn sight tougher than you look, girl.* I tried with all my might to hold on to that, but I didn't think I was nearly stoic enough to survive any amount of time alone with Charles and Frank.

Gail caught my eye and pulled down the neckline of her shirt, revealing a jagged, half-healed, star-shaped scar just above her breast.

My breath caught, "What is—"

"It's a brand," she whispered. "I fought Charles every day. *All* day. For four days. I have three more in other places."

I gaped. "But, I thought that since you had a hysterectomy, they never—" I trailed off.

269

"I was one of the first," she said, straightening her shirt, "and Charles didn't believe me. Said he couldn't accept the word of a hysterical female. The first time he—ya know—he could tell that I had been telling the truth." She shrugged and waved a hand, urging me to keep undressing and get into the water trough. "The surgery scars are obvious. But he kept me in that bunker of his anyway. Said I needed to learn my place...the natural order of things. He branded me after every fight just to remind me who was stronger and that he owned a piece of me."

Her voice caught, but she pushed on, "Every time was worse than the one before. He tried everything he could to get any sort of resistance out of me. On the fifth night, I stopped fighting. I just laid there and stared at him no matter what he did." A dry, bitter smirk curled the corner of her mouth, "He couldn't get it up."

I gaped at her.

"He needs the struggle. The power trip. That's what turns him on; and when I took that power from him, I humiliated him. There is nothing less intimidating than a limp dick, right? I made the mistake of smirking at my discovery...he beat me bloody for it."

I eased myself into the tepid water, goosebumps rising across my skin. "Gail...I'm so sorry."

She waved my words away, "I hoped that he would kill me afterward...out of spite for figuring out his game. But it seemed that God had other plans for me. Charles needed a medic, so he sent me here instead of the brothel."

I turned to look at her. She told her story so matter-of-factly, but her experience must have been an absolute nightmare. How was she so *strong?* How did she keep going?

She dipped a large, plastic cup into the water and began gently wetting my hair, her movements slow and methodical, as if the movement gave her the strength to continue. "I've been a willing partner to more men—and women—than is probably proper. The physical violation of being unwilling wasn't the worst of it. Not for me. It was the helplessness. Knowing I wasn't strong enough to stop him, no matter how hard I tried. I was powerless. That's what almost broke me."

"How can you even stand being in the same building as him—as any of them?"

"I know that they're all insecure little pukes and Charles is the biggest one of them all. The second I understood how his mind worked; I took that power back. The scars are ugly, but I earned each one by staying strong. By not giving up." Gail placed her fingertips on her forehead and over her heart while her pointed chin angled up slightly and a defiant look settled across her features. "We're stronger up here, and in here. They can violate our bodies, even kill us—but deep down, I think we scare them more than they scare us. Deep down, they know they'll die without women—but they'll never admit that truth. So, they play the overlords."

"I—Gail, I can't do this." I closed my eyes, tears stinging at the corners. "I'm not strong enough to endure something like that and stay sane."

"No one is until they have to be," she said, cupping my cheek. "But pray, sweetheart. Pray that DJ has this figured out and you won't even have to worry about being stronger than you think you can be."

Tears fell freely from my eyes, and I nodded, turning back around in the water. There was nothing left to say, she'd put it all out there on the table. But my thoughts floundered. How had my life come to this? I couldn't place all my trust in DJ and just hope that he would figure out a way to save me from this place. That was stupid. Gail's option, to just lie there and take it, was even worse. I needed to figure out something for myself, but try as I might, I had no idea what to do.

I let her wash and condition my hair then I scrubbed, shaved, and plucked myself clean and smooth. After an hour, I climbed out of the water, shivering. I oiled my skin and dressed in the clothes that had been set out for me.

As I shimmied into the yoga pants and short cropped sweatshirt, I marveled at the fact that I'd never worn a pair of actual leggings in my life. They were surprisingly comfortable, if a bit revealing for my tastes. I sat on a low stool and Gail ran a brush through my hair in silence. There would have been nothing to talk about anyhow, so I simply tried to enjoy the feeling of a friend running a brush through my hair.

A heavy knock sounded at the door and we both jumped.

"How's it going in there?" Frank's muffled voice oozed through the door, and I cringed.

With a sigh, Gail took my hand in hers and we walked toward the door. She unlocked it and pulled it open to reveal Frank's sneering face. I was struck again by how he would have been handsome if he didn't look like he wanted to do us both harm. How had people like him existed before the world fell apart? Had they simply repressed their urges? Or had they been the fiends lurking on dating apps, hunting women at bars, buying prostitutes—or worse?

"We're burning daylight here, lets go," he said, motioning for us to head back to the tent. "Charles wants her there just before sundown, so we'll have the whole night to work a better attitude into her."

My stomach curdled. Had he just said 'we'?

I whipped around and shot him the vilest glare I could manage. "You're such a creep."

"Thank you," he said with a mocking grin and a small bow. "Been trying to earn the title 'sick fuck' for a while now, but I just can't seem to stoop to the levels that DJ is willing to go. Maybe I'll get the chance tonight? I'll be in that bunker too, ya know." He leered and wagged his brows at me.

Oh, no...

"Sorry bro, but you've been replaced." DJ slid out of the shadow of a doorway as we passed and joined our little procession.

"What the hell are you talking about?" Frank looked visibly upset.

"After you ran your mouth to the boss about my little moment of...indiscretion last week, it got his gears turning." DJ's voice was the same low purr I remembered—the one that sent shivers up my spine. I withered at the memory.

"Meaning?" Frank snapped.

"Meaning Charles wants me to assist tonight."

"You're a lying sack of shit," Frank laughed but stopped dead. "No way."

DJ just eyed him with a smirk and held out his two-way radio.

Frank snatched it up, hesitating a moment before he pressed the button and spoke, "Driver Three to Command."

A moment later, Charles' gravelly voice crackled through. "Go ahead Driver Three."

"I have a Gun here who says he is assuming my duties for the night. Over."

"Affirmative. That Gun has been promoted to Driver. Driver and package are expected at Command. Seventeen-hundred hours."

Gail's eyes went wide as she began ushering me back toward the med tent. I glanced back over my shoulder just in time to see Frank take a deep, red-faced breath through his teeth before responding, "Copy. Driver Three out." He threw the radio back at a smug looking DJ.

Their voices faded as we walked away and by the time we entered the tent, we couldn't hear them at all. I shuffled to my cot and collapsed with a heavy sigh.

What the hell was I going to do?

Gail had told me that Charles couldn't get it up if I didn't fight him—but if DJ was there to take over? I wasn't dumb enough to think that *he* would have any trouble, whether I fought him or not.

I looked up as Gail approached and was shocked to see a wide grin splitting her pretty face.

"How can you smile at a time like this?" I grated out.

"Keep your voice down," she chided in a tense whisper. "I told you DJ was working on something. This has to be it. Now that he's officially a Driver, he's got access to vehicle keys—got more pull in the community. And if he's supposed to go with you to Command, that means he's finally gotten into Charles' inner circle."

"And I'm supposed to be comforted by this?" I hissed. "Were you even listening to what they said?"

"I was listening to what *wasn't* said."

I raised my brows and shrugged. All I could think of was the way he'd said he couldn't wait to have me bent over—and how he'd looked at me when he'd called me a good girl. He was either a phenomenal actor...or he was telling the truth. And I was leaning toward the latter.

"DJ is intelligent, and he knows how to work these people. I don't know how he does it so well, but he's managed to earn Charles' trust in only a few weeks. He can take over this place, I know it."

Gail's certainty made no sense to me.

"Have you ever stopped to think that maybe he's playing you and not them? What if this dark side is the real him and the gentle side is the persona he shows you so that you'll trust him?" I took Gail's hand in mine. "Have you seen or heard from any of the women that he's helped 'escape'? Were you there to see any of them actually go free?"

273

She paused, but she shook her head and pressed on. "No, I haven't seen any of them, they keep me locked up here, but he's told me how he got them out."

My heart thundered in my chest, "He's manipulating you, Gail." I wrung my hands. *How could she not see it?* "There has to be something more going on." My eyes drifted to the med corner and a new thought slammed into me. "Have you ever given him anything from the med cabinet that wasn't strictly requested by Charles or anyone else?"

Her eyes narrowed warily.

If DJ was friendly with Gail, she'd probably give him whatever he asked for and not think twice about it...and the other men in the group most likely knew that.

"Just some pain killers for the women who got roughed up pretty bad," she said, slowly. "Antibiotics for STI's. ADHD meds and antidepressants for a couple of people..." Her voice began to lose some of its conviction, "But it was always for the girls he helped."

"But how do you know that? How do you know that he's telling the truth?" I held her gaze and grasped one of her hands in my own. "Think about it. What if he needed the painkillers and antibiotics for himself? What if the ADHD meds were for him and the boys? You've just taken his word for everything. You have no proof. You're a resource for him, Gail. Nothing more."

"Girl, I don't like where you're going with this," she said flatly, pulling away from me. "He's a good guy. He's kind. Giving. He's got a heart of gold beneath the act he's got to keep up for these people. Why don't you believe me?"

My gut twinged at her words, but I pushed the feeling away. I had seen that dark fire of his with my own eyes. Had felt how his presence could silence a room. That kind of energy—that kind of danger—didn't hide easily, and no amount of Gail's pleading could change my mind.

Just then the tent door flapped open, and DJ stepped in, moving with that slow, prowling gait, like a predator returning to its den. His eyes scanned the tent and locked onto mine. The breath caught in my chest and a chill shot through me...and yet, somewhere deeper, something flared to life.

Gail shot to her feet and marched over to him. "Boy, you need to talk some sense into her—"

DJ pursed his lips, and his brows crept up toward his hairline. He made a sharp motion with his hand across his throat just as Frank followed him into the tent. Gail clammed up and I felt the blood drain from my face.

"You." Frank pointed at Gail. "Out."

She squared her shoulders and stuck her chin out. "This is *my* tent, asshole. I give the orders in here."

"This is only your tent because we haven't found a *man* to do your job yet. Careful or you'll end up in the whore house with the rest of the useless cunts. Medical training or not," Frank leered but Gail wouldn't budge.

DJ stalked toward me, eyes locked on mine, and I froze, hands gripping the edge of my cot.

"Before you throw her out, I need her to get some things for me," DJ said to Frank.

Gail whirled and stormed toward DJ, yanking a backpack out of his grip before he could say another word. I hadn't even noticed he'd been holding it. "You still got three hours before you need to be at Command. What do you need that's so urgent?" she barked at him.

"Besides a small deposit for his spank bank?" DJ pointed a thumb at Frank as he casually leaned a shoulder against one of the thick, metal tent poles, hands tucked in the pockets of his jogging pants. "Not much, just whatever meds she's still taking and some anti-inflammatories. Charles says we'll need some wound salve and a tube of burn ointment. Bandages. Tape. And what's that numbing gel you use?"

I glanced at Gail. Her face looked drawn. "It's lidocaine," she said.

"Yeah, we'll need a tube of that. Is there anywhere it can't be used? Like, if she swallows a little, it won't make her sick?" His eyes never left mine as he spoke. Something dark burned in their depths.

"It...shouldn't. Why?" Gail's voice sounded small and suspicious.

"Charles wants to see if it'll numb her gag reflex...among other things." He smirked and wet his lips, that damn dimple flashing like lewd punctuation.

My eyes flew to Gail. She had panic written on every line of her face. She had to believe me now. She had to believe that this was the real DJ. That sweet persona he put on was a complete lie and I hated that I was right about it. She turned away and began stuffing bottles into the backpack.

I looked more closely at it. Wait, that was *my* backpack!

When she was done, she handed it back to DJ and he slung it over his shoulder without any thanks as he looked her up and down and gave her a wink. She blanched and stared wordlessly at him for a beat before her wide, worried eyes met mine again.

"Gail?" I squeaked as Frank grabbed her by the upper arm and walked her bodily across the tent then shoved her out the door. Once she was out of the tent, DJ advanced toward me while Frank watched on in amusement from the entryway.

My heart landed in the pit of my stomach as I slid off the end of my cot and backed away from him.

He smiled darkly. That smile sent a jolt through me—not just fear—but heat. Something feral. Dangerous. Something I didn't have a name for. This was a game for him. He was the cat, toying with his prey before going in for the kill, and I was the unwilling mouse.

He tossed my pack over to Frank who caught it with ease and set it on the floor, then leaned against the tent door frame like he had front row tickets to a show. His eyes danced and an expectant grin split his face. I could feel the weight of his stare even as I turned my attention back toward DJ; they were two predators salivating after the same prize.

Shit.

"It really is too bad that I was never able to buy you that drink," DJ drawled as he tracked me around the furniture in the tent, pinning me with a look that could only be described as predatory. "I would give my eye teeth to have seen what I could have gotten you up to after a couple strong martini's. Or maybe I could have flipped a couple bottles and let your hormones do the rest?"

What the— "Did you read my journal?" I squeaked at him, remembering how I had felt when I wrote those words, remembering the person that I thought DJ was. How had I interpreted his personality so badly? But maybe all men were like this? The only thing keeping them from devolving into salivating cavemen being a set of societal rights and wrongs. Once those rules were removed? They turned into hedonistic brutes.

"Oh, you bet I did. 'The dimple, the smile, my mysterious hazel eyes,'" he mocked as he inched closer and grabbed for me around one of the metal poles that held the tent up.

I leapt back and dashed behind a heavy, threadbare chair in the lounge area, heart hammering in my ears. I couldn't let him get his hands on me.

He stalked after me again but instead of following me around the obstacle, he picked the chair up and threw it across the tent like it weighed no more than my backpack. It landed with a crack, and I took a flinching step backward. I had to get away. I had to get out of there. But where would I go?

Frank hooted, "This is better than a dirty movie."

I glanced his direction. He was rubbing himself over his pants and I almost gagged.

The moment my attention wavered, DJ lunged. I jerked away but he was too fast. His hand clamped around my arm and yanked me toward him. I fought like a banshee—twisting, kicking, thrashing—but it was useless. He snared my arms like it was nothing; every ounce of my strength was minuscule compared to his. In seconds I was trapped—breathless and terrified—my back pressed to his chest.

He buried his nose into my hair and growled into my ear, "You smell so fucking good," his arms tightened, crushing me to him. "And just look at you. I never would have thought you had such a lithe little body hiding under all those baggy clothes you usually wear." He called over his shoulder, "It's amazing what a pair of Lulu Lemon's can do, right?"

Frank made an approving sound.

I continued to struggle, acid fear burning in my throat, but he easily clasped both my wrists behind my back in just one of his hands and walked me over to the dining table. I grunted and thrashed but he was just too strong. "Let me go, you creep!"

"I thought we established this earlier," Frank called from across the tent laughing. "I'm the creep, DJ's the sick fuck."

He pressed me face down over the table, my wrists still clasped in his hand, and in one smooth movement, he leaned over me and pushed my legs apart with his knee. My heart lodged in my throat, and I cried out. It was that easy for him to fully overpower me. I hadn't even evaded him for thirty seconds and I was helpless. And yet, beneath the fear, an ember flared to life, pulsing brighter with each panting breath I took.

DJ's breath came in short bursts as he lowered his mouth to my ear. My knees nearly buckled, and that ember inside me grew to a flame at the touch of his breath on my neck. I rallied, gritting my teeth against the heat coursing through my body. I was *not* ok with this.

"Keep fighting but don't hurt yourself," he whispered almost too low for me to hear. "We're just putting on a little show so I can get him to leave us alone for a minute."

As if being alone with him would be better than having Frank watch the whole thing? "Get off of me," I breathed and tried to stand up.

He hissed in a breath while he ran his free hand over my hip and up my spine. His warm fingers slid up the back of my neck and tangled into my hair then clenched down tight. He pulled my head back.

"That's perfect," he purred, loud enough that Frank could hear, "Do it again...but whimper a little bit for me this time."

Try as I might, I couldn't stop the angry tears from streaming down my cheeks. I huffed, furious with myself for being so weak. For not understanding the conflicting feelings flowing through me. The angry huff turned traitor, escaping as a strangled sob.

"Oh, fuck yes," Frank moaned.

DJ chuckled, "That's my good girl."

I kept on struggling and huffing beneath him. If something was going to happen, I wasn't going to just lie there and take it, but the more I struggled, the faster his breathing became. And I had the sinking suspicion that it wasn't because he was tiring. It felt like the exact opposite. His grip on my wrists tightened and my pulse skyrocketed.

I felt his upper body shift toward Frank. "That's it. Show's over. Get the fuck out."

"But this is just getting good," Frank complained.

"You wanted a teaser. You got one. Out." DJ's tone was final but slightly breathless.

"Whatever you say, King Salami," Frank snorted then chuckled. I heard the tent flap scrape open and closed again.

Gail's anxious and irritated voice sounded outside the tent, just far enough away that I couldn't make out her words, but she was definitely giving Frank an earful. DJ still leaned over me, panting.

"Please," I whispered between gasps, "don't do this." I wriggled beneath him, but he was all cold tension—coiled and dangerous—like he was fighting himself as much as he was fighting me.

He breathed deep and groaned, "Stop. Moving."

There was a note of something barely restrained in his voice.

I froze.

Several tense moments passed—he lingered against me, breath ragged and trembling—before he finally exhaled and slowly peeled himself away. I turned to find him just a step behind me, fists and jaw clenched. He took another shuddering breath, and his eyes shimmered—with desire, lust, or unshed tears, I couldn't tell—his face was unreadable.

He scrubbed both hands over his face and let out a rough sigh, throat bobbing as he swallowed hard. "Are you okay?" he asked, voice intense and low.

"What?" I whispered harshly as I rubbed at my eyes. The tears kept flowing. "No, DJ. I'm not okay." I lowered myself into one of the dining chairs and sat for a heartbeat then thought better of it.

Standing shakily, I took another large step away from him. I needed more space. I had so many questions—but my head was too twisted up to form a coherent thought, let alone a full sentence. I swallowed hard, trying to force my emotions down so I could think.

He'd walked that knife's edge again; dancing along an ice-cold blade of possession and control, pushing me to the edge of terror, then let it all melt away into some type of tenderness, asking if I was alright. Who was hiding under that mask of restraint? Who was he really?

I had felt his heart pounding, had heard his ragged, excited breaths. I could still feel the way his voice had vibrated through my body from scalp to toenails. Goosebumps tickled up my spine. I tried to steady my breathing even as a flush crept up my neck and onto my cheeks. He just stood there dragging in deep, uneven breaths.

"I—I don't know what I'm feeling right now." My heart refused to slow, and I shivered despite the ball of heat at the center of my chest.

His head tilted as he studied me a moment then something like recognition flickered behind his eyes. The ghost of a knowing smile curved the corner of his mouth lightly as he raked a hand through his hair and took a step in my direction. But he stopped short.

"Look," he said in a voice so low it was almost a whisper, "I won't pretend that I know what you're feeling right now but judging by the color in your cheeks and the way you're breathing, it's not fear." His eyes hungrily roamed my face then drifted downward.

An image burst into my mind unbidden. An image of DJ and I in an extremely compromising position and I suddenly felt weak all over.

Nope. Absolutely not. There was no reason for my head to be dreaming up that kind of imagery after he'd just man-handled and terrified me.

"It's a little bit like the feeling you get waiting for the roller coaster to crest the top of the hill, right? Scared? Nervous? Excited?" He took another shaky breath, "They all feel really similar sometimes."

His voice was slowly taking on its normal, softer tone and I found myself nodding. My palms were clammy, my heart hammered in my chest, my skin tingled. It was similar to the anticipation of the first big drop on a roller coaster. Was that what I was feeling? Anticipation? I shook my head. In my world, this type of fear and anticipation didn't mesh.

"No, that's not it."

"What would you call it then?" He arched a brow at me.

My lips parted but I couldn't seem to form a word.

He smiled knowingly, "You can only lie to yourself for so long," he whispered.

Only, I wasn't lying to myself. I couldn't. In spite of everything that had happened over the past several days, I still, inexplicably, found him alarmingly attractive. And there was that undeniable, unthinkable pull toward him. But... "You scare the hell out of me, DJ," I whispered with a small shudder. And I meant it.

"Good," he growled, a playfully sinister light flashing in his eyes.

Just then, the tent door scraped open, and Frank stuck his head in. "Are you sure you can hold your load for another few hours?" he snickered.

DJ's face fell a heartbeat before his gaze darkened and he pinned me with a predatory look, "Not if I hang around in this tent for much longer."

What had that look been about? Had he wanted to tell me something and not gotten the chance?

He winked at me before turning toward Frank, "I gotta get changed anyway." Then to me he said, "I'll see you soon." And walked out with Frank on his heels.

My hand dropped to my chest, and I sagged as Gail rushed inside and took in the toppled chair and disrupted table. "Jesus Christ on a cracker, what did they do?" She looked me over like a mother hen then held my shoulders at arm's length. "You're alright?"

"Yeah, I'm fine. He just scared the hell out of me again," I breathed. My heart was finally slowing but that burning energy still smoldered, not in my chest, but low in my belly. It was just adrenaline. It had to be. Just the remnants of fear coiling in my stomach, nothing more. I sniffed and wiped my eyes with the backs of my hands and stood up straight. "But something isn't adding up with him." He'd said he was just putting on a show so Frank would leave us alone for a minute. "I think he—"

"I've never seen him act that dark before," Gail interrupted, sounding shocked by what she had witnessed. She grasped my hand and we sat down on a cot together. "I guess it's because he's never directed that persona towards me, but..." she paused, struggling for words, "we've been sharing this space since the end of March, and he's never once scared me like that. And he didn't even have to touch me."

"See what I mean?" I said in a hushed voice. "It's almost like he's two completely different people. Like, maybe the lines between his different persona are blurring."

"You might be on to something with that," Gail said with a far away look in her eyes. "He's never been anywhere near this handsy with any of the other girls he's helped escape either. I don't know what's gotten into him. I mean, I've seen men teeter on the edge before, but whatever he's wrestling with, I don't think it's just for show."

I nodded, relieved that she was finally seeing things from my point of view. But I was fairly sure that *I* was the reason for his erratic behavior. As small as it was, we technically had some history together, and in a world as crazy as ours had become, that would probably mean something to him. Only, how did I explain it to Gail? I knew in my bones that Gail was good and honest and trusting, and in a strange way, she was my friend. I hadn't been fully honest with her because I didn't fully trust her motives in the beginning, but she deserved the whole truth.

"I think," I took a deep breath and let it out in a whoosh, "I think it's because I met him a few hours before the power went out."

The other woman's eyes went wide, "You knew him before all this went down?"

I nodded stiffly.

"He never told me—and why are you only just now letting me in on this?"

"I didn't think it was important." Which was stupid of me. "And I didn't know for sure who I could really trust here."

Gail nodded, "And you trust me now?"

"Of course. But—" I hesitated. Would she believe the story?

"Oh, no—you don't get to waffle about this now,"

"Well, how I met him isn't strange at all, but the fact that we ended up here...together? The odds are next to nothing. And how I managed to get from the national forest all the way back to town is even crazier."

"Wait, you weren't here in town?" Gail leaned in close.

"No, I was way up past the reservoirs camping when the power went out."

"How did you—that's—you know what, just start from the beginning."

I crossed my legs, took a steadying breath, and told her everything. I told her about my photography, meeting DJ at Miller Park, meeting Dan, being stranded at the camp store and my harrowing journey home, sparing only the details about the glow and Dan's injury and subsequent healing. That would have been too much. She gaped at me enough even without those bits of mystical information.

"No wonder he was crying when he first brought you in. It must have been like he was seeing a ghost. And to have you end up here of all places." Gail shook her head. "I bet he feels like shit about it." She seemed to be contemplating her next words, "And now he feels like he's got a second chance."

"We talked for like two seconds, Gail—we didn't even know each other. We never had a first chance."

"We're living in dark times." Gail's voice was low, "Shared trauma can forge unbelievable bonds."

My stomach clenched. Is that really what was going on here? Gail seemed confident, but I wasn't convinced. I pulled myself to my feet and paced the width of the tent. "Trauma bonding aside, what do you think he has planned for tonight? Because, before he left with Frank, I'm almost positive that he wanted to tell me something."

"I assumed he was going to find a way to turn you loose before you got to Charles' house."

"And what if he doesn't?" I stopped at the center of the room. "What if getting me to Charles' place is what he really wanted all along?" My voice sounded small to my own ears.

Gail paused, pursing her lips before she spoke slowly, "I've had enough experiences in my life to know that it takes all kinds to fill the freeway and some folks just—" she cut herself off, striding to the medical shelves, and pulled out a storage tote. She rummaged through it, finally pulling three small pills out of a plastic baggie and handed them to me.

"What are these?" The tiny white pills looked harmless enough.

"Doesn't matter what they are. They'll help you not care what happens if DJ and Charles—" her words died in her throat as if she couldn't bear the thought of even finishing that sentence out loud. "They'll help you forget it even happened afterward. Take them all as soon as you can if he doesn't let you go." Her hand covered her mouth for a moment. "If you chew them, they act faster and stronger."

My heart landed in my toes as I shakily tucked the pills into the small, thigh pocket of my leggings with a slow nod. Was oblivion better than knowing? I hoped that I wouldn't have to find out.

25

Chasing Ghosts

TWO AND A HALF HOURS LATER, DJ escorted me out of the building and across the parking lot toward an old, two-tone pickup—silver and black. He was back in the Survivalist getup: dark tactical gear, ammo vest, boots, gloves. A black ball cap shadowed his face, while dark sunglasses and neck gaiter masked the rest. A rifle was slung at his back, handguns resting at his thigh and hip, while cuffs, zip ties and other gear crowded his belt.

I would have been lying if I'd said he didn't look good. Not just good, no. It was the kind of good that sent a sinful shiver through my body before my brain registered the danger. The gear clung to him like it had been stitched to fit his lean, lethal, terrifyingly competent frame. And yet, covered as he was, he didn't trigger the fear I'd expected. Hidden behind the sunglasses and mask, I couldn't see his eyes; couldn't see the wild flicker that lived in their hazel depths. I sighed to myself, heart fluttering for all the wrong reasons, and shoved the confusing feelings in a neat little box; something to unpack later...if I lived through what was to come. He was taking me to command—to Charles' house.

As he opened the passenger side door and helped me inside, he handed me my backpack.

"Buckle up," he said in a flat tone and closed the door.

I grit my teeth and slid the seat belt into place. He climbed in the driver seat and fired up the engine, put it in gear and rolled out of the parking lot and onto the road.

My first thought was that it felt weird to be riding in a car again, my next feeling was awe at just how destroyed the city was. Entire neighborhoods had been consumed by fire, large military trucks sat empty or rolled onto their sides, traffic lights had fallen, power poles with their broken cables littered the side streets. Weeds were beginning to sprout out of cracks in the asphalt and sidewalks while every lawn I could see was growing wild.

The last of the pink and white blossoms had fallen off the ornamental trees to gather in the gutters, and yellow pollen clung to the untouched rain puddles that were slowly drying in the evening sun. DJ turned onto a road that headed due west, right into the setting sun. Golden light shone through the windshield and I pulled the sun visor down. It could have been an ordinary Wednesday. DJ picking me up on our way out to dinner and a movie, except the movie theater there on the corner was deserted and a burned-out car rested halfway through the large glass doors. Black soot marred the front of the building, and I suppressed a groan. Life really was never going to be the same.

After several minutes of silence, I clutched my pack to my chest and said, "I can't believe you read my journal."

DJ glanced my direction, "I didn't read it all, but I read enough."

His voice had that hard edge to it and my stomach clenched.

"Frank went through your bag last night. He read the part about me out loud before I took it from him. Finally figured out why its so hard for me to keep my hands to myself when it comes to you."

"You know what? I don't even really care that you read it given that you're taking me to a mad man's house. Seriously, how can you do this?" I locked my eyes on the side of his face willing him to speak. If Gail was correct and DJ thought he had some sort of second chance, maybe I could tap into that—let guilt do its thing—if he could even feel guilty. He could be a sociopath. Who really knew?

"I was so excited to get to know you that I almost came back to town after you texted me that day. You were so charming and easy to talk to," I said softly. "That doesn't happen often for me."

His gloved hands gripped and twisted on the steering wheel.

Should I be fully honest with him? Could I? He was either going to let me go, in which case, I'd never see him again, or I'd be stuck with the survivalists, and it would be his fault. I might as well lay it all out there. I let out a quiet, bitter laugh. "It had been almost two years since anyone had asked me out the day you did."

He removed his sunglasses and looked at me for the briefest moment before returning to the road. There was true sorrow there, I could see it in every small crease around his eyes. Good. I wanted him to feel like a dirt bag for what he'd done and the people he was involved with. "I haven't slept with anyone since then either."

He slid his sunglasses back into place and took a deep breath, then let it out slowly.

"I tried going to a couple bars with an old friend from high school. Hated it. Then I tried the dating apps and met a guy with a Jeep like mine. Seemed nice at first and we hung out for a few months, camping and off-roading mostly, but it turns out he was sleeping with other people when I thought we were exclusive." I shrugged. "I wasn't heartbroken by any means, but I stopped trying. Figured that the right person would come along at the right time. I thought that person was you." I ran my palms across my face as my stomach did summersaults. "You were on my mind the entire time I—God, I'm such an idiot."

His shoulders sagged and he shook his head.

I ran my fingers over the pocket that held the pills as we made another turn into a neighborhood I knew well, and after a few minutes we rolled onto the main street of Kingfisher Terrace. We were back in my neighborhood. "You were never going to let me go, were you?"

His face whipped my direction, and he placed a finger over his lips then pointed to what I had taken for an automatic garage door opener clipped to the sun visor in front of him. I looked more closely and found that it looked more like a microphone than anything.

Oh, Shit. Could Charles be listening right now?

He removed his sunglasses again, eyes flicking between me and the microphone as he slowed the truck almost to a stop, "Letting you go was never an option." His voice was hard but his eyes were full of regret. "It was a ploy to keep your hopes up...keep you docile. Seems like it worked."

He turned his eyes back toward the windshield. "If I'd had it my way, I would have started your training last week when I first got my hands on that pretty little neck of yours, but Charles has his own ideas on breaking in new girls."

"What?" I squeaked. *Training? Breaking?*

"Gail is in on it too. She always is. That bitch plays the mother hen like a pro."

My heart hammered in my chest. Was he saying these things because of the microphone or because it was the truth? "I thought Gail was my friend."

He reached over to cup my chin and I slapped his hand away. "Don't touch me! How dare you. How dare you *both*."

Without a word, he stomped on the accelerator. While the engine roared, he unclipped my seatbelt and as he slowed to navigate another corner, he looked at me, eyes full of regret, and jerked his head toward the door.

He was letting me go.

I didn't hesitate. The worn, metal door latch was cold and hard under my fingers as I yanked and flung it wide. With a silent prayer, I jumped then hit the ground hard, rolling across the damp asphalt. Pain bit into my knee and elbow, but I scrambled to my feet and sprinted for the next block, pulling my pack across my shoulders and tightening the straps as I went.

The truck's tires squealed as it came to a halt and DJ jumped out yelling, "Amber, stop!"

He gave chase, boots pounding pavement behind me. Was this all an act to convince the powers that be that I had escaped? Or was it all part of some elaborate game he liked to play? I'd already learned that the chase seemed to excite him, but why would he do this so close to sundown? So close to Charles' house?

Damn it, I had to stop thinking and just run.

"You can't outrun a radio, Amber! Just come back!" he called out from behind me but I kept going. His next words, spoken into his two-way radio, faded with the distance I put between us. "Driver Five to Command, we have a code red, I repeat, code red. The package is on foot, moving toward Robin Street."

I cursed under my breath and changed directions, and he followed but didn't make any announcement about where I was actually running to. DJ may have been stronger than I was and have radio backup, but this was *my* neighborhood, and there was no way he knew it as well as I did.

He was gaining on me, the sounds of his boots pushing me to run faster, my new trail runners springing under my feet. I pushed myself harder and the sound of his boots began to fade. All I had to do was make it to the low, chain link fence, and I could hit the small stream that ran through Ellsworth Park. Ancient blackberry vines hid the stream from view, but I knew where a clear space was. Joey and I used to play hide and seek there and had built forts all over the forested section of the park with the rest of the neighborhood kids. If I could just get there, I could lose him. The chain link fence came into view. I scaled it with an ease I'd never thought possible, and I thanked myself again for committing all those hours to my fitness back at the camp store. Ice cold water soaked into my socks as I splashed down into the creek bed and followed its winding path, then ducked into a small cove, hidden by berry vines and ferns. Air puffed in and out of my lungs and my heart pounded behind my ribs as I strained my ears for any sign that DJ had figured out where I had gone.

The big motor of the truck rumbled a couple of blocks away. He'd turned back. I breathed a sigh of relief...but it was getting dark and there was nowhere safe to hide from the darkling spawn in the park. I had to get to my house and get inside somehow. I hadn't even tried last time I was there. I'd allowed the strain of my journey from the camp store and my injuries to cloud my judgement. Not this time though. My head was clear. My eyes fully open. My body was strong. I *would* figure it out.

I continued following the creek bed as quietly as I could, then climbed out at a familiar trail. Poking my head out of the bushes, I glanced left then right, and seeing that the coast was clear, charged across the street and into a childhood friend's front yard. Their side gate opened easily, and I closed it behind myself. When I was young, a chain link fence was all that separated the yards, but over the years, homeowners had built solid wood privacy fences throughout the neighborhood. A seven-foot tall, wooden fence was a harder beast to get over than a five-foot chain link, but I only needed to hop this one to get to my street.

I jumped and heaved myself over the fence, landing in a crouch and listening for any signs that I had been spotted. Silence greeted my ears, so I ran through the back yard I had just jumped into and crept slowly out of the side gate. My house was at the other end of the block and across the street. I'd have no cover whatsoever as I made this last mad dash and I still had no idea how I was going to get in. We didn't have a side gate to enter the back yard, and the garage had been locked when I had been there two weeks ago. The first story windows had been boarded up as well. Maybe I could hop the fence and get in through the back of the house?

Listening tensely, I crept down the driveway. The light of golden hour was fading and in passing, I remembered Joey and I racing our bikes up the street trying to get home before the streetlights came on. My neighborhood appeared so untouched; I expected to see the streetlights begin to flicker to life.

My memory was cut short by the rumble of an engine and I ducked into a thick hedge of budding rhododendrons. Through the branches of the shrubs, I could just make out DJ's truck rolling slowly up the road. It stopped near the end of the street directly in front of my house.

What the hell? After a tense moment, the truck rumbled past our neighbor's house and on around the corner.

I crept out of the hedge and strained my ears for the sound of footsteps or another vehicle but didn't hear anything. I had to take my chance.

I hunched through front yards and across driveways all the way down the street until I was directly opposite my house. Staring at the familiar building had my heart soaring, but something was different. My eyes scanned the house and came to rest on the garage door.

The bloody hand prints I had left beside the large, spray painted 'X' were gone.

My hand drifted to my chest and tears stung the back of my eyes. "Mom?" I breathed.

It couldn't be, but it was the only explanation. If she and Joey were still there, hiding in plain sight, living right around the corner from a psychopath like Charles, she would have known that any change in the appearance of the front of the house would have given them away.

I looked both ways then sprinted across the street, running straight to the garage door.

"Please be unlocked," I whispered and pushed up on the aluminum door. *It rolled up.* I ducked inside and pulled it closed behind me, sealing myself into the pitch-black space. I felt my way along the inside of the door until I located the manual lock and cranked it. My knees buckled and I slumped to the floor.

I was home. I was *home.*

After a few moments of simply taking in the familiar smell and feeling of the garage, I pulled myself to my feet. With arms out to feel the space around me, I shuffled to the door that led into the house. My toe hit the concrete steps. If it hadn't been so dark, I would have taken the steps two at a time, instead, I walked carefully and fumbled for the doorknob. It was locked. If everything was still in my backpack, my set of keys would be there too, but out of habit, I reached my arm out to the left, feeling for the small terracotta pot on top of the garage refrigerator that held the spare key. It was there. I put the key in the lock and let myself inside.

The back hallway was dim but smelled just the same as it had when I left that morning in March. All I could do was breathe through the tightness in my throat and the tears that stung my eyes. It seemed like years ago. I set my pack down in the hallway and removed my wet shoes and socks. House rules. No dirty shoes on Mom's clean floors. Only now, the floors were dusty and the house was still. Too still.

"Mom? Joey?" I called out while I slipped down the hallway in my bare feet. I called out again, up the stairs this time, "Mom?"

Where are they?

What if someone else had commandeered our home? I suddenly wished I had taken the time to pull my combat knife out of my pack, but I continued slowly down the hall and paused where it opened to the great room. To the left, the living room area was dark due to the plywood over the big windows but to my right, in a shaft of dimming light, Mom sat in her kitchen chair just staring out the back window. My heart soared and then promptly broke into a million pieces.

"Mom!" my voice cracked and I ran to her side.

When I touched her shoulder, she looked up at me, her face tired and gaunt, "The ghosts of both my children haunt me now," she said, her voice barely a rough whisper.

Both her children? But I was right there and Joey was just in his room. He had to be.

I shook her lightly and cried, "I'm alive, Mom. I made it. I'm home."

She'd always been thin, everyone in the family was, but her shoulder felt like nothing but bones under my palm and her clothes hung loosely across her small frame. She just looked away.

I softly took her face in my hands and looked straight into her tired, sorrowful eyes. "I'm here, Mom. I'm here." I pulled her into a tight hug and sobbed. I hugged her so hard I thought I might snap her in two. I'd missed her so much. I missed her comforting aura, her smell, her sweet voice, her loving smile. "I'm home. I'm home."

After a moment she shakily returned the hug then clung to me so fiercely I could hardly breathe. She stroked my messy hair. I kissed her cheek. And we simply sobbed in each other's arms. So much fear, sadness, stress, anxiety, and relief all escaping at the same time. Finally, she pulled away and looked at me. She smiled then, so sad but so full of hope.

"Oh, Mom, I'm so sorry. I'm sorry for not being here. I'm sorry for always brushing you off. I'm sorry for being so damn independent." Everything I had been through the last two months happened because I hadn't listened to her when she wanted me to stay home.

She shushed me gently.

"I'm just so sorry for everything," I sobbed.

When she finally spoke, her voice was rough like she hadn't spoken in days. "You're home, sweetheart. That's all that matters.

26

Reckoning

M Y EYES FLUTTERED OPEN WITH the first light of dawn, the familiar scents of home surrounded me—my fluffy comforter, my clean cotton sheets, and the faint scent of lavender in my pillow. I'd been afraid to go to bed, thinking that it was all a dream, that I hadn't really made it home, but as I looked around at all of my things lit by the muted gray glow coming through the curtains of my own bedroom window, I knew I wasn't dreaming. I smiled at the comfort, but it slipped away almost as quickly as it came.

Joey hadn't made it.

I was never going to see my brother again. I closed my eyes and summoned his image into my mind's eye. His soft brown eyes and thick brown hair that always looked like he'd just rolled out of bed no matter what he tried. His easy smile, freckles, pronounced Adam's apple and dusting of facial hair on his lip and chin. He was good and kind and funny...and my best friend. It wasn't fair. My eyes filled with tears again and my chin quivered. At least I still had so many pictures of him. Mom had been a photography nut before me, and the dozens of photos that hung on our walls were just a fraction of what she had stashed away in photo albums and shoeboxes.

I rolled over in bed to stare at my calendar. It had been a Christmas gift from Joey. Twelve months of Ansel Adams' most famous black and whites, the month of March still showing the circled, four-day weekend away from work that I had been so excited about. I hadn't once thought about my job in the student store at the community college since the power had gone out and my whole world had gone to shit.

Thinking about work made me think about school, which in turn made me think about the life I had planned for myself. I'd wanted a little house just outside the city with a big shop that would be half photography studio and half auto shop. I would have a job as a photographer with a couple of virtual and physical magazine companies that would pay me to travel and photograph four-wheel drive events all over the world. I wouldn't have much; I'd never needed much anyway. But it was all gone.

I'd been so wrapped up with just surviving in a strange place that I never had time to mourn the total loss of my life dreams. Laying in my room, staring at the things that had once defined me, I suddenly felt absolutely empty and directionless. All I had wanted was to just get home. After I was home, everything was supposed to be alright. I would know what to do next. Only now that I had finally gotten to where I thought I needed to be, it didn't feel right either.

I flopped over and pressed my face into the pillow. "Why?" I whined, the sound barely above a whisper.

My ears pricked at the sound of Mom's feet padding past my room and down the hallway. I counted down in my mind, *three, two, one...*and smiled as she stepped onto the one squeaky step on the staircase.

My beautiful, frail mother. I threw off the covers and pulled my favorite pair of baggy sweatpants off my nightstand. I had to make sure that she ate something. I snapped up a tattered old hoodie that belonged to Joey and pulled it on over my nightshirt. It was three sizes too big and felt like he was giving me a gentle hug.

Oh, Joey...

Before the sun set yesterday, Mom had taken my hand and led me out into the back yard. We sat beside Joey's grave and cried together, then talked to him until the last of the light faded from the sky. After we closed ourselves inside the house, we sat in my room and talked for hours.

"If it hadn't been for that soldier, I'd be dead too," Mom said. "He carried Joey and got us both back here safely then helped with the burial." She took my hand. "Before he left, he saw that picture of you standing on top of the Jeep hanging in the hallway." She paused before continuing again, "I don't know if I should even tell you this, you've had enough bad news already, but you deserve to know."

I looked at my mom, puzzled. "Why wouldn't you tell me about it? It's not like I knew the guy."

Mom's face fell. "He said that he knew you."

"I don't have any friends in the military, you know that," I said as I took her hand in mine.

"He recognized you from your picture in the hallway and said that you had only just met."

A muted chill ran across my scalp and down my back. I stopped breathing.

"He said that you jumpstarted his car that morning and sent him a selfie in front of that old store in the mountains."

My ears rang and my heart thundered in my chest. It couldn't be. Fate wouldn't be this cruel, would it?

"He's the main reason that I never gave up hope that I'd see you again. The fact that you were so close to that store when the power went out—"

My breath hitched as a block of ice seemed to settle in my stomach. "DJ was here?" I interrupted, my voice sounded small to my own ears.

"I couldn't believe it. What are the odds that someone you knew would be in the right place at the right time to save my life?" Mom beamed while I felt like I was dying inside. "He said that he'd come back to check on me but never did. Then the last of the military showed up and he wasn't with them. By that time, he was presumed dead, and they tried to get me to go to that mall colony. Another young man about Joey's age told me to stay put—that the Mall colony wouldn't be safe. And I knew I needed to stay here for you."

Mom's voice grew quiet, drowned out by the ringing in my ears. DJ knew where I lived. That's why he had stopped the truck in the street right out in front of the house. If he knew where I lived— "Oh, God." My free hand went to my chest.

"I'm sorry, sweetie. I know you had only just met him, but I know it's hard," Mom said, giving my hand a reassuring squeeze. "I'm sorry he didn't make it."

The ringing in my ears ceased, "He's alive, Mom." I said flatly.

"He's alive? You've seen him?"

My eyes went to our joined hands. I couldn't look at her while I dashed whatever Good Samaritan image she had of DJ in her mind. "I have. And he's dangerous." My gut prodded that I was mistaken about him, but my head just couldn't reconcile the confusing behavior I'd experienced with the survivalists and the story that Mom had just told me. "The whole group he's with are monsters."

"He's not with the gang that's been taking women, is he?"

She *knew* about the Survivalists? "Yeah. He is." I finally dragged my eyes up to meet hers. "They got me after I survived the night in a tree beside one of the old houses down by the tracks."

Her face paled. "I thought—I had a feeling that the racket those idiots made was tied to you somehow. A mother's instinct. I went out as soon as I woke up the next day. I saw the tree."

"That's where you were when I got here?" I'd only just missed her! If I had just stayed in the driveway instead of giving up...

Mom nodded and fresh tears filled her eyes. "I thought I heard a scream and ran back here as fast as I could. All I found were blood streaks on the garage."

I pulled her into my arms.

"If I had just stayed here," she sobbed, "I would have been home when you got here. I knew you weren't dead; I knew it in my gut. But I thought that they'd caught you...and I don't know where they're holed up."

Tears welled in my own eyes as I held her, my cheek resting on the top of her head. When we had both calmed down a bit, I told her about everything that had happened in the forest during my time at the camp store, sparing no details. I told her about the road home, about Dan, and glossed over what had happened with DJ at the Survivalist's headquarters. She didn't need all the details, it would just make her feel worse. But all she could do was gape at what I told her about the survivalists—about what DJ was a part of.

She was convinced that the guy with the Survivalists couldn't be the same kind soul that saved her life, carried Joey home and helped bury him without knowing her from Adam.

"No, that's not possible." She shook her head. "He—he saved me. There's no way we're talking about the same person."

"It's definitely him, Mom. I don't know what changed between the time that either of us first met him and now, but something isn't right with him," I said, pausing a beat before continuing. "Dan told me, 'There are only nine meals between peace and anarchy' and Gail said, that 'Desperate times can make good people do terrible things'." I shrugged, "Maybe that's what happened? Either way, we've got to get out of here sooner rather than later. If he knows where we live then it's just a matter of time before every Survivalist knows."

Mom shook her head, "He's known I was here since the beginning and they haven't shown up yet."

She had a point with that but everything I had experienced was still too fresh. Just the thought of him had alarm bells ringing in my head. "Even if DJ did keep you and the house a secret, if anyone else figured it out, they'd be knocking down our door in a heartbeat." The plain and simple fact was that we were not safe. "We've gotta get out of here."

"But how can we leave with the Survivalists running around town?"

"I don't know, but we've got to figure something out. Charles, the leader of the whole thing, lives somewhere in our neighborhood. He's got surveillance and a freaking bunker, Mom. That's where DJ was taking me when I jumped out of the truck." The words tumbled out in a rush, my tone of voice bordering on panic.

I watched as my mom's thin face fell. She nodded and hugged me again.

"He's just...unpredictable. Some of the things he did and said—I can't bring myself to trust him, not after everything he's done and the people he's with, no matter how much Gail believed he was one of the good ones." As I spoke the words, my gut gave a twinge.

Something kept telling me that even with as dark as DJ had become, there was still good there. But he had made his choice. He'd chosen to stay with the devils he knew. Nothing I could have done or said would have changed his mind. In my mind, I understood it, but in my soul, it just didn't sit right.

At that, mom and I lapsed into silence. So much to think about. So much to be thankful for. But the urge to sleep finally took over. She stayed in my room. I think she would have stayed with me all night, holding my hand and smoothing my hair, had I not insisted that I was really there, and I was ok. She finally shuffled off to her room as I was drifting off to sleep. As I let my consciousness fade, I told myself that I didn't care about DJ. I told myself that he was a monster and that I'd be relieved if I never laid eyes on him again.

And yet...something in my gut wouldn't stop whispering that I was missing something—that I didn't have the whole picture.

I shook my head, bringing my thoughts back to the present and pulled on a pair of warm socks.

Whether DJ let me go or I had actually escaped was irrelevant. He was with the survivalists doing God knows—*Goddess*—knows what, and I was back at home with a mother that had starved herself for almost two weeks because she had given up. She was weak and needed care before she'd be well enough to even attempt to leave here. The camp store was going to be our only shot.

Pulling open my bedroom door, I slipped down the hall in my stockinged feet, pausing to peer inside Joey's room. His bed was made, which surprised me. He never made his bed. But that had most likely been Mom. Model cars sat on a shelf above his bedroom window and his walls were plastered with import car posters and women in barely-there bikinis. I had mercilessly ridiculed him for his 'Basic-Bro' décor for years. A sad smile twitched my lips. This was all that was left of my brother. I reached over and pulled his door closed with a sigh and blinked away fresh tears before continuing on downstairs.

Mom and I met in the kitchen with a warm hug and a kiss on the cheek. She'd made up some instant coffee and set out a couple of cereal bars for breakfast. We sat down in the breakfast nook and simply enjoyed each other's quiet company for a while.

After she had choked down half her coffee and a few bites of the cereal bar, Mom shifted on her chair and leaned towards me. "I've been thinking about something I forgot to tell you last night,"

"Uh-oh," I said with a crooked grin.

She smiled back and continued, "About a week after the soldiers showed up at the door, I was out scavenging and ran into a couple out doing the same thing. I hadn't seen anyone in so long, I was a little scared to talk to them, but I'm glad that I did."

"What did they say?" I leaned forward, curiosity piqued.

"They were trying to make their way from Portland back to their apartment on the east side of Orchardville about the same time the attack on the ration lines happened. They said they were almost to the interstate bridge where the military had a checkpoint set up, when the creatures attacked from the north. They hid in an abandoned city bus while the creatures systematically took out the checkpoint."

"How the heck did they survive?" I squeaked.

"They said it was sheer dumb luck, but the way they described the attack is what really unnerved me."

She went on to describe the systematic nature of the attack and how the creatures seemed impervious to pain, which I'd noticed as well, the night I spent in the tree. The bullet from the survivalist's gun hadn't even bothered the creature.

The people told her that after the attack was over, a different sort of creature walked onto the scene. It looked like a giant mutt dog with pointy ears and a slightly curled tail. It still had thick, brown fur covering its body, but it had the same glowing red eyes as the darkling spawn—and it was huge. Close to the size of a small horse, which made no sense whatsoever, but none of what had happened the past two months did.

According to the couple, the creature waited until the fighting stopped and the darkling spawn gathered around it. Then, together as a group, with the dog-creature in the lead, they inspected each body. One by one, the creatures stopped to feed, just tearing off limbs and eating everything, including most of their victims' clothing.

Seeing that the creatures were occupied, the couple was about to make a break for it when they heard a human scream. The giant dog-creature had found a soldier that had hidden during the attack and was dragging her out of a small guard building. It had her by the back of her vest, face down, and appeared to be taking great pains not to damage her as it dragged her out into the open.

The darkling spawn gathered around the pair and watched. The poor woman looked tiny and pale as a ghost when the creature released its hold of her vest, and she sat up on her knees frantically looking for a way out. The dog-creature stood above her and stared into her eyes. Slowly—inexplicably—she raised a shaking palm toward it. It brought its nose to her hand and sniffed, then its lips curled back into a snarl and fast as a snake, it lashed out and bit her. She snatched her hand back and cradled it to her chest as the creature turned and walked away. The darkling spawn followed and then...so did the woman.

I gaped and stared at Mom, wide eyed. "What the Hell? Do you think they were telling the truth?" I asked.

Mom shrugged and replied, "They had no reason to lie, sweetheart. And you should have seen the way they talked about it. They were serious, alright. And scared to death."

"Wait." The thought hit me like a ton of bricks, my mind scrambling to connect the pieces of this puzzle. "Dan said Erik and Alma had called the creatures darkling *and* spawn." I swallowed hard. "What if that giant dog was the *darkling*, and the hairless, mutated creatures are their *spawn*?" I almost shrieked but kept my voice down. It was cloudy out and there was no way to tell if the creatures were close by.

Mom perked up at my idea, "That could be why there are so many of them. The young man, the soldier, Jones, said that the demon's numbers just kept growing and they didn't know how. What if the," she paused, waving her hand as if trying to bring something to her mind, "darkling are infecting the people and animals they don't eat somehow?" Mom's voice was low and thoughtful. "So, if darkling create the spawn, what created the darkling?"

"I have no idea," I mumbled. Except, maybe I did! "Hold on." I sprinted up the stairs to my room and dug into my pack, pulling out my journal. I thumbed through it on my way back to the kitchen then set it down in front of my mom. "Dan had me copy down verbatim what Erik had told him. Look, right here," I pointed to a sentence and she read out loud.

"'The camp store is an Outpost and is protected by The Light. The darkling and their spawn cannot penetrate the dome of Light Magic. Nothing possessed by The Dark Mother's taint can.'" Mom looked me full in the face, "Is he suggesting that these creatures were brought into existence by this 'Dark Mother'?"

"I think he is." I closed the tattered journal, "I mean, if The Light Mother created all mortal beings and has the power to keep us safe with Light Magic domes, it only makes sense that The Dark Mother, would be her opposite in every way, trying to destroy everything she built. Like God and the Devil maybe? Dan even said that Alma told him that the story of creation had been twisted to suit the needs of evil men."

"But why would that happen?" Mom furrowed her brows.

"That's like asking why good and evil exist. I don't think we'll ever know for sure, but I get the feeling that at some point, a powerful or corrupt man, someone who didn't like seeing women in positions of power, wanted to change things."

Mom flopped back in her chair and crossed her arms. I could almost see her thoughts whirling. "If you're right about this sweetie—my God—er—Goddess. This is...we really do have to leave, don't we?"

I gave her a slow nod. She picked up her cereal bar and bit down with a determined look on her face.

"Don't eat too much too fast. You need to get better, not make yourself sick," I said.

She swallowed what she had been chewing and hit me with her most stern 'mom' look. "When you walked in last night, I had been sitting here thinking of walking out into the dark."

My stomach churned at her words. I shook my head and opened my mouth to speak but she held up a delicate hand and I stayed silent.

"I had given up. I wanted to die so I could be with my children. But I prayed...to whatever deity might be listening, to give me the strength to hold on just a little bit longer. And then you walked in not an hour later."

Was it truly divine intervention or a stroke of luck? "Oh, Mom," I reached out and took her hand.

"I have to believe that somehow, I was spared from death for a reason. Three times I've looked my death in the eye, and something happened to turn it around every time. I know I never raised you guys in any sort of faith because I didn't think it was a necessary step to raising good, responsible humans. The older you guys got, the more I could see that organized religion almost caused more harm than good for so many people; and that observation just confirmed my point of view. Decent people don't need religion or an ancient text to tell them how to be good people—they just are. It just comes naturally." She sighed, "I've always known that there was more to life than what we could see, and now, with these darkling spawn spreading like a plague and all this talk of goddesses..." She trailed off.

"We're caught deep in something much bigger than ourselves," I murmured.

"If we've both been spared death or becoming one of those creatures, I have to believe that somebody or something has a plan in store for us, and we have to rise to meet it."

I nodded and something in my chest warmed. That same warmth I had felt when Dan told me all that Erik and Alma had shared with him.

Even with the darkling spawn and the survivalists lurking around every corner, I knew we couldn't quit, not now, not ever. Two months ago, I would have never thought I would be around to witness the fall of our civilization, but now I was living through it—*we* were living through it—when it would have been so much easier to simply give up.

I cast Mom a worried but resolute look and she pulled me into a tight hug, "We're going to make it, sweetheart." Her voice trembled but her grip on me was fierce. "Even if we don't know how just yet, we are going to be ok."

27

The Devil You Know

Melissa

YOU KNOW, WE HAVE ENOUGH supplies in here to stay put for a while if we need to," Amber whispered in the dim light of the garage. "But I worry with Charles being so close. How are you feeling this morning?"

Melissa glanced at her daughter still shocked every time she heard her voice. It still seemed like a dream that Amber had actually made it home, that she was really there, right by her side. "Better than yesterday," Melissa replied, her own voice low.

The skies were thickly overcast, so the creatures (darkling spawn according to the people who ran the camp store in the mountains) would be out hunting. "I'm sure I'll be ready to go soon, sweetie." Which was not altogether true. Melissa felt like a flimsy bag of garbage every day; stuffed full and barely holding together. A fact that she did her best to hide from her daughter, but Amber wasn't blind.

"You're a rack of bones, Mom." Amber gave her a flat look.

"But I've put on three pounds since you've been back. I swear, if you feed me anymore, I'm going to burst." She straightened her shoulders, doing her best to look steady, even as her vision swam.

"I know. I'm sorry. I wish we had some protein powder or weight gain. I can only feed you so much peanut butter, ya know." Amber paused her searching of the shelves to turn and smile.

Melissa's heart stuttered and she reached a hand toward her daughter. When would the surging emotions finally level out?

Amber grasped Melissa's hand and gave it a little squeeze. "I'm not going anywhere without you, Mom. I promise."

Melissa's eyes welled up and she shook her head. "Ugh, I'm such a weepy woman lately."

"We'll get this figured out and you'll get your strength back. It's just gonna take a little time. But I'm so excited for you to meet Dan, I think you two will get along great. And I can't wait to meet his wife and daughter. Imagine how awesome it's going to be to have other people around to survive with." Amber's animated whisper filled the space between them as she brushed her fingertips across the handle of the survival knife that had once belonged to Dan. She barely took the thing off to sleep.

Melissa smiled softly and sniffled. Just a couple of months ago, Amber would have balked at the simple *idea* of meeting new people. "Who would have thought my introverted Amber would be excited to get to know strangers."

"All that time alone in the camp store sort of changed my outlook on things." Amber looked sheepish. "I don't think I was ever truly introverted; I just had a hard time with certain social situations and small talk. Now that I've almost died a few times and society as we knew it is gone," she shrugged, "I suppose I have bigger things to worry about now than social blunders."

"True." Melissa nodded at her daughter.

"Maybe when—" Amber began, but she immediately went silent at the sudden sound of a light tapping on the garage door. Her wide eyes met Melissa's own as her hand went to the hilt of her knife.

"Amber? Mel?" A hushed male voice sounded from just outside.

There was only one person left among the living who would have called Melissa by her nickname. She quickly made her way toward the garage door, "DJ?" she whispered.

"Yeah, it's me. Open up." Relief crashed over her. He was back—the young man that had saved her life and helped her lay Joey to rest—but what was he doing outside on a cloudy day?

"Mom, don't," Amber stood to rush to her side, but Melissa was already disengaging the lock and pulling the big rolling door upward.

Before it was even halfway open, DJ ducked inside, a rifle grasped in one hand, while two side arms rested in their holsters, one at his belt, the other strapped to his thigh. He was wearing the same uniform he'd been in that day in the park. Melissa could have cried with relief as his grateful eyes met hers and she lowered the door behind him. But that relief was cut short as her daughter lunged at DJ.

Melissa gaped. This wasn't right. Amber would never pull a weapon on anyone. Not unless—her stomach twisted. She hadn't been there. She hadn't gone through what Amber had gone through.

DJ hadn't even had the chance to stand from his crouch before Amber set the point of her blade to the side of DJ's throat. "How *dare* you come back here," she hissed through gritted teeth.

"Amber, what are you doing!?" Melissa barely kept her voice low enough to be considered a whisper as she cranked the lock on the garage door back into place.

"Hey—woah, easy!" DJ said as his startled eyes flicked between Melissa and her daughter. He slowly raised his free hand while the other still held his rifle.

"I won't go back," Amber whispered as she pressed the tip of the knife into his neck, drawing a dark droplet of blood. "I'll kill you if you try and make me."

"Amber, stop!" The pleading in Melissa's voice seemed to stay her daughter's hand but Amber's eyes never left DJ's face.

Melissa scanned the faded red marks and the shadow of a bruise on her daughter's face. Could this kind soldier really be partially responsible? It didn't seem possible that he would have teamed up with a group of kidnapping-survivalist-nutcases. Melissa was sure her daughter must have been mistaken about his identity, but as she took in the tense scene playing out in her garage, she knew that Amber had most definitely suffered some sort of trauma at DJ's hands. There would be no way she would have acted so extremely if she hadn't.

Amber's hand trembled lightly bringing a wince to DJ's face.

Melissa knew she had to do something, but what? "Think about this, sweetheart." She placed a gentle hand on her daughter's shoulder, then turned to DJ, "Loose the guns."

He carefully set the rifle down on the concrete floor of the garage. The two handguns followed, and he very wisely kept his mouth shut while his hands went up, palms out.

"You weren't there, Mom." Amber blinked away tears and grit her teeth. "You didn't see the things he did. Didn't hear the things he said."

"I had to—" DJ started then hissed in a breath as Amber pressed the blade harder into his neck.

"You shut your mouth. I can't—I just can't." Amber's voice cracked and she took a deep breath, clearly struggling with herself.

"There is no such thing as law and order anymore, but if you do this, there is no going back. You'll have to live with it for the rest of your life." Melissa said as calmly as she could manage. "Listen to your gut, Amber. It's not going to steer you wrong."

Her daughter stood with tears glistening in her eyes for what seemed like an eternity, but then, Melissa felt the moment her daughter decided *not* to murder a man in their garage. The tension in Amber's shoulders eased a moment before her grip on the knife loosened and Melissa let out a breath she hadn't realized she'd been holding.

But the moment Amber withdrew the knife, everything went wrong.

A shadow passed over his eyes and in a single heartbeat, DJ's hand closed around Amber's wrist and twisted. He plucked the knife from her grip and in one smooth movement, spun her around, pinning an arm behind her back. With his free arm, he pulled her close, her knife mere inches from her own neck. His jaw ticked as a small, dark smirk quirked the corner of his mouth.

Amber gasped, then ground out, "You son of a bitch," she struggled and winced as the movement pulled at her shoulder. "Just don't hurt my mom."

Melissa stared in stunned silence at just how fragile and helpless Amber looked pinned to DJ's chest. His eyes were hard as granite as his gaze flicked from Amber to Melissa before settling on the well-worn survival knife gripped tight in his fist. The smirk faded from his lips as he studied the blade, turning it slowly.

Melissa took a half step forward, pleading. "DJ, don't. Please." His eyes shot back to meet hers and the breath punched out of her lungs. They were not the kind eyes of the man who had saved her life

305

and helped her bury her son. That man was gone and in his place was someone who could break Amber apart without a second thought.

Amber had been right. He *was* dangerous. How had she misread him so completely? Every time she thought she had run into a decent man, they always, *always* showed her they could never really be trusted. No matter how heroic and honest and kind they made themselves out to be, men would always be able to overpower and take advantage of a woman because they were simply bigger and stronger. And when they were charming, gentle, and kind, the disappointment hit threefold when they would inevitably betray her...just like her children's father.

Her heart pounded and her stomach roiled. She had let their doom in through the front door.

DJ blinked and his gaze returned to the knife. His fingers flexed around the hilt, and for a single, terrifying moment, Melissa thought she was about to witness her daughter's demise. And then—he tossed the knife aside, the clatter ringing through the garage like a gunshot.

She cringed at the sound as Amber cursed and wriggled out of his grasp, but Melissa could tell that DJ had simply released her. Relief flooded her system.

He raised his hands in surrender, an apologetic look passing over his face before he schooled his features into a neutral mask. There was definitely something off about him. Had it been there when he had escorted her back home during the ration line attack and she had just been too blinded by grief to see it?

Her daughter spun and backed away from him, eyes wide. "What are you—" Amber screeched than clamped a hand over her mouth. She took a moment to steady herself before continuing, "What are you even doing here?" she whispered, hands clenched at her sides.

A look passed between the two of them before DJ spoke, his voice shaky, "I left headquarters just before dawn."

"But its cloudy out there," Melissa and Amber both hissed at him.

"I know. I know. I took a truck to get me most of the way here then I left it in drive and let it roll down the interstate with the horn blasting to draw the demons away. Nobody will be looking for me until the weather clears up, and when they find the wrecked truck headed south, hopefully they'll just give up thinking I'm dead."

Melissa didn't believe a word that was coming out of his mouth, and she told him as much, with a few choice words for added emphasis, Amber nodding at her side.

"You don't have to believe me," he said as his shoulders sagged a bit and he shifted on his feet. "But I brought a peace offering." He slowly reached into his pocket and pulled out a set of keys.

Amber shrugged, "And? What are those gonna do?"

"They're keys to a motorhome," DJ said with a crooked smile.

"A motorhome is gonna be just as useless as any other broken-down car," Amber said, her voice low as she pointed to Melissa's silver sedan that took up half the garage space.

"Not an old one that was owned by a crazy doomsday prepper." DJ raised his brows.

Amber crossed her arms and glared at him while Melissa shot him a skeptical look.

"I serviced it myself three weeks ago. It runs, has a full tank of gas and it's loaded with replacement parts. It was hardened against an EMP, just like the military vehicles and the old trucks that we—that *they* use for patrols...and its only two blocks away." He smiled flashing straight, white teeth and a dimple.

Amber guffawed and it only took Melissa a second to figure out why. Charles was supposed to be somewhere close by. It had to be *his* motorhome. Melissa shook her head. "No way. Amber told me all about the people you're running with now."

"*Ran* with. Past tense. I left everything they gave me behind." He paused and shrugged a bit, "Well, I stole the truck and a bunch of ammo, but I figured they owed me for that. These are my issued weapons and uniform. I didn't bring anything else," he said to Melissa then turned to Amber. "These keys are for you. To show you I'm not the monster you think I am. You can take the RV and leave me behind if you want...or we can all get out of here. Find someplace safe. I have—had friends out in Astoria with a sailboat. I know it's a long shot, but we could—"

Amber laughed bitterly and shook her head. "You are unbelievable."

"What do you mean by that?" DJ's brows furrowed.

"You really think a set of keys is going to undo everything?" Amber spat the question with a ferocity Melissa had never heard from her daughter.

DJ flinched at the harshness of her words but said nothing.

"Why didn't you just go get the motorhome and bring that here instead?" Amber asked. Melissa agreed with her daughter. That would have been the smarter thing to do. Men and their small brains.

"I knew I needed to talk to you first. To convince you. If I would have just gone straight to Charles' place and taken the RV, he would risk life and limb to stop me. He's too close and I didn't want him to know where you two have been hiding." DJ's voice took on a pleading tone as he spoke directly to Amber. "They knew someone was still in this area, they just didn't know where. And when they almost caught you that night by the train tracks, they thought you were the one they'd been trying to find." He wiped at the streak of blood trickling down his neck. "They don't know that Mel is here. I couldn't risk ruining that advantage; it's the only one we've got. There wouldn't have been time to explain what was going on and there is no way in hell you would have gotten into any vehicle with me let alone a motorhome after how we left things."

Melissa began to understand why Amber had been so guarded about DJ. He'd looked like he was about to kill her just a minute ago, and now he sounded just like the stoic soldier that had saved her life. Something was definitely different with DJ, but as she analyzed the situation, and even though her brain told her not to trust a man as far as she could have thrown him, her gut was telling her to take him at his word, that he was speaking truth.

"I don't believe you," Amber said flatly.

DJ deflated slightly, "What can I do to convince you?"

"At this point?" Amber's gaze and words dripped with venom. "Probably nothing."

"I think," Melissa whispered, stepping between her daughter and DJ, "that we need to go inside and talk this over. The garage door is too thin. They'll hear us if we stay in here." Her head swung between her daughter and DJ several times before Amber finally turned in a huff and marched toward the house door.

DJ's eyes followed until Amber pushed the door open and stepped inside. He looked at Melissa then, his hazel eyes pleading.

Despite everything that had just happened, her gut still urged her to trust the imposing soldier before her. Melissa felt her firm expression fail a moment before she schooled her features and stepped firmly into Mom-Mode. He had some serious explaining to do.

"Leave the guns and the rest of that gear in here. Boots and bullshit at the door, young man. You're in my house now and you'd better behave yourself." Melissa used the tone she'd always used with Joey when he was being pushy or obstinate, hoping DJ wouldn't be immune to a 'mom voice.'

"Yes, ma'am," he said with a nod, the shadow of a smile brushing his lips as he unbuckled his helmet and began removing his vest.

Melissa nodded stiffly and shuffled to the house door as well. Her legs protested as she mounted the stairs, but she could not allow DJ to see just how physically weak she was, so she climbed the steps without touching the handrail and let herself into the house.

As she eased herself down into the chair beside Amber at the dining table, a ragged sigh escaped her lips. Her daughter reached out to rub her shoulder. The morning had taken more out of Melissa than she had realized, and she slumped slightly in the stiff chair.

"Are you ok?" Amber whispered, concern creasing her brow.

"I'll be fine, sweetie, just a little woozy from all the excitement."

"It's probably your low blood sugar," Amber said as she stood and moved to the pantry. She pulled out a juice box and water bottle then set it down on the table. "I suppose we should feed him too."

Melissa turned to see that DJ had made his way into the house and was standing awkwardly in the hall. "I suppose we should," she said and motioned for DJ to join them at the table.

He eyed her as he sat down, no doubt taking in her pallid skin and shaking hands. She tried to peel the juice box straw out of its wrapper but with the tremors in her hands, she couldn't manage.

"I'll get that for you, Mom," Amber said softly then shot a warning look over at DJ. With a sigh and an edge of sarcasm, she said, "Would you like anything to drink?"

"Water, if you can spare it. Please," he said, raising a dark brow. He met Amber's glare with a flat look that said he was more than ready to go toe to toe with her.

Melissa groaned internally as Amber set the juice box back down in front of her and turned on her heel, marching back toward the pantry.

This was going to be a disaster.

28

Unraveling

I KNEW THE EXACT MOMENT MY mom lost her patience with me. It was about the same time DJ had had about enough of my attitude as well. I was purposely being obstinate, contradicting everything DJ had to say, every scrap of a plan he could come up with, every reason for not doing something differently, I was there, running my mouth, being snarky, shutting him down. Mom inhaled sharply and closed her eyes while she pinched the bridge of her nose. My eyes flicked to DJ. He was leaning back in the dining chair with arms folded across his chest while his jaw ticked. His eyes burned into me. Yep. I had successfully managed to piss both of them off.

"I think I need to go lay down for a little while," Mom mumbled and pushed her chair back.

Before I could pull myself out of my own chair, DJ was up and taking my mother's hand in his, gently helping her to her feet. She wobbled slightly and he placed a steadying hand on her elbow.

"You got it?" he asked in a hushed tone.

She nodded and patted the back of his hand while a grateful, half smile crept across her mouth. "Thank you."

What in the actual hell, Mom?

I stood and shot a suspicious look at DJ as I wrapped a protective arm around Mom's shoulders. "I can take her upstairs, thanks." My tone was more than a little curt.

Mom huffed, "Oh, cut it out, you two. I can make it upstairs just fine." She took a weak step then paused. "Ok, maybe not."

Together, DJ and I helped Mom back to her room. Once she was settled with a few snacks, some more juice and some water, I made my way back into the kitchen and sat down heavily at the dining table. DJ made his way back into the garage, I assumed to retrieve whatever Mom had insisted he leave out there.

The garage door snicked open and closed again. I looked up knowing he would be standing there in the hall. His eyes met mine, sharp, calculating and completely unreadable. It felt like he was analyzing every movement, every breath I made. With hands behind his back, his head canted slightly to one side while a questioning look took over his infuriatingly handsome face.

I wanted to hit him. Hard.

"Can I help you?" I droned, trying to keep my voice flat even as my heart kicked in my chest.

Without a word, DJ produced my knife, flipping and twirling it effortlessly, the blade catching the gray, watery light as it spun. He always seemed to move with that purposeful, controlled grace, as if the practice of subtle, efficient movement was a game to him. Or perhaps, his game was trying to see how off balance he could make me? I remembered the easy way he moved and spoke to me all those weeks ago when we'd met at Miller Park and I grit my teeth. The knife came to a stop in his hands, and his gaze locked onto mine.

"Where did you get this?" His words came out as casual, but his eyes were too focused.

I blinked, caught off guard. That was definitely *not* the question I expected to hear. It took me a moment to form my words. "I found it in the basement of the camp store." I held out my hand, palm open, silently demanding that he return the blade. "Why?"

He grunted, like he thought my answer was lacking in some way. It was, but I refused to confirm his suspicions. He didn't need to know that it used to be Dan's knife. If I told him that, I would have to tell him more about the camp store and I wasn't ready to trust the likes of him with that kind of information just yet. I narrowed my eyes and took in a slow breath while my empty palm still hung in the air between us.

His jaw ticked but he held the knife out to me anyway—hilt first.

312

Just as my fingers brushed the handle, he pulled it back, a small smile tugging at the corner of his mouth. A hot ball of rage settled in my gut. That look. The teasing, the control...it made my blood boil.

"Don't make me regret letting you live," I whispered through clenched teeth, but I was powerless against the way my pulse quickened.

His smile widened just enough that the rage in my gut morphed to butterflies for the briefest moment, but the look in his eyes unsettled me. There was something there, lurking just below the surface. It wasn't true cruelty, and it definitely wasn't kindness either. It was...something else entirely. Something that felt dangerous, only not in the way I had come to expect from him.

Slowly, he lowered the handle back into my palm. This time, he let me take it. My fingers wrapped around the hilt, the flat of the blade brushing against the skin of his fingertips as I pulled the knife away. It felt cold and heavy in my grip.

"Thank you," I breathed.

His brows knit together, and I glanced down at the tip of the blade. A dark smear of dried blood still marked the steel. His blood. I almost smiled but stopped myself.

My eyes flicked up to meet his again, searching for something, *anything* that might tell me what could possibly be going on in his head, but all I saw was that same intense, unreadable gaze.

He blinked slowly and I narrowed my eyes in response, trying to keep my expression neutral, but I could feel the heat rising beneath my skin. There was something about the way he looked at me...like he knew every thought running through my head, like he could see right through me...the butterflies morphed back into a hot ball of rage. I hated the way he could make me feel so out of sorts without doing...well, *anything*.

With what I hoped was a silent sigh, I turned and moved toward the kitchen sink, snapping up a damp rag to wipe the blood from the blade. I tried to keep my movements smooth, unbothered, but my mind was reeling.

Did he know? Did he feel, even for a second, the fear I'd felt at the survivalist headquarters? The way he had grabbed me, manhandled me, all to keep up appearances. My hand tightened around the rag and shook despite my best efforts, the memory still too raw. He deserved that wound on his neck at the very least—

313

deserved to know at least a fraction of the fear I'd felt at his hands. One flick of my wrist, and I could have ended him.

But I didn't.

I'd let him live. He'd never actually even hurt me, and I had drawn blood in retaliation for the fear I had felt because of him...and I still wasn't sure if that had been a mistake or not. On one hand, it seemed like I had let him off too easy, and on the other, I felt like I had gone too far.

The rain pattered steadily against the roof and windows; the sound would have been soothing were it not for the thick tension permeating the room. I stood there, wiping at the blade long after it was clean, pretending like I didn't care that DJ was standing just a few feet away at the sliding glass door that led into the back yard, watching the rain.

The house was too quiet without mom's pleasant humming or Joey's loud music. No hum of electricity or the distant, steady drone of traffic drifting over from the main road. It was the kind of quiet that forced me to listen to my own thoughts louder than I would have liked.

I hated that I could feel him there, that I was aware of every breath he took, no matter how quiet—every shift in his stance, no matter how subtle. The tension between us wasn't new...I was certain we had both felt it the moment we'd met before the world fell apart, but it felt sharper after all we had been through, like it had grown claws; clinging, gripping, reminding me of everything I was too stubborn to admit and too afraid to speak into the ether.

"After everything we've discussed, you're still not convinced, are you?" His voice broke the silence, low and steady, but there was an edge to it.

I glanced over at him without meaning to. His hazel eyes met mine, and for an instant, I couldn't breathe. That ridiculous flutter landed in my stomach again...the one I didn't want to acknowledge. The one that made me want to close the distance between us, in spite of all the reasons that I shouldn't. A flush crept up my cheeks as I forced myself to look back down at my hands, slowly running the rag over the blade. I needed something...*anything* to focus on that wasn't him.

"Why should I be?" I asked, my voice sounding cold and distant. Or maybe detached? I was trying to be, anyway; but underneath the carefully controlled mask I struggled to wear, every nerve in my body was firing. I hated it. Hated how much I wanted to understand him, to trust him even though I was still scared shitless of him. This couldn't be healthy...

He sighed and I could hear him moving closer, around the edge of the breakfast bar, his steps soft, deliberate. He stopped just behind me, his presence dark and intense. I tried with all my might not to flinch or tense up at his nearness, but I failed. My hands stilled and I sucked in a breath.

"God, I never wanted to do any of this," he said, his voice barely above a whisper, "I hate hurting people who don't deserve it. And I hate truly scaring you."

That small statement made me instantly want to hear him out. I hated that it did, but I couldn't help it. Setting the knife and rag down on the countertop, I turned slightly and looked up at him again, this time holding his gaze. His expression was softer than I expected, almost regretful, and for the briefest of moments, I almost believed him. I *really* wanted to believe him.

"But you did." My voice wavered just slightly, and I turned back toward the dripping window above the sink. "You scared the hell out of me, DJ."

He sighed but stayed silent, so I continued, "The fact that you can morph into what that group of psychopaths expects you to be so quickly—the fact that I can tell there is a small piece of you that likes having that kind of power—" The words came out before I could stop them. The thought had been bouncing around in my skull for weeks...that the man standing two paces away from me wasn't the same one I thought I knew. Maybe he never had been. I certainly wasn't the same person I had been the day we met in that tiny parking lot. Steeling myself, I glanced over my shoulder again.

A flash of pain flickered in his eyes, but it was gone as quickly as it came. He was so good at hiding what he really felt. "I've done what I had to do to survive my entire life," he said, his voice hardening as my eyes found the window once more.

I just couldn't look at him.

"I had to keep you safe from—" He cut himself off and stepped even closer. So close that I could feel the warmth of him radiating through the oversized, tattered sweater I wore. My whole body tensed, and I held my breath, every nerve on high alert, caught between wanting to step away and wanting to lean back into him, to feel his arms gently encircle me. I shook my head.

"You have no idea how hard it was to keep them from hurting you and Gail both," he said softly. "I played along. Said an did things, did things I hate myself for. But I did it to protect you both."

My hands gripped the edge of the countertop. His words were so close to what I wanted to hear, but there was still that voice in the back of my mind, the one that kept nagging, *you can't trust him.* I wasn't ready to ignore that voice. Not yet. Even though my gut kept gently nudging that he actually *was* trustworthy.

"You're used to controlling things, aren't you?" I asked, my tone sharp. It was easier to push him away than it was to let myself get sucked into whatever it was that seemed to be pulling us together. I turned to face him full on, my eyes roaming his face. That was a mistake.

DJ's lips quirked up into that infuriating smile, the one that made me want to slap him and kiss him at the same time. "Only certain things."

I glared, "Well, I refuse to be one of those *certain things.*" My chin kicked up a notch and I folded my arms across my chest.

"Well, only certain aspects of certain things, then."

What the hell was he hinting at? I felt something stir in me, something wild and reckless...and far too dangerous to trust. I fought it down, but despite myself, my lips twitched, a tiny crack in my defenses. "You already know how stubborn I can be," I said quietly, not trusting my full voice.

He leaned in just a little, his voice dropping to that husky, low tone that sent shivers down my spine, "But I like stubborn."

Houston, we have a problem.

The air between us thickened, charged with electricity and heavy with all of the things we weren't saying. My heart hammered in my chest, and I wet my lips as I looked up at him.

Oh, this is bad.

I refused to allow myself to fall into that tangled mess. Not just yet. Shaking myself out of a momentary stupor, I turned away from him and stalked out of the kitchen, running a hand through my hair and scrubbing palms over my face. "DJ, I—I." I crossed my arms tightly over my chest as if that could somehow contain the storm raging inside me.

"You don't have to do or be anything right now," he said as he slowly followed me over to the sliding door. His voice was softer, but the tension still hummed between us like a live wire. "Just give me a chance to prove that I'm not really the dirtbag you think I am."

I stared out through the wet glass, the rain obscuring everything outside and I wished it could wash away the dark stains on my memory the same way it washed away dust and debris. I closed my eyes, feeling the heat of him again as he stepped beside me. My chest tightened as his words tugged at my gut. I wasn't ready to confront that feeling...that I knew he was telling me the truth.

"Maybe I've already decided to trust you," I whispered to myself so quietly that I wasn't even sure I meant to say it out loud. I could only hope I'd spoken low enough that he didn't hear.

DJ shifted beside me, and I felt the tension in the air shift as well. He was waiting for something...some sign that I was willing to give him the chance he wanted. I didn't have to look at him to know he was staring at me. I could feel the weight of his gaze burning into my cheek as I drew in a lungful of air and let it out in a whoosh, my breath fogging the glass.

"Cat got your tongue?" DJ asked, his voice low and careful. Like he was afraid to disturb the silence...or the thoughts whirling in my head.

"I don't really know what else to say." Which was a flat lie. There was so much I wanted to say to him—about him—about the way I felt when he was close, the way my heart jumped into my throat when he looked at me. Just a few days ago he'd told me that excitement, anticipation, and fear could feel remarkably similar at times. I barely held back a scoff at the memory.

DJ carefully stepped closer. "I don't think that's ever been true about you."

I glanced over my shoulder, just enough to hit him with a sideways look. "You think you know me that well?" The question came out sharper than I intended, but I couldn't help it. He had a certain knack for getting under my skin.

"I think I'm starting to," he replied, as his hazel eyes flashed in the dim light, flickering with something warmer than I expected. There was a rawness to him, like he was letting me see more than he should.

I turned to face him fully, "You don't really know anything about me, DJ. Shit, I don't even know if I know myself anymore." The words spilled out before I could stop them, and I worried my bottom lip. Did *not* mean to share that with him, but it was obviously too late to take it back.

He just looked at me for a long moment, his eyes searching mine, before he shook his head softly. "That's not true. I know you like hiking...it helps you think. And you love huckleberry milkshakes, your Jeep, photography, camping, and the different shades of fresh spring leaves." He paused a moment, shifting on his feet. "And you're stronger than you think you are...and more honest than you give yourself credit for."

I let out a bitter laugh and pushed away from the window. He sounded like Dan. The space between us felt too intense. I needed to move, to create some distance.

"Honest?" I repeated, shaking my head. "I've been lying to myself since I jumped out of the truck. Thinking I could just move on, forget what happened with the survivalists. Forget about you—" I clamped my hand across my mouth, like I could stuff what I'd just said back into the realm of unspoken words.

Damn it.

My cheeks flushed with heat. How could I have let that slip? I couldn't bring myself to look at him.

"You shouldn't try to forget, Amber. Everything you've been through and everything yet to come will help shape you into the person you need to be to survive this thing. I can understand if you hate me for what I've done, you can say it out loud if it helps, just don't pretend like it never happened," he said, voice gentle but firm.

The words hit me like a punch to the gut. "I don't hate you, DJ," I finally admitted quietly, meeting his eyes. My voice was too small, too vulnerable, but the truth needed to come out. "But I don't know— I'm afraid to trust you."

His lips twitched, almost forming a smile, but it didn't quite reach his eyes. "Fair enough. Trust is earned." He took a small step closer, his arm nearly brushing mine as he looked up at the gray expanse of the sky. "The clouds are pretty thick, you figure we have, what, four or five days of rain to wait out?" He glanced down at me with a crooked smile. "Give me five days to prove to you I'm worthy of your trust."

I bit my lip, trying to fight the smile that threatened to break through. "Three days. Maybe four. Tops." I raised an eyebrow at him. If he was looking for a challenge...

He grinned, dimple flashing. "I've faced worse odds."

I rolled my eyes at his playful smile, but it was half-hearted. The tension between us eased just a little. "You're impossible to dislike, aren't you?"

"Maybe." His gaze lingered on me, and I could feel it on every inch of my skin. "I mean what I said though. I'm not giving up until I know I've earned your trust, no matter how long it takes."

My heart skipped a beat at the intensity in his eyes, and I tried to brush it off, nudging his arm playfully, anything to break the tension. "You better be careful. I might start thinking you actually care about me."

DJ chuckled then, the sound deep and low, reverberating through the room. "It's a little too late for that."

The air caught in my throat. I was not expecting that. My defenses began to crack with every beat of my heart as I stood there, the silence stretching between us.

"I'm serious," DJ said, his voice soft. There was a vulnerability in his eyes that I had never seen before. "You aren't just some random person I helped escape, Amber. I didn't let you go just because it was the right thing to do. I did it because I couldn't imagine a world where your perfect smile didn't exist."

My heart stuttered in my chest, and I gazed up at him, eyes wide. I couldn't form a coherent thought, let alone a single word.

DJ stepped closer, his knuckles barely brushing my arm before he softly took my hand in his. "You don't have to say anything," his voice was just above a whisper. "Just...let me show you. Give me a chance."

I hesitated, my heart pounding so loudly in my ears I was sure he could hear it too. I wanted to believe him. I wanted to trust him, but that little voice in my head was still telling me to run, kick him to the curb before I really got hurt.

Always trust your gut, it will never lead you astray. Mom's words echoed in my mind as I looked into his eyes; eyes that always seemed to see more than I wanted him to, and finally I saw it. The truth. The sincerity. The quiet promise that he was not going to hurt me. That little voice of doubt in my mind faded away.

"Okay." I nodded with a sigh, "You have until the sun comes out. However long that might be."

"Deal." He looked relieved as he pressed my knuckles to his lips.

Oh, he is impossible!

I pulled my hand from his grasp and shoved at him playfully. "I suppose you're going to need somewhere to sleep."

"Is your room off limits?" He cocked an eyebrow at me.

"I sleep with that knife under my pillow, just so you know."

A full smile spread across my face as he raised his hands and took a step backward.

"Fluffy couch or ancient, twin sized mattress?" I asked.

"Couch?" he replied.

"Through the pocket door over there." I pointed toward the den entrance. The room where Joey and I had played so many video games and watched countless hours of television together. Where mom let us set up pillow forts and camp out on the giant sectional couch every Christmas Eve. So many memories in that room and now DJ was adding himself to the list.

He nodded and disappeared through the doorway.

"Extra blankets and pillows are in the closet." I sighed, running a hand over my face. What was he going to sleep in? His dirty uniform? Just his underwear? In the buff?

Nope, don't think about that.

I quickly switched gears, imagining Joey, tall and lanky, with his strange affinity for clothes that were two sizes too big, offering DJ a pair of sweatpants and a giant t-shirt or hoodie.

In a perfect world, they would have gotten along well, I was sure of it. And the thought of DJ wearing Joey's clothes would be much better for my mental and emotional state than imagining him lounging on my favorite piece of furniture in nothing but his small clothes. "Umm—do you need a change of clothes? Something to sleep in?"

DJ popped his head back through the doorway with what I could only describe as a coy smile, "You better be careful. I might start thinking that *you* actually care about *me*."

∞

Two days after I'd caved and given DJ the chance to prove himself, I was already starting to regret it. Not because of anything he'd done, it was quite the opposite. He was doing everything right...literally everything. And it infuriated me. He sat up at night, watching the sky and keeping an ear out for the creatures, he cooked, cleaned, set up a rainwater collection system in the back yard...he even went out scavenging. In the rain. Just to find Mom some quality supplements because she was still feeling weak.

I'd been an absolute wreck while he was gone. The darkling spawn could have been anywhere, they were always hunting, but after three nerve wracking hours, he came creeping back through the gap in the fence between ours and our neighbor's backyard. I barely kept myself from running out into the rain, throwing myself at him like some sort of lovesick idiot because I was so relieved.

He had come in through the sliding glass door, dripping and silent, his eyes glittering with mischief as he presented me with a handful of daffodils and tulips that he'd found growing in an abandoned yard. Heat rose in my cheeks at the gesture. He'd been out there, risking his life for supplies, and even knowing the danger, he'd stopped to gather *flowers?*

My relief twisted, "What are you, crazy?" I hissed at him. He just smiled, like he could see straight through my anger and into the tangled mess of feelings and emotions that I wasn't really ready to face...which irritated me even more.

I just kept pushing him away. All the trust issues I thought I had squashed were wriggling back to life like a giant roach under my boot. Every time he tried to get close, I either snapped at him or found some excuse to avoid him, so he gave the flowers to my mom instead. The two of them sat in her room talking for what seemed like an eternity, no doubt conspiring against me, and all I could do was scowl at her door trying to make sense of my emotions.

The next day I was sitting at my bedroom desk, scrawling out my feelings about the whole insane situation in my journal when mom tapped at my partially open door.

"Amber, can I talk to you for a bit?" she said softly.

Her voice had that serious tone she hadn't used with me since I'd been in high school and I knew I was in for an earful. I turned to face her, my brow furrowed. She had been treating DJ like she had treated Joey, like he was already family, a fact that rankled my feelings to no end. We both missed Joey, but she couldn't just use DJ as a substitute for the son she had watched die not two months ago. And aside from all that, I was certain he'd put her up to this.

"Sure," I said, the word came out sounding more like a question.

She slid in, closing the door behind her and patted a space beside her on my rumpled bed as she sat down. "Come sit with me, sweetheart."

Great. I tried not to roll my eyes and sigh as I placed my pen inside my journal and closed the leather cover. When I sat down, shoulders and back stiff, she gave me an apologetic smile. We had always been close, but Mom was never one for serious talks—not about relationships, anyway—and I had the sneaking suspicion that that was where this conversation was heading.

She took a deep breath, hands fidgeting in her lap before she laid a frail hand on my knee and spoke. "I've been watching how things have been going between you and DJ the last couple of days,"

My face must have copped an attitude because she squeezed my knee with a half-smile and pressed on.

"I get it, Amber. You don't trust him, and I'm not saying you should just blindly believe everything he says. But—" she paused, eyes darting around my face, "I see the way you're treating him. And—it reminds me of someone."

I blinked. That was not what I had been expecting. "Who?"

"Me," she said, her voice thick with...was it regret? "After your father left."

No, it couldn't be. Her words cut deep, slicing through the anger I had been masking my true feelings with. She had never opened up about her feelings (or anything for that matter) when it came to my father. I was at a complete loss for words. I had never asked about him either, though. I mean, we had talked years ago about how he had abandoned us and that it was ok for Joey and me to be angry, but we never talked about what his leaving had done to *her* emotionally.

As I grew up a bit, I always figured that it must have been too painful for her to speak about, so I never brought it up. I didn't need to know the specifics of their breakup; I was her kid, and it would have been unfair for her to place that kind of emotional baggage on me anyway. All I needed was my mom to be my mom and she had been the best parent I could have ever hoped for. Strict, but loving, kind and encouraging, her door was always open to discuss anything, but as I moved into adulthood, it was easy to see that she was angry, lonely, and deeply hurt.

She looked down at her hand on my knee and sighed. "When your father chose his other family over us, it destroyed me. My heart was so broken that I couldn't even think about trusting or ever being vulnerable enough to love anyone else ever again. It was safer to build walls and stay behind them. To focus on raising you and Joey and forget about having a love life or partnership ever again. You know I never dated, but it was more than that. I never even tried to move on. I just...shut everything out."

I nodded, afraid to speak. This was important and I needed to not only listen, but to really *hear* what she was saying. Her words hung in the still air, and I felt my throat tighten. Hearing her talk about her young life like this—it hit me harder than I expected. My mind immediately went to her age. She'd only been two years older than I was when my father abandoned us. Putting myself in her shoes, it struck me just how hard Mom's life had to have been. Alone in her mid-twenties with two small kids? I cursed inwardly and took her hand in mine giving it a little squeeze.

"I *really* thought that if I focused on raising you and your brother, I wouldn't need anyone else, I'd have my beautiful children and that would be more than enough," she continued, her voice shaky. "But the truth is, I was scared. I dreamed of a loving partnership, but I was too afraid to go out there and look for it. I lied to myself and turned down every man, and woman for that matter, that ever offered to get to know me on a romantic level. It wasn't until a couple of years ago that I finally realized that I missed out on so much."

And here I was, doing the same thing she had done, letting fear close me off while hiding behind a wall of anger because the truth was too unsettling. I swallowed hard.

"Mom, I—" I started but she shook her head.

She turned to fully face me, worrying her bottom lip. "You were so young when I was at my worst and I always hoped that my shitty attitude toward men hadn't rubbed off on you, but since DJ's been here, since I can see and hear you interact with him—I can see that it did."

323

"You didn't do anything wrong, Mom. You had every right to be angry. I was barely old enough to realize what had happened and I just figured that dad didn't love us enough," I said, my throat tight.

"Your father didn't love anyone, not even himself, sweetheart. It was nothing that any of us did and there was no way we could have changed a thing about what happened."

I nodded and she continued. "When you were thirteen, he called one day while you and Joey were at school. Said he had made a mistake and wanted to come back home." She shook her head and let out a bitter laugh. "Of course, I told him to screw himself and that I wouldn't fall for his bullshit a second time."

I chuckled, imagining my mom telling my dad off and hanging up on him. "You did?"

"Oh, you bet I did." A wry smile touched her lips before she turned serious again. "I'd learned enough by then to realize *he* was the problem and not me, but I was too blinded by my anger to see that not all men are like your father, Amber." She paused, eyes roaming my face before she reached over to brush an unruly strand of hair back off my forehead. "I'm telling you this because I don't want you to make the same mistake I did. I see the way DJ looks at you. That young man is smitten and he's trying for you sweetheart, he really is. And I don't think he's anything like your father."

Smitten? I glanced down at my lap, barely containing a snort as my cheeks burned. She didn't know the half of it. When we first met, I might have said he was curious about me, but now? It felt like something else—something deeper. On the rare occasion that I gathered the courage to truly look into his eyes, there was something else there. Something much different than him being simply *smitten*, as Mom thought.

The look in his eyes felt more like intense infatuation, like I had become a challenge or a game of some sort. A goal for him to charm and court and pursue. And what would he do when he finally lured me in? What would *I* do? My stomach flipped at the thought and not in the way it probably should have.

Now, all I could see was a man that I was overwhelmingly physically attracted to...and the last thing I needed was to dive in headfirst and catch feelings for someone I didn't even really know. Plus, he had never been completely honest with me when it came to

324

his true intentions...not that I'd asked him either though. I probably should have.

Guilt and a strange excitement warred within me. On one hand, Mom was right. I'd been awful to him. Cruel even. Brushing him off, keeping him at arm's length despite him doing everything he could to show me he could be a decent man. On the other hand, I had every right to not want anything to do with him.

"Well, shit," I croaked out. My heart stuttered and I took a shaky breath. I really shouldn't want *anything* to do with him, but instead, against all my better judgement, I wanted *everything* to do with him. I wasn't afraid of him being dangerous, or violent, or any of the things he'd pretended to be in that survivalist camp, not anymore. No, I was afraid of how easily he'd charmed his way past my defenses. From the second I had seen him in the park months ago, to the moment in the med tent when his eyes darkened as he'd snaked his arm around my waist and told me to 'play along' just a few weeks ago...I was afraid of just how much I wanted everything he could offer.

"I know you're scared," Mom said softly, obviously mistaking my groan and lack of eye contact for a different sort of realization.

DJ hid that shadowy part of himself so well—I was going to have to learn to do the same.

"And," she continued, "I know that letting your guard down and learning to trust someone new—especially after growing up with an absent father on top of everything you've experienced since this all started—is likely going to be one of the hardest things you've done in your life. But you shouldn't let fear keep you from experiencing something as magical as human relationships."

Thinking back on the day DJ and I had first met, I had been all for finding out just what type of person he was. Had we been able to go on a few real dates and gotten to know each other a little bit better before the world went to hell, I may not have been so put off by his...quirks. Hell, who was I kidding? I knew I would have found it exciting because I was fascinated by the idea now. But that fascination had nothing to do with the fact that I had built a fortress around my heart, and it didn't excuse the fact that I was being an absolute bitch to him.

Mom was right of course. "Shit. I—I didn't realize I was—" I stammered, waving my hand, searching for the right words. "I thought I was just being careful. I mean, I just didn't want to end up—"

"Like me?" Mom interrupted with a raised brow, her voice gentle but firm.

I looked at her and grimaced. "No, that's not what I meant," I started. She always understood exactly what I was trying to say and never took offense if I came off bluntly.

A weary smile curved her lips, the kind that held a lifetime of what-ifs tucked in behind years of acceptance. "It's alright, sweetie. I made my choice years ago and made peace with it, for the most part, but now that the world is crumbling, I know for sure that I missed my chance to ever feel the highs and lows of love...or lust," she added with a conspiratorial wink, "again...in this life anyway."

"But maybe you haven't, Mom. If good people like DJ and Dan still exist, I'll bet—"

She simply shook her head. "I'm too old for all of that, but you?"

"You might be older than me, but you aren't *dead*, Mom," I protested with a crooked smile, but she rushed on.

"Now, I'm not saying that DJ is Mister Right or even Mister Right-Now, but I don't want you to miss out on something—or someone—who could end up being good for you. Fear doesn't keep you alive; it keeps you from living."

I exhaled slowly. Even if her argument was somewhat misguided, I could see where she was coming from, but would she change her opinion of DJ if she knew what I knew? There wasn't a doubt in my mind that she would second-guess herself if she had experienced what I had at his hands...but I just couldn't share those details with my *mother* no matter how close we were.

"I just don't know if I'm ready to trust him," I sighed. It was best to keep my push-back generic.

Mom nodded. "That's okay. Trust doesn't come overnight. But being cruel, shutting him out—it's not fair. Not to him, and not to yourself."

She wasn't wrong about that, and I nodded through a long pause. I suddenly realized that she wasn't just talking about me and DJ either...she was talking about herself. About the life she could have had if she'd let herself trust again.

"I know its human nature to learn everything the hard way, but please, don't let my mistakes become yours," she said softly. "Learn from me."

She'd sacrificed so much for Joey and me over the years, including a large part of her own happiness, but now she was urging me to take a risk she'd been too afraid to take for herself. She wrapped her arm around my shoulders, and we stayed like that for a moment, just breathing and thinking about what had been said...what she had finally admitted. When I pulled back, I nodded. I had been behaving like a childish bitch and DJ didn't really deserve my wrath, did he? I was angry at the situation, not him.

"Well, this is frikkin' embarrassing," I mumbled as I scrubbed palms over my face. "Alright, I'll try to stop being so...harsh."

Mom smiled, her eyes shimmering. "That's all I'm asking, sweetie. Just give it an honest try."

We sat and chatted for a while about inconsequential things before Mom excused herself back to her room and I crept down the stairs to find something to munch on. Was I really ready to do it? Could I actually handle all that DJ was about? My mind drifted back to the moment he called me out at the Survivalist's camp after the second time he'd man-handled me.

I won't pretend that I know what you're feeling right now but judging by the color in your cheeks and the way you're breathing, it's not *fear.*

I'd been a flustered mess, barely able to form words and he'd known in an instant that I was into it, more afraid of the way my body reacted to it, than to him. What did that say about me and my emotional stability?

With a huff, I rummaged through the pantry. Was I making a dangerous choice? What if DJ's dark side was as bad as Charles'? What if his affinity for control and the thrill of the chase went beyond being an innocuous kink? Would he, *could* he hurt me in the same ways that Charles had hurt others? Gail's star-shaped scars floated across my memory, and I shook my head. After a moment, my gut said otherwise. No, DJ wasn't truly cruel, nor was he a narcissistic psychopath with a God-complex like Charles.

My hand closed around a box of snack crackers, and I headed back to the solitude of my room, turning everything over in my mind. Nothing was guaranteed anymore—not another day...not even another breath—not in the new, crazy world we were living in. If DJ was ready to draw me in, to reveal the darker self he kept such tight control over, then I was going to give him the run of his life. I didn't want to live with regrets like my mom did, and I knew from my head to my boots that if I didn't at least dip my toes in the vast pool that was DJ, I would regret it. But I would make him work for it. Make him earn every ounce of my trust and the submission I could feel him aching for. Oh, if he wanted a game, he'd found himself a player.

I sat down on my bed with a small chuckle as a self-satisfied smile spread across my face and popped a cracker into my mouth. But as I chewed slowly, the hard truth settled in my gut like a sack of concrete, and I flopped back on my bed with a groan. Before all the fun and games could even get started, I was going to have to apologize.

29

Is it Hot in Here?

I STOOD IN THE SHORT, dark hallway silently staring at the door to the den like a dragon lay behind it and I was about to do battle; breath unsteady, adrenaline searing through my veins, heart pounding in my chest. My ears strained, barely picking up the sounds of DJ moving around in the cozy room as an involuntary shudder ran up my spine and I almost lost my nerve. I had gone over what I wanted to say a hundred times in my head, but the nerves still gnawed at me. Apologizing wasn't something I did often. Keeping people at arms length made it easier to avoid ever needing to. But I couldn't ignore all that DJ had done without a single complaint. Like it or not, I owed him that much.

It's now or never.

Swallowing hard, I stepped forward and knocked, the sound feeling small in the stillness of the hallway. I half hoped he wouldn't answer, but a moment later, his slightly muffled voice sounded through the thin wood of the pocket door.

"Yeah?"

With a determined set to my jaw, I slowly slid the door open and peered inside. DJ sat on the edge of the giant sectional sofa, one boot kicked off, the other half-laced. His shirt, rumpled and damp, clung to his body in ways that literally made me salivate, and I had to fight the urge to lick my lips as my eyes traveled farther upward. His hair dripped, curling at the tips, from the rain he'd been out in moments before. A flicker of surprise and something inviting danced in his eyes as he looked up at me. All I could do was stare for a moment, and damn it all if he didn't notice, his lips curling in a way that sent my pulse racing.

Not trusting my voice enough to start speaking right away, I stepped inside and slid the door closed behind me. My heart pounded in my ears as I tucked clammy hands into the pocket of my hoodie and took a deep breath, trying to keep my cool.

His gaze bore into mine as he raised an eyebrow. "Didn't expect you to ever set foot in this room while I was in it. What's up?"

How the hell does he sound so casual?

I chewed lightly at my bottom lip and fidgeted while he finished unlacing his boot and set it on the floor, never once breaking eye contact with me. The son of a bitch knew what he was doing. I could barely think straight, so before I lost my nerve, I pulled my gaze from his and stared at my socks a moment before glancing back up at him. "I—uh—I wanted to talk."

DJ tensed for a moment. "Go on," he said as he reached for the hem of his clinging shirt and lifted. His tone was even, but his hazel eyes were sharp, like he had been waiting for this very moment.

I fumbled with the words, everything I'd rehearsed scrambling in my head as I caught a glimpse of his bare stomach. "You'd better keep that shirt on if you want to hear what I have to say," I said through gritted teeth trying to hide the smile in my voice as I crossed my arms.

"Oh? Didn't know you were paying attention," he smirked, his hand hovering near the hem of his shirt before dropping it with a mock sigh. "Guess I'll have to behave, then." He ran a hand through his dark hair and leaned forward, elbows resting on his knees.

My eyes flicked toward his biceps and then settled on his lips, which wasn't really any freaking better.

Get it together, Amber.

When I finally spoke, the words came out softer than I intended. "So, I've been...I've been kind of a bitch to you."

"Ya think?" DJ's mouth twitched as if he were fighting a smile, eyes dancing with mischief. "Here I thought you just had a strange way of flirting."

I felt heat rise in my cheeks, but I just needed to get through the apology and then everything else would be easier, so I pushed on through my embarrassment. "You've been doing so much for me—for us, and I've treated you like...like you haven't earned that second chance, but you have. And I'm sorry that I've been so shitty to you. I've just been too—"

The smirk fell from his face, and the spacious room instantly felt too small. "A real apology? Well, damn."

He stood up, closing the distance between us, and I took an involuntary step backward. I should have left the door open in case I needed to escape.

No, no...that was my faulty self-defense mechanism talking.

I knew I truly didn't have anything to fear from this man, but recent trauma and years of habitually hiding behind an emotional wall were going to take more than a single conversation with my mom or with DJ to overcome.

He slowed his advance, prowling the last few paces toward me. "I accept your apology." The corner of his mouth quirked and his dimple made a brief appearance. He took a deliberate step closer, so close I could see the rain caught in his hair and feel the heat radiating off him. It took everything I had in me not to take another step backward. His voice dropped low, his tone both amused and challenging. "You're not running away this time. Progress."

That didn't negate the fact that every instinct in my body was telling me to run, again, not because I thought he was going to hurt me, no, it was because I'd finally figured out how much he loved the chase. Even still, his presence was overwhelming, and I stumbled over my next words, looking up at him. "I-I'm sorry for doubting you, DJ. Really. I'm just...I don't know how to trust someone like you, or anyone I don't know, for that matter."

His brow furrowed and he froze, rocking back on his heels and crossing his arms over his chest. "Someone like me, huh? You think you've got me all figured out?" His tone was lightly playful, but I could sense a tense undercurrent to his words.

I shook my head. "No, that's the thing—I don't really know anything about you...what makes you tick," I met his gaze and steeled myself. "And it's really hard for me to trust someone I don't know."

He canted his head to one side, hazel eyes flickering with mischief. "You might not know much about me, but I think you know enough to take a guess at what makes me tick." He paused, eyes taking me in from disheveled head to stockinged feet. "I'm an open book, but only if you're willing to dig."

His smile fell slightly, betraying the otherwise confident aura he was projecting, his words feeling like both an invitation and a challenge.

Noted. Alright then. Here we go...

"Well, you already know a lot about my family, can you tell me a little about yours?" I asked. Family seemed to me like a good place to start, but a wall slammed down behind his eyes.

He shifted, his jaw tightening as he looked away. "I don't like to talk much about family," he muttered.

I waited, but the silence stretched deep into uncomfortable territory and my heart sank a little realizing I wasn't going to get anywhere with that question.

Possible red flag number—I'd lost count.

"Okay," I said, drawing the word out with a grimace and a shrug. I skirted around him, making my way over to the couch and plopped down in my favorite corner, just like I had done for years. Pulling a throw pillow onto my lap and curling into a ball, I inhaled through my nose.

Being friendly took way too much effort when it came to the likes of him. I could try a different angle, but one more question was all he was getting from me. "How about your favorite things, then? Or what did you like to do, you know, before all this?"

DJ made his way to the sofa, a thoughtful expression on his face, and sat down beside me. Close, but not too close. After a moment, his body relaxed a fraction, though he still seemed on edge.

"Taco trucks," he said after a moment, his voice lighter. "Could have eaten at the one near my house every day."

I blinked at the unexpected answer, my lips twitching. "Really?"

"Yeah. Throw some lime and hot sauce on there and I'm in heaven." He gave me a sideways glance, a bit of that teasing smirk returning. "Favorite movie? 'Fight Club.' Probably saw it a hundred times."

"Why am I not surprised?" Mom had every Brad Pitt movie ever made on DVD and subjected me and Joey to countless movie marathons when we were in high school. Fight Club was one of her favorites too.

"It's a great movie." His eyes lit up as he continued, voice softening. "Favorite thing to do? Riding my bike. Problems just seem to disappear as soon as I swing a leg over." He trailed off, a faraway look in his eyes.

My nose wrinkled of its own accord. Bicycles were a lot of work, not to mention the silly padded shorts serious cyclists wore. But he was obviously into fitness, so maybe he—

"Not *that* kind of bike," DJ interrupted my thoughts, a teasing note to his voice. "A motorcycle."

Pursing my lips to cover any sign that I might look impressed, I bobbed my head. "Oh, that makes more sense than what I just pictured." I thoroughly looked him over and couldn't help but picture him on a motorcycle, helmet in hand, leather jacket zipped up tight. My stomach fluttered at the mental image and my ears warmed. "Yeah, *way* more sense."

"Oh? And what were you picturing?"

There was no way I was going to let him know what I'd actually just been imagining, "You in padded, neon spandex and a weird bicycle helmet," I snickered, hoping that covered the heat rising in my cheeks.

DJ looked appalled then he laughed, "It would be a cold day in hell before I ever put on spandex shorts."

"Good," I said with a crooked smile. "Ok, what are some other things you like?"

"I really miss old restaurants, dive bars, a good whiskey," he paused, trailing off a bit before continuing with a sigh, "and my kid sister."

That last part nearly knocked the breath out of me. "You have a sister?"

He nodded, but his expression darkened as he made himself more comfortable, shifting on the cushions and draping an arm across the back of the sofa. "Yeah. Half-sister—huge gap between us. She's a smart kid...I used to take care of her a lot when she was little."

There was something raw in his voice, a pain he couldn't quite hide. "I miss that lil pipsqueak like crazy," he said quietly, his eyes distant. "And I don't even know if she's alive."

I bit my lip, wanting to say the right thing, but words were just too small for the situation. "I...I'm really sorry, DJ. I know how you feel," I whispered, remembering how I'd felt the moment I realized my brother was dead.

He flashed me a sideways glance and nodded, his usual guarded expression falling back into place. "Yeah. Well, it is what it is. But...I've got a picture of us, back when she was just a baby. I'd give anything to get my hands on that photo again."

"Where is it at?"

"My old place. Along with my bike."

"Maybe we can make a trip back to your house before we leave town?" I asked.

"Eh, it's too close to the Survivalist's headquarters. It'd be suicide." He sighed while shaking his head. "I'll just have to keep the memory alive in here." He tapped his temple then straightened up and gave me a tight smile. "Enough about that though, you ever backpacked before?"

I blinked at the sudden change, thrown by how quickly he closed off again. "Backpacked? Like hiking?"

DJ's grin returned, more genuine now. "Like riding passenger on a motorcycle."

I had no experience at all with motorcycle lingo, "Yeah, no. I didn't know anybody with a motorcycle, but I think I might have liked it."

"Well, if the world ever stops falling apart and I can get back to my old place, we'll go for a ride."

My heart jumped at the thought. "Maybe," I murmured, feeling myself flush.

The thought of being that close to DJ sent my pulse skyrocketing again and I tucked a stray hair behind my ear, focusing on the pillow in my lap. I could feel his eyes on me and I suddenly wished that I had paid more attention to my friends when they talked about guys and dating. Sitting next to him, my brain short-circuited like it had never seen a man before. I blamed the proximity—and the way he filled it. Not that dating really mattered with the state of the world, but it sure would have been nice if I could confidently go toe to flirty toe with DJ. And I still had one more thing to clear up before I could really start learning to relax with him.

Without thinking, I blurted, "Did you really read my journal?"

He chuckled softly, and I felt a mix of embarrassment and dread twist in my stomach. Was he laughing because he had? Did he know all about the immediate attraction I had felt and how often I had thought about him while I was alone, stranded at the camp store?

"No, I didn't," he said. Which surprised me.

He'd known those little tidbits that he'd taunted me with in the med tent all those days ago though. "But how—"

"Frank dug through your stuff and started reading it out loud in the bunkhouse. That's how all the guys found out about our little secret." He arched a brow at me.

"Oh, no," I groaned, leaning over and pressing my face into the throw pillow in my lap. It was worse than I thought then. I was instantly mortified at the thought that every single one of those ass holes knew my thoughts and feelings about DJ, but what really terrified me was that they now knew where I had been up in the mountains, and they knew about The Glow, the light dome, that protected the store. I bolted up, "Oh, shit!"

"What?" DJ's eyes, still teasing, narrowed slightly.

"If he read it out loud, all of them know about where I was staying and where I planned to go if I could ever get out of this freaking city." Fresh panic began to rise in my throat as I gripped the throw pillow.

He leaned toward me and tugged the pillow out of my hands with a smile. "I took your journal and your backpack from him before he got too far."

"You'd better not be lying to me right now, or I swear—"

"I'm not lying," he interrupted. "And I didn't read it even after I got my hands on it. I didn't go through your bag either."

"You promise?"

All he did was nod slowly.

He could be lying, but what point would that serve? And if he had read my journal, at least he would know what was going on in my head without me having to say anything. Still, the thought of anyone knowing my innermost thoughts made my stomach turn.

"Swear it," I said, pointing a finger at his chest.

"Must be some juicy stuff in there." An amused smile crept across his lips. "Now I'm really disappointed that I didn't."

I shot him my most convincing glower and he raised his hands in surrender. "Alright, I swear," he chuckled. "I did *not* read your journal."

Relief washed over me, and I let out a long breath. "But you could have."

DJ nodded. "Yeah, I could've. But I didn't. All those years in the military—plus my dad drilling respect into me—taught me better than that. I respect your privacy, Amber."

I glanced at him with a crooked smile, half-grateful, half-annoyed. "You really didn't sneak a peek?"

DJ smirked, leaning in slightly. "Oh, I was tempted, but I was betting that you'd spill it eventually. So, what *did* you write about me?"

My face burned, but I refused to back down now. I'd told myself I was going to give him a run for his money and even though I was feeling way out of my depth, it was time to start. "You really wanna know what I wrote?"

"Dying to." His jaw ticked and I couldn't decide if I wanted to slap that smug look off his face or kiss him. I think my mom would have called him incorrigible. I wanted to call him infuriating...but try as I might, a part of me was loving every second of this.

I hesitated, my heart hammering in my chest. "Fine," I mumbled. "I wrote...that you struck me as a cocky little turd." I let those words hang in the air a few seconds before continuing, "But your smile and that dimple—God, your stupid dimple—made my damn knees weak."

DJ's grin widened, and I felt his knee brush mine. He'd inched closer, watching my lips as I spoke. "Really?" His voice was low.

"I thought you were...I don't know, when you winked at me that day, I immediately thought you were trouble." I'd wanted to climb him like a tree, but I wasn't about to share *that* little tidbit with him.

Shit, did he just move closer?

I scooted backward a bit, nestling deeper into the fluffy cushions. I just needed to keep talking and not let him get too close. "But then, you didn't have your own jumper cables and needed a girl to rescue you."

DJ laughed, the sound low and warm, and his fingers brushed against mine, sending a shiver through me. "You really thought I was trouble?"

I sighed, my voice barely a whisper, "Oh, yeah." A nervous laugh escaped my throat. The affinity he had for hardcore eye contact made me squirm every time, but I grit my teeth and met his gaze. "The second I laid eyes on you, I knew you'd get me into trouble."

His eyes darkened, raw desire crackling between us. "You did?"

I nodded, not trusting my voice as his fingers twined with mine. Every inch of my body buzzed with the weight of his gaze. His other hand reached up, tucking a stray hair behind my ear and my heart stopped.

"You're not wrong," he murmured. "So, tell me...does that trouble make you want to run now?" His eyes roamed my face, lingering too long on my lips.

Nope, not answering that.

"I think this was a bad idea," I whispered, barely able to form the words. DJ's lips curled into a dangerous smile as his fingers trailed across my jaw, thumb brushing across my chin before trailing down my neck. My breath hitched as a shiver tickled down my spine.

"Yeah, but you're so curious now, aren't you?" he whispered. "Bet you didn't think an apology would feel like this."

I didn't. Not in a million years could I have imagined that saying I was sorry would have taken this kind of a turn...and curious was the understatement of the damned century. My eyes roamed his face, then, of their own accord, took a short tour of his body. My fingers itched to touch him, to run through his hair, which in turn sent my heart rate soaring. How did he manage to turn every interaction into a game where he set the rules and held all the power? And why did my heart race every time he gave me that look, like he could see through every false front I raised against him?

"You're shaking," he whispered, leaning even closer, his lips so close to mine I could feel the warmth of his breath.

I couldn't move. Couldn't think.

So much for giving this man a run for his money. I'd just folded like a freaking lawn chair.

Just as his mouth hovered near mine, a knock sounded at the door.

"Guys," my mom called from the hallway, her voice muffled. "You need to come see this."

I jumped back, heart racing. "Uhh—Be right there!" I shouted, eyes locked on the closed door, too flustered to even think about eye contact. That was close. Too close.

Impeccable timing, Mother.

DJ grasped my chin, gently pulling my gaze back to his and pinned me with a smoldering look, his voice dripping with promise. "We'll pick this back up later."

Oh, we will? Fat chance, guy.

He winked and stood quickly, offering a hand to help me up. After a moment's deliberation, I took it, grateful for the support. My legs still seemed a bit wobbly. How on earth was he so steady? The man either had nerves of steel, or he just enjoyed watching me squirm. Who was I kidding...it was probably *both*.

I pulled my hand from his grasp and shoved at him with a playful smirk before I tugged at my clothes and ran a nervous hand through my hair, making my way to the door, DJ on my heels. When I slid it open, Mom shot me a small smile before turning a glare on DJ. "I hope you're minding your manners, young man."

DJ chuckled, his own smile crooked. "Yes, ma'am," he said with a small nod, hands clasped behind his back.

"Good," she said before turning.

As we followed her into the kitchen, DJ poked at my ribs and I had to bite back a giggle while waving his hand away. When I looked out the window, my eyes followed the direction she was pointing—the sun was setting, and blue sky stretched out to the west.

Tomorrow might be clear if we were lucky. Time to get serious about planning our escape from the city.

30

Game of Survival

THE SPEED AT WHICH DJ LAID out his plan made my head spin. He would leave just before dawn, assuming the sky stayed clear, and make his way to Charles' place where he would systematically, single handedly, take out their surveillance and disable any vehicles he could find. Then he would just climb into the motorhome and drive it back here where Mom and I would be waiting. We'd load up everything we gathered to take with us as fast as possible and then beat feet out of town, avoiding the truck teams on patrol for the day because DJ knew their routes. We'd be home free and headed out of town. Easy as pie, right?

It was a ridiculous plan. Not only was it a suicide mission, but it also sounded a bit suspicious too.

"I don't like it," I said flatly.

Mom and DJ both hit me with a look that could have peeled paint off the walls, and I threw my hands up in protest. "I don't like it because its too easy for you to get caught going in there alone." I crossed my arms and pointed my chin at DJ. He stood in the kitchen, hip leaned against the countertop, his own arms folded across his chest. "And heaven forbid if you decide to flip on us to save your own skin either. We'd be sitting ducks here."

He ground his teeth and took a deep cleansing breath. We'd been discussing this for the better part of an hour and everyone's patience was wearing thin, but my mom was fuming.

"I didn't raise you to be so obtuse, Amber," she seethed from her seat at the table.

"No, but you did raise me to question everything and stand up for what I think is right," I shot back at her. "I think he's either going to get himself killed or if he's caught, he's going to cave and give us up." I propped my hip onto the tabletop and pursed my lips.

"Your vote of confidence is overwhelming," DJ mumbled and rolled his eyes.

Mom made an exasperated sound, "Well, do you have a better plan?" She raised her brows at me.

I didn't, of course, and after a beat, I shook my head.

"This is literally the only way," DJ sighed.

"I don't think you can do it alone," I said. "Maybe I should go with you."

"Absolutely not," Mom and DJ cursed in unison.

"You have no training and would be more of a liability than a help." DJ shook his head, jaw firm, his entire body tensing. There would be no more discussion about my tagging along.

If he thought I would be cowed by a stern look and an intimidating presence, he had another thing coming. "I'm sneaky and fast. Maybe you could be the diversion, while I go in and take the RV."

"They caught you once already, Amber."

"Only because I allowed myself to be caught! I sat there. You saw the whole thing."

"The only reason they didn't take you the night before was because the team was wiped out by one of those creatures. Had you been running down those train tracks twenty minutes earlier, they would have caught you then." He raked an impatient hand through his hair and wet his lips. "They know what they're doing."

"So, what makes you think that *you* can get past them, then?" I snapped. He'd better have a really good explanation, because my gut was telling me something bad was about to happen.

DJ was silent for longer than he should have been, shuffling his feet and avoiding eye contact.

I snorted, turning to Mom. "See? He doesn't even—"

"Because I trained most of them," he snapped then turned away, stomping back toward the den.

Mom and I shared an *oh, shit* look before our eyes shot back to DJ's retreating form.

"Oh, no you don't." I charged across the kitchen and shoved him from behind. "You're gonna need to explain that shit to me."

He reeled around, eyes hard. Flat. Lethal. It was the same cold, ruthless expression he wore at the survivalist's camp, the one that turned my blood to ice. He was a predator staring down his prey. I stumbled backward several steps before I caught myself.

If that part of him was truly an act, he was never going to bulldoze me again. This was serious, not some stupid game he could play.

I planted my feet, squared my shoulders, and let him walk right into my pointed finger which I then jabbed into the center of his chest, "What do you mean, *you* trained them?"

He was silent for a long moment while we glared at each other, neither of us willing to budge. If he thought I was pissed at him when it was just myself I had to worry about, he was in for the shock of his life. Now he was playing with my mom's safety, and I'd be dammed if I was going to let him off easy for that.

He finally blinked and relaxed his stance a fraction before he growled out his explanation. "Most of those idiots had zero clue as to how to handle a weapon safely and before I realized what an unhinged piece of shit Charles was, I told him all about what I did in the military and after I got out."

My brow furrowed. I had assumed he was a regular, run-of-the-mill soldier, but now he implied he was much more than that. "Go on."

He reached up and slowly wrapped his hand around my accusatory finger and lowered it from his chest with a sigh. "Let's go sit down. All of us." DJ's voice was flat—serious. "This might take a while."

A chill ran down my spine. Shit. This was not good.

DJ sank into the armchair, leaning back with his ankle propped on his knee, his gaze flicking between Mom and I sitting on the living room sofa. The casual pose didn't match the tightness in his jaw or the intensity in his eyes.

"We're listening," Mom said, her tone laced with suspicion.

"I was Special Ops and then I contracted with a private company that worked closely with government agencies to gather intelligence once I left the service." DJ spoke without an ounce of jest in his voice.

"Bullshit." I snorted. "You told me you worked at the martini bar on the waterfront." There was no way he could have been some intel-gathering, super-specially-trained, secret agent man.

"That's where my cover story worked, but serving drinks wasn't my actual job. I was there to keep an eye out for a specific group of people that were known to frequent the bar and gather information on them. Who they were doesn't matter anymore because they're probably dead, just like eighty percent of the population, but the government and my employers thought that they had something to do with the killings and disappearances last summer."

"Well, your employer was wrong. We know it was the creatures." I threw my hands up in an exasperated gesture.

"Yeah, but how did the creatures get here? Where did they come from? What are they really? And how do you think I am able to go out and scavenge even when it's cloudy and raining without getting killed and eaten?"

My eyes locked with his. Yeah, how *had* he gone out in the rain and come back unscathed? When he'd turned up here on a cloudy day, he'd given Mom and I that half-baked story about drawing the creatures away from him with a stolen truck. I'd been too upset to really pick it apart then, but now? "What do you know that we don't?" I asked, voice just above a whisper.

DJ leaned forward, gaze flicking between mine and my mom's, "Do you remember the conspiracy theory about the government keeping the bodies of the people that were found alive after an attack?"

Mom and I nodded in unison.

"It wasn't a conspiracy. It was true. Those people were infected with something like a virus that altered their DNA. If they survived the effects of the infection, they changed into one of the creatures."

My heart thrummed in my ears. "How do you know this?"

"I saw them with my own eyes. Worked side by side with the scientists studying them. While they tried to find a cure, my colleagues and I learned how to fight them. That's how I was able to stay alive when they attacked the ration lines, and how I was able to get you back here safe, Mel. It's how I can move around undetected when they're roaming."

"But you told me they almost killed you before Charles saved you," I pushed back.

"In a horde, they're unstoppable; I was pinned down and out of ammo. But they have territories in the wild just like animals do, and they tend to travel and hunt in small packs. But that's beside the point right now. The fact of the matter is that it was my job to learn how these creatures operate, and I learned it so well, that my employer sent me to do some more digging on how they came to be. Once I learned what was necessary about the people they thought were responsible for creating those monsters, I was supposed to call for backup and we were going to capture them by any means necessary. Only, we never got that chance because of the EMP." DJ fell silent, an expectant look in his eyes as they flicked between Mom and me.

To my right, mom let out a long sigh while I sagged forward, elbows on my knees. That was a *lot.* My mind whirled, swimming with the memory of Mom, Joey and I sitting in this same room almost a year earlier, watching the news, learning about the attacks at Yellowstone for the first time. As the thoughts swirled, I began making connection after connection between what DJ had just told us, the information presented in that news story, and the things that Erik and Alma had passed to Dan, that he had then passed to me. Mom appeared to be in the same boat and when my eyes met DJ's once more, I felt like he was reading my expression like a book.

"This isn't the first time you've heard about people becoming the creatures, is it?" he asked, voice low.

I shook my head, not trusting my voice, mind flashing back to Dan's recollection of his own attack and the spawn poison remedy Erik had prepared for him. Had DJ been looking for other people like Erik and Alma? Dan was convinced they weren't human, true, but they were actively fighting *against* the darkling and the spawn. Had the government wanted to capture Erik and Alma specifically?

"What do you know?" DJ's voice was quiet but hard as stone.

Shooting a quick glance at Mom, the look in her eyes was all the prompting I needed. She'd taught me to listen to my gut, and right now it was screaming at me to share what I knew with him, but my brain told me to be smart about it. Selective. And if we all survived what was to come and found our way safely back to the camp store, I could tell him everything I knew then, but not a second sooner.

"I met a man in the forest right after the earthquake." Thinking back to that day, it felt like years had passed. "He was stranded on the road just like I was and planned to walk to the camp store to get help. I had a bad feeling and stayed with my car, but he left. Days later, when the sun came out, I made the trip myself and I found a giant blood puddle on the road beside some supplies that I had given him for the walk. I thought he was dead, but when I finally made my way out of the mountains, he found me and told me about how he had survived."

DJ nodded toward me in a silent request to continue.

"He'd been attacked by one of those creatures and the people at the camp store saved his life." I paused, considering what details I should hold back.

"Wait, he was attacked and survived unchanged?" DJ's brows climbed up toward his hairline.

Well, Dan *had* been changed, but not in the way DJ meant. "Yeah. He said he was barely conscious the whole time but remembered them giving him some sort of..." I trailed off, not knowing how to describe the remedy or if I should reveal what exactly it had done. In the end, I chose ambiguity. "Some sort of syrup to drink that they said stopped the poison."

It was DJ's turn to be at a loss for words. He rubbed at the scruff on his chin and I could practically see the gears in his mind turning, trying to make sense of this new development. "Nothing the scientists I worked with tried ever came close to slowing the virus down let alone stopping it. Did he say where those people got it from?"

I shook my head. "The only thing I know for sure is that they said that the camp store was protected by 'The Light'. I didn't know this until after I left, but the entire time I was there, the creatures never came within a hundred meters of the place."

"So that's why you laughed off my suggestion of heading toward the coast." He scrubbed a hand over his face and leaned back in the recliner, no doubt making connections of his own. "You were up there for what, ten weeks?" he asked.

"Something like that," I replied, tone flat.

"No issues?"

"None."

"I'm suddenly really glad that I didn't try and stop you from taking that camping trip." A crooked smile quirked the corner of his mouth.

My heart stopped. "Wait, did you know something?" I stood up and moved toward him. "Did you know something was going to happen that day?" I stood above him, my voice rising a note with each word I spoke. If he had known something and let me go traipsing off into the wilderness anyway, after I'd helped him out, I was going to tear his head off and shit down his neck.

"No!" he practically yelped, throwing his hands in the air in surrender, "It's not like that. I swear."

"You had better be telling the truth or so help me..." I trailed off.

"I promise, I had no idea. I only meant that if you hadn't gone up there, we wouldn't have any real safe place to go."

I hit him with a skeptical look, but again, my gut told me he was being honest. After a few tense moments, I stepped back and began pacing the length of the living room, hoping I could trust him with the tiny bit of information I had just revealed.

Mom, who had been mostly silent through DJ's revelation, took that moment to speak up. "Now that you know we have a safe place to go, does that change your plan at all?"

"Yeah," I interjected, "you going to tell us what you were really planning to do with that motorhome?"

He tilted his head, flashing me a crooked smile. "It only changes the destination," he hesitated a moment before continuing, "And I'm sure you appreciate a man with a plan."

I scoffed, hands on my hips. "Try being a man with a plan that won't get us all killed."

He raised his brows, his smirk growing. "You wound me." He placed a hand over his heart, "I promise this is going to be quick. In and out. And its gonna work. I'm not exactly planning a vacation, but I can get this done."

I sat back down on the end of the sofa closest to DJ while Mom shifted uneasily on the worn cushions, eyes narrow. "Quick or not, you're planning to head right into Charles' territory, steal a vehicle, and drive it back here. That's suicide, DJ."

DJ shrugged, the cocky mask slipping just enough to reveal a hint of seriousness beneath it. "Maybe. But it's a calculated risk, and I happen to be very good at taking those."

I rolled my eyes, but he caught the flicker of concern I couldn't hide, his gaze softening. "Look," he continued, "this is our best shot. Charles' RV is fortified—EMP shielded, stocked with supplies, ready to run. All I have to do is get in and out before they know I'm even there. If it's cloudy in the morning, they won't risk leaving the house."

"And you want *us* to take that risk? If its cloudy, the creatures will be out and there is absolutely nothing sneaky or quiet about a giant, old motorhome. They'll hear it from miles away. If we somehow manage to slip past the survivalists, the creatures will be all over it," I snorted.

"It's a risk we have to take. If all we have time for is a mad dash from the house to the RV, then that's what happens. Everything gets left behind and we're out of here, heading back to your camp store in the woods." He paused, glancing between us, his tone gentler as he added, "You'd both be safer far away from this city anyhow."

He had a point with that last statement, but that didn't negate the absolutely asinine plan he had. I turned toward Mom with a sigh.

Mom frowned, leaning forward. "And how do we know you're not just doing this to save your own skin?"

DJ's smirk returned, though his gaze held a flicker of hurt. "Oh, come on, Mel. You really think I came all this way, let myself take a knife to the throat—" he glanced at me and winked, "—all for a ride out of town? Alone? Amber has pointed out that I could have left the Survivalists whenever I wanted, and I could have. If I really wanted to go it alone, I would have kept driving when I left them last week. But I didn't."

I felt a pang of guilt, but I kept my face neutral, crossing my arms tighter.

"Amber and I both have been through a lot, DJ." Mom's voice was tired and soft. "You understand why it's hard for us to just blindly trust you."

His jaw tightened, but he nodded. "Fair. But I need you to understand that I didn't have a choice. I've had to...adapt to survive with them, to keep my cover after I started helping women escape," he hesitated before turning his full attention my way and I caught the slight twitch in his fingers, his usually smooth manner faltering. "And to keep you safe. What I had to do to you in front of them? It makes me sick that you suffered at their hands and that I had to be complicit, then do what I did to keep them from—"

"Safe?" I interrupted, my voice sharper than I intended. "I thought you were going to assault me. More than once." I tried not to shiver at the memory.

DJ flinched, his gaze hardening, his voice a little rougher. "I wasn't. I'd never do that." His tone softened. "I hated what I had to pretend to be, but if I hadn't...they would have done far worse to you."

I clenched my fists, and I could see the tension in Mom's face as she watched us, her attention bouncing between DJ and I like she was watching a tennis match.

DJ's gaze softened, a spark of regret flashed in his eyes. "I know how it looked, how I came off," he said, a faint tremor in his voice. "And I won't lie, it—"

"We are not having this conversation right now, DJ." The words hissed through my clenched teeth.

Read the freaking room, man!

Heat crept up my neck and onto my cheeks as I huffed. Hopefully, Mom wouldn't notice, or at the very least maybe she'd just assume the redness on my face was anger and not something else I still had a hard time putting a label on. I looked away, not sure how to feel. "And forgiveness doesn't come cheap," I murmured.

He nodded, his expression solemn. "I know. That's why I'm here, putting everything on the line to get you both out. That has to count for something."

Silence stretched between us and I grit my teeth.

Mom cleared her throat, glancing between me and DJ with a wary gaze. "And you're confident you can pull this off? Get the RV, get back here, and get us out?"

DJ flashed her a reassuring grin, the playful glint returning to his eyes. "You've never seen me in action against humans, but trust me, if I can handle a mob of those creatures, a few amateurs will be a walk in the park." He looked at me with a smirk. "And if Amber's still worried, I suppose she could tag along and see for herself."

I scowled, clenching my jaw. This wasn't an invitation. We'd already established that I would be a hinderance. He was just showboating to put my mom's mind at ease. "Not a chance."

"Didn't think so." His expression softened, that annoying half-smile teasing at the corners of his mouth. He ran a hand through his hair, watching me with an intensity that sent a shiver down my spine.

"You really don't like having someone else take the reins, do you?" A flicker of curiosity flashed beneath the cockiness, like he was searching for a tell.

The heat rushed to my cheeks, but I refused to look away. "You're ridiculous."

"Am I?" He leaned in, voice dropping to a whisper, just loud enough for me to hear. "I think you'd like letting me handle things more than you care to admit."

I shot him a glare, my stomach twisting. "Let's see if you can make it through this plan without anyone getting killed."

DJ's smirk faded, and he nodded, his expression turning serious. "Agreed. I'll leave just before dawn. I'll be back within an hour with the RV, and we'll head straight out of here."

Mom exhaled, glancing at me, then at DJ. "Fine. But if anything goes wrong, you better make sure Amber's safe. No matter what."

DJ looked at her, his expression unreadable. "You have my word. I won't let anything happen to her. Or to you."

There was a long silence, broken only by the steady drip of rain outside. Finally, DJ stood and hit me with a reckless grin, like he was pleased that we finally agreed to his ridiculous plan. "I owe you a real apology and a lot more once we're safe."

I rolled my eyes, unable to hide a smirk of my own even though my gut told me that he was using bravado to cover some very real concern. "Try not to get killed first, and maybe I'll consider it."

He paused, his gaze locking onto mine, his tone playful yet somehow serious. "Consider it a date," he said as he turned on his heel and headed back to the den.

"That had better be metaphor and not an actual date," I said with a groan of mock exasperation.

"You can call it whatever you want, but I'm calling it a date," he called over his shoulder.

My gaze found my mom's and I rolled my eyes, playing along with the easy charm he was using to cover the dread we all felt. All she could do was fight a small, sad smile like she saw through his façade as well.

As he left the room, the tension in the air lingered and a deep sense of foreboding settled in my gut, but a flicker of warmth fought its way through, shining like a single candle flame in the abyss. Somehow, against my better judgment, I almost believed everything would go according to plan.

31

A Symphony of Steel and Shadow

Dan

TO ANYONE LOOKING AT HIM, Dan would have appeared to be the picture of quiet calm, smooth and placid as a wide river swimming hole, but still waters run deep, laced with invisible currents that could drag a man under before he ever realized he was drowning. He sat, back pressed against the cold metal shelving in the camp store staring out into the dark, rifle balanced across his knees. His hands were steady—out of habit more than anything—but the rest of him was fraying at the edges.

Outside, just beyond the edge of the light dome, the darkling spawn were still coming.

One by one, they hurled themselves into the barrier, shrieking as the light dome incinerated them. They'd been at it day and night since he and Kate had made it to the camp store; the incessant rain turning the remains of hundreds of the creatures into a thick, sludgy mire of ash and scorched bits of bone. The stench of rot hung so thick in the air he thought it might suffocate him.

At first, the light dome had held strong, burning the spawn to ash the moment they crossed the invisible barrier, but after two relentless weeks of rain to facilitate the creatures' endless attack, something had changed. The piles of ash that once sat flush against the barrier now appeared to spread outward—twenty feet of sludge spreading out beyond the barrier. It could mean only one thing.

The light dome was shrinking—losing power—the darkling spawn chipping away at it one self-sacrifice at a time. Their attack was systematic. Unrelenting. And they seemed to be gaining ground faster with each passing day. If they had the numbers to keep it up, they would be on the doorstep in just a few days.

Dan cursed inwardly.

It reminded him of being pinned down under fire in a war-zone. Only this time, there was no way to call for backup, no airstrike, and no escape. Erik had said that this place would be safe, but instead of a haven, the camp store felt more like a tomb.

Shifting his grip on his rifle, Dan let out a long breath. Back in the room he was sure that Amber had used during her time at the camp store, Kate slept soundly, curled beneath heavy blankets. Safe and warm and hopefully lost to the sweet world of dreams, blissfully unaware of the growing danger that surrounded them. She was all he had left—the only thing in his world that mattered.

Dan reached into his pocket, fingers brushing against the cold metal of the last two bullets for his sidearm and an ache formed deep in his chest. If the darkling spawn broke through, he would not allow her to suffer. They would not take her.

Two bullets. One for her. One for him.

Swallowing the grief like a mouthful of dirt, he shifted again and tried not to think about it. Maybe their luck would hold and the day would be clear, giving them and the light dome a much-needed respite from the attack? His eyes drifted back to the edge of the light dome as a curious quiet fell across the camp store parking lot. Where had the creatures gone? Pulling himself to his feet, he cupped hands around his eyes and peered out through the glass door for a better look.

Then, in the dim pre-dawn light, something moved. Dan froze, eyes locking on the darkness beyond the dome. His breath stalled in his chest as his gaze found a figure standing tall, resolute, and wholly alone, just beyond the border of the light dome.

A flash of silver armor gleamed like liquid under the faint light of a half-moon peering through a gap in the clouds as the figure moved, whirling a spear in a smooth, practiced manner, as if the weapon was an extension of his body.

Dan stiffened. "The hell are you doing?" he whispered into the quiet of the room, as if the figure could hear him. "Run, you idiot. Get the hell out of there before—"

Then the red eyes appeared, flickering into existence one by one. Dozens circling the lone figure, the glow from their eyes bathing the space in red like a blood-tinged pit fighting ring. Dan's stomach turned to stone. No one could survive that.

"You're gonna get yourself killed. Get outta there, now!" he hissed.

But the warrior made no move to retreat. His body shifted, stance widening. Waiting. Challenging.

The moment snapped and as a single unit, the darkling spawn lunged.

The warrior moved like a goddamn storm. Wind howled, beating against the side of the camp store as his spear sliced the air, each movement a blur of precision, power, and something almost inhumanly fluid.

Throwing knives flashed, silver cutting through shadow with effortless efficiency. A dagger found a throat. The spear impaled a skull. One after another, the creatures burst into flame then flickered out like snuffed candles.

Dan had seen trained fighters in action, had fought alongside elite soldiers in war. But this? This was something else entirely. This was an intricate dance, the hissing sound of steel meeting flesh and fire, was the music. This was *art*. A symphony of steel and shadow and fire.

The spawn kept coming, but the warrior never faltered, never missed a step. It was like he knew exactly where every attack would land before it even came. Dan tightened his grip on his rifle, awestruck, fascinated, horrified, and entranced, completely unable to look away.

Then, through the shifting bodies of the remaining spawn, something massive emerged.

A bear? Or something wearing a bear's skin?

Whatever it was, it was wrong. It was too big. Way too big—a goddamn tank on four paws. Its fur was dark and slick, thick and wild, like any normal, healthy bear, but its eyes burned red; and it didn't lumber as a bear would, it stalked like an unholy predator that knew itself to be invincible.

The spawn formed a wide circle around the two, silent, waiting.

No one could survive whatever that creature was, but the warrior didn't flee. He studied the creature, canting his head to the side. Breath caught in Dan's throat and his pulse pounded as the thing lunged, a blur of claws and gnashing teeth. The warrior rolled, pivoted, dodged, and the beast touched nothing but air. How was he so *fast?*

Then the creature struck, a massive paw slamming into the silver armor, sending the warrior crashing into the gravel.

This is it. He's done for.

Dan had to do something. He reacted without thinking, throwing open the camp store door, raising his rifle, and taking aim at the beast, finger hovering over the trigger.

Then, the warrior moved in a blur of silver. He'd only let the creature *think* it had the upper hand. The fighter launched from a crouch, spear gleaming like a bolt of lightning, he slammed it home, straight upwards through the creature's thick neck. The bear-thing roared, the sound splitting into two distinct voices, as if something inside it was screaming to be set free. Then, the dagger came down, straight through its broad skull. The otherworldly screech ended abruptly as it burst into flames, crumbling into smoldering embers.

The remaining darkling spawn froze a moment before they scattered, sprinting into the trees as if their lives depended on it.

Dan lowered his rifle, his chest rising and falling in unsteady gasps. What the *hell* had he just witnessed?

The warrior stood over the ashen husk of the beast, silent, poised, like this had all been routine. Then, with an almost casual flick, he flourished his spear, sending black blood splattering onto the mud.

Dan barely heard the soft clink, as the figure retrieved his knives from the burned out remains of the dead darkling spawn.

Then—without hesitation—the warrior stepped through the barrier protecting the camp store. Dan tensed. The once invisible dome pulsed and shimmered as if welcoming the newcomer.

That didn't happen when he and Kate had walked through it. Was this guy even human?

Then the warrior called out to him, "Dan?"

Dan's breath stalled in his throat. The voice was clear, strong, and unmistakably *feminine.*

He stared in wordless shock as the warrior reached up, unfastened their helm, and pulled it free. Dan's stomach dropped.

A *woman?*

Her face was both stunning and severe. Almond shaped eyes, deep brown and unreadable quickly assessed him. She looked younger than he would have expected but was not young at the same time. Her skin was light but carried the rich tone of a natural tan while her dark hair sat cleanly braided into a tight crown around her head. As she approached him, it was her eyes that struck Dan the most. They were ancient, as if they had seen hundreds of years, and she was tall, close to six feet. The armor had disguised her frame—made him assume...

Dan had no words and in spite of all his experience and training, he gaped like a codfish. Light footsteps crunched behind him in the gravel, pulling him from his stupor. Kate, having awoken at some point during the battle, stopped just behind him, watching with wide eyes as the woman stepped forward and removed her gloves, tucking them into a band at her waist, then extended a delicate hand toward him.

"I am Trillium," she said, her voice calm, unwavering—almost serene despite the slaughter she had just wrought. "Erik sent me." She stood firm but relaxed, as if she had done nothing more than step out for an evening stroll.

Dan blinked, still trying to wrap his head around what he'd just witnessed.

"Erik?" His voice came out rougher than he intended, but he couldn't help it. He cleared his throat. "You know Erik?"

Trillium nodded, her hand still extended. Dan hesitated, then slowly reached out to take it, feeling the rough calluses on her palm. She was *real.*

"I was sent to protect this place," she said, her eyes flicking toward the now shimmering barrier. "Erik sensed the dome weakening and could feel your fear as if it were his own." Trillium explained, "He knew he wouldn't be able to get here in time, so he asked me to secure this outpost in his stead. And to make sure that you and your family were safe." An easy smile touched her lips as she glanced down at Kate.

Dan struggled to process everything. Erik had sensed his fear? He didn't know whether to feel relieved or ashamed. All this time, he had been hoping for something to aid them, but now that help had arrived, he felt utterly powerless. Useless even. After days of resigning himself to a fate he wouldn't wish on anyone, he and his daughter were going to live.

Kate stepped cautiously out from behind him, her eyes wide with awe as she took in the sight of Trillium. "That was...incredible," she whispered. "Thank you."

Trillium's smile broadened as she shook her head. "There is no need for thanks. I only did what needed to be done." She glanced between Dan and Kate then turned her ancient gaze toward the perimeter of the light dome. "I'm glad that I arrived when I did, the dome is very weak."

The atmosphere around them began to grow brighter and for the first time in weeks, the sun broke free of the clouds, thin slivers of golden morning light spilling through the trees. Dan exhaled, relief trickling into his bones. They'd finally get a break and perhaps, with Trillium with them, she could shed some light on their precarious position.

"I can't thank you enough. Please, come in and relax. Can we get you anything?" Dan asked, gesturing to the camp store. "You must be exhausted." She didn't look it though. Her dark eyes shone bright in the cool, morning light.

"Again, I only did what needed to be done," she replied with a small bow, "But I am thirsty."

Finally, something Dan could do. "Ok. I got you, one tall glass of water, coming right up. Come on in."

She turned to follow Dan and Kate back into the building when suddenly she gasped and dropped her helm, hand fluttering before it pressed against the symbol emblazoned on the chest plate of her armor. A look of pure astonishment washed over her features then melted into something close to reverence.

Dan's stomach dropped, pure dread lancing through his core. "What's wrong?"

Trillium's eyes flickered with something distant and ancient, like a memory had just risen from the depths of time itself. "Someone calls for aid in The Light Mother's name," she whispered. "I have not heard the call in a millennia. I must go!" She turned, ready to bolt. "I'll return, I swear it."

Dan held up a hand. "Wait—" Then turning to Kate he said, "Run inside and get her a water bottle to take—"

His words were cut short as the world seemed to shift around him. A rush of wind and a sound like a thunderclap cracked the air around them. Dan whirled, and she was just...gone. He staggered back, eyes scanning the empty space Trillium had just occupied.

There one moment and gone the next. He blinked, turning toward his daughter who wore an expression that said she was just as shocked as he was, unable to believe what had just happened.

Together they gaped, and he knew this moment would live in his mind for the rest of his days. Trillium. A warrior. A myth. He would have questioned his own sanity had her forgotten helm not been laying in the gravel five feet in front of him. With an astonished chuckle, he gathered his daughter close to his side.

This was exactly how legends were made. And they had experienced it first-hand.

32

The Edge of Everything

MOM SHOOK ME AWAKE BEFORE sunrise, her hand gentle but urgent. I'd barely slept, my mind whirling for hours past dark while the weight of our situation hung over me like a wet blanket, heavy and suffocating. The knots that seemed to have taken up permanent residence in my stomach tightened into a painful grind as I pulled on my clothes and headed downstairs with Mom.

In the dim light of the kitchen, DJ was already waiting, face unreadable and set with that same calm determination that set my nerves on edge. With a rifle slung over his shoulder and a handgun at his hip, he looked every inch the soldier that I wished he didn't have to be; and when I reached for the anger I'd been nursing for days, I found only pure, gut-churning worry in its place. I did not want to do this. Not at all.

With a quiet breath, I leaned my hip against the counter, folded my arms, and met his tense gaze.

"This is it," DJ said, quickly reviewing the plan. "I'll sneak onto Charles' property, get the RV, and bring it back. You'll have to be ready to run as soon as I pull up," he took a deep breath, and I knew there was a *but* coming, "but if it takes me longer than an hour, something's gone wrong. I want you both to stay hidden for as long as it takes Mel to get her strength back and then get out of town by any means necessary."

"And what about you?" My voice came out with a sharper edge than I'd intended, my inner turmoil sneaking up into my throat, betraying the mostly calm demeanor I was trying to portray.

"You don't worry about me. I'm not that important anyway."

"That's a copout and you know it." Mom sounded pissed.

"The truth of the matter is that if I get caught, then Charles is most likely going to kill me. There's no way around it. So, if I'm not back inside of an hour, it means that I failed." He said it like this was just a regular Tuesday and not a life-or-death situation, eyes bouncing between me and Mom. "Stay hidden. Gather your strength. Then beat feet out of town as soon as you're able."

His words hung between us and all I could do was nod, swallowing the knot in my throat. I wanted to scream—to yell that this plan was stupid, that something was going to go wrong—but instead, I kept my mouth shut, trying to look strong even though I was scared to death.

He produced two handguns and stepped forward, handing one to my mom, grip first. "It's loaded. Safety is on."

Mom stared at the cold metal like it was going to blow up in her hands. With the other, he gave us a crash course in their usage.

"Fifteen rounds." He shoved the magazine into the gun with a solid click and racked the slide back. "One in the chamber. Safety is here. Off," —he flicked a small switch at the back of the weapon— "On." Then he pivoted, pointing the gun toward the window, "Aim— one hand here, the other hand here," he demonstrated everything with an efficiency that sent gooseflesh skittering across my scalp. "These don't kick much, but you're both pretty small. Keep your elbow bent a little and hold tight. Don't pull the trigger, *squeeze* it." Then he handed the gun to me with a smile that didn't quite reach his eyes.

Mom and I both nodded but I was absolutely, totally, and completely uncomfortable.

"I don't like this, DJ," I said flatly.

"With any luck, you won't even have to use them. Think of them as insurance. That's all." He sounded so sure, but I wasn't convinced.

I double checked the safety and tucked the cursed piece of steel into my belt as DJ made his way around the countertop and toward the sliding door.

My gut twisted again, and my brows knit. There was so much riding on the outcome of this whole stupid plan and above all, I didn't want him to go.

DJ must've seen the worry in my eyes because he smirked then winked, "I saw that."

I scowled in response, not trusting myself to speak.

He chuckled, his grin widening. "Don't worry. I'll be back before you know it," he teased, then with a nod to Mom, he stepped out of the big, sliding glass door in the kitchen and disappeared into the predawn light, his silhouette instantly swallowed by the shadows.

Mom's hand found mine, worry and fierce resolve battling in her eyes. "Everything is going to work out, sweetie."

I wanted to believe her, but my gut told me something was about to go very wrong. I met moms gaze, "Something bad is going to happen, Mom. I can feel it," I said, my voice just above a whisper. She swallowed hard and I knew she could feel it too. After all, she was the one that taught me to trust my gut, just like her own mother had taught her.

"Well then, all we can do is hope our gut feelings are wrong. Prepare for the worst. Hope for the best." She pulled me into a tight hug then kissed my cheek. If this doesn't pan out, we grab our bags of essentials, and leave."

"But you aren't well enough to make the trip on foot yet," I tried to reason with her, but she just shook her head.

"We come from a long line of strong women, Amber. We always find a way to survive, and I will too if I have to." Waves of determination rolled off of her with such force, I could practically feel the heat of it in my bones. She wasn't just strong, she was mighty, and I wished that one day I would have the same sense of self that she did.

I hugged her back fiercely then turned to gather my pack up off the floor. For better or for worse, events had been set into motion, and there was no going back now. We made our way into the garage and in a moment of strange clarity, I removed the gun from my belt, replacing it with my survival knife and I instantly felt better. I was more likely to hurt myself with the gun than anyone or any*thing* else. The knife was familiar. Safe. And I could almost feel Dan's energy in it. He'd carried it for more than twenty years, through all sorts of adventures and misadventures. He'd even killed a darkling spawn with it. That had to count for something.

The garage was cold and quiet as we waited for DJ to return. Mom and I crouched behind the stack of totes filled with the supplies and keepsakes we planned to take with us. The silence stretched, minutes ticking by like hours, while the knot in my stomach twisted tighter with every second. If DJ didn't show soon, I was going to be sick.

At last, the low rumble of an engine cut through the silence, distant but growing closer. Mom and I stared, wide-eyed at each other a moment before she moved to open the garage door. I froze, my heart pounding, stomach in my throat.

Something was wrong. The gnawing tension in my gut that I'd been trying to ignore flared, filling my veins with acid, screaming at me to be cautious.

"Do you feel that too?" I whispered.

Mom hesitated, hand hovering above the locking mechanism of the garage door. Her head twitched in a tiny nod.

"Let me look outside first." Without another word, I sprinted back through the house, up the stairs, and to my bedroom window that overlooked the street. My heart hammered in my chest as I moved the blanket just enough to peer outside. The morning sunlight shocked my eyes, and I blinked several times before they adjusted. At the far end of the street, I could just make out the RV slowly creeping around the corner.

It was moving too slow. DJ had said we wouldn't have much time. He should have been driving faster. *Would* have been driving faster.

"Don't open the garage yet! Something's not right!" I yelled down to my mom.

The RV rolled to a stop just in front of the driveway, but DJ didn't emerge. Time seemed to slow to a crawl as I looked down at the vehicle that was supposed to be our salvation.

Waiting. Hoping.

After several tense moments, I stared in stunned horror as the windows of the RV slid open and rifle barrels appeared.

"Mom, get down!" I screamed as pure chaos erupted. Glass shattered and wood splintered as bullets tore through the house. I dropped to the floor and curled into a ball as the bullets flew through the walls, whizzing overhead, the sound like something out of a movie. The acrid stink of gunpowder and scorched drywall filled the air as adrenaline seared through my limbs. Every instinct told me to run, but I stretched out on my belly instead, low-crawling toward my bedroom door and down the hall, flinching as chunks of drywall rained down on me.

At a pause in the gunfire, I scrambled to my feet and bolted back down the stairs and into the garage nearly blind with panic.

Where was my mom?

Bullet holes in the large aluminum door cast eerie specks of light throughout the garage. "Mom?" I whispered, ears ringing.

"In front of the car." Mom's voice wavered.

As quickly as I could, I crawled on hands and feet toward the sound of her voice. It took a moment for my eyes to adjust to the shadows, and I could have cried when I found my mom waving me over.

She hugged me fiercely then ran her hands over my face, shoulders and arms. "Are you alright?" she whispered.

"Yeah, I'm good. You?"

"Fine, thank god," she said, "But—" her voice broke as if she physically couldn't finish her thought aloud.

"Either he got caught or—" I sighed, throat tight. He wouldn't...he *couldn't*. But then again, how well did we really know him? "Or he duped us." But he wouldn't have given us guns if he was planning on turning us over, would he? My stomach churned. This was some worst-case scenario *bullshit.*

And if he was captured, I couldn't just leave him like he'd told us to do. I wouldn't. He'd stuck his neck out for me...for Mom and I both. More than once. I had to believe—

The sound of heavy boots approaching the garage door brought my thoughts to a screeching halt.

"You alive in there?" a deep and slightly amused voice drifted through the garage door.

Mom gripped my hand so tight I thought I might hear the bones crunch. Neither of us uttered a word.

"How have you been coming and going?" the voice came again. That was definitely not DJ. My heart kicked up another notch. It was the tyrant himself. The psychopath.

"Fucking hell," I breathed and shot my mom a pained look. "It's Charles."

Mom's face paled. "Shit."

As we moved silently to peer around the side of the car, my mind cranked into high gear. This was the one thing we hadn't planned for.

"Ya know, we knew someone else was in this neighborhood, we just hadn't narrowed down which house," Charles chuckled to himself. "That day Frank's men spotted you running down the tracks, I knew we'd found the one we'd been looking for."

His shadow passed in front of the bullet holes in the big garage door, blocking out some of the light.

"And a young female at that? I thought we'd hit the jackpot," Charles continued, "But you turned out to be quite the handful."

I looked back at mom and swallowed the choking panic in my throat.

"Then, just when things were supposed to get fun, you gave old DJ the slip. At first, I chocked it up to you being a slippery little bitch, nothing more. But then DJ disappeared a few days later, and I knew," he scoffed. "I knew if we could find him, we could find you."

Mom and I shared a silent curse. How had they figured out which house we were in? We'd been so careful. And neither Mom nor I had even been outside since DJ showed up.

Damn it! Is he dead already?

If he was, we had to get out of the house before Charles and his cronies broke in. "Get your bag. We go out the back and hide in one of the neighbor's houses," I whispered.

Mom nodded and we started moving as silently as possible, but the sounds of a scuffle brought us to a halt. My ears strained.

"Go fuck yourself, Frank," DJ's voice grated.

"I won't be fucking myself today. Your little girlfriend is mine now." Frank's slimy voice slithered into my ears and I shuddered.

"How many times do I have to tell you before you get it through your thick skull. She isn't here. I haven't seen her since she jumped out of the truck."

Charles huffed a laugh before the sound of fists meeting flesh filled the air.

DJ groaned, coughed then spit. "If I wanted a kiss, I'd have called your wife," his words ran together.

My heart soared and sank at the same time. Not only was DJ alive but he was still protecting us. And by the sounds of it, Charles and his followers had no idea my mom was even here.

"We can beat on him all day, you know," Charles said, raising his voice to be sure I could hear him through the garage door. "I can hear you shuffling around in there. Come on out and I'll think about letting him live."

A beat of tense silence followed as I turned toward my mom. Everything he had done—here for mom and even the questionable things he'd done to me at the survivalists' camp—really *had* been about keeping me—keeping *us* safe. And now he was about to fully sacrifice himself just for the chance that mom and I might escape. He really was a good man with a good heart. Noble even. And I wouldn't just let him die at the hands of those ass holes out of sheer fucking nobility.

"He was right. I don't think they know that you're here, Mom. You should go find a place to hide and I'll see if I can get them to let DJ go." I had no idea how, but I had to try something.

Mom made a shocked but quiet sound, "Absolutely not. He told us to hide and then get out of town. And you can't just—"

I nearly jumped out of my skin and mom covered a scream as Charles pounded on the metal of the garage door, the sound loud as a shotgun blast.

"You come out right now or he's a dead man." His voice shook with barely controlled rage.

"You're talking to shadows, you paranoid dumb fuck. I told you that I was alone." DJ's voice sounded stronger, but it held a touch of something I had never heard from him. Fear.

More sounds of fists meeting flesh cut the air and I cringed. I couldn't let this go on, not when I might be able to stop it. "Mom, I've got to try and help him."

"They would kill him and take you anyway. We need to get out while we still can. It's what he wanted us to do," Mom argued like she really thought she could convince me.

"He saved your life. He helped you with Joey. He got me out of the survivalist's camp and now he's right outside being beaten to death and we're in here hiding. It's not right," I whispered. The look on her face was a mix of pride and terror. We both flinched, heads swinging to the garage door once again at the metallic click of a handgun being cocked.

Shit!

"You know, I can see why you wanted her to yourself," Charles' voice was cocky and mocking as he spoke directly to DJ, "but a filly as wild as she is needs to be ridden by every cowboy on the ranch after she's broke to make sure the training stuck."

Murmurs of approval sounded.

"I call seconds," Frank laughed, and my stomach turned.

They were showboating. Threatening. Trying to make DJ talk.

"We worked so well together, you and I. You were supposed to be my prodigy." Charles snarled, "So talented and ruthless. *Brutal.* So much potential." His voice dropped from taunting to sinister, "You could have been a *king*, but you chose some feral little girl over power," he growled. "You're no soldier. You're not even a *man*. You're just a pathetic little dog that got himself bitch-whipped."

Another thud of fist meeting flesh. DJ gasped.

"I trusted you. And you *betrayed* me." Charles drew a ragged breath as if he were fighting to control himself before he continued. "I have a great view of the neighborhood from my roof, and I know I saw you a couple blocks over. Out in the rain. With a bundle of spring flowers in your hand."

Frank hooted and the other survivalists snickered.

"You don't actually expect me to believe that you picked flowers for yourself, now do you?" Charles paused a beat before continuing, "And the day she escaped, your truck stopped right in front of this house. Oh, did you think I wouldn't have eyes all over this neighborhood? We never saw her, but we did see you take a long look at this house. Not a tough job to put two and two together."

I looked at mom again, heart in my throat. "I have to do something," I whispered, looking into her eyes, pleading.

"It's stupid, you're going to get yourself killed, or worse. I can't let you go out there. I can't. Please don't make me watch you die. I can't go through that again." Mom's face twisted as tears streamed down her cheeks. She crushed me to her chest. "I can't lose you too. I can't."

My heart cracked. What could I do? What was the right choice? No matter which way I looked at the situation, someone was probably going to die.

"Open the door or we'll tear it down!" Charles snarled, pounding on the metal garage door again.

Mom clung to me shaking and as I squeezed her back, something deep within me began to solidify, the fire of my soul tempering my flimsy resolve into something the mightiest warrior could never hope to bend. Everything I had been through had led me to this very moment. I met Dan, survived on my own for months at the camp store, I escaped the people from Dan's town, then survived a darkling spawn attack and then the survivalist's camp. Against all the odds, I made it home to my mom with only one goal in mind. To get back to the camp store so we could live. That is where we needed to be. Where *all* of us needed to be. I knew it in my bones. Soul deep.

"I have to believe that we survived this long for a reason," I whispered into my mom's ear. "Everything we've done has led us here. We aren't going to leave DJ to die. I can do this. I know I can." I pulled back and took her fragile hands in my own, eyes roaming over her beautiful face.

Slowly, I pulled her to her feet. "I don't even know how I'm going to do this, but—"

Mom shook her head, "No."

"Do you remember what Dan said about The Light Mother?" I whispered quickly. "Erik and Alma said that she walks this earth and if there is a living goddess walking the planet, I think she would hear a prayer."

Another crash rattled the garage. "Frank, go get the battering ram. You two, break down that fence and go in through the back," Charles spat the words and boots shuffled on the other side of the door. "I know you're in there."

Shit!

"We've never prayed a day in our lives," Mom said, voice barely quiet enough to be considered a whisper.

"Well, we're going to now," I said with a note of finality. Before the world had gone to shit, we'd never set a toenail inside a church on a Sunday and praying had always seemed to possess a fundamental flaw. Perhaps it was the fact that everyone prayed to a father in heaven and my own father had abandoned me, but deep in my bones, I felt something pulse. Something older. Stronger. Wiser. Something *real.*

My chest warmed, not like fire, but more like the steady bloom of sunlight on frozen ground, melting away any and all hesitation. Perhaps it was the fact that I had never once heard a peep about a *Mother* in Heaven when the science of DNA allowed anyone to trace their maternal line? Or perhaps it was the fact that I always felt safest out in nature, connected to *Mother Earth*, or wrapped in my own *mother's* warm embrace? But at that moment, I *knew* who I needed to call out to. The one that had been there all along, before any other figment of men's imagination had even been a thought.

I closed my eyes and spoke, "Light Mother? If you can hear me— please. Please help us. We don't know what to do but these people are pure evil, and we just want to be back where we belong. Deep in the forest, safe and surrounded by your light." I opened my eyes and hugged my mom fiercely. "You taught me to trust my gut, and my gut is telling me this is the right thing to do. It's gonna be okay. I love you. Walk in Light and Truth. Now, go hide."

Mom's eyes took on a distant look then suddenly went wide. She clutched her chest a moment before nodding. My own heart beat a strong, steady rhythm, and for the first time in my life, I felt certain of my path.

"I love you too, sweetheart," Mom whispered as her fingers trailed off my arm, her hand closing around nothing but air.

This was breaking her heart, I could tell, but she put her faith in something greater than herself, just as I did.

"If Charles is as sick as he makes out to be, he's not going to kill me." No, he'd want to make good on his promise from weeks ago to teach me a lesson. "But I've got a sharp surprise for him." I smiled as I ran my fingers over the worn handle of my knife and turned toward the big garage door.

The manual lock on the garage door was cold under my fingers as I cranked it, disengaging the bars with a clank.

"Amber, don't!" DJ's strangled voice nearly cut me in half.

Charles howled a manic, hateful laugh. "That's right. Be a *good girl* and do what you're told."

A wave of loathing crashed through me, flooding my system with pure, unadulterated rage. It flowed through my veins like fire, and I grit my teeth. My hands shook and my heart pounded, but a feeling of sober certainty sat in my gut, firm and grounding, stronger than my fear and more potent than my rage.

As I yanked up on the garage door, time slowed to a crawl, everything springing into crystal clear focus. My soul filled with an intense sense of oneness, as if a light, long buried inside me, had finally broken free. The morning sun kissed my skin and every cell in my body sang.

Strange words flowed from my lips like a battle cry not heard for millennia, "Light Mother, you are the beginning of everything. We breathe you in. We bask in your warmth and Light. Protect us and give us the strength to conquer the evil that seeks to sever our connection to you."

Charles barked out a laugh. "You're praying? You think *prayer* is going to stop us?"

I blinked my eyes hard and took in the scene before me. Two survivalists wearing gunman black, kicked DJ's unsteady feet out from under him. He hit the ground hard, barely catching himself on hands and knees. A cough rattled in his chest and a spray of blood splattered the pavement. The rage in my veins settled into my bones, searing and white-hot.

"Who do you think is listening?" Charles held his arms out wide and turned in a slow circle. "If there ever was a god, he turned his back on the world a long time ago and let the devil have free reign." He laughed as he strode over and soundly kicked DJ in the face as he was hunched over while the other survivalists joined in his sick laughter.

With a groan, DJ flopped over onto his side and lay still.

So *very* still. His once beautiful face—the face that had teased and tormented and smirked, like he already knew my deepest thoughts— was barely recognizable beneath a mosaic of bruises; one eye swollen shut, nose and cheekbone caved, lips split, breath barely rattling in his lungs. They'd beaten him to within an inch of his life, and he still hadn't given mom and I away. Hadn't broken.

Goddess, please let him be alright.

In that moment I knew. Charles was a dead man. And I was going to kill him myself.

"And I'm here to dance on the ashes of civilization," Charles growled and took a prowling step in my direction as the cry of a red tail hawk split the cool, morning air.

My throat tightened and my fingers found the handle of my knife as a thrumming sound filled my mind, deep and resonant like a heartbeat. I tipped my face toward the sky and breathed deep, the sound filling me, consuming all thought. It tickled up through the ground and spread through me from toes to fingertips and I sighed at the heartbeat of the earth feeding strength and resilience through my limbs.

The rest of the survivalists arrayed themselves in an arc behind Charles and DJ's prone form, raising their rifles and taking aim. More than a dozen barrels pointed at my chest.

If any of these people were real men, they would turn their guns on Charles, but I knew they never would. Too many of them believed wholeheartedly in his twisted vision. Too many of them looked down on women, thought them to be lesser beings than men, unworthy of having a voice of their own, existing only to satisfy their whims and bring children into the world. DJ had been right all along. This snake really did have a dozen heads.

My stomach churned at their delusion. It seemed more likely that their hatred and oppression of women stemmed not from their perceived superiority, but from fear. Fear of our ability to connect with nature, to move with the ebb and flow of the natural world, creating life, and love...even our ability to simply exist peacefully in the world without the need to conquer. Because if we could connect with the goddess, they would cease to have control.

The red tail hawk called again, closer this time, as Charles sauntered towards me. I stepped defiantly toward him, removing my knife from its sheath and brandishing it, its muted gleam shining in the sunlight.

You're a damn sight tougher than you look, girl. Dan's words whispered in my mind, and I gripped the hilt of the knife tighter, glaring at the man before me.

Charles scoffed, "What are you going to do with that little thing? I'm shaking in my boots."

He closed in, reaching to disarm me, expecting me to retreat, and for a split second, I almost did, but a voice boomed in my mind, *Charge* forward, *little warrior.*

Without a second thought, I lunged. There was a moment of resistance, a slight hesitation on the blade, before the knife slid through his clothes and sank into the soft flesh of his belly—all the way to the hilt. Shock leeched onto his face, and he stumbled, his knees nearly buckling.

No gunshots rang out; only silent anticipation hung in the air as a satisfied smile spread across my face. His weak, fumbling hands found my throat and tried to squeeze, but my eyes bore into his as my arm moved of its own accord, pulling the knife out and plunging it back in twice more.

Charles groaned and dropped to his knees, taking me down with him. I hooked an elbow around the back of his neck and pulled him to me, pressing my lips to his ear, the movement almost intimate.

"You brought this on yourself," I whispered, slowly twisting the blade. I let him fall then, the knife sliding out as he listed to one side and hit the driveway with a thud.

Dripping blade in hand, I rose to my feet, face twisted with righteous, bloodthirsty triumph.

The survivalists called out in shock, eyes bouncing between each other and their downed leader.

"She fucking killed him!" one of the men gasped as he stumbled backward, nearly dropping his rifle. Charles groaned, twitching as weak hands moved to cover his wounds, deep red blood seeping through his fingers.

"Jesus—he's still alive—Frank, what do we do?" another man called out, eyes darting between me and the prone body of their leader at my feet. He took an unsure step in my direction.

Hesitation hung thick in the air like they had never even considered the outcome before them.

They were the group in power. Charles was supposed to be untouchable, but—

Frank ran a hand over his face, lip curling into a snarl. "What are you waiting for, take her alive!" His voice snapped like a whip, sharp with something akin to panic.

A ripple of uncertainty rolled through the group but as Frank spoke again, his voice was strong and steady, "She's gonna pay for this."

As if a switch had been flipped, the hesitation broke, rifles rose again, and they closed in.

I lifted my chin and raised my bloodied knife to the sky in defiance. "For The Light Mother!"

Just then, the hawk swooped low, calling to the wind as it dove between me and the charging survivalists.

I started. *Why would a bird show up now?*

The hiss of the hawk's wings faded and was immediately followed by a shadow and deafening silence—as if sound itself had been pulled into another dimension. The air stilled a heartbeat before an immense gust of wind broke the silence with a crack, pushing my hair into my eyes and debris into the air.

Enormous, iridescent black wings settled like a nimbus cloud around a tall, fierce woman in silvery armor, the chest plate inlaid with crystals of all colors in a swirling infinity symbol. Her hair, windblown and dark as her wings, was twisted into a braided crown around her head. In her hand, she held a spear tipped with a razor-sharp blade. She looked down at me and her full lips tipped up in a small smile, the expression on her face almost loving, before she whipped her head in the survivalist's direction.

Before any of them could pull a trigger, the woman raised an arm then clenched her fist.

The rifles were suddenly torn from the survivalists' grip, then—with an almost casual flick of her wrist—they sailed across the driveway and into the long grass of the neighboring yard.

The winged woman pinned them all with a hard stare and scoffed, "Guns. A cowardly weapon." Her voice was strong, commanding, and carried a light accent, a slight rolling or trill at the letter R.

The survivalists gaped, one man appearing to have wet himself. Even Frank was at a loss for words, staring dumbstruck at the figure before him.

Her gaze returned to me. "You called for aid." It wasn't a question.

I couldn't hold back the flood of tears that began to flow. I nodded, wiping Charles' blood off my blade and onto my pants leg, then slid it back into its sheath.

"I am at your service," she said, voice softening.

At the faint shuffling sound behind me, I turned to see my mom making her way over, her own eyes welling with tears. She reached out and I grasped her hand, pulling her close.

She hadn't left. Of course she hadn't. A good mother never would have.

"There were two of you," Frank finally found his smarmy voice.

"Silence! I'll hear nothing from any of you." The woman pointed a finger directly at Frank as her eyes scanned the group and her wings rose, stretching to block out the sun. They all shrank beneath her gaze like the cowards they really were.

She looked like an avenging angel, fierce and glorious to behold, like pure violence on a weak leash. My mind snapped back to the video that swept the world last summer—the naked, pregnant angel escaping what was thought to be a top-secret government facility. But that woman's wings had been white.

Are there more out there like her?

With the survivalists looking sufficiently cowed, the woman turned back toward mom and I with a proud tilt to her chin and gestured to the survivalists with her spear, "These are the evil ones?"

I nodded again, not trusting my voice, throat too tight to speak.

She inclined her head just as I noticed one of the survivalists slowly edging away from the group. I raised a finger, pointing in his direction. He looked ready to bolt.

The woman's head swung back to the survivalists, and she pivoted, stance widening slightly.

"You!" she called out, but the man continued to edge away, then turned and sprinted down the street. The woman made a disgusted sound, rolling her eyes in a very human-like way.

With an utterly disappointed shake of her head and a click of the tongue, she hefted her spear and flung it. It sailed silently, striking the man square between the shoulders with a thud, and he fell face down in the street, the spear sticking straight up into the air like an exclamation point written in blood, a deadly warning left in flesh and bone.

With a movement almost too quick to track, she produced two throwing knives and arched an eyebrow at the rest of the group, silently asking if anyone else wanted to test her aim. The remaining survivalists froze, pale as sheets.

She exhaled sharply, the sound dry and scornful, yet altogether too elegant to be crude. "Wise choice...surprisingly," She said, her satiny tone laced with steel and oozing with condescension. "I am known as Deathbringer. Kneel."

The survivalists all did as they were told, dropping to their knees as a single unit, hands in the air. The woman turned her attention back to me and mom and her tone softened, "You may call me Trillium. And you are?"

"I'm Amber and this is my mom, Melissa," I sputtered, smearing away the tears that streaked down my cheeks as I glanced over in DJ's direction. He was so still. I needed to get to him.

The hawk that had flown by, returned to land on Trillium's arm, chortling. "This is Isa. We were—" she stopped short as Charles moaned on the ground, her lip curling with distaste. "Shall I dispatch him for you?" she asked.

Her words were so casual, like killing was utilitarian, just her job. But then again, she *had* just called herself *Deathbringer.*

"He was the worst of them," I said as I released my mom's hand and quickly made my way over to DJ's side.

"Then I shall not end his suffering. This one will die slowly." Trillium sneered and rolled Charles face up with the toe of her boot.

He writhed and moaned, grimacing, teeth and lips ringed in blood.

"Pitiful," she said looking back in my direction, "and what of these other men?"

"Oh, god. DJ, what did they do to you?" I whispered as I took in his battered face. New tears sprang to my eyes, and I gently laid my fingers on his throat, searching for a pulse.

You had better not die on me or I swear I'll find a way to bring you back so I can kill you myself for this stupid idea of yours.

After a few tense moments, the light thrumming of his pulse met my fingers and I sagged with relief. His breath came in short, shallow gasps, but his pulse was strong. Not dead but terribly injured. As carefully as I could, I lifted and maneuvered his head and shoulders into my lap, brushing the dark waves of his hair back off his forehead and fought the sob that was rising in my throat.

"They were here to kill us all because we wanted to leave the city," I finally ground out. "They beat me weeks ago—beat him for trying to protect us," my fingers hadn't stopped running through his hair, "and they ruined our home."

Charles opened his eyes at the sound of our voices, his fevered gaze flicking between Mom and I. "There really were two of you," he coughed, blood speckling his face.

Without missing a stride, Mom marched straight over and kicked Charles in the ribs. "That's for what you did to my daughter, you limp-dick-piece-of-shit," she hissed then spit in his face.

Go, Mom. I thought to myself.

371

An impressed look danced across Trillium's face and had the situation not been so dire, I would have laughed. Apparently, the apple hadn't fallen very far from the tree where sassiness was concerned.

"I think they've been looking for my mom for weeks so they could take everything she has here and kidnap her. They aren't good people..." my voice trailed off.

"But?" Trillium asked.

I sighed, remembering what Gail and DJ had said back in the med tent. It felt like ages ago. "I think there are good people trapped in their organization. I don't care what happens to the bad guys, but I hope that the good people can choose what they would like to do now that Charles is...no longer a problem."

Charles continued to writhe in a slowly growing puddle of his own blood.

"I see." Trillium nodded as if contemplating what should be done.

Just then DJ began to stir. He groaned, trying to push himself into a sitting position but I held him still, "Don't move, we don't know how bad it is yet," I said, trying to soothe him.

"This is not how the day was supposed to go," his voice, gravelly and pained, still held that note of confidence.

I sputtered a watery laugh, "How are you even cracking jokes right now?"

"I have no idea. How's the face?"

"Well," I let the word hang in the air, not sure if I should tell him.

"Shit. That bad, huh?" he winced.

"He needs healing," Trillium said as she removed a small vial from a pouch at her waist. An unknown liquid, thick and deep red-brown in color coated the inside as she handed it to me, "Have him drink this."

I popped the stopper without question and pressed it gently to DJ's lips, cradling his head in my other hand. He swallowed it all in one gulp, gagged, then swallowed again. Before my eyes, the swelling in his face disappeared, the bruising faded, his ruined nose and cheek crunched, moving back into place while the dull sound of several disconcerting cracks beneath his vest met my ears. DJ gasped and gritted his teeth against the pain, eyes squeezed shut.

Whatever was happening looked to be excruciatingly painful but within a few heartbeats, he began to relax, seeming to drift in and out of consciousness.

Trillium made an appreciative sound then spoke, "He'll need to sleep a while and then eat well as soon as he wakes up." She looked at Isa the hawk a moment, then lifted her arm, sending the large bird retreating up into a tree. "Would you like him in the house?"

"We were trying to use the RV to get back to a camp store in the forest."

Trillium paused, a thoughtful look on her face, "The store that belongs to Erik?"

My chin nearly hit the concrete driveway. "Yeah, that's the one."

"I've just come from there. The store is already occupied."

"Did Dan make it?" I blurted out before I could stop myself.

Trillium smiled as she crouched and laid a hand on my shoulder and then DJ's chest. "Yes, Dan is already there." She studied DJ's unconscious face a moment, "May I?"

"Please," I said, gratefully. "Do you need a hand?"

"I can manage," she said with a small smile, then scooped up all two-hundred-plus pounds of DJ as if he weighed less than a small sack of potatoes, and carried him to the RV, her giant black wings trailing behind her.

I was about to ask how she was going to get them through the small RV door, when she took a deep breath. As she slowly exhaled, her giant wings pulsed and distorted, then twinkled out of existence.

I pulled myself to my feet, mouth still hanging open. Mom's dainty finger pushed up on my chin, closing my mouth as she took my hand in hers and marched over toward the survivalists, the gun DJ had given her firmly grasped in her hand, pointing at each of the men in turn.

The survivalists were still on their knees in the driveway and when Trillium reemerged, one man resorted to begging for his life. Trillium walked a slow circle around the group who all began to murmur pleading for their lives. Ignoring them, she turned to me and Mom, eyes settling on our clasped hands. All I could do was gaze back up at her in awe.

"I wish the bond between my daughter and I were as strong as yours," she said quietly, a note of longing touching her voice. The moment of softness was immediately replaced by the stern look of a being that was about to play the role of judge, jury, and executioner. "Leave this place. Take all you will need and never return. I will decide what to do with these sniveling pieces of filth." She turned to sneer at the group of survivalists.

One of the survivalist's voices began to rise above the murmur as he called out to the Lord his "God" to save him from the *creature* in their midst.

Trillium cackled and lowered her face to the man, her accented voice hushed but seething with otherworldly power. "Evil hume never question a lie when the lie suits their desires," she said as she pulled herself up to her full height and addressed the group as a whole. "Oppression, hate, murder, violence, genocide, all in the name of your *God?!*"

The group grew silent and with scurrying feet, mom and I backed into the garage to gather the totes of supplies and get them loaded onto the RV.

All the while Trillium continued her tirade, "A *God* that does not truly exist. A god that is a twisted version of the true Goddess that created the land your unworthy knees rest upon. A god that was created by evil men to control the masses through self-hatred, blind obedience and *fear.*" She snorted, "Such simple, stupid minds, no better than spawn filth."

She turned to mom and I as we were loading the last totes, and in a low voice said, "You will not want to be here when the fate of these men is decided. My blades thirst for blood." Her eyes flashed with a deep and fearsome power. "Walk in light and truth; you are both much more than you know."

I nodded, turning her last statement over in my mind as I shoved the final items into the RV's storage bay, then closed and latched the door.

"Let's get out of here," I whispered to Mom, taking her hand in mine.

We both turned, glancing back at our home before stepping resolutely aboard the RV. I settled myself behind the wheel of the big vehicle, keys in hand, watching silently as Trillium stood over the survivalists. She really was waiting for us to leave. Whatever she had planned must have been gruesome indeed. After checking on DJ sleeping soundly on the bed at the back of the RV, Mom sat down in the passenger seat and pulled the buckle across her chest.

Frank, who hadn't stopped murmuring in prayer since one of his comrades had taken a spear in the back, glared at me through the windshield then rallied against Trillium, rising to his feet, appealing to the survivalists still on their knees. "Would God send an angel to kill us? No! This creature is from the same pits of hell as the demons!"

Of course, it would be him that would still refuse to acknowledge the truth even with all he had just seen.

Trillium shrieked at his words, the sound a mix of a raven's cry and a hateful laugh. Her black wings began to reappear, growing steadily from beneath gaps at the back of her armor. She moved to retrieve her spear from the dead man and flourished it as her eyes took on a silver sheen, matching her armor.

When she spoke, it was as if the sky split with the sound of her voice, "You are right, *fool.* I am no angel. I am *Aeon.* Created by the Goddess herself to protect all that is good from the dark plague that has infected this planet." She took a single prowling step toward the survivalists, eyes narrowing to slits, "and I live for the hunt." Her wings stretched and flexed, black as night, seeming to distort the very air around them. "Now run." The last was spoken in a loud, sinister whisper.

With a single sweep of her massive wings, she was airborne, each mighty beat taking her higher into the air. Her raven's-cry laugh sliced the air again, "*Run!*" she screamed.

The survivalists scattered like the roaches they were, some running for the rifles in the neighboring yard, some sprinting straight up the street, and others making their way into our garage. None of them spared a single glance for their fallen leader, still struggling and reaching out to his followers for help. Not a single one. I suppressed a shudder as the first man went down, a throwing knife imbedded in his eye, then fired up the motor of the big RV. I could definitely leave the killing to the professionals.

With a sad sigh, I spared one last longing look at the house that built me. The house that sheltered my family and I for so long. So many memories. So many of the things we collected over the years. Our big, cushy couch. So many family photos. Chests and boxes filled with keepsakes and vacation souvenirs and all the tiny things that fill a house, turning it into a home.

Tears welled in my eyes again and I blinked them away. Joey's final resting place. I knew it was just a place where his body lay decomposing beneath the ground, but leaving him there, along with all the memories of him that filled our home felt profoundly wrong. "But what about Joey?"

Mom reached over, taking my hand in her own. "Don't mourn the things we're leaving behind. None of that stuff matters. Everything important is right here." She squeezed my hand tight, her watery eyes meeting mine, "Even Joey. He isn't in there. He is in here." Her other hand drifted to her chest. "His memory lives within us and his spirit is flying free."

My chest tightened and I choked back a sob. She was right, of course. The only thing that really mattered was us. Living another day, creating new memories, forging new paths that Joey would be proud of.

I swallowed hard, "The house is just sticks and bricks," I said, squaring my shoulders and putting the RV into gear. "We brought the love into it, and that love is coming with us."

We still had a heck of a drive to make, and I had no idea what the route would hold, but the morning sun shone bright as I turned the RV out of our neighborhood and onto the main road. The camp store was calling—our new home was calling—and I was going to get us there, come hell or high water.

Wind whistled through the open windows of the RV as I carefully navigated the winding road, my hands gripping the steering wheel like a lifeline. Orchardville was a maze with its blocked-off streets and abandoned cars. The survivalists had made sure of that. For several tense minutes, I was afraid we might run into more of Charles' men, but the streets were eerily empty, leaving us focused only on finding a clear path out of town.

Mom turned back toward the bed where DJ still slept, her features drawn with exhaustion but eyes sharp and alive. We'd just met a divine being; she'd come when I called out to The Light Mother for help, and she'd saved our lives, confirming all of our theories and suspicions in the process. I was still in awe, reeling from the entire experience, and as mom's eyes met mine for the briefest moment, I knew she felt the same way.

Suddenly, a CB radio I hadn't even realized was there, crackled and squawked. Mom and I both nearly jumped out of our skin. Frantic screams and broken words chattered through the speakers, and I slowed the RV, listening closely. Then I heard it, Trillium's screeching laugh, followed by gunshots and then silence. I paled and shot a concerned look at my mom.

Her hand shot out, grabbing the CB microphone and pressing the button, "What's going on out there?"

Several moments passed before the frantic and broken voice of another woman sounded through the speaker, "There's a woman— an angel—she's killing the drivers! Who is this?"

"My name is Melissa. My daughter and I were just attacked by Charles in our home. I think she killed everyone that was with him."

"Is she going to kill us?" The stranger's question caught me by surprise, but it shouldn't have. What this woman was witnessing was terrifying. I knew that Trillium was a force for good, but she didn't. "I don't want to die."

Another voice sounded in the background, "Who are you talking to?"

I stopped the RV completely. I knew that voice! "That's Gail! Gail is that you?" My voice was shrill as mom brought the microphone closer to my mouth.

"Amber?" Gail's warm voice floated from the speaker. I could have cried.

I took the microphone from my mom and practically squealed into it, "It's me! I'm with my mom and DJ. Are you ok?" My heart pounded in my chest hoping she was well.

"We're good, all the women are...even some of the men...but there are a lot of bodies over here."

"You've gotta get out of the city. We're heading to that place I told you about, you should come too, it's safe." I paused, suddenly struck with the fact that someone else might be listening to our conversation. "But I don't want to give the exact location over the radio. Ya know...just in case."

"Good call, but how will I find you?" Gail asked.

Shit, I hadn't thought of that. I worried my bottom lip trying to think of a solution, when it hit me, "Talk to Trillium," I blurted. "She'll point you in the right direction."

"Who the hell is Trillium?" Screams sounded in the background and Gail's voice edged on panic.

"The woman with the wings," I said as calmly as I could.

"There is no way I'm talking to that angelic murder machine. Do you think I'm crazy?" Her voice pitched shrilly. "Fuckin' white people bullshit—" gunfire cracked in the background and Gail yipped, "where's black Jesus when you need him?"

I suppressed a snorting laugh before speaking again, "It'll be ok, trust me. She just saved DJ's life. Talk to her."

"Where are you? Why don't you come back here and talk to her for us?"

She had a point. I glanced at mom, "We can head back and go get them. There's room enough in here for a bunch of people."

Mom nodded and I spoke into the microphone again, "I'll head your way. It might take a while. I don't know which streets are blocked, but we'll get there."

There was a long pause before Gail answered, "Wait, she's already heading our way. Should I be worried?"

"You'll be fine, I swear." I cringed knowing she had to be close to losing it.

I had months of sheltering in the safety of the glow, unraveling secrets and talking with Dan about Erik and Alma to prepare me for the kind of magic she was witnessing. She'd had nothing and I suddenly felt horrible for not giving her all the details when I was trapped at the survivalist's camp.

"I can talk to her through the radio if you want?" I offered.

Gail didn't answer, instead, she must have handed the radio to Trillium, because it was her voice I heard next.

"I see you have friends here too, little warrior." A smile touched her voice, and I was struck again at just how lucky I was...and also the odd fact that Trillium knew how to operate a walkie talkie. That was something to contemplate later though.

"I do. Gail is one of the good ones. I'd trust her with my life." Mom reached over and laid a hand on my shoulder with a warm smile.

After another long pause, Gail's voice sounded through the speaker, "You still there?"

"Yes-yes, still listening," I said, anxious to know what had transpired.

"Trillium told us where you're headed and gave us the rundown on what is going on. You were holding out on me girl," she said.

"I know, I know. And I'm sorry I didn't tell you when I had the chance."

"We'll talk about that later. There is a lot to pack up and organize here, so we'll make our way there when we can. You just get yourselves safe." Gail's voice was resolute.

"Alright. I'll see you when I see you, my friend," I said then added, "Walk in Light and Truth."

"Trillium just said the same thing. Y'all have some serious explaining to do when we get up there."

A genuine smile spread across my face, "Take care, Gail. See you soon," I said with a small laugh.

"Mm-hm." Gail's non-committal sound turned my smile into a full-blown grin as I hung the microphone back on its hook and eased my foot back on the accelerator.

Mom chuckled, "She sounds like a tough one."

"Tough as nails but warmhearted, I swear."

My thoughts shifted from what Gail and the others were doing and back to the task at hand as we moved out of the city limits and into the rural outskirts.

The landscape was littered with reminders of the chaos—burned-out buildings, shopping centers sagging into themselves, deserted gas stations, and occasional shoe or article of clothing laying abandoned on the sidewalks or in the gutter, as if their owners had just vanished mid-step. Not a soul in sight. My fingers itched to scavenge, to stop and gather whatever we could, but I knew the camp store was our priority. We needed to regroup, recharge, and most importantly, we needed to be safe. I kept reminding myself we had a group now. We had a plan. We had a safe place to live. We were going to survive.

Mom and I exchanged a few words as I drove. She was optimistic in that way only a mother could be, trying to find hope in a world that had turned upside down.

Her voice was soft as she said, "Maybe things will settle into a routine again. A new kind of normal."

It was hard for me to picture what normal might look like. I told her as much and she nodded.

"All we can do is take things one day at a time," she said softly.

I focused again on the drive. The RV was massive. Thirty-five feet long at least, with a big, old diesel truck pulling it along—and the roads weren't free from debris and obstacles. The number of abandoned cars dropped as we made our way out past the towns and into the foothills, but several downed trees and large branches cluttered the road making the drive slow and technical.

Mom and I discussed all the pros and cons of several different routes we could take to get to the camp store. I knew we couldn't take the same route that I had taken to get home, or we would risk running into people from Dan's town. Another option would have been to attempt the interstate, making our way through several small cities before heading into the less populated areas. In the end, we decided on the route I was most familiar with. The route I had taken the day the power had gone out. It wasn't without its own set of risks, the main one being the old suspension bridge that crossed the narrow span of one of the lakes. If it had been damaged, we would have to backtrack more than an hour, making our way back to the interstate and through the cities we so desperately wanted to avoid. But the day was just beginning and even if we had to backtrack, we would still have plenty of daylight to find another route.

As we approached the old, single lane suspension bridge, we both held our breath. The bridge was intact, but there was a car stalled right in the middle.

Damn it.

I stopped the RV just before the bridge and looked over at my mom. "Do you think we could push it?"

"If we can't push it by hand, maybe we could use the RV?"

That was an idea, but I didn't want to risk damaging our only means of transportation. We were still at least a twenty-minute drive away from the camp store and if we broke something on the RV, we'd have to walk. On top of that, DJ was still out like a light. "Let's give it a try then."

We climbed out, listening hard for anything that sounded out of the ordinary but didn't hear anything beside the cool breeze dancing in the treetops with a gentle swishing sound. As we made our way over the uneven, wooden surface, I glanced down at my feet. Small gaps in the thick timber planks revealed a gut-churning drop of at least fifty feet to the cold water below. I thought back to the one and only time Joey and I had gone off the rope swing under the bridge. The water was cold, even in August, and I shivered at the thought of the bridge giving way under our feet. For all that it was unnerving, the bridge was sturdy and safe and I tried to calm my racing heart.

The car, a small, blue SUV, sat with the passenger door slightly ajar. A knot twisted in my stomach as we neared it. The sun was out though, so the only things that would be out and about would be other people and any animals that had managed to evade the darkling spawn. I moved in front of my mom the closer we got to the abandoned vehicle and as I peered inside, the car stood empty, the only thing left from its previous owner was a charging cable still attached to the port in the dash.

"It's empty," I said with a relieved sigh. "If we can get it into gear, you steer, I'll push."

Within minutes, it was clear that there was no way to shift a car with a push-button gear selector into neutral without the motor running. We were going to have to use the RV.

I shot mom a look full of pure exasperation, "What a stupid car."

We made our way back to the RV, climbed inside and slowly crept toward the SUV blocking the bridge.

"Just ease up on it," Mom said, leaning forward to peer over the dash.

I did the same, lifting my chin and using the steering wheel to pull myself forward in the seat. I couldn't mess this up. I couldn't ruin the RV. My heart pounded when the bumpers made contact, the RV shuddering slightly as it came to a stop.

"Now just put your foot in it and pray the car slides straight."

"Cross your fingers and toes for me, cause if I mess this up, we are literally screwed." I took a deep breath and pressed the accelerator. The big diesel roared, and the little SUV began to slide.

"There you go, keep going!" Mom tapped on the dash with excited hands and bounced in her seat.

I held my breath as the car veered slightly then sighed in relief as it straightened out inches before it collided with the railing of the bridge. Before long, its tires screeched as it moved off the timber planks of the bridge and back onto the asphalt road surface like a cork popping out of a bottle of champagne.

I turned to Mom with a wide smile, "Thank goodness for good luck. I say we crack into a box of some cheap wine when we get to the camp store to celebrate."

"Hell-yes." Mom held up a hand, "High-five!"

With that predicament out of the way, I prayed that the rest of the trip would be easy. The area appeared to be mostly untouched, but every property bore the signs of being recently deserted. Doors stood open, and in fields that used to pasture cattle and horses, the spring grass grew long and wild, not a single grazing animal in sight. The effect was eerie, like the world was standing still, holding its breath, waiting for the other shoe to drop.

As we made our way up the curving road that ran just beside the lake reservoirs, I was struck by how picturesque they looked without a single, solitary soul out on the water. The lake's surface, smooth as glass, reflected the conifers and now fully leafed maple, oak, and alder trees in a perfect mirror. This was the way the world was meant to look. Beautiful and undefiled by human hands. It would have been idyllic had I not known about the creatures that lurked in the dense forest, likely burrowed in the ground, waiting out the daylight hours until they were safe to roam and hunt again.

My mind abruptly ceased its wandering as the RV bumped over a bridge spanning the river. We were there! My heart soared as we rounded a bend, and I saw it. The camp store. Sitting tucked in among the conifers. Cozy. Safe. And still standing. It was so much more than just a building. It was the place where I had not just existed, but I had survived. It was the place that set me on the path to discovering who I was as a person and how strong I could be.

It was home.

We were *home.*

Gravel crunched under the RV's tires as I maneuvered the big vehicle into the lot and stopped near the front door. I spotted movement from the store's entrance—Dan, charging out of the door, waving wildly. A grin split my face, and I waved back with a little squeal I couldn't hold back. It was like seeing an old friend after years apart, even though it had only been weeks.

Mom's mouth fell open, shock written into every line of her face. "*That's* Dan?" she said, incredulous. "I thought you said he was old." She blinked and turned my way, "There is no way that man is older than me."

I couldn't help but laugh. "I swear, he's gonna be fifty this year, but that's what the remedy did." I reminded her then tore my seatbelt off.

I didn't even have my hand on the door handle before Dan nearly ripped it off its hinges and pulled me out in a giant bear hug.

"You made it, girl!" he said, his voice pitched high with emotion.

"Dan, I can't breathe," I choked out through a fit of giggles and happy tears.

"Oh, sorry," he set me down just as mom came around the front of the RV.

"Mom, this is Dan. Dan, this is my mom, Melissa." I introduced the two and he pulled my mom into a hug as well. He was clearly deep in his emotions at the moment.

"You can call me Mel," Mom said with a nervous laugh. "It's nice to finally meet you."

"Likewise." A teary grin split Dan's face as he turned and called out, "Kate, get out here!"

Just then, the door of the RV opened with a clack and DJ stepped out, rubbing his eyes, still groggy after his long nap, but looking stronger than ever.

For a split second, he looked like a deer caught in the headlights. Then his expression morphed from disbelief and into stunned relief as his eyes locked onto Dan's. He didn't wait for introductions, just walked straight up to Dan, hand extended.

Dan's eyes welled up and he choked back a sob. Instead of taking DJ's hand in his own, he yanked him into a tight embrace.

DJ's arms hovered inches from Dan's back as if he wasn't sure what he should do. I shot a questioning look at my mom, and she shook her head like she wasn't sure what to make of the situation either.

DJ's arms gingerly returned the hug, and a choked sob escaped Dan's throat as he hugged DJ a little tighter, "Son. My son."

33

Daughters of the Light

IT WAS AS IF THE WORLD STOOD STILL for a moment. Mom wrapped an arm around my shoulder pulling me close as we both took in the scene before us. DJ looked awkward at first, stiff in Dan's arms, but then he relaxed, hugging Dan back like he hadn't seen him in years. And maybe he really hadn't, not in a way that mattered. Dan pulled back, looked him over, and then dragged him into another hug, as if he couldn't quite believe DJ was real.

"Danny?!" A shrill voice called out from the door of the camp store. That had to be Dan's daughter. She bolted toward DJ, dark blonde hair trailing behind her, arms wide, tears streaming down her face.

He met her hug with fierce joy, spinning her in a circle laughing as she clung to him, sobbing. "If you don't dry it up, I'm going to start crying too, Katie Bear." He set her down and mussed her hair.

"Hey." She waved his hand away then wiped the tears from her cheeks with a smile.

DJ and Dan turned to me then, matching grins on their faces, dimples flashing in unison. I stared, a strange wave of emotions rolling through me.

Then the memories hit.

Dan and I sheltering overnight in an old auto shop. He'd looked younger; darker hair, fewer wrinkles highlighting a dimple I hadn't noticed the day we had first met in the forest. And when DJ had disarmed me in the garage after I'd held my knife to his throat—after I'd held *Dan's* knife to his throat—he'd studied the blade a moment before throwing it aside and letting me go. He'd even asked me about where I'd gotten the knife later on.

Goddess, could it be true?

I blinked at them and swallowed hard, pointing at Dan. "Your dad?" I mumbled, heart pounding.

The two nodded in unison looking so at home with each other.

Side by side, they looked so much alike, I could have kicked myself for not seeing it sooner—for not asking DJ weeks ago—*months* ago when we'd first met, but I'd been too timid then. "What do your initials stand for?" I shook my head and choked back a laugh, having no such qualms about asking him now.

"Daniel James...or Danny Junior if you ask this one." He poked his little sister in the ribs playfully.

"What are the freaking odds, you guys?" I squeaked. "Holy shit."

What a reunion. What a homecoming! Was dumb luck really at play here or could this be a part of some predestined path? The thought was almost too much for my brain to handle.

"I wondered how you got a hold of that knife," DJ said, pointing his chin at the blade on my hip. "After you stuck me with it, I had to take a good look."

"She stabbed you?" Dan's voice pitched up a notch as if he were fighting a laugh.

All I could do was offer a sheepish grin and a shrug.

"She really only poked me with it, but for a second there, I really thought she might do me in." DJ's own voice was full of barely contained mirth.

Dan raised his brows in appreciation then let out a booming belly laugh.

"That's my girl," Mom whispered in my ear as she gave my shoulder a squeeze.

"In my defense, I had just escaped the survivalists and I thought you were there to bring me back."

"Looks like we've got a lot to catch up on," Dan said, joy dancing in his eyes.

DJ turned to his sister and pulled her into another hug, still laughing. "Yeah, we've got a lot to catch up on. You look great, Pops," he said as he scanned the group. His eyes turned serious as he turned back toward Dan, "Where's Emily?" he asked softly.

The air stilled. Dan's face fell, and the silence that followed threatened to suffocate us all. His shoulders sagged and he shook his head slowly, unable to find the words. The unspoken weight of loss hanging between us, thick and heavy.

I reached out, placing a hand on Dan's arm. "I'm so sorry. Let's—let's not talk about it now. We should all get settled first."

Dan nodded, and we all moved in quiet agreement, unloading the RV and settling into the camp store. Sleeping space was cramped, but we made do. DJ claimed the RV for himself, while the rest of us took the rooms inside. Mom and I shared my old room and Kate opted to sleep on the couch because her dad snored like a hibernating bear. The last room stayed empty just in case Erik and Alma returned.

Hours later, once everything was unpacked, I found myself wandering, needing to check the food storage, needing to check on the garden, needing air. The sky was clear, the air crisp as I stood in the overgrown plot, listening to the wind rustle through the trees. The crows weren't around, but I hoped they would return soon.

I reveled in the moment, feeling the glow pulse around me, as if it had waited for this quiet moment to welcome me home, but it felt worn, somehow. Like it needed a long, rejuvenating sleep. I furrowed my brow.

I sort of felt the same way. Wrung out. Mentally and emotionally exhausted. But how could that be? I'd done it. I'd made it back and we were safe. Perhaps it was because this wasn't the perfect dream I had pictured without my brother, and I imagined Dan probably felt the same with his wife missing from the group as well. Reality had been much crueler than I could have ever imagined, but it was also much more magical.

As I was lost in thought, the familiar sound of a hawk's call cut through the quiet.

I looked up in time to see not just a hawk, but Trillium as well, enormous wings spread wide as she and Isa sailed through the invisible barrier of the glow. It pulsed with power at her passing, seeming to recognize her arrival. Black wings beat twice before her feet settled gracefully in the damp grass and she made her way over to me, spear strapped to her back and a broad smile gracing her full lips.

She looked no worse for wear after her run in with the survivalists and nervous butterflies took flight in my stomach as she approached.

"Amber. Well met. I trust you arrived without incident?" She spoke as if she was from another time, and it took me a moment to fully grasp what she had said.

"Uh, yes. No issues at all. Thank you for helping Gail." I bowed slightly. It felt right considering what she had just done for me and my family.

"It is my duty and pleasure," she replied, inclining her head. "I'm certain most of them will arrive here within the week if the weather holds. We must prepare for their arrival." With a graceful movement, she motioned toward the camp store.

I turned to see everyone piling onto the back patio, wonder written on their faces, especially DJ. He'd been so injured, he probably hadn't noticed that she had wings or even registered the fact that it was Trillium that had given him the vial to drink and carried him into the RV. As we approached the patio, Trillium removed her spear, leaning it against one of the wooden pillars that supported the patio roof.

"Have you eaten since your healing?" she asked, eyes intent on DJ's face.

For once, he seemed to be at a loss for words and Dan elbowed his son lightly in the ribs. "Y-yeah. I mean, yes ma'am." He straightened his shoulders and nodded; hands clasp behind his back as if he were addressing a military superior. "Thank you, ma'am." He looked like he was fighting himself not to salute her.

"At ease, hume. The time for military formality is yet to come." Trillium said with a small smile, her voice like a calm breeze. "And how do you feel now?"

DJ relaxed slightly, "I feel great. Better than great. Energy and strength to spare."

"Very well, then." She nodded, ending that particular conversation and turned back toward me. "Before I return to the front lines, I will need to charge the Singing Stone."

Everyone looked confused but I instantly understood what she meant. My gut clenched and my heart kicked up a notch, "The stone box," I whispered.

Trillium nodded in response, "That is what generates the Light Magic that protects this place. Please, the dome is weak. It must be charged before dark." She motioned for me to lead the way while dismissing her giant wings, specks of golden light lingering for a few seconds after the great, feathered limbs had vanished.

So, The Glow really was tired, but why? "What happened to the light dome?" I asked.

To my surprise, it was Dan that spoke first, "The darkling spawn attacked the barrier for weeks." His jaw clenched, as he took a deep breath. "If Trillium hadn't shown up when she did, I don't know what would have happened."

The look on his face said he knew exactly how dire the situation had been, though. "You'll have to tell me the whole story one of these days. Is the basement still locked?" I asked.

Without a word, Dan disappeared into the house, quickly returning with a set of keys and handed them over.

With me leading the way and Trillium on my heels, we all filed into the basement and gathered around the old weight bench.

"We'll need more room," Trillium said, pointing at the exercise equipment.

Dan and DJ wasted no time in clearing out a space. While they moved the weights, Trillium explained, "The box containing the Singing Stone can only be opened by a Light Being."

But the box had responded to my touch—what did that mean?

My mind flashed back to the moment my fingers had traced the raised infinity pattern. The humming power. The edges blurring like something out of a dream.

I swallowed hard as Trillium continued, "Every Township and Outpost houses at least one Singing Stone. Some are large, some small, but they are all capable of holding enormous amounts of energy. Erik, could feel its power fading," Trillium continued matter-of-factly then turned her intense gaze on Dan. "And since you had consumed such a large amount of his blood, he could also feel that you were here and in grave danger."

Dan paled visibly, his eyes locking with mine.

So, the spawn poison remedy was Erik's blood?

I held up a hand, like I was asking a question in grade school. "Um, was the liquid in the vial you gave DJ to drink..." my words trailed off.

Trillium moved, resting a gentle hand on my shoulder, "Yes, though I do not know which Fampir that blood belonged to. There are hundreds in the snow forest that donate their blood for its healing purposes."

DJ made a choked sound, he and Dan leaning on each other for support. He seemed to be handling all the information fairly well for someone who had drunk a mythical being's blood before breakfast though.

I raised my hand again, "What exactly is a Fampir?"

"You do not need to keep raising your hand, little warrior. We are not in studies," Trillium laughed lightly, the sound taking on a quality like the tinkling of wind chimes, so different from the hateful, cawing laugh I'd heard when she'd been dealing with the survivalists. "Fampir are a type of light being, like me. Their first ancestors were created directly by The Light Mother's hand. Hume, on the other hand, were not. None of the seed children were. But that is something to discuss later, perhaps over evening meal. Now, I must charge the stone."

Trillium turned, making her way over to the pedestal, then lifted it and the box as if they weighed nothing. My mouth fell open. I'd assumed it had been anchored to the concrete floor because I hadn't been able to budge the thing, but Trillium carried it easily out of the corner it was hiding in and set it in the center of the room.

I started to raise my hand again then lowered it, "So, what happens if a human—er, a hume—touches that box?"

Trillium eyed me for a moment, "Nothing. A hume would not even be able to move the pedestal."

My heart hit the pit of my stomach. Sure, I hadn't been able to move the pedestal, but the box had definitely done *something* when I had touched it.

"Why do you ask?" Suspicion colored the edge of Trillium's words, and she raised a beautifully arched brow.

"It's just that—" my words were cut off by my mom's audible gasp.

She strained her neck, leaning toward the box, trying to get a good look at it, eyes flashing between the intricate symbol on Trillium's chest plate and the matching symbol carved into the top of the stone box. Her hand trembled as she pointed.

"My father and grandfather had that symbol tattooed on both of their shoulders." Mom's voice trembled as she spoke, her eyes never straying from the infinity symbol framed by an oval ouroboros intricately carved into the lid of the stone box. "They said it was our family crest—and that when she was a child, great-grandmother had that same symbol cut into her skin by her mother."

I knew the symbol had looked familiar the first time I had seen it, but I hadn't been able to place it. I'd been very young when my grandfather passed away, but the flash of a foggy memory played at the edges of my mind's eye. It was a warm, summer day and Grandpa was visiting from out of town. We had all gone down to the river to wade. He'd taken his shirt off and dove into the chilly water, laughing because Mom, Joey and I said the water was too cold. That was the only time I'd seen his tattoos, matching black symbols, one on each shoulder.

Trillium's eyes narrowed to slits, looking more closely at my mom. No, not just looking—she was assessing. "This is the Snow Forest seal. It represents The Light Mother. And you say this was *cut* into her skin?"

Mom nodded and wrung her hands. No doubt her heart was pounding just as hard as mine.

"It would seem that you have ancestors that are well known to the Snow Forest. Come, let me have a closer look at you."

Timidly, almost as if she were afraid of what new information awaited her, Mom stepped forward.

"I could feel the touch of the Snow Forest within you both, but..." Trillium's eyes roamed over Mom's features a moment before she reached out, laying a hand on her cheek. White light crackled from palm to face. Mom went rigid, fidgeting fingers locked down into tight fists, but it only lasted a heartbeat.

"Small in stature, but tough and wiry. Dark hair and green eyes. High cheek bones and a fierce heart. You look like her, you know?" Trillium said softly as she used the pad of her thumb to brush a tear off my mom's cheek, "I knew your great-grandmother. Aster, daughter of Astrid, Matriarch of the Crystal Lake Clan Wood Sprites."

"Excuse me—what?" I thought the floor was about to open up and swallow me whole for all the room was spinning. I closed my eyes, trying to steady myself and blindly reached out a hand. DJ was there to catch it, balancing me as my world had the rug ripped out from under it. He tucked me tightly under one arm, vigorously rubbing my shoulder. I opened my eyes, fighting the giddy feeling in my head. My knees wobbled and I wrapped an arm around his waist to steady myself.

"Oh, yes. I'm shocked I didn't notice the resemblance sooner. My long memories do become jumbled at times, but yes. Aster herself was half hume, but as the daughter of the matriarch, her scarification and fierce heart proved her a Light Being in full, and child of The Snow Forest." Trillium's eyes flicked between me and my mom, before settling on my face. "Did you touch this symbol?"

Mouth dry and head still spinning, I nodded.

"And what happened?" Trillium asked, curiosity written into every line on her beautiful face.

"It sort of hummed and got warm," I said, hoping with all my might that I hadn't ruined it somehow. *Wouldn't that just be the freaking pits.*

"This is a wonderful surprise," Trillium clasped her hands and bounced a little, armor clanking, looking almost human. "Come closer, both of you," she beckoned with sweeping arm movements.

DJ's grip on my shoulder loosened, "I'll be right here if you need me," he whispered low and steady into my ear, his voice like a lifeline. I shivered as I looked up at his handsome face. He smiled, dimple flashing, "You've got this."

I stepped forward, knees still unsteady. Mom reached out to take my hand, her grip fierce and a look in her eyes that I couldn't describe. She looked like she had known all along that there had been something different about our family. Maybe I had too? What else could explain our uncanny intuition—our gut feelings?

"Even though your lineage is distant, your Spark is still many times larger than that of a pure Seed Child," Trillium explained. "It is our stronger connection to The Light Mother that allows us to commune with the stone."

She lightly ran a forefinger over the infinity symbol and the box hummed to life, just like when I had touched it, a potent power radiating from it in waves. The lid lifted, floating open to reveal a red, satin lined interior, and sitting inside was a stone, roughly the size and shape of an egg. It was brown and rough-hewn; plain to look at. Had it been sitting on the ground outside, I wouldn't have looked twice at it, but it was attached to a short length of silver chain, and just beside it sat a tiny silver hammer.

Reverently, Trillium lifted the stone and cupped it in one hand. How could something so unassuming hold so much power?

Trillium then covered the rock with her opposite hand, cradling it like something precious and fragile. "Melissa, cover my hands with your own, and Amber, cover your mother's hands with yours," she instructed.

The moment my hands encircled my mom's, power surged through my body bringing a flush to my cheeks. Once again, I felt the earth thrumming beneath my feet, the beating sensation, pulsing in time with my own heart. "Woah," I breathed, completely in awe.

"Do you feel that?" Trillium asked, eyes bouncing between me and my mom. We both nodded. "That is the planet's well of power, linked directly to the Goddess. When you connect to that, you are tapping into her infinite light."

In an instant, my mind traveled through the ground, racing along the roots of trees and shrubs, flowing through the rich, damp soil and suddenly, I was there; touching the edge of the glow, existing in it— with it—like it was a part of me and I was a part of it. Its power vast, ancient, pure, endless, *boundless*, and part of that power lived in *me*. A warmth blossomed in my chest, so warm and joyful I thought I might dissolve into it.

Trillium's gentle voice pulled me back to myself, "Our resonance with the stone and with The Light Mother has limits, if we push past those limits, we may accidentally harm ourselves. This is a resonance of consciousness and spirit, not of the body. The stronger your mind, the stronger your resonance will be. Now, close your eyes and allow the power to radiate through you."

My lids drifted shut and I embraced the thrumming pulse of the earth. My heart rate slowed, relaxed, until it beat in time with the planet, the steady drumming, sending waves of heat through our hands and into the innocuous looking stone.

"Very good." Trillium's voice was calm and encouraging. "Now, push the power outward, to the furthest edge you can reach."

With every heartbeat, we pushed the light dome out. The Glow doubled, tripled, then quadrupled in diameter and strength. My consciousness ran over the dome, stretching far above the trees and well beyond the river, all the way into the town of Riverside. It was glorious, seeing everything all at once, but then, I could push no more. My hands began to tremble, breath coming in short bursts, just moments before I felt my mom's hands shaking as well. We had reached our limit. I opened my eyes to find everything around us brighter, clearer—as if I had been half-blind my entire life and not known it.

Trillium opened her palms, and the flow of energy slowed, like the flow of water ebbing at the slow turn of the knob, then finally, it stopped altogether leaving the singing stone hanging in the air above the stone box, suspended by the light magic. Trillium reached out and delicately grasped the silver chain. Gravity abruptly returned to the rock, and it dropped, swinging from the end of the chain.

Mom and I stood, hands on our knees, panting with mental fatigue but strong and connected to the light dome. Her eyes twinkled and a smile played at the corners of her lips.

"Well done," Trillium said, pride brightly coloring her words. "I didn't think we'd get half so far." She then picked up the tiny hammer and tapped the stone. It rang like a tiny struck bell, "Earth." She tapped it again, "Air." Twice more she tapped the stone, "Fire. Water." With a final tap, Trillium called out, "Spirit."

A burst of light exploded from the stone, chasing away every shadow in the basement, racing toward the perimeter of the glow. I felt the moment it solidified in my chest—in my gut—The Glow whole and strong once again.

"It is done," Trillium said with a deep sigh as she placed the stone and hammer reverently back into the stone box. The lid floated back into place and sealed itself tight, leaving everyone in the basement reeling, Mom and I included. "Now we eat and rest. The real work starts tomorrow."

I cast my eyes around the circle—my family, my friends—my *tribe* all doing the same, and for the first time in what felt like ages, I wasn't afraid of what was to come.

34

Keepers of The Glow

MOM AND I SETTLED INTO OUR old rhythm in the kitchen to prepare a hearty, celebratory stew for dinner. Kate washed and cut vegetables while Trillium, having removed her armor, lounged on the overstuffed furniture, talking animatedly with Dan and DJ. The scents of spiced meat and toasting bread filled the house, and I marveled at the comfortable calm that had finally settled around us. This wasn't a fleeting dream that would fade the moment my lids fluttered open. It was real. And I could have cried for the fullness in my heart.

We all ate together around the rustic table in the kitchen, laughter rising and falling like waves between bites. For the first time since the power had gone out, I felt whole. Happy. Safe. Like the danger that lurked just outside the safety of The Glow didn't actually exist. Still, a part of me ached. I couldn't stop thinking about Joey, wishing he were with us, cracking dumb jokes, making everything a little brighter just by being in the room.

Dan seemed genuinely happy as well, catching up with DJ, joking with Kate, but I could tell his smiles were worn thin at the edges. The way his eyes wandered told me he was thinking of his wife, probably wishing she could've been here to see all of this too.

Eventually, after we had stuffed ourselves full to bursting with stew, bread and even a little beer, Trillium announced that she and

Isa would be leaving at first light and excused herself, disappearing into the empty room.

Dan turned in for the night not long after, leaving Mom, Kate and I lingering in the living room, chatting about inconsequential things. Not long after, Kate's yawns told us she was ready for sleep as well. We got her settled on the big sofa with a fluffy pillow and thick blanket. Mom squeezed my hand and retired to the room we agreed to share, but I wasn't ready for sleep just yet. I was too buzzy, too happy to be back at the camp store, so I made myself a cup of hot cocoa, wrapped myself in a throw blanket, and shuffled out onto the back patio.

It had started to rain. Soft and steady. The kind that made everything feel alive. Crickets chirped, frogs sang in the distance, and my entire world seemed to sigh contentedly. I breathed in the sweet scents around me. It smelled like pure peace.

"Any chance you'd be willing to share that blanket?" DJ's deep voice floated from the shadows.

I startled lightly, then suppressed a smile. "So, this is where you ran off to."

He patted the empty space beside him on the patio bench and I shuffled over, gently settling in the seat and rearranging the blanket to cover both our laps. We sat in awkward silence at first, side by side but not touching.

"It's a nice night," I said as I cast my eyes out into the dark, shivering lightly.

DJ let out a sigh. "After everything you did today, I'm not about to let you sit out here with me and be cold. Scoot over." He wrapped an arm around my waist and pulled me flush against his side then tucked me under his arm.

I shimmied even closer, grateful for the body heat he provided. "Hot chocolate?" I offered, lifting my mug to share.

He looked down at me, features hidden by shadow, but I could just make out the curve of his smile and dimple. "I haven't had hot cocoa in years." His fingers brushed mine as he accepted. "That's good," he said, returning the mug.

"I can make you a cup if you want," I said as I leaned forward to stand, suddenly feeling a little self-conscious, not quite comfortable being so close to him.

"Absolutely not. You're staying right here," he all but growled, tightening his arm around my shoulders.

Okay then, I thought, stretching the words in my mind, as my cheeks heated. "If you insist."

"I do." His fingers were warm as they tucked a stray piece of hair behind my ear.

I shivered and it was definitely not because of the cold. For two people who really barely knew each other, we had been through hell and back together over the last month. Everything we had experienced flashed through my mind, and I settled into his side with a sigh. We'd both been nearly killed just that morning, yet it felt like something that had happened to someone else. Like the weeks I had spent away from the camp store were a bad dream and I had finally woken up, safe and sound, back where I really belonged, surrounded by friends and loved ones.

DJ's low voice brought my attention back to the present. "I want—I need to thank you."

"Thank me for what?" I asked, truly not knowing why.

He chuckled, the sound vibrating through me, "You still don't know how special you are, do you?"

I couldn't think of anything to say, so I simply shrugged against his side.

"You did what I was too much of a coward to do."

"Killing Charles wasn't an act of bravery," I pushed. It was necessary and I'd had the strength of The Light Mother guiding me.

"It's not just that." He shifted beside me. "It's the fact that you truly stood up for what you believed was right, consequences be damned. You saw the evil, the injustice, and stood against it from the very beginning." His fingers played idly in my hair as he spoke, as if he were taking strength from the strands. "I'll never forget the moment you told Frank that he hit like a bitch."

I snorted, nearly choking on my hot chocolate and DJ laughed quietly beside me.

"I think—" he started, then stopped himself with a sigh.

"You think what?" I prompted.

"Eh, it's nothing. I just...knew you were something else right then and there. That if anyone could survive this world, it would be you." He paused a moment before continuing, "And how it was absolutely unfair that you had ended up stuck with the survivalists. You're a stronger person than I ever could be, Amber."

"But I'm not though—"

"You are," DJ interrupted, "And you showed me what not compromising values looks like. So, yeah. Thank you. And I'm sorry for all the harm I caused. I don't even deserve to have you sitting here beside me."

"You've more than made up for any wrongdoing, DJ. You almost died today trying to protect me and Mom. That takes a special kind of crazy. A special kind of toughness," I said, turning to look him in the eye.

"It'll never make up for the fact that I acted like a lecherous prick when I should have torn that whole place down around their heads before Charles had even laid eyes on you. I was complacent. Complicit—" Something flashed in his eyes then, but it was gone in a moment, almost too quick to see. "—I don't think I'll ever forgive myself for that."

His voice held so much strained emotion, so much self-hatred. It couldn't have stemmed only from the things he had been a part of with the survivalists, could it?

"Well, we can call it even for how big of a bitch I was to you," I said with a small laugh, trying to ease the tension.

His mouth drew into a shadowy line as he sighed, his eyes burning into mine even in the dark.

"I understand why you did it, and even why you felt like it was your only option in the moment." I was confident that not all of that lecherous behavior had been an act. No, I was damn sure some of it had been real. I could still feel it in the way he looked at me—like he was looking at me right then—like he saw through every excuse I had ever made, every wall I'd ever built to keep every relationship at arm's length. Like he understood the why behind it all far better than I did. "And I forgive you for it. Water under the bridge."

"I wish we could go back. Start over."

My mind traveled back to the texts we'd shared moments before the power had gone out. "We can." The words jumped out before I could stop them. "I still owe you that picture." During the weeks I was alone, I'd hung the photo I'd taken of him in the park on my bedroom wall as a reminder of simpler times. It was slightly blurred and brightly backlit, but that just seemed to add to the dreamy quality of what the world had been like before it all went to shit. "And you still owe me a drink, Mr. Bartender."

"I suppose I do." He rubbed my shoulder and hugged me close. "How 'bout tomorrow night after dinner?"

"I don't know, I'll have to check my schedule," I joked.

"Tomorrow night. It's a date," he said with a wink. "And you can't say no. I know where you live, so if I have to drag you out kicking and screaming, I will."

My face warmed at the thought, and I shoved at him playfully. "Don't get too excited. I have the personality of an overdone noodle once you get to know me."

"I highly doubt that," he said, the hint of something dark in his voice.

I thought he might want to keep talking—hoped he would even— but instead, he suggested we both get some rest so we could be up to see Trillium off in the morning.

With a quick goodnight, he made his way around the side of the camp store building and out to the RV.

I lingered out on the porch a little longer, curled into a ball, wrapped up in the blanket, soaking in the night, feeling the glow pulsing with strength at the edge of my consciousness. For once, everything felt right. Balanced. The weight I'd been carrying for months finally lifted and for the first time in what felt like forever, I thought that everything might actually be okay.

I must have dozed off on the bench because the next thing I knew, DJ was gently shaking me awake.

"The CB in the motorhome is picking up a weird transmission," he said, his voice low and urgent. "It's repeating. I think... I think you should hear it."

Curious and a little uneasy, I rubbed the sleep from my eyes and followed him to the RV.

As I stepped through the door, the static on the radio was sharp at first, but then it cleared, and a voice came through—deep, echoing, fierce, and chaotic all at once.

"We are the eternal darkness. We will not be stopped. We cannot be stopped. We will gleefully feed upon those who seek to destroy us until chaos is all that exists. I am free. My children do my bidding without question, and they are legion. The light shall never again cage me. Shall never again hold dominion. The Darkness will swallow it whole. Embrace the Darkness or be consumed by it. Embrace the Darkness or die."

The hair on my arms rose as the sharp sound of static returned a moment before the transmission began again. DJ and I exchanged a look, but before either of us could speak, a voice sounded from the open door of the RV, "What is this?"

We both nearly jumped out of our skin, heads whipping in the direction of the sound. Trillium stood just outside the door like a phantom, leaning in, her eyes locked on the radio. *How had she even known we were out here?*

DJ explained quickly as Trillium stepped aboard the RV, "I was scanning the channels looking for anything that might be a problem and stumbled on the transmission."

Her expression turned ghostly pale.

"This is bad, isn't it?" My words were more statement than question.

She gave a quick nod, then asked, "How long has it been going on?"

"I'm not sure. At first it was only on one channel," DJ said, then pressed the 'scan' button. Every few seconds, the channel switched but the eerie words continued, "now it's coming in on every single one."

"By the stars," she breathed before turning on her heel. "Isa, we leave now," she called out as her feet hit the gravel, her voice urgent but steady. I scrambled after her but stopped short just outside the RV.

The hawk called out in the darkness, the sound coming from the roof of the car port, directly across from the open door of the RV as I watched Trillium sprint into the camp store. DJ and I stood gaping in the yellow glow of the big vehicle's porch light while the misty rain began to settle in our hair and on our shoulders. Just then, Isa landed on the roof of the RV and chortled, wings rustling, feathers ruffled. Her head twitched, eyes glinting as if she'd caught the scent of something foul on the wind and my stomach clenched. This was *definitely* bad.

Moments later, Trillium re-emerged, fully outfitted in that silvery armor, helm in hand, Dan and my mom right on her heels. The transmission kept repeating in the background like a sinister harbinger of things to come.

DJ squeezed my hand in his, the gesture warm and comforting even though I felt the temperature drop as Trillium addressed us.

"The Dark Mother has either been freed or somehow escaped her prison of stone," she said with an unsteady breath. If Trillium was shaken by that fact, it had to be truly terrifying indeed. "The darkling will never be able to move in sunlight...but The Dark One—Nerezza—does not share that weakness."

"Stay within the boundaries of the Light Dome. It is the only thing that can keep her at bay," she said, her tone firm. "Now that you have charged it, you will know if it weakens—or comes under attack." Her gaze met mine. "It is much easier to maintain the dome than it is to expand it as we did this morning. Seek the Singing Stone often to strengthen your bond with it."

My throat tightened, but I nodded solemnly.

"If Erik and Alma still live, they'll return here as soon as they are able—with reinforcements from Evergreen. We must protect those who remain. The Light Mother's only wish is that her children survive. That you all survive."

She looked between Mom and me. "Be wary of those who ask to join you. Accept only those of pure heart. If you do not trust someone...the Dome will not either. They will not be able to enter and will suffer the same fate as darkling and spawn if they try."

Trillium stepped forward and took our hands, her eyes shining in the soft glow of the porch light. "Daughters of the Snow Forest, stay strong. Stay true. Protect this place with all your love and light."

Then she turned to DJ and Dan. "Seed Children...guard these women and this place with your very lives. And when this is over, we will all meet again in the glory of the Snow Forest," she drew in a shaky breath, "or in The Light Mother's final embrace."

Without another word, her wings unfurled, magnificent and radiant, deeper than the night around us.

"Walk in Light and Truth," she said, stepping back, face drawn as she strapped on her helm then lowered the guard with a clink. Isa took to the sky—then with a mighty beat of her wings, Trillium was gone, soaring upward into the darkness until the mist swallowed her silhouette whole.

35

The Light Reborn

THE MONTHS FOLLOWING TRILLIUM'S departure passed quickly and without incident. Spring melted into summer, and now summer was beginning to wane into fall, the early September air holding a touch of that crispness I'd always loved, and some of the trees were just starting to blush with hints of gold and fire. We had not simply survived—we were thriving.

New faces had arrived about a week after Trillium had returned to the front lines of the war, (wherever that was) refugees from the survivalist's camp, vehicles loaded down with supplies from the city. They had made homes at the camp store, sleeping in tents while they converted the old outbuildings into living quarters. More hands lightened the workload for everyone and between Mom and Gail, a chore schedule had been worked out. We all took turns with the communal tasks, and we even had a few running vehicles—my old Jeep among them—though we only used the vehicles for large transports or distant scavenging missions. Fuel was too precious to waste. We lived simply but well.

DJ and I were on kitchen duty for the day and were just finishing the lunch dishes, stacking them to dry on the large wooden countertop that now ran the length of the covered patio. We'd turned the former lounge space into a serviceable outdoor kitchen, closer to the water supply and with more space to prepare meals large enough to feed everyone who had arrived from the survivalist's camp.

I gazed out over the garden and spotted Mom and Kate straddling buckets, picking beans. Dan was wading through the corn with a few others, their heads barely visible over the fast-growing stalks, while more folks were working in the orchard, plucking early apples and late plums from the trees. Near the edge of the clearing, a group worked to build the frame for a new gathering pavilion—something to shield us through the winter months ahead—while still others were painting the newly built bunkhouse.

Laughter and voices echoed all around me, threading through the scent of earth and herbs and woodsmoke. It was calm. It was organized. It was peaceful and I couldn't believe how much life had changed in just a few short months.

I finished putting away the leftover food for dinner, then paused, feeling that familiar prickling at the back of my neck. I turned just in time to catch DJ watching me as he stowed the last plate. His eyes sparkled with amusement. I shot him a mock glare, and he raised an eyebrow at me in a mock challenge.

I stuck out my chin and wandered off toward the garden, feeling the heat of his gaze on my back the entire way.

"Need any help, Mom?" I asked.

"You've done your chores for the day and I've got Kate here. Go enjoy the afternoon," she brushed me off with a smile.

So, I did. I wandered toward the forest's edge, trying to decide where I wanted to go. A glance over my shoulder showed DJ talking to Dan by the corn patch. They both noticed me watching and waved. I waved back, then slipped into the trees.

The forest greeted me like an old friend. The air shimmered with life, and energy coursed up through my leather shoes with every step. Since Trillium fully awakened my spark back in the spring, I'd discovered something new about myself almost every day. I'd learned that barefoot, connected to the earth, I could move faster—more fluidly. Rubber soles were a thing of the past. I'd crafted my own leather foot wraps, and I hadn't looked back.

My sensitivity had tripled—touch, sound, scent...all sharpened. It was a gift and a burden. I could feel the energy of others when they were near. Sense mood. Intention. My intuition had evolved into something more like a sixth sense. (And not the M. Knight Shyamalan kind—I didn't see dead people. Thankfully.)

I felt when DJ entered the woods. The forest shifted around me, whispering into my soul. I smiled and broke into a light run, following a trail that led to my favorite hidden place—a deep, slow pool at a bend in the river nestled beside a towering cliff.

I could feel him gaining on me, which only made me run faster. Not because I didn't want to be caught—but because I wanted to make him work for it.

I vaulted onto a mossy boulder, then leapt into the arms of a tree that stretched its branches wide over the trail then crouched low and quiet. Waiting.

DJ appeared around the bend, chest heaving slightly, brow furrowed as he realized I'd vanished.

"Amber?" he called out, eyes scanning the undergrowth on either side of the trail.

I held my breath and didn't answer.

He crept forward a few steps, and I dropped down silently behind him, mirroring his movements for a few paces before stepping so close I could feel the warmth from his body.

"Right here," I whispered and poked him in the ribs, then leapt backward.

He spun, eyes darkening the second they landed on me. Then he grinned and charged, sweeping me up over his shoulder. I yelped and pounded playfully on his back, giggling the whole way. "Put me down!"

"Quit playing," he said, swatting my backside once. "If you didn't want me to catch you, you would've kept running."

We had never tested the theory, but I was pretty sure I was faster than he was now, though I'd never be as strong. He carried me like a sack of flour until we reached the riverbank, setting me gently on a log so we were eye to eye.

My eyes roamed his face, my heart skipping a beat, hoping—maybe this time—he'd kiss me. But he just reached out and traced a line along my collarbone, up my neck to the curve of my ear. My breath hitched. I could feel how much he wanted to. So why was he still holding back?

"I keep expecting your ears to go pointy," he said with a crooked smile. "You've gotten so nimble lately."

I sighed inwardly. He was still deflecting. Frustrated and slightly irritated, I turned and hopped off the log and sat at the river's edge, watching the water sparkle in the dappled light.

DJ joined me after a moment. "C'mere," he said, his voice barely above a whisper.

He pulled me into his lap, and I melted into the space beneath his chin. It felt good. Right. Someday, I'd crack the shell he'd covered himself in since our escape from Orchardville. I'd figure him out. But for now, I figured I would have to settle for his maddening brand of affection.

Just as I relaxed into his arms, a tremor ran through the Glow, soft at first then insistent. My breath caught and I froze.

DJ, feeling me tense, stilled as well. "What is it?" he asked.

I pulled myself off his lap and up onto my feet, eyes closed, reaching with my senses along the glow's perimeter. Another buzz tickled down my spine and my eyes flew open, locking onto his.

"Light Beings," I whispered, hand drifting to my chest. Trillium had said— "They've crossed into the Dome." Without waiting, I turned and ran back toward the camp store.

The forest flashed by me in a blur as I went, my eyes on the trail, but my mind monitoring The Glow. Every being that entered sent a small ripple of recognition through me as if to say, 'We have arrived. We are finally home.' And the Glow pulsed back, like it too had been waiting for their return. I pulled my consciousness back toward myself and poured all my energy into my legs, outdistancing DJ with each step, though he was never too far behind me.

I burst out of the trees, and Mom's eyes met mine. She didn't ask. She just ran with me toward the road, Dan following suit the moment he saw DJ emerge from the forest, hot on Mom and I's heels.

We came to a stop in the road and puffed as one by one, everyone in the settlement drifted toward the parking lot.

"They're back," I called out to the group. "Erik and Alma...are back."

"They've brought so many people," Mom breathed, wonder filling her voice, "and animals too." I knew she could feel the glow as strongly as I could, we'd been channeling energy into it via the Singing Stone for months.

The clatter of shod hooves and the rattle of wagons echoed off the conifers, announcing their arrival. The sound grew with each passing minute and then the road filled with a caravan—no, a *parade*—of people and animals, carts and wagons, and creatures I didn't have names for, steadily marching in our direction.

It was like something out of a dream. At the head of the procession, Erik and Alma rode horses that looked half-woven from starlight and wind, touched by ancient magic. Both wore boiled leather armor and bore weapons like something from another age, but they didn't look like fantasy. They looked real and brimming with power. Grounded and yet ethereal. Colorful wagons, drawn by broad steeds, tinkled and clattered with chimes and bells, creating a resonant rhythm that nearly filled my soul to bursting.

As they neared, Erik scanned the crowd and locked eyes with Dan. He grinned and pushed his mount to an elegant trot, obviously anxious to close the distance. He pat his horse before dismounting. The way he moved was so fluid, so otherworldly, I found myself wondering if he could be the same man that used to make me milkshakes. Dan stepped forward, grinning from ear to ear and Erik clasped his arm before pulling him into a brief hug.

"You look well, my friend. Thank you for holding our home," Erik said, then turned to me. "But I suppose I have you to thank as well."

I stepped forward, my mom tight to my side, heart pounding. His presence was so strong, I had to fight the urge to bow while I hoped he would be pleased with the way we had cared for his home.

"And I can't believe I missed the touch of the Snow Forest on you last summer...it's so obvious now. But you seem so changed from that girl who came in every other week for milkshakes." He reached out, offering a hand and I looked up at his considerable height.

That girl felt like someone from another lifetime, not me. Not anymore.

Fighting the blushing warmth that rose from my neck and onto my cheeks, I took his offered hand. Mine disappeared in his. I was immediately struck by the realization that had he offered his hand last summer, I would have ended up a weak-kneed, melting puddle of longing, but now, I could stand firm and meet his gaze.

And what a gaze it was. He was still devastatingly handsome—but more than that, he seemed...freer, like he was no longer forced to dampen his light, hiding his true self from the modern world—like this new world allowed him to finally show who he truly was. And he was mesmerizing. I could have stood there, shaking his hand for hours and not realized any time had passed.

By the Goddess, if this is anything like what Dan had experienced with Alma, all the women at the settlement were in for it.

DJ appeared beside me and, to my surprise, settled a hand at the back of my neck, running his thumb lightly over the pulse point near my jaw, no doubt counting the beats of my racing heart.

Erik noticed, releasing my hand and smiling down at DJ. "Ah, you must be Dan's son."

DJ blinked, clearly surprised. "I am. I didn't think the resemblance was that obvious."

"It is," Erik said, "And I'd bet the strength of will runs just as deep." His eyes flicked between DJ's face and the possessive hand that now lightly rubbed at my shoulder.

What the heck did DJ think he was doing? I reached up, gently removing his hand of possession from my shoulder with what I hoped was an innocent smile and a gentle nudge at his ribs.

Dan patted his son on the back, saying so much with that one small gesture, before pulling Erik's attention away from DJ and toward his daughter. "This is my Katie-Bear—er, Kate. Just Kate."

Erik's gaze softened as his eyes moved to Kate. "It's a good thing you take after your mother and not this guy, young lady," he said while tilting his head in Dan's direction.

Everyone within earshot chuckled, then Erik turned his gaze to my mom, and his expression positively smoldered. "You must be Amber's mother," he practically purred.

Mom nodded, and extended her hand, cheeks flushed. "It's so good to meet you. I've heard so much about you and it's nice to finally put a face to the name."

I bit back a giggle. I'd never seen her look so flustered in all my life. *Oh, Mom...*

"The pleasure is all mine," he said, voice low.

Yup, the whole town is definitely in for it with that man around.

I fought the urge to shake my head at his sheer animal magnetism and glanced over at Dan. A flicker of jealousy passed through his eyes even though he smiled.

Oh, dear...

I knew he and Erik shared a deep connection, but I also knew how territorial men could be. I had noticed Dan's budding interest in my mom, even though they both refused to acknowledge it, claiming they were just friends.

As introductions continued though, Alma rode up and dismounted then pulled Dan aside with a coy smile, his eyes taking on a dreamy look as they went. DJ trailed after them. She was also even more mesmerizing than I remembered, her deep red hair glinting like embers in the dappled sunlight.

Erik announced that, because their numbers had grown, they'd brought a larger Singing Stone, capable of encompassing an area far larger than the current one, to protect the new community, and that it would be placed at the settlement's heart.

A settlement...not just an outpost or a village.

He introduced several elves, sprites—some that even knew my distant kin in the Snow Forest—a dozen more fampir, and three different kinds of fae. I was struck dumb. So many things that I had believed were simple fantasy, the stuff of faerie tales and fables, were simply milling around and getting settled, unhitching wagon teams and setting up large canvas tents. They were real.

A cry like I had never heard echoed overhead—vast, thunderous, and melodic. Two colossal gryphons swooped in and landed, their great wings billowing, catching the light like gleaming, coppery sails.

One bore a woman with a small child slung at her back. The other carried panniers of supplies while a woman—her armor similar to, but lighter than Alma's and bearing the same symbol—glided down on pearlescent, cream-colored wings to join the woman and child. Her wings were not nearly so large as Trillium's, her countenance not as fierce, but still, her presence commanded respect.

"Mama!" the child called, reaching tiny hands out towards the winged woman.

Mom and I exchanged a wide-eyed glance. I knew her at once as the woman from the angel video last summer. All real. Had I not been living in the strength of the glow, my knees would have buckled. It was all *real.*

Erik introduced the two women as the settlement's new Elementals—sisters who could manipulate the elements: earth, air, fire, and water. They would shape the land, build living structures, and help the community flourish in exchange for trade and care. The new society worked on barter, trade services, precious metals and never left anyone hungry or homeless.

The caravan of newcomers had brought livestock, pets, supplies. Everything a new society could possibly need and nothing that it didn't. They had no fossil fuel burning equipment, nothing that required electricity or batteries. Nothing that would damage or pollute The Light Mother's beautiful planet. Civilization as we'd known it had ended, but these beings were here to transform what was broken into something thriving. And I marveled at the fact that I was lucky enough to see it reborn.

A war was still going on somewhere out there, but we were far from the front lines...for now anyway. The Dark Mother still roamed, her darkling and their spawn scattered throughout the forests. Always lurking. Always hunting. Danger hadn't vanished, but hope had returned.

The Light Beings set up quickly. Wagons settled and unloaded; tents rose like magic while the scent of cook fire smoke rose into the air and my heart soared.

DJ slipped up beside me once again and leaned in. "Neither you nor my dad mentioned that Milkshake Guy was a total panty-dropper," he whispered.

I snorted. "Your dad *did* tell you how gorgeous Alma is, right?"

He shrugged noncommittally.

"So...did you really think Erik wouldn't be just as pretty?"

He glanced over, taking in the sight of Gail and so many other women completely taken with Erik. "I don't know what I expected but it sure as hell wasn't all that." He didn't *say* anything, but the heavy exhale and crossed arms might as well have been a huff.

I smirked. "Daniel James Cooper, are you *jealous?*" He hated it when I called him by his full name instead of one of the nicknames he was accustomed to, so I used it to needle him.

He looked everywhere but at me, the toe of his boot scuffing a line in the gravel of the camp store parking lot.

"By the Goddess, you are!" I laughed and shoved him lightly.

He grabbed me, pulling me into a hug, "As long as you don't look at him the way every other woman here does," he growled into my ear.

Oh, he is in for a rude awakening. Stringing me along for months and then getting jealous when my eye inevitably wandered? I'd once vowed to give him a run for his money, and I supposed I finally would.

I wriggled out of his arms with a giggle. "No promises, Mr. Mixed Signals." Then I took off, heading toward Mom and Erik. I could feel DJ's eyes burning into me.

Frustration, determination, and confusion in equal parts rolled off of him in waves. Still not making his intentions clear. Perhaps they weren't even clear to him? Whatever was going on in that complicated head of his, I was growing tired of waiting for him to sort it all out.

Ignoring the burning sensation from his gaze as it settled across my shoulders, I turned my attention outward. With so many new people and things around, I was excited to learn about the culture that had existed here, hidden for decades, *centuries*, secretly thriving beneath the nose of modern civilization. As the settlement buzzed with life and the Elementals set to shaping our new home, I felt it again—that swell of hope in my chest.

The war wasn't over, but we were building something worth protecting, something the darkness could never take from us. For the first time since the world ended, I truly believed we had a future.

Four Months Ago...

Charles

THE ANGEL THING SCREECHED a maniacal laugh as Charles' men scattered like the pitiful roaches they were. The sound sliced through his shredded body like nails on a chalkboard, each note a fresh sort of hell. Not one of those pukes stopped. Not a single goddamned one even glanced his direction as he raised a trembling arm, reduced to begging for his life like a rotten coward. Spineless bastards. Every last one of them.

Then came the roar of his diesel motorhome. The big vehicle fired to life and his bleary gaze dragged toward the street. That little bitch was driving off with *everything* that belonged to him. He should have killed her the day Frank and that traitorous shitstain DJ, had dragged her into his office reeking of demon blood and defiance. But no. His bone deep desire to crush her spirit, to watch her squirm and kneel, had stayed his hand. He'd wanted to own her. To break her. Now, he was paying the ultimate price for that mistake.

His shaking, bloodied hands clutched again at his gut wounds as if he could somehow hold himself together by sheer force of will, but Amber had gotten him good. Three times she'd driven that knife into his gut, each thrust deep and deliberate, her wild green eyes gleaming with delight like she'd enjoyed it—like she'd *won*. Three times she'd told him without saying a word that she would not bow. Would not break. And that she'd broken him instead. That smug, stubborn little bitch. Yeah, she'd gotten him good alright, and then, that black-winged creature had dropped out of the sky like she had called it down with that idiotic prayer of hers.

He gagged and coughed, blood bubbling up to splatter his lips in crimson as the rumble of his RV faded in the distance. Gone. She was gone and he was well and truly fucked. Now, all he could hope for was a quick death. His vision swam, the edges folding inward, then...darkness.

The screech of a demon ripped him from that welcome blackness and slammed him back into the screaming wreckage of his body. Cold. Aching. Still sprawled out in the driveway, but twilight had closed in around him. And the monsters were rising.

He moved with nothing but raw instinct animating his limbs, dragging himself toward the garage like a wounded animal crawling into its den to die. Even a man as broken and twisted as he couldn't stomach the thought of being torn apart by the creatures that owned the night, but maybe that would be easier, *cleaner* than slowly festering to death from a septic gut wound.

Pain screamed through his gut, draining what little strength remained in his limbs. Still, he growled and kept crawling. Inch by inch, he clawed his way into the garage until his body gave out and he collapsed on his side, panting like a dying dog. Each shuddering breath was pure agony. The shadows deepened out beyond the open door and the screeches grew louder. He didn't have the strength to stand—couldn't even close himself away from the night. This would be his last night among the living.

"Wasn't supposed to go this way," he rasped, breath rattling. "To hell with that pint-sized piece of shit." How had he allowed himself to be brought low by a damned *woman?* And to hell with that winged she-devil that refused to finish him off. "To hell with all of you," he snarled, voice dripping with venom. Hatred surged through him like poison pumped straight into a broken vein, familiar and comforting.

411

That hatred was the only thing he had left. Silence pulsed in his ears. "You can all fucking rot."

Shadows slithered on the street, claws scraping on the asphalt and red eyes glowing like ruby coals in the near-total dark. Dozens of them. "You assholes looking for me?" he croaked, the words rasping out on the edge of a cough.

Shadowy heads whipped in his direction then prowled toward the garage, slow and deliberate.

"Let's make this quick," he muttered and tried to sit up, determined to meet his death head on—face to face—but pain tore through him like white-hot fire, and he flopped over onto his side, breath hitching.

The demons stopped, just beyond the end of the driveway, a shadowy wall of low, hissing growls pressing in from the dark.

Goosebumps crawled down his spine. "What are you waiting for?" he spat. "Kill me!" His vision blurred at the edges, but still, they waited.

Charles panted through the mind-numbing pain. *Why? Why were they hesitating?*

Then, another shadow peeled away from the group—tall, humanoid, draped in a smart, thigh-length coat, a dim, yellow glow emanating from beneath its deep hood. The figure approached the garage without a sound, then stepped inside.

"This place reeks of light magic," the smooth, masculine voice said with a disgusted sniff, each word oozing across the concrete like thick oil, slick, heavy, and darker than the shadows surrounding him.

Charles couldn't move...could barely breathe. He simply lay there like a sack of rotting meat.

The figure knelt down beside him, sniffing again, "But you are not the source."

The man's head tilted, bird-like. Curious. Then he lifted a pale hand and pushed back his hood revealing an almost angelic face. Serene. Kind. Golden ringlets framed his features, cascading toward his collar like spun silk.

Not at all what Charles had expected.

But his eyes—those sickly, pale-yellow eyes—the irises almost white, made the pit of his stomach twist. Something ancient thrummed beneath the man's calm exterior. He was powerful, unnatural. Dangerous.

"What *are* you?" Charles croaked.

The man chuckled, the sound sweet and melodic, as it echoed through the garage. "What is your name, Hume?"

"Charles," he answered, the word springing from his throat unbidden. He didn't have a choice. It was a command. One he couldn't refuse.

"And who has left you with such grievous wounds, Charles?"

Again, the answer slipped from his lips before he had even chosen to speak, "A girl named Amber wounded me, but another woman left me to rot. Called herself Deathbringer."

The man rocked back on his heels and hissed through his teeth while the demons in the street raised a shrieking chorus of unearthly howls, the sound rattling the walls...and Charles' very bones.

"I know that one," he growled. "Ancient, she is. And powerful. But not invincible." He leaned in and laid a cold hand on Charles' shoulder, precise and almost tender. But those yellow eyes pierced his soul like scalpels. "Tell me, would you seek the deaths of those that wronged you if you had the power?" The man's voice was saccharine sweet. And suffocating.

"I would." Once more the words escaped Charles' throat of their own accord.

"And would you crush the very thing they stand for under your heel?"

"Fuck yes." Charles' voice was low and raw, hatred filling his chest like a second heartbeat. "Can you do that for me?" he asked, teeth grinding while his soul curdled with poison at the mere thought of Amber and that winged, she-devil bitch.

"No." The man's voice was flat and final.

Charles deflated.

"But *you* can."

Something in the man's words plucked the unhinged threads in Charles' mind. Could it be? But no. He was no dreamer. Only a realist. "That's impossible," he snapped. "I can't even sit up. Got one foot in the grave and the other on crumbling ground."

"Ah," the man whispered, crouching closer, "but you do not have to die." His voice was like a satin-wrapped dagger. "Embrace the darkness within you and you'll have power beyond your wildest dreams, Charles. Embrace the darkness—or die. The choice is yours."

If this was a dream, Charles didn't want to wake from it. This man, this being, who walked the night, side by side with the demons, and talked like a god, was offering him life. Powerful life. And revenge. All he had to do was say it.

"Yes," he rasped. "I choose life in the darkness."

The demons in the street howled, the sound like a riotous cheer and the man before him grinned flashing elongated canine teeth, then sighed, "Excellent."

Pain lanced through his gut as the man scooped him up like a child. Charles groaned, vision swimming, his head slumping against the man's chest. The heartbeat beneath his ear was all wrong—four sharp beats instead of two. What was this creature that carried him with such gentle grace?

As the man carried Charles out into the street, the gathering of demons parted before him like a black and red sea then filed in behind like dutiful guardians. Soon, they were joined by two other figures flanking them to either side. To the left, another man, and to the right, the form was unmistakably feminine, both clothed similarly to the man who carried him.

Darkness swept across his eyes and dullness began crawling up his limbs like an ashen lullaby, the coming promise of a blissful reprieve from the pain. His head lolled back on his shoulders.

"Do not give up the ghost just yet," the man said quietly. "Mistress Nerezza is dying to meet you."

Charles smiled through the pain, surrendering himself to the peaceful embrace of darkness as something ancient crept gently into his mind, vast, patient, and all-consuming.

She welcomed him home.

Acknowledgements

The bones of this book began over twenty years ago when I woke up from a dream, reeling at what my imagination and the realm of dreams had just gifted me. My mom had always told me, ever since I was a little girl, to write my dreams down, no matter how silly, crazy, or grand they might be, and so I did. And that single dream spawned an entire world filled with people, places, creatures, and cultures that were (and still are) so unbelievably real to me, that they occupied my mind day and night. It was a sort of obsession that only I was privy to, dreaming becoming more like a journey—and with a little meditation, I could bring myself back to that amazing land most nights, traveling with people, meeting with legendary beings, and learning about the world.

Out of all the folks that helped me bring this dream of mine to fruition, first, I have to thank my mom for her endless encouragement and support. I never would have started this journey without her.

Next, my sisters and brothers, both blood and found on this journey we call life. You have always been my biggest cheerleaders, pushing me to persevere even when I wanted to throw in the towel. The words 'thank you' don't even come close to expressing the depth of my gratitude. I love you all.

And my partner in this life, Jeff. You have the patience of a saint. I know listening to the keyboard clacking first thing in the morning and late into the night drives you half crazy, (especially in our tiny home) but you always give me space to weird-out and write...and that means more to me than you will ever know.

My stepmom, who went to live in The Light Mother's embrace in 2023 but told me before she left to make sure that I did all the things I wanted to do while I still could. Your beautiful smile will always be my bookmark and your encouragement, urging me to follow my dreams, will live in my heart until we meet again in the afterlife.

My dad who instilled one hell of a work ethic into me, and my stepdad for sharing my love of all things sci-fi and fantasy. I couldn't have asked for a more eclectic and amazing pair of men to help mold me into the person I am today. Thank you so much.

My small but mighty group of beta readers, y'all are the real MVP's. Thank you so much for taking the time to help me dial this manuscript in. My cover artist, sorry I was so picky. Thanks for putting up with me, girlie. And my developmental editor...your mind is worth millions. Here's to never 'swallowing thickly' again.

And to the first few folks who read this book in its (almost) final form. All of your excitement and whimsy over the characters and themes helped me actually hit the publish button. Even after years of work, I wouldn't have done it without your incredible words of encouragement. Thank you, thank you, thank you.

We're all in this together.

Walk in Light and Truth.

About the Author

LynnErin Faye believes every story should lead readers into a world of midnight mystery and wonder. She has been a storyteller since childhood, but in 2004, the image of a Darkling Spawn appeared in a dream, its glowing red eyes forever imprinted in her mind's eye. Since then, she has been building and nurturing a world of adventure, danger, and enchantment. In the waking world, she travels the country full-time in a vintage Toyota Odyssey motorhome with her longtime partner and her beloved American Bulldog. But in spirit, she resides in The Snow Forest Library, preserving the legends and lore of her world for those wandering souls seeking the magic hidden beyond the stars.

More from LynnErin Faye

Origins of the Aeon Saga
Creation's Quest (coming soon)

The Aeon Saga
Aeon Rising (coming soon)

Other Novels Set in the Aeon World
This Is The Fall: Book Two (coming soon)
Children of Earth and Wing (coming soon)
Dreamwalker (coming soon)